STOLEN BEAUTY

ARROW TACTICAL SERIES

ISABEL JOLIE

ISABEL JOLIE

Editor: Lori Whitwam

Proofreading: Karen Cimms

Cover Design: Damonza

Created with Vellum

To Dad,

On the day I shared my first story with you, you said, "I suppose, if you wanted, you could write those stories when you grow up."

I assumed you meant the hardback Readers Digests that filled the shelves in the den. But maybe you meant the books behind the cabinet doors with titles like The Thorn Birds.

We never discussed it.

You may wish we had.

But you were right. Today I'm a writer. And this story is for you.

I miss you. And love you. Always.

Everything has beauty, but not everyone sees it.

-Confucius

PROLOGUE

Sage

A shadow passed through the front lawn and a prickling sensation curled up my spine. The crescent moon silhouetted the broad-leaf trees. A quiet stillness blanketed the street. The lights in the small craftsman-style homes along Blue Ridge Road had flickered off hours earlier.

The cursor on my screen blinked. I abandoned my work in progress and pushed up off my bed. A million tiny pins pricked my thigh as blood rushed through my sleeping leg. Photos, postcards, and letters littered the comforter.

The sole light source in the room dimmed when my screen saver flicked on. I wrote the shadow off as the product of an overactive imagination. A side effect of spending far too much time indoors reading. Mom used to tell me I read too much Stephen King. She'd been right. Fear of resurrected pets and the possessed stole my sleep for years.

"If you're ever in danger, there are specific things you must do."

Sam's words came to me out of nowhere. If anyone other than Mr. King was to blame for my adult self being easily spooked, it was Sam. My brother hadn't always been paranoid. For that, I blamed the SEALs.

The clock on the bedside table glowed. I'd spent hours researching anything I could on the Cayman Islands, where my sister lived; on Origin Laboratories, the company she worked for, and on what to do when a loved one goes missing abroad.

An internal battle raged. One part said I should be in full panic mode. She hadn't returned my phone calls. Missed our weekly video call. The other part said that she gets caught up in her work. She's borderline obsessive. Forgets to eat. Works until she passes out over her laptop. And then my worrywart self would wail that she missed our scheduled online date. In the year since moving abroad, she never missed our scheduled call. Not once.

"If you don't let me know you're okay, I'm contacting the embassy and coming there. I found a flight. Please just respond."

Nothing. Six days with no response to my emails or my text. Deep in my gut, I knew something had happened. I needed to help her, but how? Her office said that she resigned. But where had she gone? Why hadn't she called?

I shut my laptop and pushed off the bed, concluding there was nothing more I could do until the US Embassy opened in the morning.

Two steps to the bathroom, and the front door hinges creaked. Two more steps, and I would've been inside the bathroom with the door closed because I'm an odd bird and even when home alone, I close the bathroom door.

Seconds later, and everything would've happened differently. Seconds later, and I'd be dead.

CHAPTER 1

Knox

Six days later

The forecast is for an unusually hot Santa Barbara day, and judging by the early morning heat, the weatherman might be spot-on for once. My sweat-soaked running shirt clings to my back like another layer of skin. I open the canteen and pour water into a dish.

The trainee at my side pants, pink tongue lolling about, her attention on the crashing waves.

"You wanna go in?" Millie's thick brown tail hangs down in a curve and slowly wags.

The early morning sun streams across the ocean as a sea gull squawks.

Up the beach, a mountain bike approaches, wheels sinking into the packed sand. It takes a second to confirm the bike and bulky rider. Judging from the strain of my buddy's monster leg muscles, he's getting a half-decent workout.

Max hops off his bike, lets it crash into the sand, and steps right up to my left side. "What's up, dog? You not answering your phone?"

"Did you call?" Out of habit, I glance at the sports watch on my wrist, one that records my run and health metrics, but doesn't connect to my phone. "Everything okay?"

"Whoever stayed over last night is still hanging around your place. Wanted to give you a heads up. Figure she locked herself out and then remembered she left something. Or you got yourself a clinger."

Max snorts at his own half-baked joke and bends down, hand out to Millie. I watch him closely, looking for any tell this is a prank. Of all the guys, he's not the biggest comedian, though. And we've mostly outgrown pranks.

"Seriously?" He nods as the dog tilts her head, giving him a better angle for scratching. "Didn't bring anyone home last night."

Max squints into the sun. "Really?"

"Why'd you think it was me?"

Max and I live in a small condominium complex with three units that open into a communal courtyard. Max lives in a back unit. One unit's vacant. Mine is the street facing unit, and from the street, you'd think the blue front door opens into a home, rather than into a multi-unit dwelling.

All along Cabrillo Boulevard, multi-unit housing can be mistaken for single-family homes.

"She's sitting on your stoop. You got a sister?" Max pats Millie's head with finality and stands.

"No." I draw the answer out. "Only child."

Max should know this about me. We both have a crew of adopted brothers from the teams. I'm Uncle Knox and even godfather to a handful of munchkins. Max has a sister, and his parents live in New Hampshire. We know this shit about each other.

"You didn't recognize her?"

He wipes sweat from his brow as he gives a negative shake.

"You didn't talk to her?"

"Why would I do that? I came out here to give you a heads up. So, you know, you could steer clear if you wanted."

"How old did she look?"

He scratches his jaw, clearly doing some mental math.

"I mean, could it be a buddy's wife? Or is it maybe a buddy's kid?"

"You mean from the Navy?"

I nod in answer. What else would I mean?

"Nah, man. No one like that. She's kinda hot. I figured she and you..."

Back when we lived in Coronado, that thought might've been valid. Ladies there love a Navy guy. But here in Santa Barbara, we're no longer hot commodities. Or at least, if that fan club exists, Max and I haven't found it in the handful of months we've lived here.

"And you're sure she's looking for me?"

He shrugs his linebacker shoulders again dismissively. "Maybe not. Maybe she had the wrong address."

That's a real possibility. The addresses on our street can be deceptive. Not uncommon at all for the food delivery guy to end up at the wrong destination.

"Not even three months out, and you got yourself a dog?" Max grins, clearly not too worried about the lost woman back at our place.

With a pat to the side of the animal in question, I explain, "Technically, she flunked out of K9 training. I'm taking her in for a little tutoring. I think she's got what it takes."

"Good-looking dog."

Millie lies down, paws out front, haunches upright, surveying the rolling waves like a lion on a cliff. "She's a big girl."

For a chocolate lab, she's got a wide chest, and at ninety-five pounds, she's big for her breed. "The guy back at the training center has a thing for German shepherds. Not sure he ever gave her a fair shake."

"You got dog training experience?"

"I bought a book."

"Well, you know, they say it's normal to pick up new hobbies."

He and I both left the Navy four months ago. Me for medical, Max for his own reasons. The black-ops security firm, Arrow Security, offers better pay, benefits, and hours. Less bureaucratic bullshit. But still, it's an undeniable transition. And given we excelled in our old world, it's to be expected that it'll take a beat to find our new footing.

"A dog isn't a hobby." The words sound more defensive out loud than they did in my head.

"You could do worse. Who's going to take care of her when we have to jettison?"

"Trevor and Stella. Besides, this is temporary." Trevor's one of the Arrow Tactical founders. He spends his days training guys. His wife, Stella, is the HR maven, and she's also a big-time dog lover.

"How'd you get roped into this?"

"I was petting Stella's dog, and we started talking." Back when I was in the teams, I couldn't have a dog. We had to be up and gone on a moment's notice. "She sent me out to Santa Barbara Dog Training Academy yesterday. They got a new crop of K-9 dogs, and she was curious about Arrow procuring one. But I got there too late. By the time I made it past reception, a police officer was negotiating a purchase of two of the successful graduates. Millie trotted up to me as I was talking to Steph, the owner of the training center. I commented on what a beauty she was, and Steph said she was looking for a home."

"So, she's Arrow's dog?"

"No. As an obedience school dropout, she doesn't meet their qualifications." As if to underscore the point, Millie licks my hand. At least she doesn't jump on people.

"Wife and kids gonna be around the corner."

I flip him my middle finger. Leaving the teams hadn't been an easy decision, but family desires didn't factor in, and Max knew it.

Special operations isn't for the aged. Thanks to an explosion a couple of years back, my hearing took a hit. And the kind of shit we do on a regular basis takes a toll on knees and shoulders. In a lot of careers, thirty-five's still young. Special Ops isn't one of those careers. I could've stayed. Moved into a different functional area. My dad spent his entire career in the military. But when I didn't pass the last medical review, it felt like a good time to go through with a medical retirement. Get the benefits and move on.

Going private offered better pay and a mix of action and strategy. Plus, Arrow Tactical has a stellar reputation among the guys.

"Come to think of it. You better get back home. That woman on your stoop could be the future Mrs. Williams." He chuckles when I glare. "You coming to the barbecue tonight?"

That question has me grimacing. I read through the invitation list. All couples.

I like that our new company is all about fostering camaraderie, and getting to know the families of those I work with is a part of that. But there are other things I'd rather do on a Friday night than bond with co-workers' families.

"You going?"

Max shrugs noncommittally and picks up his bike. "You heading back now?"

"Yeah. Gonna get this one back. Ran four miles, and I'm not sure she's used to it."

"You need me to come back with you? Just in case you need assistance?"

"How big was this woman sitting on my front step that I might need backup?"

"Wee little thing. A bit curvy." Max flashes a shit-eating grin and attempts to wiggle his eyebrows.

He's a big guy with Ken doll blond highlights and blue eyes that reel in the ladies. Even my mom swoons when he's nearby. She calls him a big lovable goof and ships him care packages every time she ships me something.

"But, you know, crazy's got more strength. Might need a witness."

"She's not there for me. She's at the wrong address." Besides, about the only people who have my new address are my military buds, Arrow folks, and my folks.

"'Kay, man." He slings a meaty leg over his bike seat. His loose shorts bunch, and he readjusts himself.

"No bike shorts?"

He just grins. "I told you, I rushed to find you. Now I'm here, might as well go down the beach a bit."

"All right. Text me if you decide to go to the thing tonight."

With a two-fingered salute, he's off, and I head back home. Millie pads along beside me with slack on the leash like a well-trained dog. Along the way, I hold the frisbee out for her to sniff, but she doesn't care for it much.

Cars line our street, taking up every inch of parking space. The North Carolina plate on a Ford Bronco catches my eye. One of the many states I've lived in. A plate from that far away means it's probably a rental, but the tag is expired. The vehicle needs a good wash. Soot covers the car. The rims are nearly black. There's an NPR sticker on the left side of the bumper and a Co-Exist sticker on the right. Possibly a college student, but we don't have too many of those near us. The college campus is about ten minutes away by car.

We're a thirteen-minute drive to the airport, a nine-minute walk to the harbor, and minutes away from the pier. Restaurants, bars, and small shops abound. The location of the place Arrow set me up in couldn't be better.

The terracotta tile roof, off-white stucco walls, and blue trim make for a nice welcome home. Mom calls it idyllic. But Mom and Dad haven't been out yet to see it in person. Not that it's worth a trip out west for. Arrow owns the building.

The leash tightens as Millie tugs. A young woman sits on the tiled step. She's leaning against the off-white stucco wall. Her hands are in her lap and her eyes are closed.

Millie tugs harder, and I let out a sharp, "Heel." The line loosens, but her tail flips and flops, intrigued by the stranger on the steps.

Judging from her pale skin, the woman sleeping on my stoop is either a sunblock adherent or she's not from California. Her dark hair is pulled back in a loose binding. There's something familiar about the shape of her face that tweaks a distant memory. High cheekbones and an angular chin. Slight shoulders. Max wasn't off his rocker. She's definitely my type. Brunette. Petite. Natural.

Max assumed she was an overnight guest, probably because she's wearing wrinkled clothes that are likely yesterday's outfit.

The closer I get, the more the stains on her loose-fitting jeans show. The cropped tee circles her neck with a washed-out yellow band. There's a faded rainbow on the front of the tee, but the way she's resting against the building, her arm partially covers the design.

She looks young. Younger than me. I'd guess early twenties. Given her clothes, she could be a college student. Maybe she just had too much to drink last night and wound up on my stoop sleeping it off.

Should I wake her or just let her rest? She's not hurting anyone out here.

Millie takes the choice away with a bark so loud it could wake the dead.

CHAPTER 2

Sage

"No!"

Bright white light forces me to squint.

I clutch my chest, curling away. The floorboard creaking. Crouching. Darkness. Black metal. The gun. It all comes back in a flurry.

I blink into blue skies. A palm frond sways.

I'm in California.

Ruff. Ruff.

An enormous chocolate Lab approaches with friendly golden-brown eyes and a wagging tail.

"Shh. It's okay."

My gaze lifts, past the dark brown fur, to the deep intonations with the barest trace of a southern accent. *Knox Williams.*

My heart, an organ I'm hyperaware of, seizes for a split second.

Knox Andrew Williams. I'd thought he might show up at Sam's funeral, but he didn't. Someone said he was still overseas. No one from Sam's team made it. They were supposed to, but they didn't.

The funeral was twenty-two months ago.

Knox's short-sleeve shirt clings to every muscle along his shoulders, stretching across his pecs and rounded biceps. His skin bears the bronzed tone of someone who spends hours working under the sun. The dark growth along his jawline is uneven. It's not a full beard, and it's darker than his ruffled sandy brown hair. He looks like he's been on vacation and decided against shaving during his time-off. It's a good look.

Aside from his appearance, it's Knox Williams's smile that stands out. That unforgettable smile transforms from uncertain, as in who-the-hell-is-on-my-step, to a friendly hey-I-think-I-might-know-you.

My body trembles uncontrollably, and my eyes sting. My body's reaction is one I'd managed to control for days, and now isn't the time to lose it.

"Sage?"

I nod, breathing through my mouth to control the flood of random emotions.

"What're you doing—"

A watershed of tears overflows uncontrollably from the depths within.

Knox steps up and pulls me into his damp chest. He reeks of sweaty, smelly guy, but I don't care because I made it. Alive.

The dog at my side licks my hand and wrist as Knox guides me inside his home and directs me to a sofa. He leaves and returns with a box of tissues.

"What's wrong? What's going on?"

He leaves me again as I blow my nose into tissue after tissue while he sets a glass of water in front of me. *Pull it together, Sage. Regain composure.*

"Are you hurt?"

He scans me up and down. Probably looking for an injury. Or signs of a recent surgery.

I blot my eyes with a fresh tissue and choke out between sobs,

"I'm sorry. I don't know what came over me. Just give me a minute."

"Sage Watson." He says my name like he can't believe I'm in his home. And I can't blame him. He was best friends with my older brother. Not me. "Take your time. Whatever's wrong, I'm here, okay?"

A weight hangs over my shoulders, a weariness that I recognize as exhaustion. A part of me wants to curl up on his sofa and sleep for days. But no. I didn't drive here to sleep.

"Someone bad…" My nose drips, and I swipe it with another tissue.

"You want some water?" He pushes the glass closer to me, urging me to take a drink, while I focus on my breathing.

Where to start? "Sloane's missing." My throat's dry, and I reach for the glass, gulping the cool tap water down. The light taste is a welcome change from the syrupy, caffeine-loaded sodas I've been forcing down on my cross-country trek.

"What do you mean, missing?"

"Sam." He blinks at my brother's name. Any sign of a boyish, friendly expression evaporates. "He left me instructions. Explicit instructions. He said if I'm ever in trouble, or in danger, to come to you."

"And you think Sloane's in danger?"

I'm not making sense. I lean over my thighs and close my eyes. Breathe. In and out. The worn-out hardwood floors have a million dark black lines scratched into the golden strips of wood.

"I'm sorry." I press my palm against my forehead. The skin is warm, but not hot. "I'm way too sleep deprived. But…" I close my eyes. *Just get it together.*

"Did you drive here?"

I nod. "Six days. Cross-country."

"You had my address?"

"I didn't." My eyes burn. I close them. *Focus.* "I drove to San Diego. To the address on my Christmas card list. The one Sam left for me. Your neighbor told me you didn't live there anymore. So I called your Mom."

"You drove from North Carolina to California?"

I sink back into the sofa, eyes still closed. The burning sensation underscores how tired I am. "You're going to think I'm crazy." The break-in might not be connected to Sloane. Or it could be. But why would someone come after a kindergarten teacher? "Someone broke into my house, and Sloane hasn't answered any texts or calls in almost two weeks."

"Did the person hurt you?"

"No. I escaped. But Sloane…"

"Where did you see her last?" He sits on the edge of the sofa, leaning forward, as if straining to hear me. Because I'm not making any sense. None of this makes sense.

"She's been in the Cayman Islands." I half-expect him to give me the same attitude others had. Other people who didn't know Sloane. "She's been doing research. For a small research company."

"What kind of research?"

"Cellular regeneration. Sloane moved to the Caymans about eighteen months ago. But she's disappeared. I finally reached someone within her company, and they said she resigned, but I know she didn't. She wouldn't just…" I should've stayed home and made more phone calls. Maybe contacted my state senator. But when the man with a gun broke into my house, my instincts said to follow Sam's instructions. To do exactly what Sam told me to do.

"It's okay. Take your time."

My fingers quiver uncontrollably. Is it my blood sugar?

"She missed our scheduled call. And I've sent countless emails. Texts. Voice messages, not that she listens to those, but she'd see the missed calls."

"And she hasn't returned your calls?"

"No. The last time I checked messages was from the road. Near the Tennessee border. I should check again. Do you think it's safe?"

Knox crosses an ankle over his knee. Grains of sand coat the edge of his sock. I can't read his expression.

"I know. I sound..."

"Like a concerned sister. And I'm glad you came to me. But why not call? Why drive here?"

I swallow, hard. "The person who broke into my house. He had a gun. One with a silencer. Sam showed me those. He owned some, too." Knox nods. He knows what I'm talking about. "I hid until daybreak. Grabbed the bag Sam left for me, the one he packed and told me to use in case of emergency, added a few things to it, and drove here. I stopped at the Tennessee border. Read through Sam's instructions. The detailed ones I hadn't paid much attention to because I didn't think anything like this would ever happen. But when I stopped, I followed everything. Point by point. Turned off my phone, switched out my license plate with the one he packed in the duffel, and have only used cash to pay for things. He left me ten thousand dollars in an envelope. For emergency use."

I risk a glance up. This sounds crazy. I sound like I'm out of my mind. I'm living a nightmare.

"He packed a license plate for you?"

"The sticker on it is expired. I was afraid I'd get pulled for that. But he packed a screwdriver, too. Told me to switch it out...once I crossed state lines."

"You did good." Fresh tears threaten at the corners of my burning eyes. "I work with a company that specializes in finding missing people. Among other things. You came to the right place. We'll find Sloane."

So many people told me to relax. She'd be in touch. That maybe my sister really found love. Would that be so hard to believe? And boats are notorious for not having a reliable signal. The person from her office said that she'd fallen in love and planned to go sailing. There could be a reasonable explanation for her not calling me. Just give her time. That's what Jimmy said. And my neighbor said the same thing. There's probably a reasonable explanation.

When the man broke into my home, I didn't go to any of them. The only voice I heard was Sam's.

"Driving here was crazy, right?"

His dog's paw scratches against my leg, asking for attention.

"No. Not at all. Although a plane ticket might've been a better way to get cross-country." There it is. The mocking grin.

"I followed Sam's instructions." If I did something stupid, the blame falls on Sam. "Sam said to avoid airports. A car can't be as easily located."

"Sam told you that?" The twist of his head and the slow measured words relay his disbelief.

"More than once. He told me what to do if I was ever in danger. Made me run through the list of steps every time he visited." The last time he came home, we went through the duffel together. He updated the printed instructions.

Knox stretches his arm out along the back of the sofa. His eyebrows crowd together. "Tell me about this guy who broke into your house."

"He was dressed in black. He wore gloves. Thin gloves. Not the kind you wear in snow. His gun was thick, metal, but a handgun. Boots, but not Doc Martins, you know, the black leather military looking boots. They were more like hiking boots, just dark."

"And a silencer was attached to his gun?"

"Yes."

"Sam showed you how to use a silencer?"

"No. But he taught me how to shoot a gun. And he stored his stuff at my place. I'd sit with him while he cleaned everything. Sloane thought he was paranoid, and I agreed, but I played along because it seemed to be important to him. I listened. Learned everything he wanted me to learn. He packed two handguns and two boxes of ammo in the duffel bag for me. I took the weapons out and put them by the spare tire. I wouldn't trust myself to use a gun, but I didn't feel right leaving them behind since Sam wanted me..." My lower lip trembles. I close my eyes and clench my teeth, willing myself to maintain composure. I made it this far, I've got this.

Knox squeezes my knee. "You haven't slept much, have you?"

"No." I could barely sleep when I stopped. I would stop on the side of the highway, crawl into the back seat, and endeavor to sleep. "There were two hotels. Paid cash at both. Sam said I couldn't use credit cards."

"The light blue, almost gray Ford Bronco with NC plates. Parked in front. That's yours?"

I nod and sniffle.

"Your stuff in it?"

Once again, I nod and dab my eyes.

"How about you give me the keys? I'm going to check it out."

"To make sure they don't have a tracker on it?" I googled what trackers look like when I was at the rest stop in Tennessee. Sam didn't go over that with me. But he talked about how you can be tracked.

"How do you know about trackers?"

"Books. TV. A little from Sam." Those lips turn up in amusement, and my stomach tightens. "You've got to believe me."

"I believe you." He taps my leg. "You're safe here, okay? I'm gonna go out, check the car, get your stuff, and then you're going to get a shower and some sleep while I do some research. Sound like a plan?"

CHAPTER 3

Knox

Holy shit, Sam. What the hell were you up to?

I get telling his sisters to come to me if they're in trouble. Totally normal to leave instructions to those you love, should something happen. When you're on a team, the unexpected is always possible. But guns? Avoiding airports? Ten grand in cash?

And Sloane's missing?

She was two years younger than me, and I didn't know her that well. But, according to Sam, she'd been studious. Pretty sure she went all the way and got her PhD in some brainiac science.

While I never knew her well, Sloane is Sage's last living close relative. Given all of Sage's childhood health issues, there's no way she wouldn't leave a way for Sage to reach her. Not willingly. Of course, by the same logic, it's unbelievable that she'd move to another country and leave Sage behind.

People change.

There's no denying life's truths.

People also make mistakes.

After exiting my apartment, leaving Millie and Sage safely

indoors, I scan the street. Visually search the parked cars for anyone sitting innocuously inside. Scour the front yards for a seemingly benign flower sniffer or a beggar blending into the streetscape. No suspicious persons. All clear.

In the Bronco, a crumpled Time Out bag and an empty cup with a straw clutter the front passenger seat. There's also a frayed sweatshirt she won't be needing during our heat wave. I lift it and shake it. Nothing. Of course, there's nothing. What did I expect would fall out?

In the back, I locate the black duffel. Typical go bag. A go bag for his sister. *What the hell, Sam?*

Under the spare wheel panel is a Glock 17, unloaded. A SIG P365, unloaded. Can she even shoot these? Four boxes of ammo. She shoved them in this space with no care. At least the guns were unloaded.

After placing everything inside the duffel, I zip it up, close the back, and do a cursory inspection of the undercarriage. All clear.

Sage drove across the country. At the direction of her brother who has been dead for almost two years. I shake my head as I step back from the car. A conversation stirs in my memory.

"Hey, man, I let my sisters know if something happens to me, and they need anything—"

"Nothing's going to happen to you."

"I know, I'm just saying...you're the one I'm sending them to."

"Honored." I clapped a hand over my chest and looked him straight in the eye. "But nothing's going to happen to you."

Where were we? The timing is fuzzy. We were on base. Maybe. Coronado?

Why not an aunt or an uncle? I didn't give it a second thought. Was Sloane into something that had him suspecting they might one day need protection? Or Sam? But no, Sam as the reason doesn't add up. The explosion occurred two years ago. Whatever is going on can't possibly be related to him.

Of course, if Sage knew the truth about her brother's death, I'd be the last person she'd come to for help.

The sun shines over the San Rafael mountain peaks. It's early morning, hours before noon. The golden yellow ball beats down from a flawless blue sky.

It feels like Sam might be up there, looking down on me. Watching to ensure I step up. Honor my word. Protect his kin. Repay him.

As I re-enter my place with the black duffel strap slung over my shoulder, it's with a steadfast determination to help Sam's sisters. Both of them.

Inside the house, Millie sits up on the sofa lapping the side of Sage's face with her long pink tongue. Sage has her arm around the dog, and she's squirming. Smiling. It's an endearing smile that reminds me of her as a kid. So much better than the tears. I might even catch a trace of a giggle.

"Millie. Get off the sofa."

The dog turns her head, making it clear she heard me, but instead of getting off, she lies down, resting her head on Sage's thigh.

I scowl at her disobedience but let her stay. The sofa's nothing too great, as it's one that's been around the block. A dog stretching on it won't hurt a thing.

Sage had a heart and double lung transplant when Sam and I were at the Naval Academy. During my last two years of high school, she'd been back and forth at Duke Hospital. It had been touch and go. The family, our community, the school, everyone rallied behind her. Congenital heart defect and additional complications. The transplant had been a success, but recovery had been a bumpy road that first year. It took a lot out of Sam. The worry and concern from afar weren't easy on him.

When we were in high school, his sick sister consumed his parents. Sam could've raised hell or resented his youngest sister for all the attention she garnered, but he didn't. I've never met a family so close. Seeing how close the Watson kids were made me wish I had a sibling. The last time I saw Sage was when Sam and I graduated from the Naval Academy. Almost didn't recognize the dark-haired beauty with her doe-like brown eyes at graduation. She'd been flirty too. Full of herself. Post-surgery, she'd blossomed into a new person. Older. Mature.

A few more drinks, and she might've had me seriously thinking about crossing a line that would've severed my friendship with Sam. And she was seventeen. A no-go.

On the stoop, I'd estimated she was in her twenties, based on her smooth complexion and her slight frame. But, if memory serves, she's only five years younger. So that would put her at twenty-nine, almost thirty. Still beautiful in a natural, girl-next-door way. And god, she looks so much healthier. Even exhausted with matted hair, she practically glows.

I always thought of her as a fighter. If someone thought they could scare her by showing up with a gun, they seriously underestimated Sage Watson. She took what might knock someone else down and dug her heels in. She went to Carolina, against her parents' wishes. Insisted she wanted to live a normal life.

"Are you still a teacher?"

She jumps a little. She saw me come in, but I suppose after what she's been through, any sound risks rattling her. Exhaustion paints her face, from the bloodshot eyes to the sleep-deprivation bruises below them.

"Kindergarten. It's summer break."

"Still live in Rocky Mount? Or did you move to…" I wrack my brain, trying to siphon through the stories I heard over the years from Sam and my mom. "Durham?"

"Asheville. Moved there a couple of years ago."

That's right. "I've heard good things about Asheville."

"I like it." Her health medic bracelet clinks against an Apple Watch with a black screen. No doubt the battery is dead. Which means nothing is monitoring her heartrate. Does she need it to?

"Did you pack your medicine? Do you need me to—"

"I'm good." Her arm tightens around Millie's thick neck, and her head jerks, like she's in danger of falling asleep on the spot.

"Shower first? Or sleep?"

Those eyelids snap open, and she shakes her head. "I…if you point me to a hotel, I'll stay there."

"You're staying here. You need sleep."

"But—"

"Sleep. You're no good to anyone if you collapse. I'm going to do some research. See what we can get on Sloane's phone records, credit cards and such."

"But…I didn't pack…I don't have any of—" A yawn forces its way out.

"I have resources. I'll get what I can. When you wake, we'll talk. You can barely keep your eyes open. If you crash, you're no good to Sloane." I bend down and offer my hand, as that's more appropriate than scooping her up and carrying her, which is what I'd prefer to do. "We're going to tag team this. You got here. I've got the baton now. I'm gonna pull what I can. When you wake, we'll convene and decide on a course of action."

She stumbles two steps past the sofa…and screw it. I bend, scoop her legs, and lift. She's light in my arms, and all my protective instincts surge. If someone's after Sam's little sister, they'll have to get through me first.

She's not the frail girl I remember, but I'm still not letting her fall. And I'll be damned if I'll let some sick fuck hurt her.

"You don't need to carry me." She pushes her palm against my chest, and I shift her in my arms.

"Shh."

"I'm okay, Knox."

"Are you getting angry with me?" I grin, liking the combative strength. "Here you go." With care, I set her on the bed and back away, moving to close the blinds.

"You don't need to baby me. I'm okay now."

"I'm looking out for you. There's a difference. Now, rest." She glances up, and I'm hit with those dark brown irises lit with amber flecks. I don't think I ever realized how similar her eyes are to her brother's. It's been a while since those eyes came to me in a dream. Chances are good that recurring dream is returning tonight.

I flip the light off and close the door. Give my head a shake to clear the irises and resist the familiar funk that's descending. I've got a lot to do.

CHAPTER 4

Sage

Light peeks through the slats of the closed white blinds. Drool dampens the pillowcase. The black screen on my watch serves as a reminder the charge is dead and has been for days.

I'm in Knox's bedroom. I made it. Drove cross-country by myself. I followed Sam's instructions. And Knox remembered me. Unfortunately, he likely remembers everything.

The king size bed is crammed against the corner. There's no headboard. Nothing hangs on the generic white walls. There's a tall dresser between the bedroom door and another door, which is opened to reveal a white tile floor and a frosted plastic shower curtain.

I wipe sleep from my eyes, remembering how sweet Knox had been. Comforting me. Carrying me, for crying out loud.

Does he remember me throwing myself at him all those years ago? He must, but he's apparently let it go. It was a long time ago. And I'd been inexperienced. Feeling invincible. Like I had a new lease on life. I didn't know better. Not really. With luck, he'll never mention it. It shall be the event we never speak of.

The rumble of deep voices filters into the bedroom.

"And you say this is Saint's sister?" There's a two-inch crack below the closed bedroom door. The voices are near.

"Yeah."

That's Knox. He must've told whoever is here about me.

I push off the bed. My black duffel is on the floor beside the dresser. I dig out my toothbrush, careful to avoid jostling the boxes of ammunition, and head to the bathroom. With a splash of cool water on my skin, my eyes open and my breathing deepens. My fingers comb through tangles, but there are too many. I give up and pull it back.

"You know anything about her?"

"Other than what we dug up online?"

"Not Sloane. Sleeping beauty."

Sleeping beauty? How long have I slept?

Sharp red creases mar one cheek. Pillow lines. I splash more water over my face, dry it with a disheveled hand towel, and exit the bathroom.

"My dad took a job in Rocky Mount after he retired from the Army. My junior and senior year of high school, I lived a few houses down from the..."

Knox sees me and smiles. The other man blinks.

Knox's guest has broad shoulders, broader than Knox's, and he's noticeably taller, too. Judging by his closely cropped hair, tank top, and cargo pants, he's a military guy. Given he knows my brother's nickname, maybe he served with him.

I laughed when Sam told me his nickname. Saint. As if.

"You feeling okay? Can I get you something?" Knox asks.

The view through the den window is of another building with terracotta roof tiles and robin's egg blue trim around the windows. The fading sun casts a rose-colored hue over the stucco walls.

"What time is it? How long did I sleep?"

"It's around eight. Thought you were going to sleep through the night. You must be hungry."

I should eat. I'm not hungry at all, but I need to eat to take my meds.

"Hi there." The tall man extends his hand, but my gaze falls to his beefy bicep. I've met quite a few of Sam's Navy friends in the past, and none had the physique of a bodybuilder.

"Sage, this is Max."

A bit groggy, I'm slow to react, but he doesn't seem to notice as his meaty hand swallows mine and he gives it a polite shake.

"I brought some food over from the barbecue," Max says, his gaze now on Knox, whose back is to us as he opens the freezer and shakes an ice tray. "You're welcome to it."

Max snaps a red lid off a clear plastic bowl that is sitting out on the counter.

"Did I keep you from going somewhere?" I ask Knox while peering into the plastic bowl of what appears to be shredded char-grilled chicken.

Knox waves a hand dismissively as he pushes a glass of ice water my way. "Nowhere I wanted to be."

Still a bit dazed, I sit on one of two bar stools next to the narrow kitchen island with a glazed white tile countertop.

"You know, I knew your brother," Max says. In a nanosecond, his facial expression says it all. He's sorry for my loss but isn't sure what he should say about it.

Knox slides a plate over the tile. Shredded chicken, potato salad, and sliced cucumbers in what appears to be a vinaigrette fill the plate. "From the barbecue," Knox says as an explanation. "They always make too much." He crosses his arms but doesn't make a move to fix a plate for himself. "Did some research on Sloane."

"And?"

"July twenty-fourth is the last time her credit card was charged. Almost two weeks ago. But the auto payments she's got set up are still going through. No subscriptions were canceled or paused. No cash withdrawals to indicate she planned to go somewhere. Last cell phone location is in the Cayman Islands."

"How'd you get her credit card information?" I couldn't have told him what kind of credit cards she had, much less where she banked.

"We have resources."

Sam's emergency duffel comes to mind. Alternate passports and identification. Resources, indeed.

"I can't get over you driving cross country," Max says. My stomach becomes unsettled, and I rub the area. "You just...your first thought was to drive to Knox?"

Knox glowers at Max.

"It's okay." I set the fork down and rest my palms on my lap. "I must look like a lunatic. It's just...when someone broke into my house, Sam's instructions...they were all I could think of. Everything Sam told me came flooding back." He didn't just tell me once. The instructions were in the last letter I received from him. A letter I memorized. Splattered pasta sauce covers one corner of the creased stationery.

"How'd you escape?"

I swallow down rising bile, remembering the cramped cabinet. "I hid."

"And when he left, you what? Loaded up and drove here?"

"I waited until morning." My voice sounds weak. My hand over my belly is doing nothing to settle the queasiness.

"No one closer?" Max asks. I don't miss the finger movement he sends Knox's way, a hand signal to hush and let him talk. Or rather, ask the questions.

"I have some friends in Asheville." My best friend Jimmy lives in Asheville. He possesses a torrid hatred of guns and a passion for bookstores. "No one who would know what to do."

"The police?"

I probably should've gone to the police. Should've called 911. But then they would've asked me questions and left me alone in the house. And if that guy was still around, I'd be a sitting duck when he returned the next night.

"Do you not trust the police?" Max presses. "Do you think they're involved?"

"No, nothing like that." I don't actually know any police officers. "I just…" The man in black wore hiking boots that thudded on the floor. I can still hear the rhythmic plod. It's as if moments pass where I'm trapped in a movie or television show. "My sister's missing. When I ran…" All I could hear was Sam's voice telling me to go to Knox. "I just… I followed Sam's instructions." I force my gaze on Knox. In some ways, I barely knew Sam's best friend. In others, I knew him well. I'd met his parents. Didn't miss a single one of his high school soccer games, home or away, except for when I'd been in the hospital. Followed his progression through the Naval Academy and later, the Navy.

I wasn't top of mind for him. I don't fool myself about that. I probably never crossed his thoughts. Coming here might be the dumbest thing I've ever done. Why would I expect Knox to help me? Why would Sam? He was probably thinking I might need a guy to give me advice on buying a car or a house. Sam probably never imagined I'd drive all the way to California. But no, Sam specifically said danger. A man breaking and entering my home with a gun and not stealing anything? That qualifies as danger.

Knox's sinewy hand covers mine, dwarfing it. Thick veins cross the back of his hand, leading up to his knuckles. Healthy veins that would be easy for a needle to puncture to draw blood. Short, clean nails with healthy nail beds. But it's the warmth I feel. The heat travels through my center and pulses into my extremities.

"Don't worry. We're going to get to the bottom of this," he assures me.

"You think I'm crazy."

He squeezes my hand with the lightest of touches, meant to comfort. Logically, I'm fully aware of his purpose, but still, my belly flips. My nerves have always frayed around him.

"You did the right thing. The smart thing. You trusted your instincts."

I risk a glance away from our joined hands to his face, afraid I'll see amusement or teasing. The lines by his eyes don't deepen. Sincerity flows through the depths of his familiar gold-tinged, honey-infused brown eyes.

"Thank you."

CHAPTER 5

Knox

Max crowds Sage, on the ready with questions.

"Can you step outside with me for a minute?" I pointedly ask him.

My apartment unit has a front door that leads to the street and a side door that opens into a shared interior courtyard. Max steps to the side door, but given there's no air conditioning, the chances are great that windows are open, and I don't want to risk Sage overhearing, so I redirect him to the front.

Millie hangs back, planting herself beside Sage and the plate of food.

Outside, I scan the street. There's a typical mix of automobiles. One motorcycle snagged a street parking spot. A woman pushes a baby carriage on the sidewalk one block down. Nothing out of the ordinary.

"What's up?" Max asks as he crosses his arms, making his biceps bulge and his pecs rise like cleavage. Since leaving the team, he's been bulking up. A hobby of his, for sure, but something that could slow a guy down. Now that he's no longer a frog man, he's free to aim for Rock status. It's a hobby he's become obsessed with.

"I need you to lay off her. She's legit."

He tilts his head, doing that thing he does when he disagrees. "You into her?"

"What? No. Why would you even ask that?" From the get-go, he's assumed the worst about her. And now he's assuming the worst about me.

"Don't get pissy. I just see the way you look at her."

"And how is that? She's Sam's *little* sister." *Jesus.*

I step farther out into the front yard and peer down the driveway. With one unit empty, we have an extra parking spot.

"She's not so little anymore, is she? The background report puts her at twenty-nine."

"I've known her for ages. Since she was in middle school."

"So, you're not interested in her? Like at all?"

"No." He knows he's pissing me off, and that just pisses me off more.

"Well, while she's here, maybe I'll ask her out."

I whip around. "What?"

He chuckles. "Yeah, that's what I thought."

"That girl in there…" I point at the blue front door, "she's gold. One-of-a-kind. That girl fought through hell and survived. She's not just Saint's little sister. She's his reason for being a saint. The only guys who deserve to date a woman like that are men who are in it for real. To do right by her. And the last I checked—"

"Yeah, yeah, that's not me." He holds up a defensive hand. *Yeah, that's what I thought.* "So, did you two date?"

"What the hell is with this line of questioning?"

"I'm just picking up vibes, man. And in my experience, women don't drive for a week straight to get help. Her 'Oh, I didn't think to call the police' raises questions. And 'My dead brother left me a note two years ago' isn't the best excuse either. But if you're positive she's not some psycho stalker, I'll drop it. I'll sleep with a gun by my bedside and the window open in case I hear gunshots at night, but I'll drop it."

"Jesus, Max. Stalker?" I give him a lethal glare, disgusted by where his thoughts are going. "If you have questions that will help us figure this out, fine. But watch how you ask the questions. Don't make her feel like she's a suspect."

"Noted. Just be careful you're thinking with the bigger head." The guy can be a total fuckwad. "The scenario she's drawing doesn't hold water, which doesn't make her a suspect, but it does mean there are questions."

"What scenario has she drawn?" I'm gonna lose it on him any second now.

"Someone kidnaps her sister and then sends a hitman to kill her. And her brother packed her guns and ammo in a duffel bag." Max steps forward, hands on his hips. "Let me repeat that. A hitman. I know she's your friend, and she's our teammate's little sister, but we gotta look at all the angles here. Who sends a hitman to Asheville-in-the-middle-of-bumfuck Carolina? Let's say someone has her sister. Why worry about a sibling? What could she possibly do? She lives in a Podunk town in the middle of nowhere."

"It's the age of the Internet," I say with an edge. But he isn't wrong. We need to look at all angles. Why would anyone consider Sage a threat? Why would Sam prepare her for this scenario?

"Not to mention. Did you see what Erik sent over?" Another one of Arrow's founding partners, he heads the tech side along with a woman named Kairi. They work interchangeably, only Erik is a gruff bastard while Kairi is always amenable. "She's got hundreds of friends on Facebook, Instagram, Pinterest, and TikTok. You don't think one of those friends might have been a better choice than driving cross-country?"

"I told you. She's a sweetheart. She's the type of person with a lot of connections. But that doesn't mean they're close connections." Erik's still looking into both of the Watson sisters. He only shared the account information for me to verify he was looking at the right person, but he's got a team diving deep. He says there could be leads in those posts and comments.

The two of us don't have social accounts. We deleted them ages ago as we climbed ranks. But, from what I remember, you could become friends with someone you barely knew, or even not at all. The report also said that her posts were school-related, and she hadn't posted since June. The woman is a kindergarten teacher. Where does Max get off being so suspicious of her?

Frustration rips through me. I pace in front of Max, sorting through his points.

The front door opens. Sage holds out my phone. "Someone's calling. I thought you might want to get it." She glances between me and Max. "Everything okay?"

With four broad steps, I reach her and take the phone. "It's Erik." I hold the phone up to Max so he can see our colleague and the source of our background reports is the guy on the line. Pushing the door open wider, I gesture for Sage to head back inside where the dog awaits her. "Everything's fine," I reassure her, then with a press of the button, answer Erik's call on speaker, following her back inside. "Hey, man. Did you learn anything?"

"Am I on speaker?"

Max enters and closes the door with a slam. His hiking boots thud on the wood.

"That you are," I announce, giving Max a look that I hope communicates to quiet the fuck down.

"Can you pick up?" Max's gaze catches mine. My heart rate kicks up a notch. I select the phone option, then press it to my ear.

"You're off. What's up?"

"The woman who arrived at your house. We got it right? Her name is Sage Emory Watson?"

"Yep."

"Age twenty-nine. Birthdate November twenty-second, 1994?"

"Yeah." Trusting, concerned, baby brown eyes meet mine. I wink, letting Sage know everything will be fine. "That all sounds right."

"She's listed as missing. Her house burnt down three days ago. Arson is suspected, but the investigation is ongoing."

CHAPTER 6

Sage

Knox's jaw clenches, and he jams the phone flat up against his head. His fingers cover his other ear. What he's hearing isn't good.

When you witness bad news being delivered frequently enough, you develop an instinct, almost like a sixth sense. When his troubled eyes meet mine, I know. My stomach bottoms out.

"Is it Sloane?" Knox's Adam's apple flexes in his throat. "Is she hurt?" Movements slow around me. Max steps closer. Millie's nose rubs my fingers. The scent of vinegar tickles my nose.

"Nothing like that," Knox says. "I'm gonna put this back on speaker. So if you have questions, you can ask Erik."

"Who's Erik?"

Max answers from behind me. "Our tech guy. He manages a team of worker bees all over the world. Give him a keyboard with Wi-Fi, and he can find anything."

Knox sets his phone on the counter, face up. His palms press against the edge of the curved tile and his forearms flex. One thick vein bulges.

"What is it? Where's Sloane?" I ask, staring at the phone like it's a Magic 8 Ball with all the world's answers.

"He doesn't have more information on Sloane. It's you," Knox answers.

"Me?"

"Your house burned down three nights ago. I take it you haven't turned on your phone?"

"No, I was..." I blink, processing what this would mean. "Oh, my god. Jinx."

Knox's warm hand covers my shoulder. "Jinx?"

"My cat." My fingers cover my mouth. *My home.*

"You left your cat?" Max asks with an abundance of skepticism. I can't blame him. Who leaves behind their cat?

"He's an indoor-outdoor cat. He hates being indoors. My house backs up to a preserve. Really, the grade is too steep to be buildable much past my house. It's in the mountains. He roams those woods like, ah... He's a Maine Coon. He's huge. Oh, my god. He must be..." He'd be in the woods, scared. But he's a hunter. He'd find food. He'd... *but Jimmy.*

"I've got to call home." Frantically, I pull away. "I've got to get my phone. It's probably dead. I've got to—"

"Stop." Max halts me with his body. "Turning your phone off was smart. You can't turn it back on. Your hunch someone is tracking it could be correct."

"But I have to let my friends know I'm alive."

"Did you tell anyone you were going away?" Knox asks.

"No...I...I didn't. I was so scared, and I just wanted to get away and—"

"Hey, I get it." Knox caresses my shoulder. The movement soothes and warms...*but my house.* "No one knows you're out of town?"

"I texted Jimmy. Told him I had to go and not to worry..." I chew on a nail, as realization Jimmy has probably been frantic dawns. He'd be the one to call me, to tell me about the fire.

"Why would someone want to burn your house down?" The voice from the phone breaks into my thoughts, bringing me back to the kitchen.

Someone showed up at my house with a handgun with a silencer attached. And something has happened to Sloane. "I have no idea." I pace the middle of the floor, willing my heartrate to slow down and for my brain to kick into gear. "That man who broke in. He didn't look through anything. It was like...he was looking for me. Only me."

"He didn't look at your computer?"

"I threw a blanket over it. It's an old laptop. But he never lifted the blanket. I watched him through the crack in the cabinet I hid in. I don't know what he did downstairs, but I have a home office. Well, it's more of a craft room. But when I left, everything looked like it was in place." *Shit*. Jimmy must be freaking out. He's probably called a million times. "I've got to get my phone."

"Wait. You're listed as missing. You are safer with whoever is after you thinking—"

"Are they searching for my body?"

"There isn't an update in the local paper," the voice on the speakerphone says.

Max's stony stare is completely unreadable. I turn to Knox, pleading. "I have to call Jimmy. He's going to be worried sick."

"Who have you contacted about your sister?" the speakerphone asks. "I read your emails. But did you visit anyone? Go to the police?"

"You read my emails?"

"You have a Gmail account and use the same password on every website." Is he annoyed with me? "We need you to think about this. Your emails get more frantic—"

"She never responded to me. Something is wrong."

"I understand that. But we need to know everyone you spoke to. Did you drive to the police station and talk to someone there? Did you contact the US Embassy?"

I massage my temple, kneading the dull, throbbing pain. "I didn't go to the police. I called the US Embassy. I have no experience with this. I mean, her employer said she resigned, and I didn't believe them, but I assumed she'd call. I didn't want to be overly dramatic." *Oh, my god, I'm an idiot.*

"Do you know who you spoke with at the embassy?"

"I wrote her name down on a piece of paper. I was going to give her one more day to call me back. She was going to look into it. It just seemed so unlikely that something would really happen to Sloane, like I just kept thinking she would turn up. But…something has to have happened, right?" I search Knox's face. "I screwed up. I should've gone to the police on the first day after she missed my call. But Jimmy told me not to worry. That she'd show up. She can get very absorbed and…"

Knox pulls at a stool and gestures for me to sit, but I can't sit.

"Listen," he says, "you did what most people would do. Give it some time. And she's in another country, which is an added complication. But think. Did she send you anything? Videos? Documents?"

"Letters."

"Emails. That's what you mean, right? Do you have multiple email accounts?" The tech guy's voice startles me.

"No. Letters. It's what we do in our family. Sam started it. We write letters to each other."

"With stamps?" Max asks, both eyebrows raised.

"Yes. Why?" Who cares about our family's letters?

"Where'd you store them?" Erik asks.

"In a wooden chest." I close my eyes, realizing the fire would've destroyed it. "My dad made me the chest. I kept all the letters in that." The tips of my fingers cover my mouth. That chest holds all of my letters from Sam, all of them except the instructions he placed inside the duffel.

"You think they burned a house down for letters?" Max asks.

I didn't say that. But Max isn't asking me. I can't believe my home caught fire.

Knox runs his hand back and forth over his head. "Not sure. If they knew they existed…maybe. Chances are they knew you weren't home, so they didn't do it to kill you. Could've just been sending a message." Knox's eyes flash to mine. "Or someone's flushing you out."

"What? Like hoping I'd run home to see the fire?"

"Maybe. If you were nearby, it'd be hard to stay away from the ruins, right?"

Ruins. He's talking about my home. "Is it that bad? Did the fire destroy everything? Is there a news article I can read?"

"Or they're looking to see who she reaches out to confirm she's alive," Erik says. "That's absolutely what they're doing."

"You can't reach out to anyone. Not yet," Knox says.

"As of right now, the fire department hasn't uploaded any reports into the database on the fire. It's hard to know what caused the fire without those reports," the speakerphone announces.

"Look." I wrap my fingers around Knox's wrist, above his thick watchband. "I'll tell Jimmy he can't tell anyone I'm okay, but I have to let him know. You remember him, right? My grade. Jimmy Ringelspaugh."

"I don't remember—"

"I have to call him. He's going to be worried sick."

"He lives with you?"

"He lives in a house in a different neighborhood. But we moved to Asheville at the same time. I can't let him think…you know, they never found Sam's body. I can't…I can't let someone else go through—"

Knox pulls me in for a hug and my face presses against a hard, muscular chest. To breathe, I turn my head to the side. Pressure on the top of my head has me wondering if Knox just kissed my hair.

"All right. You can call him. But from one of my phones."

Knox and Erik go back and forth about what phone I should

use and how the call should be handled. The scenario is straight out of a movie, but it's also what I'd always imagined Sam's work life had been like. The reason he became so paranoid.

Why would someone set fire to my house? Sloane is a scientist. Could they think she sent me something proprietary? If so, they couldn't be more off. Sloane never talks to me about her work. She assumes it's over my head. And it is. She's a cellular biologist.

Eventually, the men agree on a small, cheap looking phone. Knox hands it to me and asks, "Do you know his number?"

Jimmy has had the same number since high school. I take the phone from Knox, venture out the side door for some privacy, and dial.

"You've reached Jimmy. I'm unavailable at the moment. It's no longer 1995. Text me. If you leave a voicemail, no one's gonna hear you, sweetie pie."

Of course, my call will appear as an unknown number. There's no way he'll answer. But Knox told me I can't text. Nothing in writing.

So I dial again.

"You've reached."

Hang up. Dial again.

"Hello? This is Jimmy."

"Jimmy, thank god you picked up."

"Sage? Is that you?"

"Yes. Where are you?"

"At home. Where the hell are you?"

"Is anyone there?"

"No. It's just me. Bart's at his office. Are you okay? Why haven't you returned my calls? Or my texts? Where are you?"

"Babe, you've gotta calm down."

"Are you serious right now? What the hell, Sage?"

"I know. I know."

"Does this have to do with Sloane?"

"I think so. But look, you've got to listen to me. You can't tell anyone you've spoken to me. And quit saying my name."

"Why? What's going on? Do you know? Did you hear about the fire?"

"Yes. Can you feed Jinx for me? See if you can find him?"

"I've been over there for days, asshole. I thought you were dead. Your neighbors think you're dead, too. I couldn't find Jinx, but two of your neighbors have been putting out food for him. They're supposed to call me if they see him. Where the hell are you?"

"You're not gonna believe it."

"Sage, your home burned down, and the fire department suspects arson. I've waffled between thinking you were dead or someone kidnapped you. Bart asked me to see his therapist. I stood there crying while firefighters searched your house for a body."

"Were any of them hot?"

"Are you serious right now? Do you think this is funny?"

"No, no. Of course not. It's gallows humor surfacing. I'm so sorry, Jimmy. My brain is–"

"Where the hell are you?"

"California."

"Cali? What the fuck? Why? What is going on?"

"Okay, Jimmy. I'm going to need you to chill. And you're going to need to remember to keep it quiet. I don't want to put you in danger."

"Jesus fucking Christ. Hold on just a minute." The phone goes silent.

"Jimmy?"

An uncomfortable silence weighs over the distance. But it's not a dial tone. He hasn't disconnected the call.

"Okay. I'm back. I'm calm. Tell me. What is going on?"

"I don't really know. Someone broke into my house. He had a handgun." I pause, rubbing my hand over the tightness in my chest.

My eyes burn. This situation is surreal. "I ran. Well, I hid and then ran when it was light outside."

"You drove away." He says it matter-of-factly.

"Yes."

"I think they've been looking for your car. Searching for the license plate. I told the firefighters and the police that your car was missing."

"It's okay. I switched out the license plate."

"How did you have an extra license plate?"

"Sam left me one."

"Why...you mean in that giant duffel he left you?"

"Yeah. Don't tell anyone about that. Did you?"

"No. I thought about it. But I figured it burned in the fire. But I also wondered if maybe Sam wasn't the paranoid freak I assumed he was. Like he somehow did something to bring someone's wrath down on you and Sloane. And he knew it was a risk, so he taught you how to shoot a gun."

It's hard to swallow. "Jimmy."

"Sorry. It's just...I've been worried sick. I thought you might be dead."

"What do the police think happened?"

"If they have theories, they aren't telling me. I'm not family. If anything, I'm a suspect."

"Oh, Jim—"

"I don't think I am now. One of them found me tissues. And I fully cooperated."

"Well, don't tell them anything more, okay?"

"You think the cops are in on this?"

"No, nothing like that. But Knox and Max want me to stay low. Just in case the people who are after me burned the house down to locate me."

"Who's Knox and Max?"

"Knox Williams. Max works with him."

"Knox Williams? From Rocky Mount Senior High?"

"The one and only."

"So, wait…let me get this straight. A guy breaks into your home, and you drive to your secret long-time crush? In California?"

A tap on the window grabs my attention. It's Knox, watching me from inside his house. I give him the thumbs up signal, and he signals the same back to me.

"Are you staying with Knox?"

"I can't tell you. But I'm safe. And I'll be back as soon as I can."

"You really think this is about Sloane?"

"It's the only thing that makes sense."

"If I'd listened or been more concerned when you first told me about Sloane, maybe this wouldn't be happening now."

"It's fine. And you did believe me. But you believed she'd turn up."

"Well, yeah, because…" His voice trails.

"It's the rational thing to expect."

"But you're okay now?"

"Yes, I am. How bad is my house?"

There's a pause. And I know.

"There's good news and bad. Which do you want first?"

"It's totaled, isn't it?"

"Jumping to the bad news. So now let me give you the good. Insurance will cover a new build. You rebuild it exactly like you want."

"That's your idea of good news?"

"And better news. Remember when I took photos of all of the furniture you crammed into that house?"

He did. He took photos from multiple angles. "You wanted me to post everything to sell."

"Sage. You had rooms that were so packed with furniture you couldn't enter them."

My parents lived in a four-bedroom home. I couldn't bring myself to sell their furniture. And then Sloane left things with me.

And all of Sam's stuff. Tears sting my eyes. "The fire destroyed everything?"

"And now you get to furnish your house with style. That's the good news." I swipe at a tear and look off into the street. "You happen to live near the furniture capital of the world. Unfortunately, Mitchell Gold went under, but we'll get–"

"Jimmy." It sounds like a whine, and I have to swallow before continuing. "I don't want to think about it."

"You may not see it yet, but your place needed an overhaul. Any visitor would assume you suffered from a hoarding disorder."

"Jimmy."

"Okay. Okay. We'll talk about it later. And now you're with *the* Knox Williams."

"Yes. And I'm safe." My throat hurts. I want to curl in a ball and cry.

"And you went to Knox because you were following the freakish instructions Sam left you?"

He read all of Sam's letters after the naval officer visited me. "Yeah."

"You know, I wondered if that's what you were doing. But then I thought Sam hasn't been around in two years, and we always thought he defined unhinged."

"I panicked. And I didn't want to put you in danger."

"Right. Well...thank god you're okay." A muffled sound comes through the line. Then a sniffle.

"I'm okay, Jimmy. I'm so sorry."

"Can I call you at this number?"

"Ah, I'm not sure. How about I call you?"

"Okay. Well, can you tell me, I mean...is Knox as god-like as ages ago?" Another sniffle. Jimmy tries to be tough, but he's a tall, leggy softie.

"More so."

"Figures. Men like him always age well."

"His hairline is receding a little, but he somehow looks even more attractive."

"Still in shape?"

"Jimmy. The guy was a SEAL."

"He's not anymore?"

"No. He works for a security company now."

"Like a mall cop?"

"No. Like protect the rich, at least, I think. I don't know, really. But he said they can help me find Sloane."

"And he's going to keep you safe?"

"Yeah, he is."

"I still can't believe you haven't returned a phone call or a text in a week." The fire in his accusation smolders, and his pain reverberates in my chest.

"I'm sorry. It's just...everything Sam told me to do clicked. Sam's voice was all I could hear. I was afraid to turn on my phone."

"I get it." He sounds resigned. "Well, there will be payback."

"What do you mean?"

"When you bang Knox, I get details. I want all the goods." I roll my eyes. Not that Jimmy can see. "Roll your eyes all you want. But take your chance, go for it, and take lots of mental notes. I need you to feed this inquiring mind."

"It's not like that. And you know it." Jimmy really knows it. He's quite familiar with my sordid history.

"It could be."

"I'm not his type." I imagine he dates Baywatch babes. Blonde, buxom, tall, tan, and blue eyed.

"Then he's a fool."

More like off-the-charts hot with unlimited options.

The door cracks open. Knox sticks his head through the opening. "You about done? Erik has some questions for you."

"Hey, Jimmy, I gotta go. But I'm fine. And I love you."

"Love you, too, Sagie. And if that guy doesn't see the beauty in you, then we were wrong. Not only is he not god-like, he's undeserving of the Norseman title."

I look up from my seated position on the stoop. Knox's ruffled hair swirls about in loose, erratic waves, no doubt from his constant tugging on the strands. Anxious eyes sear my skin with a mere look. His height and build convey strength and ability, and his concern radiates conviction. Like Sam, he risked his life for his country, to make this world a better place.

Jimmy has never been more wrong. Knox Williams absolutely deserves our adulation. The man is beautiful, inside and out.

CHAPTER 7

Knox

"What's she doing?"

"Finishing up her call." I pull the side door closed, watching as she wraps things up with her significant other. It's no surprise Sage is dating someone. But it's puzzling she would drive cross-country without looping him in. She followed her dead brother's instructions instead of going to this guy. It doesn't speak well of him.

We'll have his number after this call. Erik can gather basic information on him. Run a background check.

I back away from the window, but not before gaining a good view of her backside. Those jeans hang loose over her legs, but the denim hugs her bottom tightly, revealing firm, full contours. A sliver of skin, the curve of her waistline, shows between the bottom of her cropped tee and her jeans.

She turns, and I twist to avert my gaze. The last thing she needs is to think I'm ogling her.

Max types away, presumably on the team Slack channel.

The screen door slams behind Sage with a creak and pop.

"Everything okay?"

"All things considered. Thanks for letting me call him. He was worried." She sets the phone on the kitchen table. "He said that he told the cops my car is missing. And they suspect arson. I asked him to not tell anyone he spoke to me."

She shoves her hands in her front pockets.

"Good. If he tells the police, they'll update their report. Once they upload the police report, anyone with access to the server will have the information," Max says.

She shifts on her feet and moves her hands into her back jeans pockets. The action presses her chest out and lifts the hem of her cropped tee, exposing a wider stretch of smooth skin and the dip of her bellybutton.

"Jimmy said they've been searching for my license plate. I guess it's good that Sam gave me an alternate plate."

"I find it fascinating Saint packed an alternate license plate for you," Max says, crossing his arms over his chest in a way that makes him look like a bouncer at a bar with a queue to enter. His stance says he's calling bullshit on her story, but he's running the wrong angle.

"I'll go move your car," I say, giving Max my best stand-down expression. "We have an extra spot." Millie pads over to Sage and sniffs her feet. "One of our colleagues, Kairi, the one who works with Erik on the tech side, has some questions for you. Can I set you up on a laptop? She prefers to communicate on Slack, which is like a system for texting. Keeps everyone in the loop. She's got a team of minions doing research for her."

"Sure."

Max stands and gestures to my laptop. "Here, you can use this one. I'll go with Knox to move your car."

Given I don't exactly need help moving a car, I figure Max has either learned something or he has more questions.

The second the front door closes behind us, Max says, "Erik made some headway."

"Is that right?" The streetlamps flick on. A passing car slows for a speed bump. I wave at a neighbor several houses down.

"What do you know about her sister? Sloane Watson?"

"Like I told you, I didn't know her well. Back in high school, she was studious. Quiet. Head of the debate club. If I remember correctly, she won a STEM competition and was nominated for homecoming court, but that would've been two years after I left. My memory could be off."

"So, she's attractive and smart?"

I stop in front of Sage's car and cock my head at Max. "Why?"

"Interpol's been watching her."

"Seriously?" *What the fuck?*

"Erik went to file a yellow notice, you know, missing person's alert, and received an alert from a contact within Interpol. Her name flagged on a case file. Nothing so serious as to warrant a purple notice, or official watch, but still."

"Was Interpol watching her specifically, or her company?"

"The assumption is the company, but we're getting confirmation. Wanted you to be aware."

"What kind of work was she doing that would warrant monitoring?"

"Kairi said there are international laws regarding research." Kairi works remotely, so I've never met her in person, but all the guys respect her. "She found research papers from Sloane on stem cell research and growing tissue. Both are areas governed by international law. The Caymans has a notoriously lenient legal environment. And she chose to do research there. That alone might have put her on a list. It could mean nothing. But, given she's MIA and someone appears to be targeting her sister, I'm relaying the information. Sloane might be guilty of breaking international law."

"Guilty or not, I'm still going to find her. I owe it to Sam."

Max crosses his arms and stares down the bridge of his nose. "Sam?"

"These are his sisters. He's not here. And that's on me."

"Jesus, Knox. For the thousandth time, that wasn't your fault. You gotta let it go. Sam's death is not on you. And I know damn well the shrinks told you the same damn thing."

I swing the keys around my index finger, remembering Sam. His last wave. More of a casual salute. I blink the memory away.

"His death might not be." The military shrink did say as much. "But I'm the one he asked to look out for his sisters if something happened to him. And that's where we are." I clap him on his back. "Let's move the car."

I get into the driver's side, and Max opens the passenger side door. The dash is dust free, the seats shiny like someone polished the leather. It appears Sage takes good care of her vehicle.

"You worried someone's going to track her to California?" Max asks.

I adjust the rearview and press the button on the ignition. It's one of the new Broncos that's smaller than the classic. Better gas mileage. Four-wheel drive. "Normally, I'd say no. But they burned down her house, so…all bets are off." I sling an arm over the seat as I reverse to back out of the parallel spot.

"You know, if this is about Sloane, it's possible Sloane mailed her something she didn't even realize she had. Maybe that guy who broke into her place wasn't after Sage at all. Maybe he just wanted something Sloane sent her. Couldn't find it, so they burnt the house down to be safe."

I pull out into the street, only to whip left into our drive and the line of parking spots for our place.

"That's an interesting thought. Could be why the intruder didn't look hard when he broke into her place. Maybe he sensed he wasn't alone, and they didn't hire him to kill. Could be after she left, they ransacked the place, still couldn't find what they were looking for, and they cut their losses. There's some logic to it. I mean, who mails letters these days? Especially internationally?"

"And you trust this girl? Sage?"

I put it in park and kill the ignition. Max is a teammate. One of Sam's teammates. Brothers for life. "I know you've always got to assume the worst in everyone, but these are Sam's sisters. They're good people. Both of them."

"And if they're not?"

"I'll stand by them. Do everything I can for them."

Max's expression is stoic. Unreadable. But I don't need to read him to understand him. This is Max being Max. Figuring out where his team stands before the mission starts. Evaluating the angles. "And if she's trying to loop us into something—"

"Seriously? What could possibly be her end game?"

"I'm just saying. I'm having a hard time buying that she'd drive across the country to find you. There could be some other reason for pulling Arrow into this…whatever this is. Think about it. Interpol is involved. Getting Arrow involved could be a last resort to save her sister."

"Did you not see her when she found out about her house? Her home? And how would she even know about Arrow? When Sam was alive, we didn't work there."

"All I'm saying is keep an open mind. I can tell you're into her, but there are a lot of questions right now."

"She has a boyfriend. She's an old friend. A family friend. These are Sam's sisters, and I'm going to help them. Both of them. And, by the way, Ryan called earlier. Erik updated him. He said Arrow's on board to help."

Ryan didn't serve at the same time as Sam, but he's stayed close with the commanding officers. He's heard of Sam. Knows we lost him in Syria. Ryan's got a sister of his own. He'll do right by Sam.

And Max is being Max, but he's got his head up his ass if he thinks Sage is playing us. I hope our theory that they were just eliminating incriminating evidence is spot on. It's the best scenario. That would mean no one is coming after Sage. But right now, we don't know. Right now, we are far too light on intel.

CHAPTER 8

Sage

KAIRI

Do you know any of your sister's colleagues' names?

The message board shows first names and comments. To the right, I can see that multiple people are accessing the board as I type. Multiple people, people I don't know, are reading all of my responses. My unhelpful, woefully inadequate responses.

So many of my conversations with my sister were pointless.

Why didn't I ask more questions when we spoke?

The weather. Jinx, my rescue cat. My school kids. Frustrating crap that came up during her move. When she first moved, I'd ask if she met anyone.

She never did. Said most of her colleagues were married. Referred to her boss as "my boss." She liked him, although he'd frustrated her, too. She complained about his frequent mansplaining and that he desperately needed a nose wax.

She had a relationship with one colleague. Not a direct boss but a level higher. She refused to have sex with him until she got confirmation from HR that she wouldn't be breaking any rules. But he moved to Switzerland months ago. I asked if she'd keep dating him, and she'd told me it was just sex. I've never known if Sloane is really as unemotional as she claims, or if she says things like that so I won't worry about her.

SAGE

Her direct boss was Dr. Haussler. She dated a colleague named William, but he moved away around six months ago.

Somewhere out there, people I'd never met were reading and processing. Probably searching for Dr. Haussler online. There'd only be one of those in the world, right? And that was her boss at the beginning.

KAIRI

Do you know the first name?

SAGE

No. And I'm not 100% that's still her boss.

I never asked. Why would I? Do normal people ask for the first names of people they'll probably never meet in person? Do normal people know the names of their siblings' colleagues?

SAGE

Sloane is a clinical researcher. Her field is generative cell therapy. Her passion is organ bioengineering.

Her work is way over my head. Light years. At least, that's always been my assumption. I both hated and loved that my sister put her career behind my illness. Or at least, for years, I looked at it that way. Jimmy helped me see it differently.

Your experiences inspired her interest in cell therapy. Stop reading into it. Don't put her choices on your shoulders.

Of course, it was her experience, too. She didn't live in a hospital like me, but she spent far more time in a hospital than the average kid. Her luck of the draw with a sick sibling. Really, my entire family's poor luck.

KAIRI

Was she happy at her job?

I stare at the question.

Happy? Obsessed is more like it.

I sent her photos of my back yard, of plants, Jinx, Jimmy…of anything to remind her a world existed outside the lab. She sent me letters.

. . .

SAGE

Her boss pushed what she called anti-aging research. Still in her field, but it didn't match up with what she expected based on the job description.

Sloane didn't go into details. But in one of our video calls, we debated it. Me saying that anti-aging research helped to lengthen lifespans, and it was worthwhile. After all, some called it longevity research. Sloane believed investing in lab-grown organs could save more lives and generate billions in profit, unlike what she called "the wrinkle initiative."

KAIRI

Anti-aging research like skin care? Creams?

SAGE

No, still cellular. One of the drugs they were testing is Rapamycin. It's a drug that kidney transplant patients use.

SAGE

It has a lot of uses. She only mentioned it to me because she asked if they had added it to my drug regimen.

KAIRI

We'll look into it. Was the company she worked for a subsidiary of Lumina International?

SAGE

Not sure. Why?

KAIRI

Having trouble locating Origin Laboratories employee records.

SAGE

She paid US taxes. There has to be a record.

We didn't discuss details, but in some off-handed conversation she'd complained about taxes. In order to maintain US citizenship, she had to continue paying federal income taxes and contributing to Social Security.

KAIRI

Do you have any of her tax records?

Seriously?

SAGE

Any documents I had probably burned with my house. She stored everything she didn't want to move with me. But I never went through her boxes.

Max stands and stretches. "I'm gonna head home. See you two tomorrow."

"Do you need your laptop back?"

"That's Knox's. I was just using it. You're good."

Knox steps up behind me and scans the exchanges. "Are you good on meds? Do we need to get you anything?"

"I'm good." Everyone close to me worries about my meds. The worry is a holdover from my childhood. But they don't need to worry. I don't have a death wish. I'm proficient at managing my medication and have been for over a decade.

"Later," Max says, then disappears through the creaky side door.

"When will you need refills?" The question feels personal, but he's not prying. He's just concerned. Which is nice of him. There's no way for him to know it's a sensitive subject.

"Ten days."

Knox's lips scrunch together.

"I can get a refill here."

"And when you do, you open up the possibility they'll find you."

He's right. I should have thought of this. "How long…I'm supposed to be back at school, setting up my classroom in two weeks' time. I mean, do you think someone will still be looking for me?"

"I'm not sure. We've still got a lot to figure out." He leans closer, touching the trackpad to scroll through the questions and answers. He smells of fresh soap, a masculine brand. And something else too…a light scent, like just-out-of-the-dryer laundry. His jaw flexes and his eyes narrow. I can practically hear him wondering how long I'll be in his space, messing up his routine.

"I can look for another place to stay tomorrow. I have—"

"You'll stay here."

"I don't want to impose—"

"Didn't you say that Sam told you to come here?"

Is this what he meant, though? Was my brother actually envisioning me arriving empty-handed on his friend's stoop?

"You're going to stay with me." The matter-of-fact statement leaves no room for argument.

"There's no way they have any idea where I am." My phone remains off. Sam's packed duffel included ten thousand in cash. The trip cross-country took about a thousand in food and gas, but I still have plenty.

"You're staying with me." He points at the screen and the latest Slack.

KAIRI

We're good for tonight. Regroup tomorrow.

"Kairi's team is global. Someone on the team will keep digging through the night."

"So, we could have answers in the morning." Steps closer to finding Sloane. Figuring out what is going on.

"Possibly."

"Should we go to the cops?" Why didn't Sam tell me to go to the cops if I was in trouble? Why didn't I think to ask him more about his instructions? *Because you thought he was paranoid and should possibly be kicked out of the military.*

"No. Not yet. The scenario that they burned your house down to flush you out is still too likely. And local cops can't help locate your sister in another country. We'll have a team meeting tomorrow to discuss strategy. We might bring in the FBI. Or maybe someone from Interpol."

He crosses his arms and his lips curve together. His eyes glaze over in a faraway expression, like he's processing information. It isn't the first time I've seen that thoughtful expression.

He blinks, and his face transforms back to the present. With a loud exhale, he says, "I'm guessing you'd love a shower."

A shower and a Xanax. "I'm really so sorry. The last thing I wanted—"

"Stop. You're Sam's sister. And an old friend. Follow me. I'll set out clean towels for you and give you some time."

Guilt nags at me. I'm forcing him to host me. Of course, what did I expect? I showed up on his doorstep.

When I exit his bedroom after a much-needed shower, I find him at his breakfast bar, reading on his laptop. I stop, frozen, taking in the tortoise rimmed glasses.

Knox has always been a gorgeous specimen, but with the added splash of humanity, he slips into breathtaking. The hot professor on campus. Or the muscular computer nerd. Put some cowboy boots on him, and he could star as the urban cowboy. He could be the cover model for so many romance novels. That is one thing Sloane and I had in common. We both love reading romance novels. For her, it's a guilty pleasure. One she's reluctant to admit to. But I've seen her Kindle.

"Feel better?" His lips spread into a slow grin.

"Yeah." My belly twists.

He closes the laptop and pushes off the stool. "Can I get you some tea?"

"You drink tea?"

"Decaffeinated. Helps me sleep. Want some?"

"Sure."

I slide onto the stool as he opens a cabinet and removes two plain white mugs, then steps to the stove and picks up an already steaming kettle.

"Did anything new come up while I was in the shower?"

"Nothing concrete. Based on the location of the labs your sister worked for, we suspect she was conducting ethically gray research." Steam rises from the mugs as he pours the hot water. "Origins Laboratories is a relatively new business entity. We're looking into who was funding them. Trying to uncover any connections. Which is why anything you can remember, any names, any piece of information could be helpful."

"Sloane wouldn't do anything illegal." But after she disappeared, my imagination went wild. "It's possible she discovered something. If she did, she'd threaten to turn them in. Sloane refused to drive above the speed limit. She's big on rules. She isn't someone who could be convinced to break the law." He slides a mug over to me, along with a squeezable bottle of honey. "I've read about research studies that went belly up because of transgressions. One of my theories is that she discovered something and they're trying to prevent her from being a whistleblower." Slowly, I stir the tea bag in the hot water. "But I don't like that theory, because I don't see why they'd keep her alive."

"Tell me about these transgressions."

"Oh, I mean things like admitting people into the study who shouldn't be admitted. Or selectively choosing which patients get the placebo. That kind of thing. And truthfully, I don't even know if it's applicable to what Sloane was doing. I know that one of the big questions with Rapamycin, for example, is what the ideal dosage would be for someone taking it for longevity purposes. Not for organ rejection, but just for, you know, anti-aging. The drug suppresses the immune system, so it's a fine line to walk. But it's kind of hard to imagine an anti-wrinkle solution as being whistle-blower worthy."

He raps his knuckles against the counter. "We're not going to figure it out tonight."

"My sister is still alive."

I can't allow him to believe she isn't. No one believes Sam is alive, and I live with that. I can't be the only one who believes Sloane is.

"Has she contacted you?"

"No. I can feel it." Rather than take in his reaction to my explanation, I pick up my mug and enter the small den. If forced to explain, I'll sound crazy. Or wishful. But I knew when my father died. I felt it in my chest and went to his house and found him. Deep in my chest cavity, I felt the moment his life ended. It was the same with my mom. Admittedly, I'd been sitting by her side, holding her hand. But I hadn't been with my dad. It's the reason I know Sam is still alive, and so is Sloane.

"Tell me about Asheville. You like it there?" The sofa cushions sink with our weight as we each take our places on opposite sides of the sofa.

"I do. Have you ever been?"

"Nope. But I've heard good things."

"It's pretty great. Lots of artists…glassblowers, painters, pottery makers, chocolatiers…all kinds." Small businesses thrive throughout the downtown area. "Very entrepreneurial." Knox smiles with his eyes. The tortoise rim glasses set off his familiar, warm, honey-brown irises. He's probably the most handsome man I've ever been around. "I like those glasses."

He lifts them, rubbing one eye with the butt of his hand. "Forgot I was wearing 'em."

"It's a good look."

He holds the frames out, looking them over before setting them onto the coffee table. Millie lifts her head from where she's sprawled out on the floor, decides they aren't food, and lies back down.

"Vision isn't what it used to be. Wearing those glasses when I'm on the computer is supposed to help."

"Have you thought about Lasik? Does the military approve of Lasik?"

"I had Lasik. About five years ago. My vision's still pretty good. Those glasses help with eye strain. If you're wondering why I left the Navy," he side-eyes me and sucks in the side of his bottom lip, giving me a thoughtful half-smile, "it wasn't vision. It's not like that these days. Maybe for pilots, but… no, my hearing took a beating."

"They have hearing aids, though."

"What if one gets knocked out while we're on a mission? Docs said it might improve, but it didn't. Just as well. I'm thirty-five, pushing thirty-six. Joints have taken a beating. Nothing too bad. Still active. Still working. But…the things we do. Did. It's better I move on than be the team's weak link."

Not when other lives depend on him. I understand. Sam shared some of what they do.

"Sam said they take body and soul."

"Body, I'll grant you. Soul…if they take that, then you've stayed in too long."

"That's a good way of looking at it."

"I got to do what I wanted. Had a good run to the top. For a while, it felt like winning every day. I was good at it, you know? But there comes a time when transition is necessary."

"And so now…what exactly do you do? You went to what Sam called the privates? A security company?"

"The privates." The nostalgic grin has me smiling, too. "Yeah, we didn't talk too kindly about the privates. But this one's a good one. After I took a medical discharge, an officer recommended I reach out to them. Arrow Tactical Security. Best phone call I ever made. Ryan, he's one of the founders, came down and met with me. Hired me on the spot. Better pay and benefits than the Navy. And they really care about our health. There's this guy, Trevor, another one of the partners. He works with us, mindful of injuries. Keeps us healthy."

"But what exactly do you do?"

"Security. For sure, that's a big piece. Handle ransom demands. We take jobs…mostly international…for governments when they don't want to get involved. It can sound sketchy but unlike a lot of the privates that are motivated solely by money, Arrow is fully funded. The founders are motivated for all the right reasons." He tilts his head and looks me straight in the eye. "We find missing people. You came to the right place, Sage."

"All that sounds like… I mean, how much will it cost?"

"You don't need to worry about that."

"But you're using employees. Resources. That has to—"

"One of the partners is loaded. Jack Sullivan. Billionaire. More money than anyone could spend in a lifetime. Family money. Owns Sullivan Arms." He says it like I should recognize the name, but I don't. "They make weapons. Guns. Jack bankrolls Arrow. He's a good guy. Former Navy. CIA too. He's looking to do good. He definitely looks out for his fellow servicemen."

"Did he know Sam?"

"Maybe. Who knows? Pretty tight-knit community. But Ryan had heard of Sam, and he told me Arrow is all in."

"And Erik? And Kairi? And those others on the chat earlier?"

"Erik and Kairi are partners, too, but I've never met them in person. They live up north. They're not former military. Their background is in intelligence. Max is actually considering training so he can work with them."

"Not you?"

"Nah, I'm not much of a computer guy."

That half-smile plays across his lips.

Lips that once, a long time ago, I stared at too long. Back when

I misinterpreted that half-smile. The memory brings heat to my cheeks. He'd backed up. Couldn't get away fast enough.

How many times have I wanted to apologize for that? For embarrassing him? For being completely inappropriate. It was so long ago. I hope he's forgotten about it. But there might not be a tomorrow. There's no time like the present to apologize. You can't bank on having another day. "I'm sorry—"

"Haven't you said that enough? You have nothing to be sorry for. I'd be mad at you if you didn't come to me. I'm sorry about your house."

I don't want to dwell on my house. Not right now. "Well, as Jimmy said, on the bright side, there's insurance. And, thanks to Sam, I've got USAA."

"They're good."

"Jimmy knows someone who works for them. He's going to have them come out."

"He won't tell them where you are?"

"Oh, no. He won't."

He stares at me, like he's trying to determine if I'm telling the truth. And it's a good thing I am, because there's something about sitting so close to him, about being the sole focus of his attention. I feel bared. Open. Raw.

Millie approaches the sofa, glances at Knox, and hops up beside me, curling so she nestles into the side of my leg. Such a sweet dog.

There's no day like today. The words play in my head as my fingers sift through fur.

"You know…I never apologized for that time I…" Tried to kiss him? Threw myself on him? "Never mind." I dig my nails deeper into Millie's coat, scratching her back. "You probably don't even remember."

Why would he? Why did my thoughts go there? I never should've brought it up. It was so long ago. A childish mistake. It's the honey brown eyes coupled with tortoiseshell spectacles and the proximity.

"You think I'd forget a beautiful girl kissing me?"

Deep indentations on the edge of the coffee table capture my attention. Heat singes my cheeks.

"You do not need to apologize."

I'm such an idiot. I should've never brought this up.

"Or be embarrassed."

A light coat of dandruff rises on Millie's thick chocolate brown coat. The tips of Knox's fingers touch mine, and I swear my heart palpitates.

"Sagey–"

"No one calls me that." It's a childhood nickname. Sam and my parents used it. Well, my parents called me Sagey Bean. And Jimmy uses it, but no one else. "I shouldn't've said anything. But I've wanted to apologize for a long time, as I'm sure it threw you." I push up off the sofa. "Here, I'll sleep on the sofa. Where do you–"

"You're not going to sleep on the sofa. You'll take the bed and I'll sleep out here."

I can hear the determination in his voice. And I'm too shaken by his touch and this conversation to argue. Besides, Knox, like Sam, sticks to certain southern ways, and this is a losing argument. He was raised to be a Southern gentleman, and that means he'll take the sofa. Another reason I need to find a hotel.

He pulls back the light blue comforter on his bed and grabs a pillow and a blanket for himself. He stands in the doorway, hand on the light switch.

"Thanks, Knox. I'll be out of your hair soon."

"For the last time, I'm glad you came to me." He flicks the light off but remains in the doorway. "Sage, just so you know, if you weren't my best friend's little sister, if I wasn't leaving the next day, if you had been eighteen, if any of those things had been different, I promise you, I wouldn't have pushed you away. Now, get your sleep, and in the morning, we'll work on finding Sloane."

The door closes, along with any chance for sleep.

CHAPTER 9

Knox

Ryan Wolfgang, one of the Arrow founders, pushes back from his desk. He doesn't smile, but he has a reputation as stern and standoffish until you get to know him. The guy has freakish ice-blue eyes that contributed to his nickname, Wolf. His positive attributes, mainly being a good leader, fair, intelligent, and disciplined, make up for his chilly vibe. Besides, one could argue that Trevor, his counterpart at Arrow, compensates for the no-bullshit chilliness. That guy always has an upbeat smile. He's the quintessential you-got-this coach.

"Ryan, this is my friend, Sage Watson. She's the one—"

"Sage, it's a pleasure to meet you." With two strides, he stands before us, hand held out for Sage to shake. He does a double-take at Millie and her wagging tail. She's wagged nonstop since this morning when we left my house, walked to the coffee shop for breakfast, then to the office.

The conference room door opens, and Stella, our Human Resources director and Trevor's wife, steps out. Polite introductions ensue. She brushes her hand over Sage's arm in a friendly, welcoming way that's all Stella. Despite her blue-tinged hair, her smile possesses a motherly vibe, and her outfit, a pencil skirt and silk blouse, colors her professional.

To Ryan, she says, "After your meeting, let me know what resources you need." She gives a brief nod to me and speeds down the hall.

"Let's step into the conference room. Erik's expecting our call."

Ryan heads into the long room and we follow. Sage tugs on my pinky finger, distraught. "You're sure about the cost? Shouldn't I ask?"

"No. We've got this," I tell her, placing a hand firmly on her lower back to guide her into the conference room.

"No." Sage's fierce tone halts my motion. "When Sam told me to come to you, he didn't mean for you to spend a small fortune helping me."

Wrong. Sam would want his sister safe and healthy at any cost.

"These men are family. Not by blood, but we're all former military, and we now work together. We defend each other. And as I explained, we also have the luxury of being well-funded, so finances aren't a concern. And you're my family. So that makes them your family. Got it?"

Her lips purse and her brow wrinkles. She doesn't get it, but she will.

In the conference room, the large monitor at the end of the room flicks to life. Kairi appears on the screen with a BabyBjörn strapped to her chest.

"Hi, guys," Kairi says. "Erik got pulled on another case, so I'm filling in."

"What'd you learn?" Ryan asks, leading the charge from the end of the conference table. He gestures at the empty chairs for us to take a seat.

Someone, presumably Stella, laid out coffee, water, and small snacks on a side table.

"Hey, guys, sorry I'm late." Max rushes through the door,

followed by my friend and colleague, Felix. "Trevor said we were getting too fucking tight, so he added on a mobility session."

With Sage at my house, I skipped the group session this morning and went on a quick five-mile run. "Yoga?" I shoot him a grin just to razz him up.

"That's exactly what the stuff is, and Mr. Bendy loves it," Felix says and leans across the table with a hand extended. "Nice to meet you, Sage. I'm Felix. Sam and I served together. With this guy." He jerks his thumb in my direction, then nods to the screen. "Kairi. How's it going?"

"Good. David's mom isn't feeling well, so I'm home today with her. Just a heads up if I get interrupted." Kairi's husband, David, is a pediatrician. He doesn't have the luxury of working from home.

"You guys are so lucky to have family right there," Felix says. "Man, Maria would kill for that."

Ryan raps the table with his knuckles. "What'd you learn, Kairi?"

She reaches down, and the screen switches from her to a photograph of an aerial shot of five buildings surrounded by trees.

"This is the campus for the entity Sloane Watson's tax returns show she worked for. We finally located the personnel files. According to her file, she resigned and her employment discontinued on July twenty-first. Three weeks ago."

"That's not accurate. She and I spoke in July. You can check our texts. She would've mentioned if she was changing jobs. She didn't resign. I know she didn't."

Sage's dark brown eyes jump from Max, to Felix, to Ryan, pleading her case.

"If that's true, then someone within the company must be preparing for inquiries," Felix says.

"Kairi, are you showing us this complex because you think Sloane Watson is still there?" Ryan asks.

"No. This research center gets too much attention. There's no barrier around this complex. People come and go freely. Lumina is a leading biotech firm headquartered in Switzerland with approximately forty-six thousand employees worldwide. "

"But she didn't work for Lumina," Sage says.

"No, but Lumina International is the primary investor in Origin Labs, where she worked. The complex on screen is Origin Laboratories property. It's not technically a division of Lumina, but it's probably set up this way for tax purposes," Kairi says. "Lumina International is a large conglomerate with individual CEOs for each entity. Some entities have CEOs for specific geographic regions. All those CEOs are here right now. My guess is they're having a conference in the Caymans for the location. I mean, she could be held here, but if she's being held against her will, that would be ballsy. And to be quite honest, based on the annual reports, Lumina is a reputable firm. Now, what's interesting is that Origins Labs barely got a mention in Lumina's annual report. They invested one hundred and twenty-five million in 2022. Since that investment, Origins Labs hasn't expanded any infrastructure."

"Sloane talked about the space," Sage says. "It impressed her. Said it was state-of-the art and like nothing she'd worked in before. Brand new construction." Sage's face lights up. "She sent me photos." Her excitement dims. "But they might've burned."

"She snail mailed you photos?" Felix asks.

"We both like getting mail. So, yeah, we mail each other. Sam, Sloane, and...I mean, we texted and emailed too...but she always included photos in her letters to me."

Kairi's voice breaks through the speaker in the room. "We called Origins inquiring about your sister. Under the guise of a cousin trying to locate Sloane. We ended up being transferred to a Lucia Oliveira, an assistant to Lumina's Global CEO. Based in Zurich."

"Why would an investor field employee inquiries?" Ryan asks.

"We're not sure. It's possible that for various accounting or tax reasons Lumina set Origins up independently but they are really running the show. International business structure isn't something I completely understand. I've reached out to someone to look into it. But my guess is however they have it structured, it's all about tax avoidance. A contact at Interpol confirmed they were monitoring Origins Laboratories but wouldn't share more information. Said it was above my pay grade."

"I'll reach out," Ryan says.

"Contact names in Slack," Kairi says. "And by the way, the yellow notice is in effect. Sloane Watson is now officially listed as a missing person on the Interpol network."

"Any proof of life?" Ryan asks.

I glance to Sage, but she doesn't wince at the terminology.

"She's alive." Sage answers with absolute conviction.

"Has she been in touch with you?" Ryan asks, but we all know she hasn't. She answered that exact question yesterday.

"No. But I know it. The same way I know Sam is alive. I can feel it."

And with that last comment, Sage's credibility gets shot to hell.

Max and Felix shift in their seats, angling their bodies to the static screen mounted on the wall.

Ryan visibly swallows and raps his knuckles against the table. "Alive or not, we've got someone out there who is coming after you, so we've got a case. Knox, you and Felix take the lead. Pull a plan together and let Stella know what resources you're going to need. That includes your team, Kairi. I'm gonna make some calls. Run it up the flagpole with our Interpol friends. If I need to, I'll reach out to my brother-in-law at the NSA."

"Speaking of Sam," Max says, "he packed a duffel bag for you, right? It included guns and cash. And he told you to come to Knox if you were ever in trouble?"

The way he's asking her, it's as if he's putting her on trial. And he wants everyone in the room to hear it all, even though it's all documented in our network.

Sage nods. The fingers of one hand rub back and forth over her knuckle, as if she's self-soothing. "He also got me alternative identification. A North Dakota license, a US passport, and an EU passport."

"Did he create a similar duffel bag for Sloane?" Ryan asks.

I should've thought to ask her that yesterday.

"Yes," Sage answers. "I only know because Sloane and I both talked about it. We both worried he was suffering from PTSD or some condition that was making him paranoid."

"Did she take the duffel bag with her when she moved to the Caymans?"

"Possibly. She moved some furniture and boxes to my basement before she left. I never went through the boxes. She was going to park her car in my garage but decided to sell it instead." Sage sucks on her bottom lip, thinking. "Sloane doesn't like guns. She refused to learn how to shoot one, so Sam wouldn't have given her one. But she probably would have kept the false identification."

Kairi speaks up. "Can you messenger me the IDs you have?"

Sage looks to me.

"Yeah. We'll send them up today," I answer.

"Can't promise anything. But there might be a marker to indicate where Sam got them. If Sloane's on the run, she's probably using the alternative passports. If we can find who made the passports, we can probably figure out what alias she's using." Kairi's gaze falls on Sage. "But that's an off-the-wall idea. Don't get your hopes up. If it's quality work, we won't be able to tell."

A loud crash sounds through the speaker. Millie sits up at attention.

"Guys, I gotta go," Kairi says. "Keep Slack updated."

Felix taps Max. "Let's go pull any satellite photos of the islands. Compare over the prior ten years, see if we see a bigger facility on a nearby island. Also look for interior photos of these buildings. Let's see if we can locate any facilities on the island or nearby islands that might hold someone."

"We'll join you," I say. It's unlikely we'll discover anything from aerial photos, but it's a possibility.

Felix shakes his head and cuts his eyes to Sage. "We got this. Take her up to the roof deck. Get some fresh air."

I study Sage. Does Felix see something? Is she not feeling well?

When I met Sam, he'd been an old soul at the ripe age of sixteen. And the reason had to do with his littlest sister. She'd been born with a congenital heart defect, and I'd never seen a guy so concerned about a sibling. He'd call to check in after we walked out of a movie. Didn't go camping. Missed many a weekend party to sit with his sister at the hospital. She'd been in and out of the hospital. And then the big day came. Heart and double lung transplant. We'd been at the Naval Academy, and he rushed home to be with his family.

Out of habit, I lead Sage to the stairwell. It's only three flights, but I hear her inhale and halt. "Do you wanna take the elevator?"

"I can handle the stairs, Knox." Her smile smacks my chest. Not a punch, but more of a heated massage pad right over the sternum. She's been through so much, and yet she practically glows positivity.

"You take your medicine this morning?" She rolls her eyes as if I'm nagging her. I get people fussing over her drives her nuts. I'd be the same damn way. But Felix told me to get her fresh air and... "You doing okay?" I'm not sure I trust her to tell me if she's not.

"As good as I can be, you know, given Sloane." *Right.*

She frees Millie from the leash, and Millie lunges forward on the stairwell, nearly knocking Sage down.

"Hey," I yell at the dog. Her tail wags as she bounds up the stairs, completely disregarding me.

Sage laughs. "It's fine. It's instinct. She's pushing ahead."

"Instinct, you say? Need I remind you she's an obedience school flunkee?"

"Maybe she's just a better pet."

She passes through the threshold and into the bright California sun. A few scattered clouds mix in with the blue sky. The silver bracelet on her wrist glitters.

The Arrow building is about eight blocks back from the ocean, but from the roof, you get the view and remnant ocean breeze. If you step closer to the edge, palm trees line the streets. Bikers, rollerbladers, scooters, and pedestrians traverse the sidewalks and the streets. The ambience reeks of vacation. Santa Barbara reminds me of parts of San Diego. It's much smaller than San Diego, but the beach vibe is similar and, like San Diego, it's expensive as hell.

Sage takes in the view, and I take in her. She's so completely different than I remember, but some things are the same. Her warmth. Genuine kindness. It almost oozes out of her pores. Tom Petty's words about a good girl come to mind when I look at Sage. Back then, she was a kid. But now, I'd hate to think of a bad boy—again, Tom Petty's words—coming along and breaking her heart.

"What was your cat's name?"

"Pascal."

"An orange tabby, right?"

"He was a mix. Longer hair but a total mutt. We got him from the pound." She smiles fondly.

"He was a cute guy." He greeted everyone who entered the Watson home unless Sage was bed bound. Then he camped out on her bed, like he knew she needed him.

The cat died when we were in high school. All I remember about it is Sam saying the surgery would cost thousands and his parents couldn't afford it, and I remember Sage crying and saying she wished it had been her.

"My cat now is a lot like Pascal. But he's about twice the size."

"Jinx?"

She grins. "Yeah. I hate that he insists on being an indoor-outdoor cat, but I suppose when it comes down to it, everyone's got to live their best life, right? For Pascal, that meant tons of treats. For Jinx, it's hunting time."

"He's a hunter?"

"Oh, yeah. He brings gifts." She raises her eyebrows and then scrunches her nose. "Gross gifts." She pushes forward and leans against the wall. All humor is gone, and her eyes narrow, studying me. It's a side of Sage I'm not sure I've seen before. "The way you look when I talk about Sam. You don't believe he's alive."

The last thing I want is to kill Sage's hope. It's one of her beautiful traits. But I saw Sam die. Max searched for his remains with me. The explosion incinerated everything within half a block radius.

"Knox?"

My hands grip the nearby railing that lines the wall around the top of the building. "What did they tell you?"

"Who?"

"The Navy. When they reached out?"

She blinks. Her eyes are glassy. *Oh, sweet thing, please don't cry.*

"They said he was missing in action. Presumed dead." Her soft touch warms my wrist. "Were you there?"

"Yeah, I was." The saliva in my mouth builds. I swallow instead of spitting because Sage is beside me.

"Tell me about it." She leans against the wall, crossing her arms over her belly, below her breasts. "I want to hear what happened."

An image of the bar flicks on. The wobbly barstool. The shattered mirror behind the liquor. A broken man's altar.

"You were in Syria," she prompts.

"Yep." Damascus. Off duty. We were heading out in the morning. One night out. Alcohol wasn't officially sanctioned, but the bar across the street from the hotel wasn't deemed dangerous. "There were bullets fired. Down the street. Nothing we should've gotten involved in."

Nothing we were supposed to get messed up in. Not when everyone knew we were American. Even out of uniform. One look at us and they just fucking knew.

"Sam went to check it out."

The weight of the random girl on my thigh, the dusty air, the grit on my skin, it all comes back.

Sage doesn't want to hear this.

"Please tell me."

"More shots fired. Rapid. Assault rifles." With a great amount of reluctance, I set the woman aside. Stepped outside, scanned the street. "Sam entered the building…this abandoned wreck of a building… and it exploded. A massive explosion." The searing heat is as much a part of my memory as the stench.

"And that's why…"

"Sage, that explosion knocked me flat on my back, and I was easily fifty yards away. The explosion blew out my eardrum. There's no way—"

"But you didn't find his body."

My memory is probably unreliable. When I pushed off the ground, it had been chaos. Charred wasteland where the building had been. I suffered from tinnitus for days. If it hadn't been for the random girl on my lap, a random girl I'd met in that bar and had every intention of fucking, I would've been with him. I might've seen something. Picked up on someone speed walking away. A glance back laced with fear. A warning to run.

Of course, I can never tell her. If I hadn't been breaking protocol, if I hadn't been drinking, moving in on a nameless woman, Sam might be here today.

Sage holds onto hope because they didn't uncover his body. If she'd seen the explosion, her hope would be obliterated.

"Whether I'm right or wrong, he wouldn't want you carrying this. Holding on to this." She's stepped closer and she's lightly touching my arm. "If I'm honest, there's a part of me that hopes he's working undercover somewhere. That me showing up at your place will trigger something and he'll show up and…"

She lets the words trail. I'm not sure at this point who is comforting who. Nothing good can come from talking about Sam.

The silver medic bracelet on her wrist glitters in the sun.

"How's your health? Are you good?" It's a needed conversation change.

"Yes." Her smile is weak, and I hope it's because her thoughts are still on Sam and not because she's sugarcoating the truth. There were a lot of meds in her black duffel. I finger the bracelet.

"My parents gave me the bracelet. I don't have to wear it. I choose to." She rubs the silver. Her allergies are engraved on the backside of the flat piece. "You saw my medicine." It's not a question. "I'll take them for the rest of my life. Immunosuppressants. Prednisone. Statin. Antihypertensive. All things to keep my body from rejecting my donor organs, manage my blood pressure and risk of infection. I know you remember me as someone who had to be taken care of, but I'm self-sufficient now. I'm good at taking care of myself."

"I can see that." A part of me wants to ask about her life expectancy. I vaguely remember Sam talking about it back then, about how many years the surgery bought her. But it's not an easy question. There's always Google.

I brush back her soft hair, silky to the touch. Breathe in her light, sweet scent. My heart pounds within my chest, noticeably rattled, as if I ran miles.

She tilts her head back, and my gaze falls to her pale pink lips. Dipping my head, brushing my lips across hers, would be the most natural thing in the world. If she raised up on her toes, lifted herself inches higher, we would kiss, like we did so long ago, after she received a new lease on life.

Kiss her.

CHAPTER 10

Sage

My lips tingle. His chest rises and falls inches from mine, and his pupils grow into dark pools. Heat from his touch envelops my waist. Awareness of physical symptoms rises. Shortness of breath. A rising heart rate. Light-headed dizziness.

"Hey, guys—"

My knees wobble as my lungs kick into action, and I suck in a gallon of air. Knox's firm grip on my elbow steadies me, keeping me upright.

"I can come back," Felix calls, his steps grating the white gravel roof.

"No. It's fine. We were just…" There's white dust on the rim of Knox's running shoes, and a pocket on his cargo shorts is ripped and frayed. "I was filling her in on Sam."

That's exactly right. He'd been telling me about my brother, and my fantasy-filled brain interpreted it as me starring in a Hallmark movie. My brain needs to channel *Criminal Minds* instead. A little Reed brilliance. I still haven't heard from Sloane. Someone came after me with a gun. There are many more important things than teenage crushes. Unavailable, pointless teenage crushes.

"You know, I have some pictures of Sam." My gaze sweeps up Knox's lower extremities, well-developed calves and loose, tattered shorts that brush the top of his knees, to Felix. "Was thinking about it, and if you want them, I can share them. Give me your email." He shrugs and tilts his head in an almost bashful manner. "He was a great guy. One of the good ones." His lips scrunch and he rocks back, uneasy.

"He *is* one of the good ones." I offer him a smile, but don't miss the silent exchange between Felix and Knox. Sure, Knox just told me all about how my brother supposedly couldn't have survived. But in reality, he provided evidence Sam could be alive. They never found the body. Maybe he went behind the building. There might've been an underground bunker. "But I'd love those photos." With a deep inhale, I add, "Thank you."

"Ryan's contact at Interpol briefed him," Felix says, twisting slightly to address Knox. Felix has thick, black hair and a deep tan that contrasts with his bright white teeth when he smiles. His relaxed demeanor makes it hard to picture him firing guns at people or practicing hand-to-hand combat. "They've been monitoring the research center since shortly after it opened. In return for their investment, Lumina gained two board seats and controlling interest."

"Sloane viewed investment as a positive. It was important to her because she said her research won't generate revenue for years, possibly decades." Knox's gaze travels back to me. Is this something I should've mentioned yesterday? How is it important?

"They got a tip that the research facility was breaking international law, which is the reason it hit their watch list."

"What law?" Rule-abiding Sloane wouldn't willingly break the law. Unless she disagreed with the law. How many times growing up did she tell on me to my parents? She's the queen of rules. She only uses reusable shopping bags. In school, she measured any skirt or shorts she wore to ensure she didn't violate the school policy on length above the knee. It drove our mom crazy, because she kept telling her it was a recommended guideline, not a public school dress code.

"Under current law you can't grow an embryo in a lab beyond fourteen days," Felix says.

Sloane's dream was to develop organs in a lab setting. She was convinced she could do it, and doing so would fundamentally change so many lives. People wouldn't have to be near death's door before receiving an organ transplant. Success rates would rise.

"Our contact says it was a credible tip, but they had no proof. Only rumors. When Lumina invested, given they're an international conglomerate, they determined any questionable practices would cease. It's been a low priority for them. Sounds like it's a file that hasn't been opened since the last round of funding."

I squint into the sun, filtering the information through the prism of Sloane's comments. "Sloane was excited about the work they were doing, but she wouldn't cross ethical boundaries." The temperature on the roof must be hitting the nineties, yet my fingers, palms, and forearms are chilly. "If she discovered anything like that, she'd…" She'd whistleblow it. They'd have no choice but to silence her. Or… "It's rumors, though, right?"

Felix's sunglasses cover his eyes, but he's frowning, and an uneasiness settles in my stomach.

"One of the reasons for studying embryo development is that many congenital abnormalities develop at the beginning, and I guess the hope is they can learn ways to combat those abnormalities? I don't know. But that wasn't what Sloane's research was about. She was studying cell development for organs. She was fascinated by embryonic stem cells. And I guess how those cells develop into organs. Her research held promising signs for organ creation. In labs. Ethical organ creation. That's what she said."

"With stem cells?" Felix asks.

"Yes. I think. If I understood her correctly. She was really excited about research coming out of Massachusetts that used adult skin cells to regenerate functional human heart tissue." My gaze falls to the gravel underfoot. "I didn't understand it, but it sounded promising. When she took the job with Origins, she was going to be doing research similar to what was done by the group in Massachusetts. She sent me pictures. Honestly, though, it didn't look like an organ to me. If someone walked into her lab, I don't know what they would think. But I know Sloane wouldn't do anything that warranted the police watching her."

"Hey, I'm just relaying what Interpol shared. Ryan's contact is going to send over what they have, but it doesn't sound like it's going to be much to go on."

A horn beeps on a nearby street. Up here on the roof, our view is mostly of rooftops and bendy palm trees. It's easy to forget there's a bustling town below.

"You guys staying up here?"

"Nah. We'll head down with you," Knox says.

He places his palm against my lower back as we exit, and it's kind of incredible. But I can't read into it. Knox and Sam are alike. Natural protectors. He'd be like this with any woman who needed help.

We follow Felix back down to the second floor. Empty cubicles fill the open area between the stairwell and the conference room from earlier. Offices line the exterior walls. Stella peers out from one office.

"Sage?"

"Hmm?"

"Can you come here for a minute?"

"We'll be back in our office," Knox says. "On the far wall."

Golden sun pours through the large windows lining one wall of Stella's office. A photo of Stella in a white cocktail dress shoving cake into her groom's face sits beside an oversized computer monitor. He's wearing a suit, and he's got the kind of big laugh that even frozen in a photograph brings out smiles. Or at least, I'm smiling.

Stella pushes her office door closed and leans against it. I hover near a chair, uncertain if I should sit or stand.

"Knox mentioned you might need refills on your medications."

"Well, not for another..." She stills, and I swallow back the impulse to keep my information private. "I have over a week's supply left."

"If you write down what you need, Kairi can handle getting refills for you."

"I can get them..."

"To be safe, we'd rather handle it. Just in case someone is tracking. If anyone is looking for you, your prescriptions would be an easy place to start."

Right. A splash of blue flowers decorates the top of the notepad she hands to me. I dutifully write them all down. Twenty-one pills a day. Used to be more.

She reads the list. "No birth control pills?" I blink. "Might as well let us get everything you're going to need."

"No birth control pills." I take enough medicine as it is. Someone like me...I shake my head as heat warms my cheeks from embarrassment. But there's no reason to be embarrassed. "That's it. It's everything. Right there." I should give her my prescription card, but if it's not in my name... "How're you... There's no way an insurance company is going to approve those meds."

I need those prescriptions, and at times I have issues with the insurance demons.

"It's okay. Kairi's husband is a doctor. He's helping us."

Without insurance, my meds will cost a small fortune. I have around nine thousand in cash, but—

"Don't worry about the money. It's on Arrow."

"Thanks, but—"

"Really, don't think twice about it. We've got you." Her hand falls to the doorknob. "I'm not sure what your schedule's going to be like while you're here in Santa Barbara, but if you ever want girl time. Walk on the beach. Glass of wine." She lifts her shoulders as if conveying she's good for whatever.

"I don't drink. It's my..." The butt of my hand rubs over my scar. A subconscious movement. "But I appreciate your offer. And you know what, we can meet for drinks. Lots of delicious mocktails these days. Or a walk. I walk at least three miles a day, so that, I can definitely do."

Stella beams. "Tomorrow morning? These loons get up before the crack of dawn. I could meet you and we could walk the dogs."

"Millie would probably like that." Knox might think she needs more training, but from what I can tell, the Lab is dog perfection.

"I'll bring you coffee. Do you drink caffeine?"

"One cup." I don't overdo coffee and eat like a pregnant woman, mainly avoiding unpasteurized cheeses, but there are mixed studies on coffee. I choose to believe the positive research. And my life is all about moderation.

She walks around to her side of the desk, grabs a pad of paper, and scribbles away, filling the pastel stationery with Knox's address, which I had, but also Arrow's address, the best grocery store, coffee shop, best pizza and delivery options, and her favorite clothing stores. She reaches into a drawer and digs out a tourist map of Santa Barbara. By the time I leave Stella's office, I have everything I need to subsist while hiding out in this seaside town.

A light breeze wafts through the open window. Knox was apologetic when he explained the windows needed to stay open during the heatwave, as the unit doesn't have air conditioning.

Millie stretches out on the floor, tongue lolling out of her mouth.

"She had a big day, huh?" I ask Knox.

He's resting on the sofa. There are three bikes parked in the alcove that's designed to hold a dining room table. Three rubber trunks line the back wall behind the bikes. Shelves on the wall hold bins, and there are a couple of gun cases, the cloth kind, perched against the corner.

"She's acting like it. But I have to imagine at the training facility she had full days. Unless they let her sleep a lot of the day."

I crawl down on the floor beside her to scratch her ear. There's a pillow and blanket neatly stacked on the floor beside the sofa. I didn't notice it this morning.

"I can't...you need to help me find a hotel. You're doing too much. All the guys are doing too much."

"No, we're not."

"Yeah, you are. I don't think Sam was expecting this..."

"Maybe he was." He folds his arms over his stomach. "I've been thinking about the duffel he packed for you. I have a theory."

"Yeah?" I take a seat on the sofa beside him. Any theory about Sam is of interest to me.

"I think Sam might've been doing some additional work on the side."

"Sam wouldn't break the law." It's the second time today someone has implied my siblings are criminals.

"I agree. I was thinking more on the covert side. Like you said. Opportunities come up. At any rate, it would explain why he gave you and your sister such explicit instructions. And options. If he got found out, he might've been worried someone would come for his family."

"Like who?"

"Cartels are notorious for it. The CIA has been known to poach our men. Others, too."

"You think this has to do with Sam and not Sloane?" It's what I secretly hoped, but...I also recognize that no one buys into my hope. He squints and stretches out his arms. I can't tell if he's thinking about the answer or about how to answer me.

"We need to find your sister. There's no question that's a priority. I suspect this isn't the scenario your brother was planning when he prepared you. Obviously, we're light on intel, but my hunch is what's going on has nothing to do with Sam. But Sam prepped your sister too. Which means she could be hiding under an alias. She could be safe. Maybe she hasn't reached out because she can't. Or because she's afraid of bringing the danger to you. But wherever she is, she's probably scared."

"And she's probably not in the United States."

"There's a good chance she's not." He clicks his tongue. "There's also a good chance she discovered something in that lab that someone wants to keep quiet."

He's not saying anything I haven't already thought of a thousand times today.

Knox reaches down beside him and drapes the comforter over his body like he's preparing for bed.

"I can't let you do that." I push off the sofa, looking for my shoes and bag.

"Seriously, it's comfortable."

"Well, then, I'll sleep out here. You take your bed." He grins. Full on grins. I point at his room. "You go."

He shakes his head and pushes up off the sofa, letting the comforter pool on the floor.

"The only solution I see is for us to share the bed." He shrugs, like it's no big deal. And it's not from his perspective. My palms are clammy and my heart rate increases, all from talking about it.

"I can get a hotel room which is what I should've done to begin with."

"Not gonna happen. Come on." He extends his hand. "I promise to be a gentleman."

"It's not that!" Obviously, he can control himself around me. He hasn't so much as touched me again since earlier today on the roof deck when I foolishly hoped for a kiss. "I'm not going to force you to share your bed with me. I'll be fine out here."

"Sage?"

"Yes?"

"It's not a big deal. We can put pillows down the middle of the bed if you're worried your boyfriend will object."

"Boyfriend?" I half-laugh the word.

"Jimmy?"

"He's my best friend. But not my boyfriend."

"Huh." He scratches his jaw. "Did Sam like him?"

"Yeah, of course. Sam and Jimmy have always gotten along."

"Hmm."

"That's a loaded sound if I've heard one."

"Don't you find it interesting? Sam liked Jimmy, but he directed you to come to me. Not the man who you're close to and lives in your town."

"Jimmy is the guy you go to when you're furnishing your place. Especially if you want to stay away from the big box stores and go with something of high quality but contemporary design. He's the guy you call when you can't decide which top goes best with a skirt. Unless you want to wear Birkenstocks with said skirt. But otherwise, he's your guy. When it comes to guns, he's the guy who will help you make a protest sign or know when there's an upcoming demonstration."

"Good to know." A slow smile spreads, and I can't help but wonder what he's thinking. "Think you can keep from throwing yourself at me, or do we need to place pillows down the middle?"

"You did not just say that." I bite my bottom lip, grinning because he's grinning, and this discussion is borderline mortifying. "I promise not to throw myself at you."

"Think you can trust me?"

"Yes." He's mocking me. "But this is crazy. You have one bedroom. I should not be crashing here."

"Sage. For the last time, there's nowhere else I'll let you stay. The options are for me to take the couch, or for us to share the king size bed in there. It's plenty big, and I promise to behave."

"Okay."

"Okay…what?"

"Okay. I'm going to owe you big time. I don't know how I'm ever going to repay you," I add, muttering more to myself than to him. With what I'm sure are ruby red cheeks, I grab my toothbrush and toothpaste and head into the bathroom.

When I exit, the overhead light is off and he's lying in bed, reading on his phone. He's shirtless. And perfect. Defined muscle, sun bronzed skin. Lickable abs.

He pats the mattress beside him, and I obediently walk around to the vacant side of the bed.

"You said Sam stayed with you when he was on leave?"

"Well, Sloane and I shared an apartment in Durham and he'd stay with us. When I moved to Asheville, he'd usually stay with me. He liked the mountains and whitewater rafting and hiking and mountain biking. You know, all that stuff he loves to do. It's all in Asheville."

His teeth gleam and his eyes are black pools in the dim light. There's nothing sexual about the way he's looking at me, but my body is oblivious. A ray of heat travels from my shoulders down to my core.

"What kind of stuff do you like to do? Are you an indoor girl?"

"I like to be outdoors. Hiking. I'll do whitewater rafting in a raft, but not in one of those little boats."

"Kayaks. Not your thing?"

"Sam tried to teach me once how to roll. Water went up my nose and I nearly drowned. In general, I prefer activities that don't require waivers with a line in all caps stating you may die."

He chuckles. It's a light sound, one that brings out a silly smile. I obviously can't see my smile, but I feel it plastered on my face.

"I've been meaning to visit Asheville. I have a little side business, and some retailers that carry my product are in Asheville."

"What do you sell?"

"Knives. Gear. With the gear, I'm pretty much a reseller. That business has been slowly growing for the last five or six years."

"What do you like best about it? Your business?"

"I like it all. Testing the product. Marketing. Website design. Logistics. Developing relationships with retailers. What do you like about teaching?"

"The kids. I didn't originally want to teach kindergarten. I wanted a little older. But I'm where I'm supposed to be. They're the cutest. And I love seeing how much they grow from September to June."

"I can see you as a teacher."

"Like your mom?"

"Yep, just like my mom. She loved her kids, too."

He rolls onto his back, exhales, and closes his eyes.

With his eyes closed, I peruse his resting form unrestrained. Unruly chocolate strands, let loose since his departure from the military, tuft in wild angles. His chest is mostly smooth except for a smattering of dark curls along the center. His muscles relax, presenting a smooth plane. He has the body of an athlete. I mean, he's more than an athlete. He's an entrepreneur who does brave things like find missing people. But he works that body. A body that, if Sam's accounts are true, has been abused and pushed beyond comprehension.

The thin comforter lies low across his waist and drapes over his legs and above those legs the sheet drapes over a noticeable length. Does he have an erection? Or is that his size when he's flaccid? *Nope. No. Nada. Cannot go there.*

My eyes snap closed and I roll onto my side, facing the wall. I will respect Knox. He's my brother's best friend, and he's doing me an enormous service. As a friend. I will not gape at him. Or have inappropriate thoughts.

The bed sinks. The bathroom door closes. I roll over as a light comes on below the door crack and the shower turns on.

I am absolutely invading his privacy. Cramping his space. Tomorrow, I'll ask Stella about that empty unit. It's in the building and perhaps it's close enough Knox will approve.

CHAPTER 11

Knox

Ice cold water glides down my throat. Sweat beads along my forehead. At almost seven in the morning, the outside temperature is mild, but I pushed it hard on my run.

Millie's sprawled in the living area, alternatively watching me and the bedroom.

Sage is still asleep. I hate the idea of waking her. Her body needs sleep. When I emerged from the shower last night, she was sleeping soundly. Thank god. I must be a masochist encouraging her to sleep in the same bed with me while promising to behave. I foresee many late-night showers in my future. My body reacts to hers. I'm attune to her presence. Why? She's cute. Attractive. Beautiful, even, but it's not like she's the first attractive woman I've been around. Maybe I'm more aware of her presence because she's untouchable. She could never be just a hookup to me. She's my best friend's little sister. And more than that, she's been through so much. One of the things that stands out to me when I think back on those years when she was pretty sickly, she never sought sympathy. She didn't want to be the center of attention. And her inner strength. That shone through even when she was a kid. Grace. That's what she possesses. The grace to accept whatever comes her way and to hold her head up high and push forward. She's not one to give up. I respect that about her.

And, yeah, those thoughts in the shower last night? Completely out of line.

Soreness pulses through my knees. Only eight miles today, but too much of that was on unforgiving concrete. Tomorrow, I'll need to bike or swim. Later today, I'll meet up with Trevor for a lifting session.

I refill the water bottle with filtered water, set it back in the fridge, and pad softly through the apartment.

I nudge the door open with the back of my hand. Light filters through the cracks in the closed blinds. She's sprawled out across the mattress, hair askew, the sheet kicked to the side. Her pajama shorts have risen up her hips, and my gaze runs along her smooth thigh to the slope of her ass. The pajama top she's wearing has twisted upward, exposing a smooth midriff. The position she's sleeping in is awkward. Her face is to the side, both arms spread out like she might have at one point been sleeping on her belly, but her torso rolled sideways.

Back in the day, she was too thin. The kind of skinny that had nosy people doing double takes and whispering. It was worrisome. I'd been a teenage dude, and even I'd noticed and worried. Sam sure as hell had, constantly trying to force her to eat, but her body was working too hard, struggling to pump blood, to breathe. As my dad would say, she had trouble keeping meat on her bones.

Talk about a medical miracle. There are no bones jutting out along her ribs now. Smooth skin and curves where they're supposed to be. Curves I shouldn't itch to explore. She's Sam's sister. She is here for protection.

Last night's cold shower helped, but I still returned to a bed with her in it. And given I'm staring at her now and getting a chub, it's clear I'm one horny bastard.

A shower every night isn't a long-term solution. Besides, at some point Sage will figure out what's going on, no matter how quiet I am.

Her eyelashes flutter. She rolls onto her back, and I spring into action, grabbing clothes and stepping into the bathroom.

What the hell is wrong with me?

Sam told Sage to come to me so I'd keep her safe. She's safe here. I will keep her safe and honor her brother's request. And figure out what's going on with Sloane. Then send Sage on her way.

When I exit the bathroom, Sage is no longer in the bedroom. I find her sitting at the island bar with a small glass of milk.

"Morning. Hope I didn't wake you."

She smiles. "No, not at all. I don't usually sleep late."

"Did you sleep okay last night?"

"Yeah, I did. Did you?" Those brown eyes drip with concern. "I know you're probably not used to…" Pink blooms along her cheekbones. "I mean, I know you have…but not like a friend." She slaps her palm down on her thigh. "I'm gonna ask Stella about that unit that's empty. I don't—"

"You'll do no such thing." Across the way, I'd never know if something happened during the night. "Besides, I sleep better with you in the bed."

Her chin lowers, and she studies me like she can't decide if I'm being straight with her. I hadn't actually thought about it, but I slept well last night. She'd also rolled to the middle of the bed, and it had been…nice.

"I'm about to head to a soccer game. Can I convince you to join me?"

"Soccer? Like a pro team?"

"Felix's son. Three and easy. Cute as all get out." I love going to the Saturday games. It's been a good way to bond with the guys, too.

I've been debating volunteering as a team coach for the local kids' league. Probably not for the three-year-olds. I don't have that kind of patience. But I played soccer a ton as a kid. I've got some tricks I could teach.

"Do you think we might have time to stop and get a coffee?"

"Absolutely." Damn. I should've made her a pot. "You know, I do have coffee." I point at the coffee pot sitting on the counter then open a tall, skinny upper cabinet. "The filters are right here."

"I figured I'd walk to the place down the street and get a coffee, but if we're going to go…oh, do I need to get dressed? Are you going now?" She's up and emptying the rest of her milk in the sink and turning on the faucet.

"No rush. Game starts whether or not we're there. But yeah, it starts at eight. The league hates parents."

She smiles and shakes her head like I'm ridiculous. "Trust me. Those parents have been up way before eight."

"Why do you say that?"

"Kids." She shrugs. "They're notorious for not sleeping late. I'm a kindergarten teacher, remember? I talk to a lot of parents."

Right. She would. I watch her backside as she pads through the place to the bedroom. Millie gets up and follows her. Clearly, loyalty isn't the dog's strength. But I suppose I'd rather trail Sweet as Pie than Mr. Stern and Commanding, too.

Sage has been dressed casually since arriving in California. Tight fitting tees cropped short around the waist. Baggy jeans or short shorts.

But when I imagine her teaching her class, it's a 1950s portrait. She's sitting in a chair, and kids surround her on the floor, looking up at her with admiration. Her flowery skirt spills down to her calves, and the pattern matches a thick headband. She's holding a book out to the side, maybe sounding out a word or a color or whatever they teach you in kindergarten these days. In my imagination, she's in her element.

We need to figure out what's going on so she can return to her classroom. To her kids. To her life.

"Is Max going to be here?" she asks as I slam the trunk closed.

"Nah. Max doesn't care for kids' games." Or kids. I side-eye her, wondering if she's crushing on the tank. She wouldn't be the first.

"But you do?"

Felix stands on the sideline of the field, arm thrust in the air, waving at us like we can't pick the crew out of the parents lined up along the soccer field with folding chairs.

"I like sports. I'm thinking about volunteering as a coach next season."

I've got our chairs tucked under one arm. Sage has Millie's leash, but her attention is on the three-year-olds with jerseys down to their knees. The little tikes are cute, but as a soccer player, it's painful to watch the game too closely. The coach does his best but calling it soccer is a stretch.

Maria, Felix's wife, shouts, "Hey, Knox," but she never puts her phone down. Her thick black hair is tied back in a ponytail, and she's wearing a visor that protects her from the sun as she videos the game. Phones are recording all down the line, with proud parents either clicking or videoing. There's one woman on the corner of the field with a 35mm camera and a long lens. She lowers her camera and shouts, "Kick the ball, Lucy!"

Yes, with three and easy, it's unisex. Boys and girls toddling around, sort of chasing the ball.

"This is the cutest thing I've ever seen," Sage says at my side.

Ryan gets up and shifts a chair to the side, making room for two more. "Don't bother," I tell him. "We'll start a second row."

Stella jumps out of her chair when she sees Sage. Trevor heads my way, and Stella points at Trevor's vacant chair, telling Sage to take his seat.

"Wasn't sure you were gonna make it," Trevor says. We're ten minutes late, but the game only lasts thirty minutes. Still, it's not our kid.

"Aren't Ryan's kids playing later?" The sporting complex features nine soccer fields. They split one soccer field into three fields for the littles. Games last all day, with the age of play increasing as the day progresses.

"At eleven. The ladies were talking about going to the playground, then the game, then lunch."

"Sage may want to join. I've got the dog."

"We can find a lunch place that's outdoors," Trevor offers.

"Where's your dog?" Stella always has Charlie, their dog, with her.

"Charlie's getting older." Trevor folds his arms, his attention on his wife. "Took him on a run this morning and Stella insisted he needed to rest. Plus, she's worried about him in the sun and heat."

"Did he do okay with you on the run?"

"He's slowing down. He tries, though."

"That's tough. How old is he?"

"Nine. He's still got good years left, but Stella might be right. I should probably shorten his runs."

"You're questioning if your wife is right?" That earns a snort.

"I would never."

Ryan joins us. We're all three standing in a row, facing the field, a few feet behind the line of chairs. None of us has a kid in the game, so we can do this without looking like total jackasses.

Felix screams at the top of his lungs, as if a gold medal is at stake, "Go, Ryder! Kick the ball!"

"Got an update from Erik this morning," Ryan says.

"Any leads?"

"Nothing of interest in the file on Lumina or any of its subsidiaries. Right now, we're accessing video footage. But there's not a ton of surveillance on the island. A handful of intersections. Parking lots. Open air markets. Courthouses, police station. Hotels."

"Can't imagine she's at a hotel."

"Agree it's doubtful. Kairi reached her landlord, but the landlord doesn't live on site. She's not behind on rent."

"Sounds like her condominium isn't one of the parking lots with video surveillance?"

"Unfortunately, no. I'm not sure we're going to get any leads remotely. Jack and I talked earlier. We're going to send a team over."

He's wearing sunglasses, as we all are, and I can't see his eyes. His focus appears to be on the game. But damn if I don't feel like throwing my arms around my new boss. He doesn't owe me shit.

"I can pay for it." He holds a hand out to stop me from saying more. "Really. I have a side business."

"We got this. You're one of us. And Jack knew Sam. Like I said, Arrow is all in on this one."

I choke back emotion. It feels damn good to know your team has your back. "Thank you."

If he acknowledges my gratitude, I don't pick up on it.

"We did learn that a couple of years ago someone reached out to the *Sunday Times* in London about a subsidiary of Lumina. Claimed to have an exposé worthy of coverage."

"What happened?" I can tell from his tone it didn't end well.

"Person disappeared without a trace. The *Sunday Times* correspondent reported it to the police, and somehow or another it landed with Interpol."

"No follow-up?"

"If there was any done, it's not in Interpol's file. But..."

I get where he's going. "If Sloane tried to play whistleblower–"

"Right." My gaze falls on Sage. *Shit*. Sloane is her last living family member. She might have some cousins, but...if we don't find Sloane, it'll hit her hard.

Trevor claps me on the back. "She thinking about making her move here permanent?" He's looking at Sage.

"She's been here two days." She's laughing at something Stella said. Alex, Ryan's wife, is scratching Millie's head. Sure, Sage fits in, but she'd fit in anywhere. "She digs Asheville. And from what I hear, it's a shit ton more affordable than the West Coast."

These guys pay me well. But even with a higher salary, it's a challenge to live here. Everyone and their mother wants to live under the California sun, and that drives prices through the stratosphere.

"Well, when the two of you cross that bridge, come talk to us before you make any decisions."

"I think you're misunderstanding the situation."

Ryan chuckles and heads back to his wife. I stare at his retreating back because I think I missed the joke.

"I like her," Trevor says.

"Sage?"

"Yeah. Of course." He shrugs like something is obvious.

"I like her, too. And?"

"I can tell you do."

"Is this your version of talking smack?" You can take the guy out of the Navy, but not the Navy out of the guy. I get it, but…

"Hate to break it to you, but you can't stop looking at her."

"What're you talking about?" She's with my dog. "She doesn't know anyone here. I'm just making sure she's comfortable." She holds her hands up, clapping and whistling. A kid scored a goal. She's wearing sunglasses and one of my baseball hats. She's pretty fucking adorable.

He smirks like a jackass.

"She's my best friend's little sister."

"Pretty sure the little sister thing is null and void when she's over twenty-five. Oh, and he's dead."

I grimace from the slap of the words.

"Sorry. That was harsh. But you know what I mean."

We both stand there, arms crossed. One man yells about a bad call. He's yelling at a volunteer ref at a three and easy game.

"You're positive he's dead, right?"

I get why Trevor's asking. One sister has a go-bag complete

with credible, expensive alternative identification, and one sister is missing. "If he survived that explosion, we would've heard from him. It's been two years."

Trevor nods. "That's my conclusion. Which means it's all about the missing sister. We'll figure it out."

We will. We'll track her down.

Felix jogs down the sidelines.

"Where's he going?" I ask Trevor.

"Maria says he's become lactose intolerant, but he refuses to adjust his eating habits. When we got here, he was in the restroom."

To the side of the field, near the playground, there's a public restroom facility, and I watch Felix hightail it into the building.

"Guess it's good Maria's videoing the game, huh?"

The parents erupt into cheers, clapping and yelling. It's not clear at all who won. Everyone's happy. Both teams line up to get snacks.

"Well, I'm coaching on a different field. See you later on field nine."

He catches Stella by the side, lifts her, and lays a sloppy kiss against her lips. She laughs. The two of them are good together. No kids other than his stepson. I wonder what the story is there, but I'll never ask. Not my business. Kids or no kids, one thing's indisputable. Trevor's one happy guy.

Our team's parents fold chairs while another set of parents unfold them, taking over the grassy spots along the white chalked line.

I meander over to the ladies. Ryan took off with Trevor. I guess they coach the same team. So, it's all the ladies plus me and Felix until lunch.

"Can I carry anything for you ladies?" I've still got the two folding chairs I brought.

It's Alex who sidles over to me. "Can you carry the other handle on this cooler?"

"Sure thing."

"I'm gonna put it in the trunk. We'll have it at the playground."

Felix bulldozes his way to his kid and tosses his son around in the air like he's a ball. The kid laughs hard, knees bent, arms flailing. Maria tugs on Felix's arm, admonishing him to be careful.

Alex and I follow the crew, walking a little slower. "Sage told us all about her sister."

"Is that right?"

"Showed us pictures. You think you'll find her?"

"What kind of question is that?" Alex sometimes assists on criminal investigations, but she's a behavioral scientist and a professor at UCSB. "Have you got doubts?"

"I think Sage is an optimist." My insides sink because what she's implying is that she's wrong to be optimistic right now. It's something I've tried hard not to think too much about, but we're grasping at straws. It's why I'm glad Ryan's sending men. When the tech nerds can't find anything, it's time for boots on the ground. And she's been missing for over two weeks now. Statistics aren't in our favor.

"She obviously adores her sister. I think she might even have some matchmaking in her."

"What do you mean?"

"Seemed to think her sister was all that. And she'd be a good fit for you." I don't miss Alex's teasing expression. Definitely teasing.

That's the problem with these married couples. Every single person needs to be matched up pronto.

"Sloane's not my type." She's never been my type. From what I remember, she doesn't speak much. Or smile. Hardly ever looks you in the eye. Talk about a unique set of siblings.

"What is your type, Knox? I've been meaning to ask you. You know, I work with a lot of single grad students."

Sage approaches with a wide, relaxed smile and glowing cheeks, partially hidden beneath the rim of the faded ball cap. She's in shorts that hang low, leaving a stretch of smooth waistline beneath today's tight-fitting tee, and beat up Converses without socks. The conversation drops, but I give Alex's question consideration. If I had a type, it'd be casual, natural…and yeah, sweet. Kind. Real. Strong.

Trevor's words play in my head. As always, the man is right. Sage Watson is over twenty-five. She's a grown woman. There's no reason to feel guilty for being attracted to her. Except that she's got a heart of gold and deserves the best. And given I live on the opposite side of the country from her, and I don't do difficult relationships, I'm not the guy she deserves. Not only that, I'm not looking for a relationship. And she's definitely the relationship type.

CHAPTER 12

Sage

There's a surfer off in the distance, straddling his board. The waves are rolling in with ease, so there's nothing for him to surf. He's wearing a tight black wet suit, which, given the chilly temperature of the Pacific, I expect is a surfer's uniform in these parts.

The old school California beachfront restaurant opens onto the ocean and offers a walk-up counter to order. Old surfboards hang from the rafters inside, and slightly faded turquoise paint covers the building. There are some tables out front in the sand, but Knox's friends secured a long table on the patio.

"I'll take a golden ale. You want anything?" Knox asks.

I tear my gaze from the shoreline to the waitperson. He's a young guy, with a sunburnt nose, cheeks, and flaming red ears. After a second of fumbling in my bag, I pull out a small container of sunscreen. "I'll just have water. Thanks." With a cautious smile, I pass him the travel-size sunscreen tube. "And here. Take this. Please."

He doesn't understand. "You're burnt," I say, and point at my nose, then my cheeks, then wave my hand all over my face. He's burnt everywhere.

He's slow to grab the tube from me, but he does eventually take it.

"I'll take water, too," Maria says. She smiles sheepishly as the orders go around the table. Maria, the kids, and I are the only ones who opt for non-alcoholic beverages. I don't drink alcohol. Is she like me, or is she pregnant? The way Alex grins at her, I get the feeling I'm not the only one to have picked up on the possibility.

But then Alex turns her attention to me. As does Stella. And I blurt, "I don't drink alcohol for medical reasons."

Why do I do that? Make things awkward. If Jimmy were here, he'd say something funny. He'd guide the conversation. Have everyone laughing. I fiddle with the napkin on my lap, fully aware they must think I'm odd. They turned their attention on me because I'm new. They were being nice. Stella helped me get my prescriptions. No one was wondering if I'm pregnant. She probably assumed alcohol might interact with one of my medications.

"With all the calories in beer, I should stick with water." Ryan pats his belly. The sun sparkles against the grays mixed in with his short, dark strands. Alex presses her lips to his shoulder and whispers something in his ear.

I look away, giving them their private moment. Alex might be the tallest woman I have ever met, but with her husband sitting beside her, clasping her hand, she looks, well, not petite, but delicate. Like a retired runway model next to a former professional athlete.

I'm sitting on the opposite end of the table from the kids. There's a pole that supports the deck near the table, and that's what I've got Millie's leash looped around. The waitstaff brought out a dog bowl of water and Millie is stretched out beside the bowl, basking in the sun.

Knox is in a conversation with Trevor. One kid holds a phone out, asking something, and Alex pushes up from her chair and walks to the end of the table. Stella shifts her chair closer to me.

"I should have your medication on Monday."

"Thank you. I can't believe…it's so expensive without insurance."

"Happy to do it. Let me know if you need anything else."

It's the way her eyes look at me. It's hard to describe. There's curiosity there, but she doesn't want to pry. She's polite but curious. It's one of many standard responses, but I've found people glaze over if the explanation gets long winded.

"The medication. I don't know if you know what it's for, but…I had a heart and lung transplant. A long time ago. I'll take this medicine for the rest of my life. And there are things…" I glance at the golden ale, "I won't partake in. Some random foods I can't have. I mean, you'll meet some who do drink alcohol, but it's not recommended."

I plan on taking care of my organs. In order to receive them, someone else had to die. And another person out there didn't get her transplant because I got it instead. The responsibility is not lost on me.

"You feel good these days?" I feel, rather than see, Knox's gaze.

"I do. I'm…my doctors are pleased. It's been twelve years. I'm doing better than good." The side of my hand rubs my breastbone. I pull on my necklace so the heart charm rests above my t-shirt and switch to playing with the charm. I'm doing really well. There are others who are doing better. They have transplant games for athletes who perform phenomenal physical feats, proving that for some there are no limits.

"It's amazing what we can do these days." Stella says it with awe, and that's a feeling I share. If I'd been born a hundred years earlier, I would've died during childhood. It's something I think about in every cemetery when I check the dates and see the tombstone of a child. That would've been me in the eighteen-hundreds. Or early nineteen-hundreds. My mom would've probably chosen a stone that read something along the lines of "Loved by all."

By the time we've finished lunch, I've talked too much about the advances we are making. They've tested pig organ replacement with limited success. It might not happen in my lifetime, but it's completely reasonable to expect that in the future, there will be labs dedicated to growing organs and possibly even limbs. Every year, we learn more and more, leading to advances in helping with diseases like cancer and Alzheimer's. Sloane's a part of the team ushering in the golden age of medicine.

After lunch, the group disperses. We're close enough to Knox's place we could walk, but we drove his Sequoia, a bigger and more luxurious SUV than mine, although his is easily ten years old.

"Why don't I walk back so you can head straight to the gym?" There's a facility nearby the Arrow guys use for training. I overheard Trevor and Knox mentioning plans to meet.

"It's your first weekend in Santa Barbara. I've already worked out for the day." He lifts his shoulders like it's no big deal, and this thought is just occurring to him, which it probably is. "What do you say to a tour?"

"Well, you've gotten in your workout, but I still need to get mine in."

"Oh?" He brightens like I've brought up one of his favorite subjects. "What do you do?"

"A daily three-mile walk. I mean, I know it's not exercise for someone like you, but I enjoy it and my doctors…" I close my mouth before I share studies on the benefits of walking. Knox isn't questioning me and I'm sure he doesn't care about an exercise regime someone like him wouldn't consider exercise.

"All right. How about this? We'll head back, drop Millie and the car at the house, and we'll do the tour on foot. I promise we'll get over three miles in. And if you want, we'll swing by the beach so you can get plenty of speed walking in too."

Refusing is on the tip of my tongue, but his expression isn't just sincere, it's a mix of hopeful and boyish. He's a handsome man when he's serious, but this expression has my stomach twisting and flipping. I mean, not that that look has anything to do with me. Maybe he's genuinely not in the mood to lift weights today. Who am I to judge? I hate weightlifting. I can't think of anything I'd rather do than spend an entire day with Knox.

"Okay."

"Okay?" He slaps his hands together, grinning, like I gave him something. As if. I get a Saturday afternoon with *the* Knox Andrew Williams.

The first stop along our tour is State Street. The touristy street is a twenty-five-minute walk from Knox's house, or around thirty-five hundred steps according to my watch. Quaint, artsy stores mix with wine shops, clothing boutiques, and restaurants with sidewalk seating. A portion of the thoroughfare is closed to automobile traffic.

The cute storefronts with awnings and hand-carved signs hanging over expansive windows displaying arts, crafts, and clothes give the street a classic Main Street aesthetic. Many of the buildings are stucco, and the terra cotta gleams golden-tan under the sun high overhead. Almost everyone's wearing shorts, although there are some brazenly strolling around in string bikinis or shorts with a bikini top. Baby strollers and retirees blend into the pedestrian crowd with ease.

It's a hot day, and while it wouldn't be noteworthy back in North Carolina, people here keep referring to it as a heat wave. There's not a cloud in the sky, but there's also little breeze this many blocks from the ocean.

A crowd inside a tavern cheers as we pass.

"Do you watch sports?" Knox asks.

"Not really," I admit. "I'd rather read than watch television. Watching a sports game has never struck me as a rational use of time. I mean, I'm a North Carolinian. I do like college ball."

He grins so wide he gives me a flash of white. He tilts his head back and claps his hand. I feel like clapping too, simply from his burst of happiness. "I knew I liked you."

"What team do you pull for?" It's been a long time since Knox lived in NC. My guess would be the LA Lakers. That seems to be the Cali team of choice if the signs in the bars we've been passing are any indication. But he said college ball, so maybe UCLA?

"I still pull for the Heels," he answers. "I mean, it depends on who's playing. But I'd say I watch more extreme sports than anything else. Things that inspire me to get out and do."

I grin. "Pretty sure watching someone jump off a cliff wouldn't inspire me to get out and do."

He snorts and directs me to cross the street, pointing the way to the promenade.

"It's more along the lines of snowboarding. Skiing. Motocross. Cliff jumping…they don't show that too much."

"Same thing. Still goes." I am extraordinarily lucky to be alive. It would be irresponsible to take that kind of risk.

We cross half a block in silence, with me staring into store windows and Knox reading a text.

"So, you work for Arrow. But I noticed boxes stacked in the second bedroom. And it looked like a postage machine on the table. Do you run your side business from home?"

He tilts his head, then switches sides, positioning me on his left. "Say that again."

I repeat the question.

"Mostly we ship through a fulfillment location, but some items I fulfill. Until the volume warrants me outsourcing shipping. Part of the side business hustle."

"I get it. I have a side business too."

"You do?"

"Don't look so surprised." I playfully push his arm, which is a bad idea because the burst of energy from touching his skin sets butterflies loose in my belly. He just grins and I shove my hand into my shorts pocket. "An Etsy shop. It was easiest to set it up that way. Jewelry."

"Oh, what're you doing while you're out of town?"

"Actually, I, ah… with Etsy, you can set yourself on vacation. Halting orders kind of thing. Before I turned off my phone, I logged in and set it on vacation mode. It's more of something I do when I have the time, anyway. But I'm building up a pretty good following."

"What kind of jewelry do you make?"

"Well, like this." I finger my necklace. The beads form the image of the heart chakra.

"That's really cool." The pad of his thumb runs over the beads, and I wonder if he can feel my heart pitter-pattering away. He swallows, and my breath catches when his gaze focuses on me.

We continue walking until we reach the end of the pier on the promenade. The temperature over the ocean is noticeably cooler. The long, broad pier holds restaurants and shops. There are surfers working waves perilously close to the pilings, but out here, we're far beyond them. Which is a good thing because I don't like watching people risk their lives needlessly. There are miles of ocean nowhere near a barnacle clad pier.

"One day," Knox says, his tone deep and wishful, "I'd like to do more with woodworking. Maybe I'll get good enough you can help me sell some stuff on Etsy."

"Absolutely," I tell him. "I'll help in any way I can." That should be obvious. I showed up out of nowhere and am camping out in his apartment, taking up half his bed.

"I figured you would. You're good like that. Always have been." I'm not sure how he can say that. Given our age difference, we didn't hang out like friends.

"Do you still keep in touch with anyone from Rocky Mount?"

"Not really, no, I don't." He scratches the side of his neck thoughtfully. "I think if I had my social media accounts, I probably would've. But we tend to cut those in our line of work."

"And I guess high school was a long time ago."

He grips the railing, looking out over the white-capped ocean, breathing in the crisp, salty wind. "That, it was."

"I still remember your senior prom."

He cocks his head with a questioning smirk. "What, exactly, do you remember?"

"Well, I wasn't there, obviously. But I remember you dropping off Sam at about six or seven in the morning. He got out of the car still in his tux, but his shirt was undone at the collar with one of his shirt tails hanging out, and he was barefoot, carrying his dress shoes." Knox grins wide again, perhaps remembering. "I always imagined you guys partied all night and that you must've had the absolute best time."

"That was a pretty wild night." He leans against the railing. "Good times."

"And Caroline...she was your date, right?"

He nods slowly, as if he's digging into the recesses of his memory bank. "Yes, she was."

God, I'd been so jealous. I'd really wanted that experience, too, but it wasn't meant to be.

"What about you?" I glance sideways, hoping he's not about to ask me about my nonexistent prom experience. "Who took you to prom?"

I'd planned to go. Bought a dress. But I spiked a fever a couple of days before and, given the gym would be packed, didn't go. "It was..." Inadvisable. The word from some adult at the time pops in my head. "Not in the cards." I force a smile. It's fine. I'd been hugely disappointed, but it was a really long time ago.

"How was college? Did you make up for lost time?"

"What kind of a question is that?" I grin at him, masking the mix of emotions that arise when I remember those years.

"I don't mean anything by it. It's good to let loose."

"That's something I really wouldn't know about."

"That's too bad. I remember Sam saying he worried that you

were spending too much of your college days taking care of your mom."

Yes, and no. I had freshman year. But my first truly wild night ended horribly.

"Ew. What happened to you?" I can still see the fraternity boy's face twisted in disgust.

I finally moved on from "What's wrong with her?" a question adults and kids alike lobbed at my parents like I wasn't standing right there, and then discovered another hurtful question replaced it.

"I didn't mean to bring up a bad topic."

I blink away the memory, remembering that I'm here with Knox and that all happened a long time ago. "No, it's okay. Mom didn't get sick until my sophomore year, so…"

"So you had your freshman year. Good." He crosses his arms over his chest, looking amused. "Any good regrets?"

"What's a good regret?"

"Oh, you know, a wild night that you regret but at the same time makes for one helluva good story."

I scrunch up my nose, searching my memory for one good story. "That's not really the way I roll," I admit. There's no point in pretending to be someone I'm not. "What about you? Any great regrets?"

His amused expression transitions to something I can only describe as rueful. His gaze falls, and I can't help but wonder what kind of regrets he might be thinking of. A lost love? Caroline? Something that happened on a mission? Sam started changing those last few years, becoming more serious, his eyes more haunted.

"Honestly, I didn't have the typical college experience either." But they had weekends and some wild times at the Naval Academy. Sam told me. "But I did have a great high school experience. We had some good times." He looks over me, fondness evident, like I'm a part of those good memories. "I'm glad you came out here, Sage. It's not a great situation, but I'm glad we reconnected. I'm glad you came to me."

His words—or no, the intensity of his gaze sucks the oxygen right out of my lungs. A bout of light-headedness overcomes me, and I lean into the pier, looking off to the ocean, closing my eyes to soak in the cool breeze and regain my wits.

"So, you said you're not dating Jimmy. Are you dating anyone back home?"

"No." I shake my head. "Jimmy and Sloane think I should try a dating app, but I just…that's not me."

They both use them, basically everyone my age uses them. But, when all my friends were getting used to app dating etiquette, dating wasn't on my bingo card. I got left behind on the social spectrum. And I'm okay with that. There are more important things that I need to be doing with my life.

A faint fish scent taints the fresh salt air, but I don't mind. With my eyes closed, I inhale deeply, taking it all in.

"You can tell me if I'm out of line here. I won't mention it again. But earlier today, one of the guys pointed out that, well, you're over twenty-five."

I'm staring down thirty. Older than I expected to be if I'm honest. Where is he going with age? I twist to face him, all the light-headedness gone.

"The timing's off. I get that. What with Sloane missing. But we're going to find her."

I lift my sunglasses onto my head. A strand of hair whips into my mouth. I'm at a loss for the next steps and inordinately grateful for Arrow's help. My hope is she's hiding, like me, and she's safe. She's alive. I know it. I feel it.

Knox cups my chin and removes the wayward strand. Like always, his touch radiates through my skin.

"I'll just say it." He drops his hand and shoves both of them into his shorts pockets. "Would you be interested in going on a date with me?"

"Like a date date?" My heart flutters and stomach somersaults.

"Dinner." He lifts his shoulders. "We live on opposite sides of the country. I probably shouldn't have said anything. Forget I said–"

"I'll go." His smile spreads slowly. "I'd love to go to dinner with you." There's no reason to stress about whether it's a date. I'll be leaving soon. School starts back. But, in my list of dreams… dinner–date or not–with Knox Williams is one of those dreams so big I'd never write it down. What's the point in writing something down you'll never be able to check off?

"Good. Tomorrow night?"

I mean, technically, we've spent the entire afternoon together. Neither of us paid for lunch because Ryan picked up the tab for everybody. Still, a date–or a sort of date–isn't about spending money. It's about getting to know each other and that's what we've been doing. But I'd thought we'd been friends getting reacquainted. I didn't shower this morning, my hair is up in a ponytail, and I forgot to pack deodorant.

"I'm going to get us reservations at a good restaurant." His lips aren't exactly smiling. He's not teasing. Is he flirting? Or asking me?

"You don't need to—"

"I want to treat you to something special. You okay with that?"

He steps closer and removes his shades. My heartbeat slows. He cups my chin, his nose rubs mine, and then his head dips closer and his lips brush over mine. Tingles cover my skin all over. The perimeter fades, and all I see is him. Attentive dark eyes so intense I feel his gaze in my quivering knees. Cool, salt-tinged breeze envelops my heated limbs and fills my lungs. The side of his index finger caresses my cheek. The corners of his lips turn up into a shy smile.

"Also wanted to do that."

The boyish smile returns, and I'm dazed. He links his fingers with mine, and we return down the promenade. My heartbeat hits a staccato rhythm.

Blessed unicorns and all things merry. Knox Williams just kissed me. On his own volition. Because he wanted to.

I'm fairly certain my heart will never beat in the same rhythm again.

CHAPTER 13

Knox

Sage's cheeks glow. She looks up at me like I'm all that and more. I'd be lying if I said she was the first to look at me like that. But she's the first that makes me feel like I need to do everything in my power to prove her right, to live up to what she sees.

As a SEAL, especially based in San Diego, a fair share of women expressed interest. But I was never sure if it was the trident or me that earned the come hither looks. And the thing about a trident, sure, some say it's forever...and yeah, in some ways it is. But it wasn't my forever.

Sage possessed the hero worship eyes way back when. She was far too young and in high school. I saw it as more of a little sister thing. I'm an only child, but from television and movies I gathered younger siblings chased after older siblings.

When she came on to me at barely seventeen, she threw me. For a few reasons. One, the obvious one, the move was completely unexpected. Two, I'd seen her as a kid until an hour before that moment. But I felt that kiss everywhere.

I'd backed up and almost fled the scene, unsure my dress slacks would hide my reaction. I'd still been in my whites, and that suit had fit well my first year. Four years later, those pants gripped tighter. I'd gained muscle everywhere, ass and thighs included. As a graduation gift, my mom bought me new dress whites, a sign I wasn't the only one who recognized the pants were pushing the line of decorum.

I chalked my reaction up to having spent too much time at the academy and not enough getting laid. Besides, she was my best friend's little sister. And she was seventeen. I was shipping out and she had college in front of her. So many reasons to put that kiss behind me.

And here I am, over a decade later, with her slender hand in mine. My reaction to our kiss? Powerful. But this time, she's old enough. I'm no longer in the Navy. And her brother sent her to me for protection. A responsibility I hold sacred.

Everywhere we go, I scan the crowds. Alert. The chances whoever came after her would find her here on the other side of the country are slim. But it is a possibility. If it's connected to Sloane's disappearance, which is our leading theory, then in all likelihood, the man was a hired gun. A professional.

"Did you get your three miles in?"

She checks her watch and grins. "I did."

"So, walking. Is that required by the doctor?"

"Not necessarily. My cardiac therapists wanted me to run. And I did for years. But I hate running."

That has me nodding along.

"Why are you smiling?" She touches my arm in a playful gesture and I tug on her ponytail. "Do you hate running too?"

"Me? Nah. I love it. It's one of the things I'm good at."

"Yeah. Of course. You. Sam. Tons of people."

"Doesn't mean a thing. If you didn't like it, you did the right thing by switching up your workout plans."

"Do you think?" Her question rings with doubt.

"Absolutely. If Trevor was around, he'd give you an earful. If you don't like what you're doing, it won't stick."

"You can't tell me you liked everything you had to do in the Navy. Sam told me–"

"Well, not everything. But that's different. Lives are at stake."

"Not so different." She looks serious again.

"What do you mean?"

"I mean, I've been given a great gift. A second chance at life. And with great gifts, comes great responsibility. So, I worry I should push myself harder. Make myself run. Give more back to the community."

"I'm not so sure that sounds like you talking." She side-eyes me, and the look is confirmation. I called it. "Who said that? Mr. Watson or Mrs. Watson?" I snap my fingers. "Mr. Watson."

She laughs a full-throated laugh. My hand falls on her lower back. Not because I need to guide her, but because I want her near.

"Dad. How did you know?"

"I can just hear him saying it. He sounded like a preacher most of the time."

"He did." She's grinning, and the look on her face is full of fondness.

"Sam hated it."

Her eyes widen and her steps slow. "He did?"

"Yeah, he did. You didn't know that?"

"No. I mean…by the time Sam and I got to spend real time together, as equals…Mom was sick."

"Well, it used to drive Sam crazy because he said that your dad was as wild as they came. Your grandparents, I guess, used to tell all kinds of stories. And so did your dad's friends. He always felt like the preacher version of your dad wasn't who he really was."

She's quiet for a couple of sidewalk squares. My arm comes back to my side. We've turned onto my street.

"Maybe Dad had to grow up unexpectedly, ya' know? Sick daughter. I'm not the only one it impacted."

I pause and reach for her wrist. "All that's behind you now. You know that, right? And your dad, Sam, all of them…they didn't hold that against you."

"I know." Her head moves up and down in a short, jerky nod, but her lips are in a straight line, and I'm pretty positive she doesn't know it at all. Or if she does, she chalks it up as one more thing she needs to live the best life for. Because they all sacrificed for her to live.

It's a heady responsibility. Not too dissimilar to survivor's guilt, something the shrinks would go on about back on base.

Back at the apartment, Millie lounges in her dog bed. Sage scratches behind her ears, and her heavy tail thumps against the floor.

"What do you want for dinner?"

We could've stopped for dinner on the way back home, but all the outdoor patio tables were taken in the restaurants along the way. I could find us a restaurant, turn tonight into our first date, but I don't want to do that. No, I want to pull out all the stops for Sage. She deserves it. Sam would expect it.

She's removed the baseball hat, and a few stray strands frame her face. From what I can tell, she's not wearing any makeup. Her skin glows, something I'd like to think stems from our first kiss. Well, our first proper kiss.

She stands before the refrigerator, the door open, probably searching for food. My gaze falls to her shorts, or more honestly, her ass. "Do you like fried rice?"

I rarely eat Chinese food, mainly because of the grease. A younger me had no issue with it, and as much as I work out, I don't really have an issue with it now, but you can't spend as much time as I do in the gym and not grow a healthy awareness for what you're putting into your body. Still, I'm not about to tell Sage no. "You want to order Chinese? I have menus—"

"You have everything we need to make it. Eggs, frozen peas, corn, rice. Won't take me long to whip it up. It's on the lighter side, but I'm not feeling like a big meal. Unless you are?"

"No, that's...but wait, I can—"

"You're letting me stay here. Cooking dinner is the least I can do."

"How about this? You leave the recipe with me, and you go get a shower?"

"What? Why?" Her lips form a little oh and those dark eyes widen. "Do I smell?"

"No." I bark out a laugh. Tempting is what she smells like. It's all I can do to keep from pressing her against the counter and letting her feel what she does to me when we kiss. But that's not how a gentleman treats a lady. I don't often live up to Mom's behavioral expectations, but for Sage, I want to. "Fried rice may not be in my recipe wheelhouse, but I think it's something I can manage. Let me do this for you while you go wash off the day. And in case there is any question, that's not because you need to shower." My thumb caresses her cheek, chest rising as I suck in air. "I simply want to do something nice for you."

And then my lips are brushing against hers. She tastes like a mix of lemon and sugar. Her tongue twirls against mine and the tips of her fingers dig into my waist. She moans, and the sound goes straight to my dick. I'd happily lift her, place her on the counter, and kiss her until she begs me to do more. But I will not do that.

My forehead falls to hers, and the pad of my thumb dries her lip. The tips of our noses touch and her eyelids flicker open. It's hard to swallow. Hell, it's hard to breathe. A change of subject is needed.

"Tomorrow, I was thinking we might go for a hike? There's a canyon nearby. If we strike out early, we can avoid the sun. Have plenty of time to rest in the afternoon. To get ready for our date?"

Because yes, I will take this girl on a date. A real date. The kind a girl like Sage deserves. And then? I don't know. We live on opposite sides of the country. This doesn't completely make sense. Maybe all we'll have is a date or two while we search for her sister. A brief connection before we part ways. Whatever we have, however long we have it, I'm going to treat her right.

CHAPTER 14

Sage

My pulse? Still racing. And it's not at all because of the vertical climb through a sandy trail with next to no shade. I'm walking on air. It's a cheesy thought reminiscent of the oldies tunes the nurses at the hospital liked to play on a low volume in the reception area.

I never dared to imagine I would one day feel this. So light. Carefree. My facial muscles burn from the smile I can't calm.

He's kissed me five times. Knox Williams has kissed me, Sage Watson, five times. And he's been the one to initiate. Every. Single. Time.

I cannot wait to tell Jimmy. But then again, I can. Because talking about it out loud will allow reality to seep in and risk puncturing my atmospheric cloud. Jimmy will ask if I'm still coming back at the start of the school season, and I'll say yes, of course. And then a heavy weight will hang in the air with the reality that soon I'll be back in Asheville. Soon, Arrow's band of detectives will figure out what my sister has gotten herself into. Once she's rescued, no one will have a reason to chase after me, and I'll have no reason to be here under a blue sky, hiking with Knox, hotter-than-the-gods, Williams.

But before all that happens — and I want it to happen because we have to find Sloane—I can enjoy this hike and memorize every second to replay for years to come.

Sloane is okay. We're going to find her. I feel it in my gut, just like I feel it in my gut that one day Sam is going to come home. But before that happens, I do hope, as selfish as it is, that I get my date with Knox tonight.

He's convinced a date means a fancy dinner, but to me, it feels like we've been on one continuous date since the soccer match yesterday morning.

For as long as I live, I'll remember our kiss on the pier. His tentative expression. The slow way he moved in, gradually eliminating the space between us. The soft press of his lips. I wish I had it on video.

"You doing good?" Knox calls from behind me. The trail is narrow, and we're staggered, me in front. And my mind's been lost in la-la land.

"I'm good." It's the understatement of the century.

Millie has been off leash for most of our trek, but she's stayed close. Up ahead where the trail splits, she waits for us, recognizing the pack has a decision about direction.

"It's a quick sprint to the top if we take the vertical. Or, if we curve left, it's a flatter route, but longer."

"You know this trail well, huh?" Everything Knox does, he does well. Just like Sam.

"If I'm on a mountain bike, I'll go left. If I'm running, I'll go straight." He's stepped up behind me and his fingers curve around my hip. I suppress a purr. What I really want to do is lean back against him.

It's how I woke up this morning, with his warmth cocooning me and even though my skin is slightly damp with sweat, I'd love to lean into his hard, muscular chest. I look over my shoulder, lifting my chin, hoping for another kiss.

"Maybe when we come back, we'll bring a pair of mountain bikes. Have you been drinking your water?" And now he's concerned. Concerned enough that checking on me ranks above kissing.

"Yes." I force a smile and lift my half empty bottle for proof, not that he can see how much is inside the gray-blue metal container, but it's a lot lighter. Besides, I'm mindful of hydration. If I fall behind, my tongue feels parched, serving as a signal to up my water intake. He's wearing sunglasses and, while I can't see his eyes, I feel them scanning me from head to toe, checking for issues. "I'm good. Really."

Millie's ears perk forward, attention trained on me until the second my foot angles to the right, choosing the more challenging path. She charges forward, her question answered. I chug back water, not bothering to slow my pace to drink.

"My kind of girl," I hear Knox say from behind me. "Going for the challenge."

My life has been a challenge. I could say that to him, but I won't because then he'd feel sorry for me. I don't want sympathy. Sympathy is a disservice to those who had it harder. To those with complications. To those who didn't get to live as long as me. It's a disservice to me, because damn it, I am strong. And lucky. And grateful.

My only regret is that my life came at such a significant cost. Two lives. My donor. And the person on the list who didn't get an organ. Others might not look at it like I do, but it's the reality of the situation. In some ways it's a burden. I'm living for three.

I charge up the last straight bit, using my hands for balance, letting my fingers dig into the sandy packed soil. My leg muscles strain, and there's pressure against my bottom, and suddenly I'm lighter. The view of dirt transitions to flat ground, blue sky, and vista across the town to the ocean as I clamber to the peak.

"Wow." I lift my hand to my brow, shielding the sun. Millie sniffs the area, tail wagging.

"You did it." Knox is full on grinning. Sweat stains his t-shirt and beads along his neck. He's freshly shaven and the missing facial growth shaves years, giving him the look of a college-aged Knox. Well, a college version who spent a ton of time in the gym. Which, given he attended the Naval Academy, he probably did.

Knox holds his hands up for a high five. I thrust my arms in the air, hands out, stretching. Our palms slap against each other.

"Atta girl." My grin miraculously widens. "Let's rest a beat before we head down."

I narrow my eyes, resting my balled-up hands on my hips. "I don't need to rest." And surprisingly, it's the truth. I feel great. Maybe not transplant-games-great, but I'm doing good. I mean, sure, I'm not GOAT quality, but I don't need a break.

"Are you kidding? This is the best part of the hike." He waves, gesturing to the expansive view of land blending into the sea. "The view."

He finds a flat spot of dirt and sits. Millie trots up and presses her nose into his face. "Life moves pretty fast. If you don't stop and look around once in a while, you could miss it."

"Who said that?" I ask as I claim a spot of earth next to him. Not so close we touch, but close enough the butterflies in my stomach take flight.

"I say it."

"No." I shake my head, grinning. "That's a quote. I've heard it before."

"It's from an old movie. Before your time."

"Puh-leaze. I'm not that much younger than you."

"What is it? Six years?"

It's actually five years and four months, but who's counting? "Something like that."

He lifts his baseball cap and wipes his brow. His hairline is slightly damp, but he's wiping it like it itches. And then he tilts his head and looks at me. Still wearing those shades, but he's got that so sexy grin and my heart stills and it's like I can't breathe.

"Who would've thought at thirty-five, I'd be sitting here looking out over a California vista with Sam's youngest sister, wanting nothing more than to kiss her?"

That flighty heart? It's completely stopped now.

"Ever since yesterday afternoon, it's all I can think about. Every second on this trail. I've wanted to grab you. Kiss you." He shakes his head, looking off into the horizon.

The sun is behind our backs and my brain shouts, "Well, kiss me!"

But I'm a dating neophyte. My dating history is minimal. Mortifyingly so. For a sizeable chunk of my life, I suspected I might be asexual. But instead of beating myself up, I finally came to realize that when you feel like crap and breathing is a chore, sex isn't appealing. Leaving the house is dreadful. Carrying on a conversation exhausting. And then, I don't know, I just fell so far behind everyone else. And even once I was healthy, given my uncertain life expectancy, I've focused on giving back and in the time I gave myself, doing things I wanted. Filling out an online dating profile wasn't on the list. Really, putting myself out there, scaring myself…not on the list.

Knox's shoulder brushes mine, pulling me out of my trance. Did I think my heart stopped? Wildly inaccurate. It's about to thump through my ribcage.

"What're you thinking?"

I'm not sure what to tell him. I wish I had a brilliant answer for him. Something other than my brain short circuits when he touches me. In the distance, the golden sun flickers against the ocean. Tiny bursts of blended light across the vast stretch of deep blue.

"Hey." He exhales the word. It's a sensual sound that has me clenching my thighs. "Look at me." I swallow and force myself to breathe. My bare arm brushes against the fabric of his T-shirt.

"I think you should kiss me." *Did that come out too breathless?*

His lips curl, and somehow he's closer, his presence sucking up all the oxygen.

My eyes close as he brushes his lips across mine.

"Damn. I really like kissing you." He deepens our kiss and pulls back, tangling his fingers in my hair. "Correction. I love kissing you."

"I love kissing you too." He touches my knee, my thigh.

"You make me want to do all kinds of unspeakable things to you."

"Unspeakable?" I should probably stop repeating his words.

And then his lips are on mine. A hint of cinnamon. A fission of energy spirals wiping all thought. His hand is against my nape, keeping me right where he wants me. His kiss is sensual and I somehow feel it everywhere, a surge of sensations through my extremities and deep in my core.

A thick, wet tongue leaves slober on my cheek.

"Ew." We both pull back, only to be met with a wave of unappealing dog breath. "Millie."

Knox chuckles and slaps her haunches. He gets up and offers me a hand. "I'd be upset, but she's helping me stay in line."

"You don't need to—"

"Yes, I do." With one firm pull, I'm up, off the ground. "Here. I'll lead on this first part. It's steep. And if you slip, I can catch you." His cocky grin has my insides flipping in all kinds of directions. There's no wonder they voted him Biggest Heartbreaker his senior year of high school. I still have the yearbook because I kept all of Sam's yearbooks for him. Or, well, I suppose I did have them. I doubt they survived the fire.

I follow Knox, letting the sight of his muscular shoulders and firm butt lessen the impact of the realization I probably lost some important mementos in that house fire. I've tried hard not to dwell too much on the fire. It'll be there for me to face when I return home and after the team finds Sloane.

We reach the straight down-drop section, the part that I used my hands to climb, and Knox spins, holding his arms out for me. Millie's already past him, waiting farther down the trail, tail wagging, watching.

"Jump," Knox says. "I'll catch you."

One million fantasies collide. I bend my knees, think better of it, crouch, and put a hand on the ground for stability.

"Jump," he urges.

In what must look like the weirdest maneuver ever executed, I push off the edge from a near crouching position into his open, waiting arms.

As promised, he catches me. His chest is so hard my breasts ache pressed against his muscular planes. With my arms clutching his shoulders, he lets my body slide down his. It's a slow, magical, dreamy journey for my toes to meet the ground. And then he kisses me.

It's like we're dancing without music. I have an urge to kick my foot up, just like in the old movies. His palms fall to my ass, and—oh, my god, he's touching my butt!

He cups my butt cheeks, pressing me into him, and his groan rumbles through me. Heat and unruly sensations course in my nether regions. He breaks the kiss, and his thumb caresses my cheek. His chest rises and falls as fast as if he's been running, and I become aware I'm breathing rapidly, too. He takes my hand and presses his lips to my knuckle, then we head off, side by side. The trail is too narrow for us both, and he leaves the packed dirt and takes the side of the trail. His hiking boots flatten the clumps of grass and kick loose rocks.

A roar of engines splits the silence. It's not the sound of a car.

"Motorbikes," Knox says, scanning the trail in the direction of the sound.

Off in the distance, two riders on mud-splattered motorbikes come into view. They're wearing helmets with face shields. One is dressed in red, the other in black. Red clay dust spins behind them, and the noxious scent of exhaust wafts through the air.

"They look like advanced riders," Knox observes.

"I didn't think motor vehicles were allowed this far up the trail."

"They're not but…every now and then you see people doing it anyway."

About a foot past us, a patch of dirt poofs in a mini explosion. Odd.

Millie stops up ahead. Her head tilts and her tail lowers.

Another dusty poof. Just beyond Knox's shadow.

"Shooter. Get down!"

CHAPTER 15

Knox

It's the motorbikes. *Fuck.*

The one wearing red has stopped. His gloved hand holds a revolver. The sun blazes down on his face shield, forming a mirrored surface, and in it I see myself and Sage.

"What do you want?"

Sage is crouched on the ground where I shoved her behind a bush. I'm not carrying a gun. Weapons aren't allowed on this trail. But these fuckers clearly don't care.

My fingers dip into my pocket and wrap around a pocketknife. It's not ideal, but I've got this knife and a couple of rocks within reach. On the ground two feet away lies a lengthy limb.

"All we want is her."

There's no fucking way.

I bend and whisper, "When I say now, you take off running. Through the woods to the right. Do not look back."

"Why do you want her?"

"Back up and you don't die."

Hands held high in the international language of defeat, I say, "Now, let's not do anything rash." Sage peers up at me with scared brown eyes. "Now," I repeat, this time in more of a shouty whisper.

Crouching to remain below the bush line, she heads to the area to the right of the trail.

I hang back, kneeling near the closest bush. I prep the stick and blindly feel for rocks to throw, keeping my attention trained on the men. I can easily take one, but not both.

"There's no point in running. You're not going to get away," the man in black calls.

Fuck me for not carrying a gun. Sage is a good thirty feet into the woods. The distance between us is getting too great.

I take off for her, hoping like hell they can't see into the shadows.

An engine revs as I catch up to Sage.

My body shields her. One hand on her elbow. Guiding her in case she slips.

Millie yelps. Her tail curls between her legs.

Dirt flies.

Mother fucker.

"They're shooting at us. Just keep going forward."

Go.

There's a thick grouping of trees up ahead. Those bikes will have to leave us and go around.

Eyes trained on the cover.

Arms out for balance.

Cover Sage.

Her foot slips. Pebbles cascade down the decline.

I catch her elbow. Lift.

Another pop. A poof of dirt right by my leg.

Fuck.

I press her down below the hedge. Peer above.

My visibility is shit.

One engine revs. He's retreating.

Or picking a different path.

I grab my phone. Tap fast.

Under fire

La Cumbre Peak

Midway down

Unarmed

W Sage

2 moto bikes

My gaze roves over Sage. She's crouched where I placed her. One foot above the ground. Quivering.

"Shh. It's okay."

"Should I go–"

"No." I scan the trail. This is a popular trail. These men have balls. We're almost at the bend where there'd be more hikers. How'd they know we were here?

Sage grips my leg. Her hand trembles.

"Are you okay?" I don't see blood.

"I'm fine." Fear coats her words, but she's strong. She'll be okay.

Millie's at my side. She yelped. With an eye on the pass through the brush, I run my fingers through her fur. She flinches. Blood soaks my fingers.

"They got Millie."

If she's too injured to make it down, I can carry her around my shoulders. I visualize the maneuver. Fuck. It'd put us at a disadvantage. I wouldn't be as quick to respond.

They have motorbikes. One of them could grab Sage and drive off. We can't just hide, waiting.

"Stay here."

I backtrack, limb in hand, and wait behind a tree. The first bike comes around the bend at a cautious speed. As he nears, I lunge.

The thick stick catches him on the collarbone, and he flips back, bike and all. In a flash, I dig my knife into the wheel. I scan the ground but don't see his weapon. The bike's on top of him. He moans and squirms.

The other bike approaches, engine revving, gun raised. The ground is too uneven to steer a motorbike one-handed and shoot a gun, but still, I won't hang out here. Sage is on her own. I take off back to Sage, ducking as a bullet whizzes by.

I pause, taking cover behind a tree. He's stopped. Checking on his buddy.

I take off.

I'll secure Sage. Find a place to hide so I can tackle them should they trail us. Commandeer a gun and take them out.

I find Sage where I left her, shielded by bushes, cuddling the dog.

"You okay?"

Millie's hackles line the center of her back.

"She's not whimpering. Maybe it grazed her?" Sage's voice cracks with concern for the dog. I can't see the tears, but I hear them. *How the hell did they find us? And who the fuck are they?*

"It's gonna be okay." I smash Max's name on my phone. The rumble of the engines tells me they haven't left the spot where I knocked one down.

One ring. "Where on the peak?"

"Close to the bend where it levels out. I'm unarmed."

"Cops on the way. I'm too far out."

"We've got shrubs for cover." In other words, shit cover.

"Sirens will be a diversion. Stay put."

"Two tangoes. Shot my dog." Fury has me seeing red. You don't fucking shoot animals.

But they missed me. Under pressure? Cocky? Inexperienced? Amateur? Doubtful. Shooting while moving has a high margin of error, but maybe they weren't aiming to hit, just to scare.

A movement to the northeast has me covering Sage's back. A bird lifts off, wings spread wide.

Beyond the brush, there's a clear expanse. A boulder. Then a bend that takes us to a frequently traveled trail section.

The engines grind in the distance.

What are they planning?

If they shot into this, with luck, they might get us. What are they doing? Waiting for us to move?

Have they positioned themselves to take us out when they get us in the scope?

A high-pitched squawk cuts through the air.

Fresh earth mixes with the faint scent of exhaust.

He used a silencer. Didn't want to attract attention.

The rolling sound of a siren resonates in the distance.

I glance down at the phone.

RYAN

Hold tight. OTW

Who the fuck would go to so much effort to get Sage? A kindergarten teacher. It's Sloane. Has to be Sloane. What the hell has Sloane gotten herself into? Sam said she was off-the-charts brilliant.

The wail of sirens grows closer.

MAX

5 min ETA

A twig digs into my knee. Sage shakes her hand. An ant falls to the ground. Millie's tongue lolls out of her mouth. Panting. No movement beyond the brush. Nothing on the peak. The engines are silent.

The cops can't drive to us. The trail head is wide enough for a car only at the base.

I want to run. Round the bend. But there's no reason for the risk.

There's been no movement. No revved engine.

Pale blue flashes against the boulder in the bend.

Crunch. Crunch.

The low rumble of an engine runs up the trail.

The front of an ATV comes into view. A cop.

I rise, holding an arm out.

"Stay back," I warn.

If the fucker shoots, he's shooting me.

The cop sees me and floors the ATV.

"Shooters. Over there," I tell him, pointing toward the peak.

Revving engines rumble in the distance. Are they leaving?

"Are you hit?" the cop asks.

"No."

"Positive it's a shooter?"

"Got my dog. Saw the guns."

The cop's wearing a helmet and sunglasses. Another ATV rounds the bend. My protective instinct kicks in. My hand falls to Sage's shoulder. Knees bent, ready to lunge.

Matching uniform. I relax. But my hand remains on Sage.

The engines up the trail are distant, but the ones around the bend grow louder.

Another ATV, three mountain bikes. Park rangers. No motorbikes. Those ATVs don't stand a chance of catching up to a motorbike.

All but one of the uniformed first responders goes off searching the canyon, but they'll never find them. One cop says she's bringing us down. I place Sage behind the cop, then sling a leg over, sandwiching Sage in. If anyone's out there, a bullet will go through me to get to her.

I call to Millie to jump up behind us, but she's not having it. She trots down the trail. She's favoring her front leg, but there's not a lot of blood. A good sign.

Max is waiting at the base. He's surrounded by SBPD. Doesn't take me long to download what's happened. Arrow Tactical has a lot of connections on the force, and apparently they're all down on the need to get us to safety.

Officer Sanford wraps things up with a, "I'll reach out if I need more information."

We climb into Max's car. I get in the front seat, but that's not where I want to be. I want to be in the back with Sage and Millie. But at least back there, Sage can lie on the floorboards if needed.

"Any update?" It's the first question I ask as soon as the car doors slam.

"Yeah." He holds a hand up in recognition of one cop managing traffic in the parking lot. A crowd is forming, thanks to the sirens. "We're doing a car switcheroo in twenty." Max glances in the back seat. Sage's arms wrap around Millie. She's panting but looks okay. "Then I'm taking your obedience school dropout to the vet."

"Where're we going?" Sage asks. Her voice is frail. Frightened.

"To a safe house. Instructions will be in the car. You two are to stay there." Max's gaze alternates between the rearview and the road.

I shift and scan our rear. If someone's following, I'll see. If I find the fuckers coming after her, I'll kill them all.

"Do you have a gun?" I ask Max. I can't fucking believe I didn't carry on the hike. But gun laws being what they are in California, I didn't. Still, I had Sage with me.

Max gestures to the glove box. "Someone back there?"

"Not yet." I pop open the glove box, pull out a Glock 19, and check the slide. Loaded. My nerves settle. Sage's frantic eyes set off all my protective instincts. "Lie down on the seat," I tell her. "No one's back there. Let's just...be safe."

CHAPTER 16

Sage

I can't stop shivering. I'm freezing.

Why is this happening?

The shooter could've hit Knox. Every single one of those bullets came closer to hitting Knox than me.

Sam told me to come to Knox, but surely he didn't imagine this scenario. He wouldn't want me to put his friend's life in danger. No one else can die for my life.

I've journeyed from fantasy to nightmare in one Sunday morning.

The radio is off. I intuitively understand Knox can't handle noise right now. He's still wearing sunglasses, but I can tell from his minute movements that he's scanning the side view and rear view constantly.

We changed cars in a parking garage. We've been driving for at least thirty minutes, weaving through the streets. Felix met us in this car and gave me a ridiculous wig with a baseball cap. He also had two duffel bags. Said someone from the office went to Knox's place and packed for us. Max promised to get Millie to the vet.

Who would shoot a dog? Of course, they weren't aiming for Millie. They were aiming for me. Or Knox. So they could take me? What would that even mean? For what?

The terror of the night someone broke into my home strikes with a force that stings my eyes. Why?

Think, Sage. Why would someone want you?

Could it be as simple as I'm Sloane's last close relative? The last person who would pursue finding her?

Maybe they think I know something. I can't do anything about them believing I have knowledge I don't have, but I can give Sloane's disappearance visibility.

"I need to go public."

Knox acts like he doesn't hear me. He's following the GPS map on the car, but he has it set to silent. We're on the 101 in sluggish traffic. There's a sign to my right that reads, "Welcome to Carpinteria. The safest beach in the world."

"If her disappearance is all over the news, they won't have any reason to come after me."

"You don't really have anything to go public with."

"A missing person campaign. A US citizen working abroad is missing. I need to get it out there. I'm the only one in the United States who will make a big deal about Sloane's disappearance. Think about it." He's completely disregarding me, but why didn't I think of this before? "The women who are most likely to be abducted are women without family connections. The women who won't have anyone looking for them."

"Are you talking about serial killers?" He flicks his turn signal for an upcoming off ramp.

"Maybe. I don't know." That's probably exactly what I'm thinking of. "But think about it. If it was evidence they wanted to destroy, they did it. Right?" I'm in the back seat because he claims it's the safest place for me to sit and he's wearing sunglasses so I can't see his eyes, so I raise my voice. "The only reason to go after me is to keep me from chasing her down. That has to be it. I don't know anything."

"We'll talk to the team." He's dismissive. He's also focused. I'll let it go until we arrive at our destination. Then I'll talk to the team. I could be on to something. I've seen missing persons alerts before in the news. That's what I need to do. What I should've been doing all along.

We turn onto a relatively busy thoroughfare with stoplights and businesses. Glimpses of the ocean flash between cross streets. Far off in the distance are mountains. It's a picturesque seaside town. We can't be far from Santa Barbara.

"How much farther?" We're headed to a safe house, or at least, that's what Max called it. But, looking around, with people on bikes and scooters and cars with surfboards attached to the top, it feels like we've arrived in a smaller Santa Barbara.

"Three minutes."

There's a gruffness to his tone I don't recognize. Is he angry? "I'm sorry about what happened. If you want me to leave—"

"Hush."

"I'm sure Sam—"

"Sage. Get down."

I slink farther down in the back seat. We're sitting at a stoplight. A car pulls up beside us. But we're in an SUV and we're higher than the car. All I can see is the turquoise surfboard strapped to the top. Our windows are up, but our car vibrates with the bass from the music of the neighboring car.

The light turns green. We turn left, leaving the surfboard car behind. We turn left again, and the front of the car rises. A garage door opens. Knox pulls in and almost immediately, the garage door descends. There's a vibrant town right outside that garage door. A city street. Well, a beach town street.

"Where are we?"

"Home for now. Stay in the car while I clear the house."

His car door slams and I watch him through the windshield, gun in hand.

This doesn't feel like a safe house. I imagined a place in the mountains. Hidden in woods. Maybe a small A-frame deep in the mountains accessible by a single winding road. A structure where no one can see if you turn on lights or light a fire in the chimney.

The lights flick on in the garage. Knox steps through the door and slides his gun into a holster on his waist. It's difficult to stop staring at the gun. My car door opens.

"Come on. I'll get our bags."

"Where are we?"

"Little town called Carpinteria."

I saw that on the sign. "What happened to the safe house?" I reach for a duffel, but Knox raises a shoulder, lifting the bag closest to me out of my reach.

"This is it."

"We're in a town."

"There are lots of Airbnb cottages on this beach. No one will notice us. We'll look like a couple renting the place. And we're close enough to HQ we can easily meet up if needed."

The interior garage door opens into a narrow hallway. A washer and dryer sit in an alcove, and on top of the washing machine sits a sample size plastic bag of Tide detergent. There's a half bath beside the alcove. A cheery watercolor beach scene hangs over the towel rack. The hallway opens into a kitchen and an open living area. From the den are glass sliding doors that open onto a deck with an overhang.

A wide stretch of sand separates the cottage from the ocean. Beachgoers are lying out, and a couple of surfers straddle their boards off in the distance.

"But anyone can approach?" I'm a kindergarten teacher, not a security expert, but this location feels way too exposed. Those men found us on a hiking trail.

"The glass is bulletproof."

"Knox, I don't want to sound like I'm complaining, but he found me after I followed every precaution. I haven't turned on my phone."

He removes his sunglasses, places them on the counter, and leans back against it with his arms crossed.

"We believe they found you through Jimmy."

"No." That's not possible. Jimmy is my closest friend. He's wrong.

"Our best guess is they have listening devices in his house."

"Is Jimmy in danger?"

"Unlikely. They must've watched to see who came around after your house fire. If they wanted to hurt him, they've had plenty of time. All they wanted was your location."

"This doesn't make sense." I pace the room, trying to recall exactly what I said to Jimmy.

"Another theory is someone has a hit out on you. Our tech team is scouring job posts now."

"Why would anyone–"

"It's just a theory. If there's a posting, I'm not optimistic our tech guys will find it. Any postings are usually pretty nondescript until the job is awarded."

"Someone would post something like that on what… Craigslist?"

"No, it's a…" He rubs his hand through his hair and sighs. "It's a part of the internet most people don't know how to access."

"And…the listening devices?"

"Jimmy's the only one who knew you were in Santa Barbara. The running theory is they listened in on your conversation. Either that or he sold your location."

"He wouldn't. There's not enough money in the world. If they're listening in on his conversations—"

"We have someone heading to Asheville to investigate. There's no point in guessing. Right now, we're guessing."

"I guess I can't call Jimmy to warn him?"

His lips pucker and his facial muscles flex into a scowl. I don't like that look.

"No." He checks his watch. "We connect with the team in ten. In the meantime, let me show you around."

He's all business. Stern. Strict. Goodbye, flirty Knox; hello, Mr. Lawman. When faced with bullets, he turns into steel, and I turn into a bumbling, freezing mess.

"As you can see, this is the living area. Fridge is stocked. Half bath in the hall. We passed it. Bedroom in here."

I follow him through to a small bedroom with windows out to the ocean and an ensuite bathroom. He dumps both duffels on the mattress.

"There's only one bedroom?"

"Actually, the cottage has two. But they outfitted the other bedroom as a safe room. Follow me. It's got a thumb print recognition scanner and I need to get you set up."

"How did you…when did you learn all of this?"

"When Felix delivered the car."

That's right. He talked to Felix and Max while I stayed with Millie. Then they transferred me into the car Felix brought. Their eyes darted around as if bullets might whiz by.

"This is surreal." It's the only word for it.

Two years ago, Sam gave me specific instructions. Was he envisioning this deranged scenario? I'd thought he'd been out of his mind. Paranoid because of whatever dangerous secret missions they sent him on. But he couldn't have foreseen this. Whoever is after me could've killed Knox. I could never live with myself if my situation caused him to die. And it's hard to see how me sitting in a safe house helps Sloane. I should be focused on finding her.

Knox swings a framed print of a beach scene to the left, revealing a panel with a glass screen. With his touch, the black glass glows and a keypad appears. He presses four numbers, then his own thumbprint, and has me press my thumb to it. The device clicks. He opens a door to a hall closet. Blue and white striped beach towels are stacked neatly on all four shelves. The wall of shelves slides to the right, revealing a windowless room.

"It's soundproof. Walls are bulletproof and fireproof. You're safe here. If anyone comes." His gaze cuts to me, his expression unreadable. "But they won't."

Monitors line one long built-in desk that encompasses the length of the wall on the left. Two ergonomic chairs with wheels are pushed up under the long desk. The monitors are dark. There's one sofa on the opposite wall, and in the far corner of the room is a full-size refrigerator. There's an interior door in the far corner, which I presume is a bathroom, or maybe it's a closet with food, or both.

Someone needs to wake me because this is out of a movie. And I hate scary movies. A friend of mine once talked me into watching *Saw,* saying it was a good entry level horror flick. I didn't sleep well for months.

"Does it hurt?" Knox's question confuses me until his gaze pointedly falls to my sternum. The butt of my hand is massaging the area.

"No." Although I'd be lying if I said my heartrate was at a resting pace. I exit into the hall, through the magical linen closet. I don't know what gadgets might exist in that freaky room, and I don't want to know. My eyes burn. My fingers tremble.

I want to go home. To my house. Take stock of the damage. Decorate my kindergarten classroom. I want to call up my sister and scream at her because she clearly made some very bad decisions. No, better yet, I want my brother to appear and tell me the last two years were all part of a dream and he never walked into a building that exploded and for him to say, "Wow, your dreams are getting intense. Guess that new ticker's doing a great job of getting oxygen to the brain."

Behind me, I hear the motorized movement of doors sliding. I head back into the den with a view of sandy beach, rolling waves, and a beachgoer hanging out beneath an umbrella off in the distance. All normal. Except that I'm standing behind bulletproof glass.

"Let's take the call in the kitchen. You want anything to drink?"

My throat is tight. Scratchy. Dry. "I'll get some water. Do you want anything?"

"Water. Thanks." I think I feel his gaze on my back, but when I turn, he's focused on his phone and moving to the kitchen table. He sets it down flat.

"Hey. Kairi?"

A voice emanates from the phone. "Hi, Knox. Give us a sec. Ryan is joining."

The water in both glasses vibrates in my trembling hands. It looks like what I imagine water looks like during an earthquake. Knox's eyebrows come together as he zeroes in on the glass.

"How's the place?" It's a woman's voice asking. Possibly the same woman, possibly different.

"It works. What've we learned?"

Seated in a chair at the table, I rub my forehead. A dull pain aches. My brain can't process this. I slide the glass of water farther away from me. I'm not sure I can swallow.

Click.

"Hey, team. SBPD are still on the scene. They found tracks from the trail base. Looks like they followed you to the base, then took an alternate trail up."

"Any shell casings?"

"No. Looks like they cleaned up after themselves, but like I said, they're still on the scene. When you guys struck out on the trail, do you remember any nearby vehicles?"

Knox's eyes flash to mine. "Two parked vehicles when we arrived. One open top Jeep. One small four door sedan. Both empty. No one pulled up after us."

"Well, they did, but you didn't see them. And someone broke into your place."

"Can you tell when?" If Knox is surprised, his face doesn't register it.

"After Stella packed your bags."

So that means after the incident on the trail.

"How'd you determine timing?" Knox asks.

"I went back to your place to get Millie's dog stuff. Someone ransacked your place. Place was fine when Stella stopped by."

"Probably because they were still getting off the canyon." Knox says.

I close my eyes, giving thanks to the universe that an innocent party didn't cross paths with these gun-toting psychos. What would've happened if they encountered Stella?

"I need to go public," I say. Knox turns his stern gaze on me. I don't know who's speaking on this phone. They don't know me. "This is Sage. I've been thinking about it, and it's the only way this ends. I don't have any information. Or if I did, they destroyed it. The only reason for them to come after me is to keep me from making Sloane's disappearance a major news story. Once the story's out there, there's no reason to come after me."

"That's one theory," a masculine voice says.

"Let me run it by Interpol." I think that's Ryan's voice. "It's conceivable they can help us get the missing persons word out on a global scale since there's already a yellow notice on her. It'll be far more effective than going to local media here in the States."

They all talk more, going back and forth in a calm, direct manner. As if this is all normal. Something people go through every day. As if now that I'm in a bulletproof compound that from the outside looks like a small Airbnb beach cottage, there's no rush or urgency. It's a business matter. No reason to freak out. Or get worked up. No reason to have a heart attack.

"Hey, are you okay?" Knox asks after disconnecting the call.

"I'm fine."

Warmth envelopes my shoulder. The nape of my neck. I'm lifted from the chair. "You're safe. There's no reason to worry."

I jerk in his arms. "Are you out of your mind? You almost got shot. Millie did get shot! I can't just sit here. I need to do something."

His lips brush my temple. We sink into the sofa. "You're freezing."

He toes off his hiking boots. Bends and lifts my feet.

"What're you doing?"

"Removing your shoes. We're going to lie together."

I cannot swallow.

"Clothed. To warm you. To calm you. I think you might be in shock."

"I'm not in shock."

There's a blanket lying on the back of the sofa, and he tugs it over us. A thick cobweb dangles in a single loop from the plain white ceiling.

"Come back to me, Sage."

Body heat warms my right side. I roll into Knox. His fingers coax tangles from my strands. Tender. Caring. His thumb brushes my cheek, back and forth, the tip of his nose over mine. And then his lips. Soft. Tender. The press of his lips to mine warms me. Sweet and caring.

I've returned to dreamland and don't want to wake.

CHAPTER 17

Knox

Sinful sugar. I could hold her and kiss her all day. She curls her body against me, her thigh gliding over mine. Beneath the blanket, heat circulates between us. Her shirt rises and the pads of my fingers touch bare skin, tracing the curve of her hip to her spine. She vibrates against me, a long, slow thrum.

Everything about her is arousing, but most especially in this proximity. My lips press to hers and she opens for a sweet, tender kiss. It's not going anywhere. My rock-hard dick might think otherwise, given she's pressing down on him, rocking into him. All I want is to warm her up. To bring her out of the negative void. Doing more would be wrong. She's shaken up after today. Terrified. Holding her. Kissing her. It's to make her feel safe. While I'd love nothing more than to remove her clothes and sink into her, I won't. We haven't yet been on a date, and I swear I will treat this girl like gold. I owe it to Sam. To her.

She is so fucking sweet. The pressure on my hipbone intensifies. With closed eyes, her fingers wander across my shoulder, to my neck, into my hair. I press my lips to the corner of her mouth, gobsmacked by the sensual creature undulating against me, clearly wanting and needing more. My tongue traces the seam of her lips, eliciting an intoxicating moan. She grips my hair and directs my mouth back to hers, demanding a deeper kiss.

Her hips flex against me, the movement sexy as fuck. I shift her so one of my thighs is between her legs. We're clothed but fuck if her movements don't feel good. It's so good that if she keeps on, I might lose control right here fully clothed. The last time I lay on a sofa making out like this with a girl with no intention of moving further must've been back in high school.

Her shorts have ridden up, exposing her round butt cheeks. The tips of my fingers sweep the center of her legs. Her panties are damp. Fuck me. She's so turned on. Arousing doesn't cut it. I want to flip her over and follow a deep, undeniable instinct. Tear off these shorts. Plunge into her. It would be the most natural action.

But this is Sage. I won't. Can't. Fuck. I want to.

She rides my thigh, working herself over me. With each thrust of her hips, my fingers glide against her panties. One finger, one very bad finger, inches the fabric aside, to her curls, to her heat. Other fingers join to cup her vulva, and fuck if she doesn't like that. Desire flares like a blinding, deafening explosion.

And she freezes. Her muscles spasm. Her lips part as she shudders through a release before relaxing against me.

Holy shit. She just climaxed on my hand. That might've been the hottest thing I've seen. She mewls. Relaxed. Contented. My cock throbs.

The top of her head falls against my shoulder, the tip of her nose brushes along my neck, and her breathing slows, evening out. I flatten one palm against her butt.

I'm too on edge to fall asleep. So I lie there, holding her, feeling the soft thud of her heartbeat against my ribcage as her breathing settles into a slow, steady rhythm.

This is a first for me. Holding someone with no ulterior motives. Only to be there for her.

I press my lips to the top of her head. If this happened, if we happened, my parents would be over the moon. Mom used to ask about the Watsons all the time. And here's another first. Me thinking about my parent's reaction. Me envisioning a future with someone.

My phone vibrates in my back pocket. With ease, I shift, hoping not to wake her. If it's HQ, I've got to answer. But it's a text.

FELIX ROSARIO

Call me

Would it kill you to give me a little more than that? Like me, Felix was Special Forces. We're going through the same things. Adjusting to life outside the military. I left because my body told me time's up. He left because his wife had a baby, and he missed his kid's birth. It was a wakeup call for him. He also clocked his twenty and retired.

With my thumb, I tap out a quick response.

ME

?

The phone vibrates. Felix's name lights the screen. But it's not just a call. It's a FaceTime call. *Dude. Video?*

I shift as smoothly as I can, careful to keep my finger off the accept button until I'm across the den and behind the closed bedroom door.

I answer the call, holding the phone away the way folks do for a video call. "You can't text?"

Felix's brown head and black crew top take up most of the space on the screen. Behind him is a window and a view I recognize as the building that's across the street from Arrow.

"Your place was under surveillance."

"Did you see them?"

"Max approached. Got tags. Guy spotted him when he snapped a photo. Pulled out a gun."

"Seriously? In broad daylight?"

"Cars and pedestrians passing. Fire exchanged."

"Holy shit. Is Max okay?"

"He's fine. Down at the station answering questions. Guy got away, but we ID'd him with visual recognition. Jasper Villanova. A known hired assassin. Dual citizenship to US and UK."

Fire exchanged. Right on our street. Baby carriages and kids walk on our street. "Any collateral damage?"

"No. Got lucky. But we had a call with Interpol."

"Yeah?"

"Ryan relayed Sage's suggestion. Requested an international missing persons PR campaign. Blow it out of the water. See if applying pressure to locate Sloane cancels the hunt for Sage."

I collapse back on the bed and hold the phone up to the ceiling. I have a view of Felix's head and a smooth white ceiling. "I'm not convinced Sage's theory is correct. Everything he said today indicated the plan was to take her alive."

In the military, interrogation would be the first reason to take someone alive. To gain information. The other reasons would be to blackmail, threaten, or negotiate.

"Interesting. But Interpol said no dice on the missing person campaign."

"It's not their call." We don't need them to hit the media.

"You sure you can trust her?" Felix adjusts the camera. He watches me. Closely. I suppose this is why we're on a video call.

"She doesn't know anything, if that's what you're getting at."

His lips purse. He nods. "The Interpol contact Ryan mentioned earlier? He's based in London. Tristan. He's the one who campaigned to keep it quiet. For the short-term."

A derisive snort escapes from me. Completely unprofessional, but you just gotta love people who are halfway across the world calling shots.

"Yeah, right?" Felix says, catching my distaste. "But, to give the guy credit, he didn't make any demands. Just expressed doubt it would be effective, and he promised to keep digging on his end. There was a lady from Interpol on the call, too. She shared that they monitor the black-market trade. Origins hit their watch list because they received an anonymous report that they've been violating international law on how long they grow and develop cells. Fourteen days is the legal max. Doesn't sound like it's a top priority for Interpol, though. The logic in holding back on the PR campaign was two-fold. One, they didn't think it would ultimately deliver Sloane to safety. And two, the lab Sloane worked at is still operating out of the Caymans. She said places like that will relocate overnight if the heat gets turned on. If they are, in fact, running some kind of illegal operation."

Sloane almost lost her sister when she was waiting on a transplant list. Is it possible she somehow rationalized being a part of the organ trade? No, she's a scientist. Not a surgeon. "There's no way Sloane would be involved in something illegal." I say the words, but not because I completely believe them. I've been around the block enough to believe that perspective plays a role in moral decisions.

"Tristan said all the black-market businesses these days have legitimate fronts. Given Sloane's a cellular scientist, his running theory is wrong place, wrong time. She stumbled on something. But they want to keep her working."

"So, he believes she's alive?"

"That's his theory. He suggested they want Sage to force Sloane to do something she doesn't want to do. Do you know if she has any surgical training?"

"Not to my knowledge."

"Well, regardless, this Tristan guy's theory is interesting. He said that, based on what we're telling him, Sage is the only person they can hold over Sloane."

"It's an interesting theory. But they burned down her house."

"Just a messenger. It's a running theory."

"Did our guys in the Caymans find anything?"

"Not yet. Two are running surveillance on the facility. Two are floating Sloane's photo."

"Nothing?" I push off the bed, frustration simmering.

"These things take time. You know that. They just hit the ground an hour ago." The screen shifts, and I get glimpses of the ceiling and the floor. It's another reason I hate video calls. He comes back into the picture, but this time he's sitting at his desk, and it looks like he's set his phone down on a charging dock. "Just wanted to tell you to stay tight. Whether they're looking to abduct her or kill her, she's on someone's list, and that someone has deep pockets."

"Did our guys land in Asheville yet?"

"Don't think so. Why?"

"She's worried about her friend Jimmy."

"You think he'd sell her out?"

"She said he's her best friend. She's worried for his safety."

"Kairi's team is behind the listening device theory. Her team said that if anyone checked her social, which is set to public, he'd be the one they'd watch to try to locate her. Kairi didn't find anything in his texts or email, which is why she sent someone out to check his place. See what we're dealing with. What kind of listening devices they used. Or if someone went old school and tricked him into sharing her location."

"Old school phishing. That's a conceivable angle. I've never met the guy. It's possible he's a dumb fuck and bought some story about someone looking for her. Insurance or something. He's supposed to be helping her. Knows a guy from USAA." An insurance cover could definitely work on an unsuspecting person. "The guy's a schoolteacher. If they got forceful, he might cave pretty easily."

The bedroom door opens. Sage squints, one hand on the doorframe, the other on the knob. "You think they'd go after Jimmy?"

CHAPTER 18

Sage

Knox blinks with surprise but quickly morphs into business mode.

"If you're concerned about him, let me call him." Desperation rings in my tone. I didn't go to Jimmy out of a desire to protect him. If something happened to him because I left…

"Not a good idea." He glances down at the phone in his hand. "Or that's my gut reaction. Felix will check with the team. Let's clear it."

"Do you need his number?"

"No." The speaker on the phone lends Felix's voice an artificial quality. "I'll be in touch."

I don't hear a click, but the call must've ended, because Knox sets the phone on the bed, face down.

"This is crazy." I'm a kindergarten teacher. Jimmy teaches history. "I worried Sam was suffering from extreme paranoia when he left me that duffel bag. And now look at all that's happened."

Knox pats the mattress, encouraging me to come sit beside

him. I comply, but there's an uneasiness I can't rub out of my chest. "You don't think they'd hurt Jimmy, do you?"

"We're looking into it."

I rest both hands behind me and tilt my head up to the ceiling. My eyes burn.

"It's unlikely. He's the only one who knew you're in Santa Barbara, right?"

Jimmy is the only one I called. But… "They were in my house. My letters. If they read them…more than once, Sam told me to find you if I was ever in trouble. He included your address. The one in San Diego. And your phone number, but an old number. It was disconnected."

"That number got on some spam list. When I changed providers, I went ahead and changed the number."

"After the explosion?" My chest sinks, and I squeeze my eyes closed, willing away the nagging doubt. Sam's alive. *I know it.*

Knox brushes my hair behind my ear. His fingers drag along my cheek with a comforting warmth. A five o'clock shadow covers his jaw, a sign he didn't shave this morning before our hike. Unbelievably, our hike happened today. It feels like days ago.

"I should've never come here."

He cups my face between his strong hands and tilts my chin until I'm looking directly into his serious, commanding eyes. "You are exactly where you should be. We're going to find Sloane. And I'm going to keep you safe."

"But at what cost?"

"At all costs. That's what Sam would want. That's why he sent you to me. He knew."

My heart skips under the warmth of his gaze. He dips his head, his lashes flutter closed, and he presses his lips to mine.

I reach for him, for his shoulder, the curly hair at the base of his neck, and he maneuvers us so we're lying down across the width of the bed, side by side. Much like the sofa, only I'm not straddling him. His hand warms my waist, the exposed skin cool. He slides down, bunching my shirt as he moves.

He's propped up on an elbow, and I'm below him. Kissing him. Reality dissipates. The warmth along my ribs spreads, and his thumb drags across the bottom of my bra.

Holy shit. He's touching my bra.

His lips caress my neck. Just his lips touching my skin has me breaking out in goosebumps. The rough stubble of his jaw sands my skin. His nail scratches against the underside of my breast. My thighs squeeze together. His teeth tug on my bottom lip. And the bra gets pushed higher. Along with my shirt.

A chill falls over me. My chest squeezes. Panic lurks. It's too much. I'm up and off the bed and out the door. My breaths come in quick, short bursts.

Through the large window in the den, a large yellow ball, the sun, descends below the navy horizon. I focus on the sun. On my breathing.

I sense rather than see him.

"Hey." He's timid. And he shouldn't be. This is all me. But it's also...what are we even doing? I should be concerned about my sister. And Jimmy. "I'm sorry. I should've never..."

If he saw me, he'd realize how true of a statement that is.

"Are you okay?"

"I'm fine. And I'm sorry about... It's...ah." Jeez, I must come off as such a tease. "I'm sorry."

"What are you sorry about?"

How to answer that? For not knowing what I'm doing. I'm acting like I want to do more with him and yet...I absently rub my chest. He's speaking to me, but what I feel is Brandon's disgust. Clothed, I'm all right, but...and it doesn't matter. "We need to focus on finding Sloane."

I swallow. Glance to the kitchen.

"Are you getting hungry? Let's see what's in the kitchen." My muscles stretch with the length of each extension of my leg, heel to toe, shoulders back, arms at my side for balance. Distance. I'm losing my mind. It's a highly unusual situation and I'm losing my mind. Prioritize. "When do you think we'll hear about Jimmy?"

"Soon."

I open the refrigerator and glance Knox's way. He's standing in the middle of the room. There's no phone in his hand. He's watching me.

I implore him with my eyes. *Trust me. You don't want me. You don't want this. I might bring out your protective instincts. I do that to people. But you don't want me. I'm a mess with a pending expiration date. And if I get sick again, it's not good for anyone. Drop this. I am not what you want.*

He sighs, bows his head and plods to the bedroom.

I let out a matching sigh of relief. He heard me.

CHAPTER 19

Knox

A chill permeates the evening air. Two reclining chairs and a small table with four seats beckon but sitting isn't on the agenda. The overhang on the deck screens the inside view. I've checked every angle from the beach and the side of the house.

Once we're in for the night, I'll lock up and set the alarm. In an ideal world, we would go for a stroll along the beach and take in the stars. Truth is, we could probably get away with it, but I won't chance it.

I'm already chancing enough with my shenanigans. What the hell is it about Sage that I'm turning into a hormone-laden teen? Kissing her every chance I get. It's not appropriate. Horrible timing. And what is the point? We live on different coasts. I don't do difficult relationships. And Sage deserves better.

She's inside, probably wondering what I'm doing. But I need the air. It's too tense in that house.

My phone vibrates, and I pull it out of my back pocket.

"Hey," I say in greeting.

Max responds with, "All good on the western front?"

The people next door are outside on their deck. The smell of hamburgers on a grill wafts through the breeze. A mother and son head out onto the sand to toss a frisbee.

"Slow." Keeping Sage safe is important, but I itch to be doing something. "You got any news?"

"We've got eyes on Jimmy."

"So that's confirmation he's safe and sound?"

"Affirmative. Kairi's team cleared him. No suspicious banking activity. He's referenced in the police report on Sage's house."

"Sage said he's her best friend."

"Right. So, right now, he has a bunch of guys over. They had dinner. Now they're hanging out, drinking. Once his guests leave, the plan is for our guys to go up, ask him to step outside, and talk to him. Convince him to let them search his place for listening devices."

"If Sage talks to him, they won't need to do any convincing."

"Good point. I'll relay that to them."

"It's late on the East Coast. He's still got people over?"

"And they've been drinking. They may hold off approaching him until morning."

"Copy that." The statement is habit more than anything else. I push off the back wall with my back foot, knowing I should head inside.

"What's going on there?"

"We ate dinner. Sage is getting a shower. I'll let her know Jimmy's safe." If I let her call him, he'd probably clear the house pronto, but if there are listening devices, we don't yet know where they are. If anyone is watching the house, they might get suspicious.

Sage enters the den in loose sweatpants and another tight short sleeve tee that accentuates her chest and skims her belly button. This t-shirt has the phrase Keep Asheville Weird scrawled across it. A wet, black braid curves around her neck, ending just above the peak of her breast.

"Talk later." I end the call, slide the phone into my back pocket, and open the door.

Her almond-shaped eyes avoid mine as her socked feet slide across the wooden floor.

"Jimmy's safe. We have confirmation. He's with a bunch of friends right now but we're going to talk to him later."

"He's pretty social," she says with a fond smile.

"I'm going to lock us in." She stands in the middle of the room, arms crossed below her breasts, like she doesn't know what to do. I busy myself checking locks and securing the alarm.

When there's nothing left to lock, I take a seat on one end of the sofa. She curls up on the opposite end, tucking a blanket around herself. Her freshly scrubbed skin looks dewy beneath the lamp's glow. A scattering of freckles spreads from her cheeks across the bridge of her nose.

Our conversation at dinner had been fine. Slightly stilted. She'd had questions about Arrow. How we're funded. When I reminded her that Jack owns a gun and weapons manufacturer and told her how much money a billionaire earns in interest each year, she accepted they could afford to take her case and do all this pro bono.

The television is off. The phone digs into my ass, and I shift and pull it out. It's one issued to me by Arrow, with government-level security measures. I'm scrolling through our team Slack channel, searching for team updates. She's got a book spread out on her lap, but she hasn't turned a page in a while. It's a book she found on the bookshelf in the den. I think it's Tom Clancy.

"Not your favorite book?" I prompt. *Talk to me. Don't read.*

She flattens her hand over the pages and gives me a sheepish smile. "Just a lot going on in my..." She holds her hand up and gestures to her head.

"I get that. I've been on missions where I couldn't have settled my mind to read a book if you paid me. What kinds of things are you thinking about?"

She looks straight ahead at the dark television screen. Her shoulders are tense, raised. So much so that if she were lifting weights, I'd encourage her to lower her shoulders out of fear she'd strain her neck muscles.

"You're not scared, are you? We really are safe here. I know it might not be a television-style safe house, out in the middle of nowhere, but we're safe. We blend in. And they built this house like Fort Knox." Yeah, I'm exaggerating a notch, but we're far safer than we would be back in my apartment.

"I'm not scared." She dips her head, and her lips scrunch together. It's like she's puckering them, ready for a kiss. I'd like to give her that kiss, but I will not. Nope. I'm going to be a Boy Scout. "I'm just thinking about…back home."

"I told you, he's fine. I'm sure by tomorrow we'll get a call that they've spoken to him, cleared his house."

She nods. But her eyes are sad.

I nudge her leg with my foot. The blanket wrapped around her is thick, but the nudge wins me her gaze. "What's going on in that head?"

"I'm sure a lot of my friends are worried. I haven't turned my phone on in over a week. That worries me. I don't want anyone to needlessly worry about me." I raise an eyebrow. "But I'm not about to get on my phone and text anyone. I mean…unless…if I get on your phone, can I do a post? Just letting everyone know I'm okay?"

"Hmm. I'll ask the team if there's a way we can access it through a VPN. Or something untraceable. But it's a definite no until we get clearance. These days there are computer brainiacs who can trace anything."

"Do you deal with that a lot?"

"Some. More so now. In the Navy, there's a group that deals with it. I wasn't in that group."

"Tell me about you. I mean, I know you can't tell me about your government missions. That's top secret. Sam made that abundantly clear." Her eyes widen in emphasis, but then she reaches out and softly touches my leg. "But tell me about you."

"Pretty sure you know everything." She's looking at me like I'm out of my mind, but there's not a lot to tell, and she's known me longer than almost anyone. Until high school, my dad was in the military, and I wasn't great about keeping in touch with people after a move. Social would've helped, but my mom distrusted it, and I didn't care enough to push for access.

"Tell me about your most recent girlfriend." Jessica flashes in my head. Telling Sage about a woman I casually dated appeals about as much as a plant-based hamburger patty. "Or, I know." Her voice rises an octave or two. "Tell me about the most important girlfriend. Or your first love."

"Love?" It's hard to keep a straight face. I've never thought of anyone as my first love. First sex, sure. Melanie Prescott, junior year of high school. "I'm not really a lovey-dovey kind of guy."

She giggles. It's cute. I'm teasing her, but I'm also more or less playing it straight.

"Seriously." Her full lips glisten. She's got a smile that's about as girl-next-door as you can get, but in the homecoming queen-next-door kind of way. She's the girl who wins the crown not just because of her looks, but because she's nice to everyone, every clique, even all the girls.

"Seriously," I repeat, raising my brows for emphasis. She tilts her head, the smile slips, and she feigns annoyance. "You really want to know?"

"Yes. I want to know more about Knox Andrew Williams."

She says my full name like it means something. Like I'm special. She could care less that I've left the teams. "Okay." I shift on the sofa so my back is against the arm rest facing her and stretch my legs out until my feet fit snuggly against her thigh. She lifts the blanket and covers my feet, cocooning them in warmth. "You may not like what you learn."

"I doubt that. You're Sam's best friend." The present tense reference to her brother jabs at me, but there's no point in correcting her. I've already tried. "Sam didn't date much, did he?"

I can't recall Sam dating anyone regularly. I wouldn't call us man whores, but relationships weren't on our radar. A couple of guys on our team were married, but most of us were single. Two guys got divorced. Our jobs didn't really cater to serious relationships or long-term commitments.

"No."

Her lips curve up, and I register happiness, but her gaze is on her fingers, like she's somewhere else. "He always told me if he met someone, I'd be the first to know." She lifts trusting brown eyes to me and shrugs. "I'd always ask, and he'd always repeat that line back to me."

"Doesn't sound like a line to me. It rings of the truth. We spent a lot of time on the move." In our line of work, I always figured it was better to be focused on the job at hand.

"Well, that's Sam. What about you? You're what…thirty-six now?"

"Thirty-five." The gruffness in my tone aims for comical.

She giggles. Score. I like that I can make her laugh with so little effort. She grows serious. Or at least, that's how I interpret her narrowed eyes and the tilt of her head. "But no serious relationship?"

Disbelief rings through her question. I let out a sigh and skim the past twelve or so years since Annapolis. Hook-ups, sure. Dates. Plenty. "I've dated. Have had some exclusive relationships."

"Is that how you define serious? I might be out of touch with the lingo."

"Well, when you have the we're-not-seeing-anyone-else talk, it elevates the relationship. Above, you know." I don't hide my smirk. "And there were one or two in there that I dated more seriously." Stopped using condoms in two different relationships. In my book, that's damn serious, but I'm not about to share that with Sage. Not right now. "But, you know, we reached the bridge."

"The bridge?" She's amused, sure, but she's genuinely curious.

"You know. It's when you've been dating for a while, met each other's families, and questions start getting asked. Or life events force a discussion. Let's take Chere, for example. She and I dated for about two years before I got stationed in Japan. I liked her, loved some things about her, but didn't see us getting married. We faced the bridge. I'd never ask her to do a stint in another country if I didn't see us getting married." I've known plenty of guys who had the shit or get off the pot moment for the same damn reason. "There was another woman. Jessica. I just had one too many assignments abroad, I guess. We just kind of grew apart slowly. She's the one who ended things. She was ready to settle down, and I wasn't the guy she wanted to do that with."

"So, the bridge is marriage?"

"It's what I call it." I link my fingers and stretch out my arms. As I deepen the stretch, the muscles along my shoulders burn. "That's my love life, in a nutshell." I nudge her thigh with my big toe. "Your turn."

What I wouldn't give to pull her on top of me right now.

"I don't really have anything to share."

"I'm calling bullshit on that. How old are you?" I'm teasing her. Pretending to be oblivious. When she tried to kiss me the first time, she wasn't yet eighteen. Back then, I'd been highly attuned to her age.

She covers her face with one hand, spreads her fingers, and peeks through the cracks.

"Hiding?"

She drops her hand and stretches her fingers across the blanket. "Well, you know my story."

"No." Her gaze shoots up. "I mean, yes. Your younger years. The wonder years, so to speak. But not your twenties. Sam told me the big highlights. College. Teaching. Your love life never once came up in discussion."

"Those weren't really wonder years for me." She slaps a palm over her mouth, then drops it. "I hate when I do that. I'm sorry. I'm lucky. And I had a great childhood. The best family. I'm very lucky." She repeats the words like it's her mantra.

"Hey, I'd say you have every right to vent a little. Bum heart and all."

Sam's the one who showed me how to act around her. To treat her like I would any other kid.

"True." She cracks a smile. "But I'm also very lucky and fortunate, and I know others who weren't so lucky. Anyhoo…this is not a pity song. But I…you know, after the transplant, I stayed close to home. Then, I got to go to college, but had some complications. And then during college, Mom was sick." She picks at the blanket. "Then Dad. Then I moved. Oh, and let's not forget Covid. I had to be more careful than most. I mean, yeah. It's…yeah, I dated, but no one serious."

"No one to chill out with during Covid?" During Covid, I lived in San Diego and more or less spent time outdoors. Ignored warnings. I mean, I wore a mask if instructed, but…

"Jimmy. We were Covid buddies." She peeks up at me through her lashes. "It was a sacrifice for him, you know? He had to really restrict himself because he couldn't risk bringing anything back to me. I mean, in Asheville, people battened down for a while, but even when restrictions loosened, he took all the precautions. For me. Which is why, like, I get you questioning him. But he'd never sell me out. Ever."

"One of these days I'm going to have to meet this Jimmy," I tell her, and she grins. I really like that smile of hers. It warms me up in ways I do not need to think about.

"All right. So, no first love?" She says that phrase like it's magical. Grinning, I shake my head, but I'd really like to pry into her history. "Any missions you can talk about?"

"I could…but then I'd have to kill you." She laughs. Another easy score. "So, no serious relationships for you. Does that mean you're a strictly casual sex kind of girl?"

Her cheeks flame beet red. And I remember how she froze up when my hand wandered. Holy shit. Could she be? But that's not possible, is it?

"Earlier, did I go too far? Did I make you feel uncomfortable? I would never want to force you to do something you aren't comfortable doing." Attempting to remove her shirt was a dumbass, wrong move.

An air of determination envelops her. "I'm not…I don't…" She flattens her hands on her thighs and spreads her fingers out wide, then starts over. "I don't show people my chest. My scar is…" She wiggles her fingers and huffs. "It doesn't matter. I'm not…we aren't. Let's just talk about something else."

Her cheeks are flaming red. Her eyes are dark as night, and they seemingly merge with her pupils.

"You think I don't have scars? I've been in the military for over a decade. I've got scars that I don't even remember how I got them. I've got buddies who've lost limbs. You think they don't deserve love?"

"No." She blinks rapidly and stares straight at me like she needs me to believe her. "That's not what I'm saying."

"I've got some nasty scars on my back. Don't bother me much 'cause I can't see them, but they're fucking there. From an infection. Look below my knee. Spread that leg hair." She looks where I tell her, but her hand doesn't come near my leg. I bend forward and point. "See this white line? Machete. One hundred and fifteen stitches."

"Someone took a machete to you?"

"Yeah. Me. Dumbass move." I point to a series of scars on my forearm. "Dog bite. I was eight. Sweetheart, you live long enough, chances are you're going to have scars."

Her timid expression stirs something in my gut. Unease. Concern.

"My scar is… It's not like your scars. Yours are barely noticeable. Mine, it's raised and…" She rubs the side of her hand against her sternum. I've seen her do that a few times, and I'd bet big bucks that's where the scar is. Between her breasts. Makes sense. Heart and double lung transplant.

"It bothers you?" Enough to keep every guy at bay?

"No." I narrow my eyes, silently calling bullshit. "Well, yes. I mean, there are Facebook groups of people posting their scars with pride. Others get tattoos to cover them… I have friends who wear tops that show them off. But my scar is just different."

"Why do you say that?" She shifts on the sofa, moving farther away from me. "Did someone—"

Her gaze cuts to the ceiling.

"Wait. You're telling me a guy made you…" In a flash, I'm touching the blanket over her legs. I can't not touch her. "Trust me. If someone can't see past your scars, they're not worth your time. And they need some metaphorical glasses too. Because there is so much more to you than one lousy scar."

"You haven't seen it." She braves a glance at me, and I stroke her cheek softly with my thumb.

"Not yet. And if I do, I can promise you, I'll see past the scar." She's skeptical. I see it in the expanse of her pupils. So I push forward. "My body hums with arousal when you're around. Every time we kiss, I feel it, deep within. This attraction…what's going on between us…a scar won't lessen my desire. Trust me." I wait for those timid eyes to look up at me. To see I'm playing it straight. "I want you. If you were any other girl, I probably would've had you by now." It's conceited to say, but it's my track record. "But you deserve better."

Those words are true, too. Which makes me wonder why I'm giving in to this at all. Sex won't be casual to her. She'll be sharing something she hides. She'll be trusting me. I can take her to dinner, but am I the guy to give her more? Will we be around each other long enough to know if we're a fit? If more makes sense? She's special. Of that, I don't have any doubt. But practically speaking, there are thousands of miles between us.

CHAPTER 20

Sage

I push harder against my sternum, wishing to smash the doubt. I hate that part of me. Sloane doesn't possess insecurity. She's what they call a spitfire.

Tall, gorgeous, brilliant, and healthy.

And what does any of that matter? What are we doing? Why are we talking about my scar?

I'm here to find Sloane. Someone was shooting at us today, and I'm sitting here with doe eyes for Knox Freaking Williams.

The back-and-forth motion of the rough pad of his thumb combined with the way he's looking down tenderly at me is… I have to close my eyes. His proximity makes it hard to think.

"I have to be back in Asheville soon. School starts. I've got to get my classroom ready."

The sofa cushion sinks as he shifts, readjusting around me. "You know, I travel a lot for work. I can travel on the weekends, too. We can connect. When you go back, it won't be goodbye." He shifts on the sofa, and cool air fills the gap between us.

I sit there, processing what he has said. He would travel on the weekends to see me? After we find Sloane, he won't be responsible for me. But it's sweet that he's thinking about seeing me when this is all over.

"Ready to call it a night?" That's an abrupt change of subject. "The place is locked up. Slack channel's quiet. Nothing we can do but wait. Let's get some shuteye. It's been quite the day."

Understatement of the year.

He enters the bathroom while I dig around in the duffel bag. It's the same black bag I threw in my car a week ago, only there are some additional clothes and a toiletries bag filled with brand new travel size options of basics such as toothpaste, mouthwash, body wash and soap, a razor, and tampons. My brother had a toiletry stash in the bag already, but the supplies are running low. Stella even included tampons. Not needed at the moment, but I'm touched by her consideration.

I'm not supposed to start for another three or four days. Which means if I had sex right now, I wouldn't get pregnant.

Where did that thought come from? I have no business thinking about that.

Do you really want to die a virgin?

The pesky, nagging voice irks me.

Sex isn't a big deal. Not to me. I mean, I love reading about it in my books. I love a good romance, even when the guy is a complete and total ass. But when I have gone on dates in real life, I usually don't feel any attraction. I've been on dates that I didn't even want to kiss. So I didn't. I always assumed the problem was me. Like maybe my sexual appetite wasn't the same as others. Wondered if my low libido might be a side effect of one of the gazillion pills I take every day. Yet I really loved kissing Knox.

The bathroom door swings open, and Knox steps out. He's in black briefs that fit him like a glove and the same t-shirt he was wearing earlier. He's so gorgeous, from the bulge in the front of his briefs to his muscular thighs and calves to his biceps that stretch the gray t-shirt with the bold Navy letters.

"Stella didn't pack pajama pants for me. I hope you don't mind. I can put on shorts or jeans—"

"No, no. That's great. It's great."

A smirk plays across his lips, probably because he just struck me incoherent. He double-checks the windows, and I gather a bundle of pajamas and toiletries and slip behind the safety of the bathroom door.

In the bathroom, I brush my teeth and apply lotion all over. I shaved in the shower earlier this evening, and my skin is smooth and silky.

Girlfriend, I'm not one to harp, but as your friend, you gotta deal with that. Seventies bush is fine if that's your thing, but the bush can't extend past the fence line. Trim that shit. Jimmy said that to me two years ago when we'd arrived on the river. I was in a one-piece, the kind lap swimmers use, so I already stood out in the field of bikinis and low cut one-pieces. I'd gone back to our stuff and slipped on my jean cut-offs to tube down the French Broad.

I glance down at my crotch. There are no hairs past the panty line. I'm not full bush anymore either. After Jimmy mortified me, I went online and bought a bikini trimmer and watched a YouTube video on trimming. But my dark curls are still pretty abundant. I didn't really expect anyone would see them other than me. I mean, other than doctors. But they see *everyone*.

I want you. And if you were any other girl, I would've had you by now. That's what Knox said. Again, treating me differently. I slip my long sleeve Carolina T-shirt over my head and look in the mirror.

My cheeks are flushed. My eyes are bright.

Knox being interested in me has been a fantasy. But if our kisses mean he's interested, then why wouldn't I take advantage of this?

Whether or not we find Sloane, I need to be back in Asheville. My job is in Asheville. My life is in Asheville.

I swish mouthwash and spit it out.

I'm always beating myself up, feeling like I'm not living enough for the person who gave me her organs. She died in a car wreck. Twenty-six years old. I am now older than she was.

Part of living is experiencing things, right? She'd want me to have sex, right?

Unlike Knox, I packed my pajamas. A long sleeve T-shirt with a crew neck and loose, light cotton pants. It's probably the opposite of sexy. The clothes I packed are clothes I rarely wore so wouldn't miss them when they were stowed away in the emergency duffel.

His declarations are going to my head. My nerves riot. My brain short circuits around him. I should go to sleep.

Knox is lying back on the bed, beneath the covers. He's holding out his phone, reading something. His gaze cuts to me and I flick off the bathroom light.

"I left you the same side as before. Is that okay? I didn't ask back at my place." The moon is full and a pale light casts a glow across the room, intruding through the cracked shutters.

"Why would you?" I grin. "It was your place. I'm sure you don't get many visitors who expect to share your bed."

"I don't get many visitors I would allow in my bed." His hand slaps against the empty side of the duvet cover. He leans forward and tugs it and the sheet down, creating an opening for me.

I come around and slide in. The cool sheets chill my skin through the cotton PJs. In the bed, I roll onto my side, only to find he's put the phone down and is on his side, facing me.

I could get lost in Knox. His sheer perfection. Topaz brown eyes, wavy dark hair that falls over his brow, lips that alternate between breathtakingly stern to relaxed in a nanosecond. Kick-ass Navy fighter to goofball. Or maybe he doesn't transform into a goofball anymore. I just remember him that way, back before the stern kick-ass man infiltrated his psyche. He was the guy who'd follow Sam into my room on a mission to make me laugh.

Only, as he inches closer, he's not stern. And there's no trace of the jokester either.

I want you.

His stare is both covetous and hot. This moment is dreamlike. Tingles zap through me. I don't want to blink. Swallow. Or do anything that might alter this mirage. When we find Sloane, I might have to thank her for getting herself into a mess.

His lips brush against mine and I close my eyes. Breathe. He nips. Licks. I open and our tongues meet in a slow and sweet reunion. He tastes like minty toothpaste, and I smell a whiff of freshness, like he reapplied deodorant. His leg brushes mine, and I wish I didn't have these long pants on so I could feel the coarse hair along his legs. He's so much bigger than me. Taller and broader. But lying down like this, beside him, it feels like we fit perfectly.

His thumb caresses my cheek. He lies his head down on the pillow. I'd like to keep kissing, but he smooths a finger over my lips.

"We're going to take it slowly."

"Why?" The question sounds a little whiny, and he chuckles.

"Because that's what you deserve, golden girl."

I'm not as perfect as everyone assumes.

"But, why?" I repeat, looking straight into his eyes. "We live on different coasts. I appreciate you wanting to treat me right, but..." Somewhere in the recesses of my mind, clarity lights. "You know, we aren't guaranteed tomorrow. Only today. And of all days for that little saying to be true, I think a day when a bullet whizzed by it bears repeating."

He grimaces. "I had no idea we'd been followed. I should've—"

I place my finger across his lips. "Stop it. My point is if that bullet had hit, I would've died without ever having..." I can't quite say it.

"You're a virgin." It's a statement. Judgment. Pity. Man, I hate pity.

"No." I'm not a liar, but this shouldn't matter. "Of course not." I brave a glance into his eyes. There's no pity, but maybe there's curiosity.

"I just...don't have a lot of experience." There. That's the sugar-coated truth. He reaches out and caresses the side of my face, from my cheekbone, along my jaw, brushing my hair back. Tingling sensations course along my skin, and I fall into his dark eyes, darker in this heated space.

"Your first...someone earlier, he was a jerk?"

I nod, a half-truth. I don't want to admit I'm almost thirty and haven't done this. But I do want this with Knox. While he wants it, I want it. I might never have this chance again.

I reach for him, edging toward him beneath the covers, seeking the closeness from last night on the sofa. He kisses me, and a buzz goes through my body, a low hum that has my lower belly clenching. We're getting the hang of this. His hand falls on my hip and he inches back, enough so he can see me, but our lower bodies remain aligned.

"Beautiful, if we're going to take things slow, it's not a good idea to play around too much in bed."

"What if I want to play around?" He blinks, and my heart pitter-patters in a wild, erratic beat. *Live while you can.* "What if I want to do all the things? Right now?"

"We don't have to rush." His fingers tangle with my hair and his nails lightly scratch my scalp. His muscles are tense, and the way he's looking at me, it feels like he wants more now, just like me.

"I know we don't have to rush, but what if...we do?" I brave a glance up to meet his heated gaze. "What if we just enjoy tonight? Something could happen tomorrow and—"

"You're safe here."

"You never know." I'm not thinking of the men in the canyon. I'm thinking of friends of mine who died on the waitlist. Or those who got the organ and then... My theory has always been sudden is better than a long sickness. The hospital sucks. But sudden is always possible and… "We're not guaranteed tomorrow." And I may never get this chance again. He could change his mind.

He reaches for my hand and lifts it to his lips, pressing soft kisses along my fingers. He hums, and the vibrations thrum through the tips of my fingers into my bones. He's weighing all the options. And I'm scared. But excited. I'm probably out of my mind.

"Are you ready?"

You have no idea.

"To let me in? To trust me with your scars?"

CHAPTER 21

Knox

Lying next to me, draped in cotton from the base of her neck to her ankles, she still oozes sensuality. I should roll over and call it a night before things get out of control. Instead, I can't stop touching her.

If her hand wandered lower, she'd find evidence of my support for her proposition. But her hands mimic my movements. Exploring my shoulder, my jaw, my hair. A light flurry of fingertips across my chest.

Lying on her side, she squeezes her eyelids shut.

Her hand grips the bottom of her long-sleeved tee. The bottom of the tee rises, exposing a smooth, pale curve from her hip down her waist to the bottom of her breast. My chest tightens incrementally as she carefully exposes skin. I'm so fucking hard it's borderline painful.

I should shut this down.

The fabric hovers above the swell of her breast. My hand covers the curve from her waist to her hip, the tan, weathered skin a direct contrast to her pearlescent hue. The span of my fingers nearly covers her ribs. Her heart palpitates into my palm.

My thumb sinks into the flesh of her breast, and I force my gaze upward, my breaths shallow, muscles on edge.

"This okay?"

She nods. Her elbow points precariously to the ceiling, frozen. Nervous. She doesn't need to be nervous. Scars don't bother me. Scars symbolize survival. The only way a scar forms is if you survive.

She shifts onto her back as I take over the lifting of her top. Her arms stretch above her as the hem rises over her nipples.

I inhale deeply, breathing in her faint scent, and take in my first view of her breasts. My mouth waters, and I dip my head and suck a creamy peach nipple into my mouth, twirling my tongue. She gasps and her thighs shift.

I lift my head and brush a finger over her swollen bottom lip. "Feel good?"

She gives the slightest of nods, eyes wide. Too wide. Nervous.

Yes, there's a scar. Thicker in some parts, narrower in others. It's not as straight as one would expect from a surgical scar, but skin doesn't always heal as expected. The line is similar to a misshapen lightning bolt, raised in parts, flat in others. Subtle blues and cream. I bow my head and press my lips along the seam. Her strength. Her heart.

When I reach the dip in her clavicle, I lift my head, wanting to taste those sweet lips. There's a single tear gliding down her cheekbone and I brush it away.

"You're gorgeous. All of you."

I wrap an arm around her, holding her close against me as I tug that long-sleeved tee over her head, using one hand. Once it's past her head, the sleeves get stuck on her forearms and she maneuvers herself out of it.

Brown, wavy strands scatter wildly around her. And god, the look she gives me. It's awe and wonder.

And fuck, yeah, this wasn't my intention. Not this quick. Not right away. But every single part of me wants to make her mine. Now. And I can't remember any reason we should wait. Not when we both want this.

When our lips meet, our tongues intertwine, and hunger drives away patience. Our teeth clash, and she elicits little moans as our bodies grind against each other. I could take her right now. Push our pants down, slide into her warmth, but no. We might be on a fast track, but I'm taking this slow. She said she doesn't have much experience. I'm going to blow her mind. Make her forget every jerk who came before me. Especially the ass who made her second guess her beauty.

I taste her, alternating my lips and teeth and tongue all the way down her throat to her breasts.

"Gorgeous." I cup her breasts in both hands. They fill my palms. Truly fantastic tits. I dip my head, administering attention to the other nipple, loving how she squirms and the sexy-as-fuck noises I don't even think she knows she's making.

She's putty beneath my hands and tongue. And that scar...god, I get not liking some part of yourself, but it's not a blemish. It's a symbol of her strength. There's nothing ugly about fortitude. I kiss it all over again because it's her. Because it's something private that she's sharing with me.

As I administer kisses, my fingers trail lower. Pushing below her loose pajama pants, below her cotton panties. The tips of my fingers brush against silky curls. I spread those curls apart and find her sleek seam. She's fucking soaked.

I sit back on my heels. If it weren't for my briefs strapping him down, my erection would stand out like a flagpole. Her gaze locks on the bulge. I grip the band of her pants, careful to catch those panties too, and with both hands, tug. She squeezes her legs together and bends her knees, and with a relatively smooth move, I drag the material over her ass, thighs, and knees. I press my lips to the outside of her knee, then finish slipping the pants off and toss them onto the floor behind us.

"Now. Spread those legs."

Her chest heaves, and those teeth sink into her lower lip as she smiles.

You like that? So do I.

Timidly, she spreads her thighs. I lift one leg and kiss, then nibble at her calf. She grins and gives a teensy giggle. I position myself below her and use my finger to spread her twisty black curls.

"What're you doing?" She's up on her elbows, watching.

"I'm going to taste you. Find out if this gorgeous pussy tastes as good as I think it will." My tongue rides up her slit. She gasps. "God, you're sweet."

Sweet and smooth like silk. I love how trusting she is. How needy. How she squirms and gasps. I slip a finger in as I circle her nub. Her channel's tight. Velvety smooth. Liquid heat. She contracts against my finger, and I add another, stretching her.

She mewls and pants. But it's when my teeth graze that precious bundle of nerves that I earn a "Knox!"

She half rises off the pillow, eyes shut tight, hands in my hair. Her breaths calm and she slowly sinks back onto the pillow.

"Wow," she breathes.

Yeah, baby, I agree.

There's a wet spot on the front of my briefs. I want her so fucking badly, but I need a condom. The two open duffels are on the floor. I clamber off the bed and rummage through my bag. In my wallet, I've got two. Can't imagine Stella added any to the duffel when she packed it for me. I find the billfold and grab the two gold foils.

"What're you doing?" She's curled up on her side with the sheet tucked up beneath her armpits.

"Getting these." I hold out the condoms between my fingers and stalk toward her, tossing them down on the side table with the lamp. Her pale skin glows in the moonlight. Standing beside the bed, I push down my briefs.

Her gaze goes straight to my erection. I'm not sure how to interpret that expression. It's a little too much like fear.

"We don't have to. You can always change your mind."

"No. I want to." Her tongue darts out, wetting the seam between her lips.

I reach down and tug on the sheet, dragging it down the bed. "No hiding."

She welcomes me back onto the bed with a timid smile. Our bodies align, skin on skin. She rocks against me as we roll together, kissing. The feel of her against me. Soft skin. Her heat. Nothing between us. God, I really wasn't going to do this, but fuck me if I can remember why I was holding off.

She spreads those thighs, making room for me. With every rock of her hips, she positions me farther down against her, wedging my needy cock against her wet slit. My eyes practically roll into the back of my head. It would be so easy, one minor adjustment to line up my crown.

But no. That, I will not do. I haven't lost all my wits.

I strain and reach for the foil pack and tear it with my lips. Within seconds, I'm covered.

I kiss her and nuzzle her with my nose.

"You sure? You want this? Now?"

She nods, and I grin.

"Gotta use your words, baby. I need to hear you."

"Yes. Please."

I hover over her, waiting for those eyes to meet mine. And when they do, I ask, "Do you have any idea how badly I want you? Want this?"

She squirms below me. Her fingers twist her nipple as her hips rock. Those darks eyes plead. *Fuuuck*. She's a goddess.

I slide my tip through her center. Through her curls, dipping into her heat. My tip disappears. I close my eyes because she feels so fucking good.

She grips my biceps. It's a light touch as she moans. A plea for more.

I sink farther into her. *Fuck, she's tight.*

I reach beneath her, lifting her ass, gaining a better angle. She stretches. And I go a little deeper. So fucking tight. So sweet.

But it's not just her tight little cunt gripping me. She's tense. Frozen.

"You okay?"

"Yes. Just..." She lies there, chest rising and falling rapidly. Her nails sink into my skin.

"Does it hurt? Are you—"

"Let me adjust."

Was she...she said she wasn't a virgin, but how long has it been?

My muscles strain. A drop of sweat rolls down my temple.

"Breathe, baby." I lift my hips, retreating. Her nails dig into my back.

"There. Now...move." Her voice is breathy and her thighs brush my sides as she spreads her legs, lifting, asking for more.

Slowly, I allow my hips to flex. I study her every movement. Easy to do with her eyes squeezed shut. The lines across her brow relax as her hips roll, mimicking mine. Welcoming me.

She looks like she's relaxing into it, but I'm not sure this position is working for her. I pull out, and she whimpers.

"Shh," I console. "Let's try it this way."

I position her on her side, capture her thigh in the crook of my arm, and slide back into her warmth. Ah, fuck, she feels good. But her muscles are still tense. I lower her leg and reach around her, working her little nub. Kissing her shoulder, pressing against her, deep into her, loving every sound that escapes.

CHAPTER 22

Sage

Knox is inside me. I'm having sex. I'm actually having sex.

And it…hurts. The more he moves, the better it feels, and what he's doing with his fingers has me squeezing my thighs, and oh… the sensations from when he used his tongue swirl back. It feels good. All of it. But he's behind me, and I kind of want him back in front of me, so I can hold him…and touch him.

"Does that feel good?"

"Uh huh." It's all I can get out. I'm probably supposed to be doing something more, but I don't know what. I can't do much in this position, on my side. It's… He's stretching me and it's…oh…it feels good, but really, it's what he's doing with his hand…

"That's it, baby. Right there. Let it go. Relax. Give in to it."

His deep, rhythmic tones coax, a constant reminder that I am with Knox…like really with Knox. My hand rises of its own accord, and I tease my nipple, twisting it.

"That's it. That's it."

His fingers work my clit, the rhythm fast and hard, while he fills me, stroking in and out.

"Let go, Sage. Relax."

It's his hand, really. What he's doing as he cups me, like he did on the sofa. He's stretching me and there's a fullness. I like it. Being with him like this. It's—

"Jesus, you feel good. Fuck. I am never gonna get enough of this."

My muscles seize, and a wild animal sound escapes from within me.

Knox's hip movements become frantic, the rhythm lost. And I'm curling over, but then I'm on my back, legs up in the air and Knox pounds into me.

Bliss. Sore. Blissful soreness. I open my eyes to see him close his. His facial muscles strain, the blood vessels in his neck bulge, his arms flex, and…oh…he pulses, deep within me. I can feel it… it's the strangest feeling. But a good feeling. A really good way to end what at first didn't feel so good.

He lowers himself and presses his lips to mine. My arms wrap around him, and I want nothing more than to hold him tight as our heartrates calm.

"Damn, girl. I think we both needed that release."

He pushes back up like he's doing a push up and slides out of me. There's a slight pull… Some discomfort.

He stills. "There's some blood. Are you okay? Did I hurt you?"

I look to the side, avoiding his gaze. My palm covers my scar.

"Are you about to get your period?"

"Not for a couple of days." The answer flows out. But that was the wrong thing to say. I should've let him think that's it. But no…that could gross him out. Who wants to have period sex?

He smooths his hand on the sheet below me. I close my eyes, and the mattress shifts. His feet hit the floor and the light clicks on in the bathroom. I reach for the sheet and pull it around me. Chilled and alone, I curl onto my side.

The toilet flushes and the water runs. Based on the volume of the sounds, the bathroom door is open. He hasn't gone running to the other room. Yet.

His warm hand coaxes my shoulder. "Slide over. Make room for me."

I do as he says, shifting more to the middle of the bed…closer to my side, giving him room. The bed sinks with his weight, and then I'm captured by a big, strong arm, and he pulls me against him, my back to his side. He's still naked, and heat rolls off his body. He brushes my hair with his fingers.

"Sage, I'm going to ask you something, and I want you to be honest with me, okay?"

There's a pressure on the back of my head. Like maybe he's kissing my hair.

"Were you… Was that your first time having sex?"

My eyes burn. "Was it that bad?"

"Are you kidding me?" He lets out a chuckle. "Hey, roll over."

I'd prefer to dig a hole and bury myself, but I did just have sex with him. And it's Knox. I wanted him to be my first. Time to own it.

My insides are a mix of sad and cozy, fluster and agitation. I read about this. It's the after-sex emotions. The reason they told us teens in the hospital to be wary of sex because we were already dealing with so much. But wasn't all that supposed to go away as an adult?

His enormous hands maneuver me so I'm curled into him, my head on his chest. He adjusts the pillows so when he lies back down, he's propped up, then plucks at my chin with his thumb and forefinger.

"Look at me."

I lift my eyelids to face him.

"What we just did…was amazing. I…" His gaze flits to the ceiling. "It's been a long time since I felt that kind of connection with someone. But—"

My gaze falls and I brace myself for whatever he might say.

"Was that your first time?"

My face heats, and I press my cheek against his chest.

"Why didn't you tell me?"

My shoulders lift.

"Hey…look at me."

I feel like a pouty teen but force my gaze up to his. He doesn't look angry. Maybe mystified. Maybe…amused?

"If you'd told me, I would've done things differently."

"If I'd told you, you wouldn't have done it at all." I shift back so my head is on the pillow and I can see him. "There's no need to make it more than it is. And I know I should've been honest, but given my age…I mean, it's embarrassing."

He lets out a snort that's half laugh. "It's nothing to be embarrassed about. But you've waited this long. I'd think it would be important for it to be meaningful."

My heart cracks, and I tug the sheets up to my armpit. *It was meaningful to me. I've had a crush on you since I was twelve.*

"I mean, not that it wasn't meaningful, but—"

"It's okay." My nail traces the edge of Knox's nipple. "I know we live on opposite sides of the country. I know that once we find Sloane I won't see you again—"

"Says who? Don't think you're getting rid of me that easily."

I keep my gaze down. He did say he wants to see me again. And he's saying it now, again, even after seeing the scar. It didn't bother him. All those years it's bothered me and yet he kissed the raised skin.

"Just…help me understand. Are you religious?"

"Not at all, actually." I shift back onto the pillow. He rolls on his side so we're facing each other. He's not looking at me with pity, mere curiosity. "When you spend your childhood thinking someone on a cloud hates you, you open up to other philosophies. The prosperity gospel was fairly common back home, but it didn't work for me. I received no comfort in thinking that I somehow deserved what was happening to me, and all I had to do was pray for it to be okay when that clearly wasn't the case." He reaches out to caress my cheek. I capture his hand and press my lips to his thumb. "Science comforts me. I prefer to understand the mechanics of my condition rather than believe someone up there played favorites. I don't find comfort in the phrase, 'God works in mysterious ways.' People back home loved to say that. I never knew how to respond. *Okay. Thank you?* I'd rather understand. And Sloane…she's like me. Sam too, but…it was Sloane who became a scientist. I think it had to do with her spending so much time in the hospital…you know, with me. She saw me wasting away, and…"

He brushes my hair back, leans forward, and I think he's going to kiss me, but he rubs the tip of his nose against mine… And the intimacy, us lying here naked, lightly touching, the comfort and warmth, it's incredible. This must be what love feels like.

He leans back on the pillow, and I miss his touch, so inch closer.

"So, not religious, but yet…" He wants an explanation for my lack of sexual experience.

"I didn't plan on being an almost thirty-year-old virgin. It just… For a long time, I didn't feel like having sex. I suspected, actually, that I was asexual. Which is a legitimate thing."

He caresses the side of my face, down my throat, to the top of my scar. "Based on what we just did, you're not asexual."

"No…but…" Now I'm smiling. He's right. "But back then, when you don't feel good, when it's hard to breathe, sucking face doesn't rank high on the to-do list."

"Sucking face?" The corners of his lips turn up in amusement.

"It's what we called it in the hospital. Me and a few other kids who spent a lot of time there. Some kids were bound and determined to have sex before they died. Two on the oncology floor got busted." Olivia and Rex. Olivia died a couple of months after that. I don't know what happened to Rex. "Anyway, that wasn't me."

"But when you were seventeen, you looked great. You were what…six months post-op?"

I had been doing great. I'd felt like I was on top of the world. Hence the reason I felt brave enough to go for a kiss at Knox's graduation. His rejection knocked me back. Mortified me. Plus, I got pretty sick shortly after that. College was better. Sophomore year I lived in a dorm. And then when I tried…yeah, the scar was still really ugly. Hooking up with a drunk frat guy who'd been unable to control his reaction probably wasn't the smartest idea.

"In college, it just, it wasn't a priority. And then Mom got sick, and she needed me. And then Dad…"

"What happened to your Dad? Sam didn't talk much about it. I didn't know your dad had a drug problem."

"He didn't. Shortly after Mom died, he was in a car wreck. Minor. Sort of. It caused some back problems, and he was taking pain meds. The prescription ran out and he found a source. It was laced with Fentanyl. This was back before people were even aware that could happen. At least, I hadn't heard of it. It wasn't really publicized back then. It was rare, I think."

"Hmmm." His fingers roam my arm, my shoulder, the curve of my neck. I could lose myself in this bliss.

"And after he died?" The question is gentle yet probing.

"It was a difficult time. I wouldn't have made it through if it wasn't for Jimmy."

"And Jimmy's gay?"

"Yeah. He met someone from Asheville and there wasn't any reason for me to stay close to Duke…so I moved when he did, and I don't know…"

"You moved to a new city and still didn't date? Didn't meet anyone?"

"I've dated. I refuse to do the online dating thing. I'm missing the gumption, I guess. But I've been on dates. Honestly?" I wait for him to nod. He wants honesty. I can give him this. "I get really nervous before a date. It's not something I really enjoy. I have a tendency to bail; to make up excuses. It's just…I don't like dating."

"You seemed to enjoy our time at the pier. And the soccer game. And hiking." He's got this incredulous expression, but I'm pretty sure he's teasing me. An outgoing person like him would never understand. I playfully push against his shoulder and the sheet falls, a big-time reminder we're both naked.

"But nothing we did felt like a date. And…I mean…I've gone on dates. I'd just rather not. I'm pretty sure I could count on one hand the number of dates I've been on since moving to Asheville."

"Creature of habit?" He softly cups my breast and smooths the pad of his thumb over the nipple. My breath catches at the warmth of our budding intimacy. "I'm going to guess you like to spend time with your friends?" I nod and suck in my lower lip. "What else do you do in your free time?"

"Hike. Read. Draw. I like crafts."

"Solitary pursuits."

Again, I nod. That's who I am.

"Well, here's the thing, my solitary girl. I wish you'd been honest with me because I would've done things differently. But I don't regret what we did. As a matter of fact, I hope we get to do it again."

Really?

"Don't look so shocked." His hand abandons my breast for my shoulder. "I'm honored to be the one you chose."

"I chose you for my first kiss. When I was seventeen. Remember?"

There's a blood vessel protruding in his forehead, strained from lying on his side like this, and I reach for it, softly smoothing it with my finger.

"Like I told you, if you hadn't been jailbait, I might've overlooked the fact you were my best friend's kid sister."

"I've never been more embarrassed in my life."

"You didn't need to be. I walked away on principle. No other reason. I've always thought you were special. Full of beauty. Inside and out." He presses his lips against mine. Just a press, and then he's back on his pillow.

His eyes drift closed, but my thoughts race. I had sex. And I really liked it. It was better than I expected. And obviously, Knox is being the gentleman and saying all the right things. All the things one would expect him to say. But he really didn't seem to mind my scar. There are Facebook groups dedicated to scars, and so many others are proud. They don't let them bother them. Maybe now I can be braver, too. More like the others who are leading such amazing lives.

Knox's arm jerks and his chest rises. He's fast asleep. I can't believe I finally did it. We did it. Knox and me. I just hope in the morning things aren't awkward. I've read about the morning afters. Now, it'll be my turn to experience one. My stomach squirms and flips. But I close my eyes and focus on my breathing. I'll need my sleep to face tomorrow.

CHAPTER 23

Knox

She's deep in sleep, her melodic breathing pattern denoted by the slight movement of her ribcage. It's early. Judging from the golden rays peeking through, it's just past daybreak. A sheet covers the curve of her hip down the length of her body. During the night, after retreating to the bathroom, she put her panties back on and one of my basic white t-shirts.

If I were a selfish man, I'd wake her with my fingers and tongue. My body wants her. But I won't do that to her. She'll be sore and needs her sleep.

I'm as quiet as possible getting out of bed, which, as a soldier trained in stealth, is pretty damn quiet. After I get a coffee pot going for her and leave a note, I'm careful to lock the door behind me and set the alarm.

The early morning hours on the beach are calm. It's low tide, and the packed sand stretches far. There's one lone surfer in a meditative trance. The low tide waves are too calm for action, but there's more to surfing than getting up on a board.

On a normal day, I'd clock seven miles, but the stretch of beach gets busier the farther down I run on unfamiliar terrain. My gut stirs uncomfortably.

Sage is safe at the house. There's no way anyone can find us.

But that's what you thought on the hike.

I change direction, headed back to the house, pushing it double time.

What happened last night probably shouldn't have happened, but we're both consenting adults. By anyone's standards, she waited long enough. Although I do wish she'd been honest with me.

What would Sam say about us? He sent her to me to keep her safe. There's no way he'd want me crossing this line. He'd want better for his sister.

She lives on the other side of the country, and as a rule, I've avoided long distance relationships. But I'm no longer in the military. Maybe long distance is more manageable for civilians? Day by day. That's how to take it. That's what I've always done.

I promised Sam I'd look out for her. I didn't realize how seriously he took that promise until she showed up at my door, but now that she's here, I'll be looking out for her for the rest of her life. From afar or by her side.

By her side. That phrase is loaded. But it also feels right. But I'm getting way ahead of myself. We've spent a couple of days together. That's it. And we have last night. If I wasn't her first, would all these thoughts be hounding me? Would I be sitting here thinking about protecting her forever? Yeah, I would. Because of Sam.

But last night definitely put a spin on things. And she actually thought she wasn't good. Last night was incredible. It wasn't just a hook-up. The emotions I felt. The connection. No, that comes from caring for someone. But none of that changes that it's only been a couple of days.

Sand coats my calves and ankles. Sweat soaks my shirt and drips down my brow. I kick my shoes against the piling, remove them, and tiptoe back inside. Stillness greets me. The coffee pot's full. In the bedroom, she's still asleep on her side. She hasn't moved.

Showering is out of the question, since doing so would wake her, so I head back into the kitchen, knock back a bottle of water, pour myself a cup of Joe, and login through the VPN to check in.

There's a list of updates on the group board.

MAX

Surveillance outside J Ringelspaugh home. Plan is to approach him this am.

KAIRI

On site team checked out Sloane Watson apartment. Place still holds her stuff. Doesn't appear she packed to leave. Her desk is clear. No computer.

KAIRI

Neighbor at apartment complex recognized photo. Said she hadn't seen her in a few weeks. Never spoke to her.

KAIRI

Sloane Watson's US bank accounts and credit cards remain open. No one has accessed them.

. . .

KAIRI

Last known location based on phone GPS at Origins Laboratories. Last night the team checked the office grounds. Nothing of interest.

A text on my phone comes through while I'm reading the group board.

MAX

I'm headed your way. Need anything? Your dog's with Stella.

ME

Vet cleared her?

MAX

Yep. She's got a shaved patch on her shoulder. No stitches. They used glue. Stella says she can stay as long as needed.

ME

You didn't want her?

MAX

Nope

He's such a hardass.

MAX

See you in thirty.

Half an hour?

I head back to the bedroom. She's still sleeping, but she's rolled onto her back. She's sexy as fuck, sprawled out against the white cotton sheets, dark hair twisted around her shoulders. The cotton tee does little to hide the perky nipples my mouth waters to taste. I love how she squirms with the scrape of my teeth. It's strange to me that she thought anyone worth his salt would have an issue with her scar. An imperfect lightning bolt between her soft, pillowy breasts. Unique, unforgettable beauty.

I adjust myself and lean over her, brushing my lips to her forehead. She blinks slowly with sleepy eyes.

Her brow wrinkles and her hands clutch the sheet, tugging it up, but I block it, unwilling to lose our intimacy from last night. I cup her breasts over the tee and tease her nipple with my thumb, rubbing back and forth.

"Morning," I say.

She twists on the bed, rolling onto her side, her dark eyes blinking awake, slowly taking me in. "Did you exercise?"

"Went for a run." I bend my head and get a whiff. Then I push up off the bed. No need to expose her to that. "I'm gonna hop in the shower. Coffee's on, but you may need to heat it in the microwave. Max is on his way over. I'll be out of the shower in five."

As I close the door, she's rubbing her eyes, waking up from what I hope was a deep, restful sleep.

True to my word, I'm out with a towel wrapped around my waist with minutes to spare. She's still lying on the bed with the sheet tucked up under her armpit.

"Your turn. I'll go scrounge up breakfast."

With my back to her, I throw on a T-shirt and fresh running shorts. I hear the bathroom door click, put on fresh socks and running shoes, and head into the kitchen.

There's a sleeve of a dozen plain bagels, and I pull two out to toast them. I set the carton of eggs out on the counter. I'm not a chef by any stretch, but I know my way around breakfast. It's the first breakfast I've cooked for her, so I'll need to wait to learn how she likes her eggs.

Whoever stocked this place knows his way around the frozen food aisle. There must be twenty frozen food options stacked in the freezer. No vegetables or fruit. They loaded the pantry with protein powder and bars. Looks like we're set on flour, sugar, spices. No meat that I can locate. I'll need to make a grocery run if we're going to stay here long.

The side of the house trembles and the walls emit a low-key grumble. The garage door.

I swing open the side door and watch as Max's Toyota 4-Runner pulls into the empty bay beside the Land Cruiser Felix brought us.

The door glides down behind him, sealing us in the garage. He hops out, opens the back door, and waves me over. He's got three bags of groceries and another duffel.

Max heads in first, and I almost slam into his back when he comes to a sudden stop.

"Morning," Max says, but he's not speaking to me. I step around him, a bag hoisted in each arm, and understand.

Sage stands where the den meets the kitchen, hair dripping wet, a solid sheen of black. The moisture has spread down her tiny T-shirt that's missing the bottom half, and she's wearing sky blue running shorts that are so short I'm fairly certain when she turns around, half her ass will hang out.

"Hi…" She waves her hand timidly. "I…ah…not all of my clothes made it."

"Looks good to me." I recognize that tone. It's his pickup tone. My head whips to Max.

"I guess we're not really going anywhere, right?" Her timid tone has me doubly annoyed with Max.

"Max just brought us over some fresh groceries, so we're good. It's not like we're locked down here, but—"

"How's he treating you?" Max, who typically has the tenderness of a cactus, hovers near her, infringing on her personal space.

"All good." She flicks those golden-brown eyes my way. I shove the bags up onto the counter and suppress the urge to grab her hand and pull her into me.

"If he gets on your nerves, I can stay with you. Knox can cover back at HQ."

"Are you kidding me right now?" I grip the counter. Who the hell does he think he is, flirting with her?

"Oh, so, it's like that, is it?" Max asks with a mischievous grin. "You told me she was a friend."

"She is a friend." And he's playing with fire.

Sage steps around Max, still timid, and positions herself next to me. She stands on her toes and peeks into the paper bags.

Max crosses his arms over his chest and smirks.

I don't get the cocky smile playing across his face.

"Cool, man." Max bends and lifts the black duffel he carried in. "Brought a secure phone you can use." He digs it out and offers it to Sage. She glances to me, and I give a quick confirmation nod.

"It's also monitored. Just FYI," Max informs her. She takes it, but it's clear she's confused.

"The team monitors all communications. Safety precaution."

"I'd like to call Jimmy," Sage says. "I know he's worried."

"Got an update on the drive over," Max says. "Our guys made contact with him this morning. No one has approached him about you. No one has asked your whereabouts, other than concerned colleagues and neighbors. He willingly let our guys into his home, and they easily found two listening devices. Looks like whoever is after you may have burned your home down to smoke you out, which is one scenario we considered."

"Did Jimmy let someone into his house recently? Cable company? Gas?"

Max gives me a head shake in the negative. "Looks like they broke in to install the devices."

"Did we leave the devices in place?"

"No. Pulled 'em. Getting them to Kairi and Erik so they can check them out. Expectations aren't high they'll lead anywhere." Max sighs and glances at his wrist. "I'm gonna head. If you need something more than what we've packed, let us know." His directive is at Sage, but he's all business. There's no sign of flirty Max. The guy was just messing with my head.

"You're sure you weren't followed?"

"What do you take me for?" Max is several inches taller than me with linebacker shoulders. He's skilled, but he's also hard to miss. He's one big freaking guy. "Last night, I crashed at Trevor and Stella's old condo near the office. No one followed me there. We're taking all the precautions." He tilts his head and studies Sage. "You need more clothes?"

"Well, not all of my clothes made it."

"Stella said you had some dirty clothes?"

"I'd been meaning to stop by a laundromat."

"She's having them washed. We'll get 'em to you."

"This is my shirt, but I don't know whose shorts these are."

"Not mine," Max says, and I can't help but chuckle at that vision. "Knowing Stella, she grabbed some things from her closet."

"That was nice of her."

"She's HR for Arrow. And she's Trevor's wife."

"She gave me a lot of information about Santa Barbara. She was at the soccer game, too."

"Did Rafael's team win?" Max asks.

"It was a bunch of three-year-olds. If someone kept score, I didn't see," I tell him, walking him out to the garage. I leave Sage sorting through the groceries and close the door behind me.

"So, you and Sam's little sis," Max says as soon as the door clicks.

I narrow my eyes and cross my arms. Regardless of what happened last night, she's hardly little. "What of it?"

"Nothing. I like it."

"You do?"

"Yeah, man. I do." He opens his car door and, before climbing inside, adds, "She's better than a dog."

I shoot him the bird, and he chuckles. I stand there, arms crossed, dealing with a mix of pissed off and flummoxed emotions, on guard until he's out on the street and the garage door has closed.

When I re-enter the house, Sage sits in a chair by the kitchen table, legs crossed. She looks up when I enter.

"Can I call Jimmy?"

"Sure." Her feet hit the floor. I was right. Her ass cheeks hang out below the hem of those ridiculously short shorts. The curve blending from her thigh to her ass is delectable. Damp, dark waves cascade down her back.

She reaches the hallway and looks over her shoulder. "I didn't think to thank Max for this." She holds up the phone. "Can you thank him for me?"

"Are you interested in Max?" She wouldn't be the first. I don't believe she is, but after last night…why would she bring him up to me?

"No."

"Good. Because I'd hate to have to end him." She cracks up at my joke and spins to go into the room to call her buddy. As unsettling as it is, deep down, I'm not sure I'm joking.

CHAPTER 24

Sage

The phone rings. And rings.

Come on, Jimmy. Pick up.

"Hello?"

"Jimmy!"

"Sage? Holy shit. Hold on." Silence descends. I strain to hear anything at all. Click. "Where are you? Oh. Never mind. I know you can't tell me. Are you okay? Are you safe?"

"Yes. Things are crazy. But yes, I'm safe. Or at least physically." I crawl up on the bed, back to the headboard, butt on the pillows so I can see if the door cracks open.

"What do you mean?"

"Well, a lot's happened." I want to tell him exactly what's happened, but is that juvenile?

"Any leads on Sloane?"

"No. But they've sent people to search for her. It's probably what I should've done."

"You can't think like that. But they said they've got you somewhere safe."

"Yeah. Just me and Knox." I let his name hang there in the air between us.

"Is the stud muffin making moves on my girl?" I can hear his smile if that's even possible.

"I'd say he made a big one."

"Whoa. My head may explode. I have so many questions. I don't know how to prioritize."

"It's okay."

"Can you video? I need to see your face."

"I don't know if I can. I'm on this weird phone. It can probably video, but—"

"You don't know how to. Got it. So, Knox. Like, you're getting it on? What are we talking about here? Making out? Holding hands? With you, a guy can never tell."

"All the above?"

"All...*what?*"

"Yep... finally." My tone hits the highest pitch, and yes—it's juvenile.

"No. Way."

"Yes. Way." My cheek muscles burn from the wide, uncontrollable grin.

"How did that even work? Was he like...yes, someone is shooting at us. And we're going to send big, burly, scary men to check on your friend in Asheville. And I'm so turned on by all of this I'm going to jump your bones."

"Oh." All humor evaporates. "Were they mean to you?"

"They were no joke. Like, let's just say, if they asked questions, I would answer out of fear they'd begin yanking out teeth or fingernails. What the hell have you gotten yourself into?"

"It's not me. I swear. I haven't done anything. It's Sloane."

"Sloane's such a rule follower. It's hard to imagine her getting caught up in... What is this? What exactly is going on?"

"I have no idea. But I know Sloane's in trouble. She still hasn't returned any of my messages."

"You aren't returning messages. No one can reach you. Do you know how many people have contacted me to make sure you're okay because you haven't returned their messages? And we're supposed to be back in school in one week. Seven days, Sage."

"I know. I know." We have two weeks to prep our classrooms before the first day back. Lots of meetings. "Did the class lists come out?"

"Sage. Seriously? Okay. Let's try this again. Let me tell you what happened here." I nod, not that he can see me. "Two men came to talk to me. I thought it might be my lucky day, because one of them was very Ian Somerhalder. But he opened his mouth and... yeah, no. Straight and narrow. And his buddy Mr. Clean Cut was all, 'We're going to hold you upside down by your ankles and shake out the change.'"

"No."

"Not really. But they had a vibe. And they told me that someone could be listening. That I had to watch what I was saying. Where I went. It's like *Mission Impossible* came to Asheville with taller Tom Cruises. And I let them in my house because, A, I have nothing to hide, and B, they said it would help you. You know me. I'll do anything to help you. But do you know what they found?" I open my mouth to answer. "I'll tell you what they found because you will not guess this one. They found listening devices. In my home. And this is after your house burns down. I asked if your house was not an accident—which Timothy Jones from the fire department believes a gas leak caused it, by the way—but Somerhalder's doppelganger didn't seem to think that. They really would not tell me much. Just promised me you were safe and that you would be in touch. They wouldn't even confirm you were with Knox."

"I'm so sorry you had to go through that."

"Me? I'm fine. I'd be a helluva a lot finer if you would answer your damn phone."

"I told you. I can't turn it on. It can be tracked."

"Can I call you on this line?"

"This is supposed to be a secure line. It's like government level secure or something. You can reach me at this number."

"How will you know if your sister calls?"

"They're checking messages. But, at this point, they believe something's happened to her, too. Her credit and debit cards haven't been used."

"Damn." The word comes out as a sigh. "She really is missing. I can't believe you haven't been calling me every single day."

"I know. But I can't. Just from our one conversation, they found me."

"That's what the secret agent duo said. Unbelievable. Are you any closer to finding Sloane?"

"Not yet. But if anyone can find her, they will."

"Who the hell are they? Like ex-Navy SEALs? Rambo wannabes?"

"I don't think Rambo was a SEAL."

"Sage. Who. The. Fuck. Cares? Who are these people?"

"They work for a security company."

"Bullshit. I had an alarm installed on my house, and these men do not work for CPI Alarm Systems or any CPI competitor."

"Don't be a dumbass." I'm grinning, and he's grinning too…I can hear it in his voice. "No, they handle special cases, like missing persons. The CIA and FBI are both clients. But I think that's for cases where the US can't be officially involved."

"This is surreal, Sage." A heaviness falls over the line. It is. All of it is. "You know, those men, they said that they may have burned your house down to flush you out. Like, they studied you and knew that you would reach out to me. Why would they do that? Did Sloane tell you trade secrets or something?"

"I swear, Jimmy, no. Sloane and I, I mean, you know. What she works on in the lab is so over my head. She was excited. She was making headway. I know that. She was frustrated at times. Her boss pressured her to work on cellular rejuvenation for anti-aging purposes, and as you know, she's really into cellular re-growth for organs, but…she never seemed scared or worried. And none of that would be worth abducting her."

Sam, our paranoid sibling, had been the one worried about unthinkable scenarios. Any email could be read, so he rarely emailed. He'd drop letters off to me and wouldn't send them through the military base. He got Sloane and me into the habit of mailing letters too. But he's been gone for two years.

"You said a man broke into your home and he had a silencer on his gun."

The cylindrical device on top of the handgun had been a silencer. I recognized it from Sam's stockpile. "Yes."

"Did you see if he had any restraints dangling from his waist?"

"Like handcuffs?"

"Yeah, or rope or anything?"

I think back to my limited view through the crack in the dresser. "It was really dark. I couldn't see much." Not even his face. His steps were heavy on the wood. Methodical. I turn my attention to the clear blue skies outside the bedroom window. "Why?"

"It's just a comment one guy said. When he found the listening device. He said that they were dealing with professionals. And the other guy, the Somerhalder guy, said… yet they missed. He didn't say more, but it got me thinking. Sloane is missing. She's a scientist, and she has no one in her life other than you."

"That's not true."

"Really? I know you love her, but come, now. She's as frosty as they come. And that's me being generous. What if they want her to do something, like build a nuclear weapon, and she's refusing, and they want to threaten your life to force her to do it?"

"Okay, first, whatever books or movies you're into, it's time for a change."

"I'm serious."

"Sloane wouldn't be able to create a weapon. That's like…I don't know what kind of specialty that requires, but Sloane is a cellular biologist. That has nothing to do—"

"Weapons come in all types. Some people think Covid was a viral weapon that escaped."

"Okay, well, then, she'd need to be a virologist, which she's not."

"Maybe. But something's not right here."

"No shit. I'm in a safe house." A garbled sound comes across the line. "And I made out with Knox Williams."

"And you said he's still hot."

"So hot."

"Still has his hair?"

"Still there."

"I want to join you. So I can see for myself you're safe."

"Just hang tight. If someone is out there watching you… Jesus, Jimmy, just stay safe, okay? I couldn't bear it if something happened to you because of—"

"Because of what, Sage? None of this is your fault. You recognize that, right?"

"I do, but…I keep thinking, what if that bullet had hit Knox? That would've been my fault."

"How do you figure?"

"I involved him. Maybe I should've never come here."

"Says the woman who has yet to see the charcoal remnants of her home. Look, just…what's the plan? Have you talked to the school?"

"No, not yet. I'm hoping I'll be back in time."

"Will Knox come back with you?"

"No, his life's here." The side of my hand rubs up and down my sternum. There's a rap on the door. "Come in."

The door opens and the legend himself leans on the doorframe. "I'm whipping us up some breakfast. Anything you don't eat?"

I always joke that I eat like a pregnant woman, steering clear of unpasteurized cheese, but I'm not about to say that to Knox after last night. "Hey, Jimmy—"

"I heard. Go watch over the food preparation. Keep in touch, okay?"

"You stay safe, okay?" If something happens to Jimmy…I wasn't exaggerating. I could not live with that.

"Call me back because I need to hear more about the sex!"

And it's only then, for whatever reason, I remember I'm on a line that's being monitored. That's mortifying. The team listens. *Christ on a cracker*. "I'll call you back. Love you."

In the kitchen, Knox opens a crate of eggs. "How's Jimmy?"

"Good. Scared for me."

"Understandable."

"Do you think he's safe?"

"There shouldn't be anything to gain from doing something to him."

"Why not bring him here?"

He lets out a sigh and leans on the counter. The muscles in his forearms flex with his weight. "If someone's watching him, they may slip up. Could give us some leads. Our guys out there are doing surveillance, just in case."

"Because right now we don't have any leads, do we?"

"Our men in the Caymans are coming up empty. But, sometimes in a case like this, it can take some time. Our tech team is going over everything they can get on Sloane." He swings the fridge door open. "What do you like in an omelet?"

"I'm really not very hungry." I rub my stomach. Reality is settling in and… I'm not a big breakfast eater, anyway. I usually get my walk in before I eat. "Could I… Is it safe for me to go for a walk?"

"On the beach?"

"Yeah." Through the window, there's a lifeguard stand, and the lifeguard putters by along the beach on an ATV four-wheeler. The scene outside feels about as safe as conceivable.

Knox snaps the egg carton closed. "I'll eat a protein bar. Let me get my shoes on and we'll go."

"You don't have to go."

"Do I look like someone who wants to spend the day cooped up inside? A walk sounds nice."

"But you've already exercised."

"I have." A grin plays across his features.

"This won't count as exercise for you." Of course, it won't. He's like Sam. It's not exercise until your clothes are drenched.

"It counts as something I want to do." The look he gives me sets a thousand butterflies free.

"Did you tell Jimmy about last night?"

"Why?" Unease sets in, like I've been caught doing something I'm not supposed to do.

"Just curious. If you told him about me, it's one thing, if not—"

"I told him." I catch a trace of a smile before he turns to head outside. He holds the door for me and I step through into the California sun.

"Is there a speed you need to go on this walk of yours?"

"No, not necessarily."

"How're you feeling?"

At this, I give him the side-eye.

"Like, are you sore?"

Oh, that. "I thought you were asking me if I felt like I could make it down the beach. You saw me hike yesterday."

"I'm not questioning your health, Sagie Bean."

My face breaks into an ear-splitting grin. "I haven't heard anyone use that name since…"

"Not since Sam," Knox finishes for me.

"Right."

"But, to get back to it…you're not sore?"

"No, not really."

"And you told Jimmy what, exactly?"

"What're you getting at?" I push my arm against his.

The tide's coming in. The sun is high over the mountains to the east. My bare feet sink in deep sand with bits of broken shell.

He peers down at me, and it's clear he's expecting me to say more. This conversation feels juvenile, but… "I told him we made out."

"Made out. So that's what the kids are calling it these days?" I exchange smiles with an older woman walking her dog on a leash.

"You can stop teasing me." I've always been behind the curve. But I'm finally okay with that. It's who I am. "I forgot the line is monitored. So I guess your team knows now, too." I can't believe I forgot that.

"I don't think it will be exactly news to them." We grin at each other, but I'm still all kinds of embarrassed. "So, there's something else I want to know."

"Okay." He squeezes my hand gently, and the action sets me on edge. What could he possibly want to know?

"Your, ah…health status. You're healthy now, right? That's what you said."

"I am."

"And we've got all the meds you need. You're good?"

He emphasizes the word good, and I let out a deflated sigh. He's seen my pill stash, so I can understand why he'd repeatedly ask.

"I'm good. I promise. I'm really good."

"I remember Sam saying something about life expectancy."

"It's just statistics. And I was young…that's to my advantage. There are Facebook groups out there of people who are going on thirty years post-transplant. That's what you're getting at, right?" Thirty-six percent of people survive more than ten years after a heart and lung transplant. If you focus too hard on percentages, especially in the post-twenty-year data, which drops to a six or seven percent survival rate, it's scary. But as my doctors say, and as I continually counsel myself, each person is an individual. My doctors are optimistic."

"So, the life expectancy figures…they don't apply to you now?"

"I'd say that yesterday my chances of dying by bullet were much higher than organ failure."

"That's not funny."

He's right. It's not funny. Yet I laugh. And then the next thing I know we're running along the beach, splashing in the water, and it's as if all is right in the world. And yet, there's a gun tucked into a holster on a belt around Knox's waist hidden by the untucked shirt he's wearing.

CHAPTER 25

Knox

A glimmer of light, a bright reflection off on the hill, has me covering her with my body, angling her behind me. A man seven feet away, legs out, feet in the sand, looks up from his book, a curious expression on his face. He shifts in his seat to see what caught my attention.

"What? What is it?" Sage stutters.

It's a relatively flat beach, with cottages tightly packed together. I might've seen someone closing a sliding door. A window. Light reflected off a ring. The shoreline is the lowest elevation, and every row of houses rises higher above sea level. Far away, in the hills, houses with an ocean view look out upon us. We're on a public beach, and someone could be watching from any one of these houses.

"Knox?" Her grip on my wrist strengthens. A plastic shovel halts midair. The mother watches me instead of the bucket her kid asked her to fill.

"Yeah. Sorry." I wrap an arm around her shoulder and pull her up against my side.

The houses thin as the beach narrows near rocky terrain. The shoreline curves up ahead. In almost every window, the sun reflects off the glass, creating a mirror facade. My vision's solid, but behind any one of these doors or windows could be an assailant. I'd never know.

"Is walking the only form of exercise you can do?"

"No. But it's my favorite. I find it helps clear my mind, and it's cardio, but it's not too stressful. I tried biking, but–"

"How about we go back to our place and we do some Pilates or yoga today?"

"Is something wrong? Did you see someone?"

"We're too exposed out here."

"They couldn't possibly track us." She's simply saying what she overheard one of us say. Theoretically, she's right. But they found us once. And we still don't know who they are, or why.

"Let's wait until we've gathered more intel. It's...best to play it safe." I already ran the length of this beach. Scanned the terrain as I went. But it's a different experience with Sage out here beside me.

My experience comprises little protective detail. They deployed our team on missions more along the lines of extraction or infiltration. But that's no excuse. I know better than to parade her along a public beach.

Back at the cottage, we rinse our feet and head inside. I lock the door behind us, set the alarm, check the windows, and check my phone for any updates. There are none.

After I find a workout routine on my phone, she stretches out on the floor, legs spread wide, and leans over one long leg with the grace of a gymnast, leaving the smallest of gaps between her torso and thigh. I sure as hell don't have that kind of flexibility.

"Are you going to sit there and watch?"

"Will it bother you? I rather like the view."

She rolls her eyes to the ceiling, but the flush of color in her cheeks says she might act annoyed, but she likes it. And her acting job is piss poor. She's too sweet to pull off angry. She alternates her stretch to the other leg, then flattens to the ground between her two outstretched legs.

"Have you always been this flexible?" These moves are familiar. Call it yoga, Pilates, or plain old stretching, but anyone who doesn't do it, no matter how macho, is begging for injury. For me and my brothers, it's serious business. Still, Mr. Bendy, I am not.

"I guess." Her fingers spread out as she flattens her palms against the hardwood floor.

"Do you want me to get you a towel? I can ask Max to bring a couple of yoga mats."

"A couple? Are you going to join me on the floor?"

Mirth fills those sugary sweet eyes. And yeah, I can imagine quite a few things I could do to her stretched out on the floor like that. We could move those tiny shorts to the side, and I could come up behind her… I close my eyes and force myself to redirect my gaze out the window.

An overly bright voice speaks through my phone, telling her to begin by getting on her hands and knees. My semi-hard cock does some stretching of its own. I shift on the sofa, adjusting my shorts.

Her back forms a dome, as instructed. The cotton of her tee stretches smoothly across her back. No bra. Her chest presses out, and she looks to the ceiling, lengthening the lines of her smooth neck where my lips traced last night.

The band of her shorts slips higher up her slim waist. The hem lifts too, exposing the curve of ass cheeks and a strip of white cotton. I swallow. My mouth dries.

Her hair's back in a ponytail, and it flips around with the movement of her head. It's a nice, thick ponytail, one that could be fisted and used to direct… Jesus, I have to get hold of myself.

I grab the laptop and connect through the VPN. Read through the project updates.

BLUESKY

Contact made with S. Watson neighbors in 3B. No valuable intel. Report posted.

RYAN

Interpol shared watch list. Mtg at 1300 PST to review.

MAX

Dropped supplies. All good.

BLUESKY

Does watch list include all known aliases? Database pulling zilch on three.

RYAN

Plan to attend the 1300 mtg. We'll review.

I glance up from the phone. She's stretched out in a downward dog pose. The heels of her feet are flat on the floor. Ass in the air, nipples poking through thin cotton. She's a little low, but not too low for me to grip those hips and push…

All right. *Get a grip.*

She peers up at me, the tips of her chocolate waves sweeping the floor.

She swoops down into a plank but tilts her head and gives me a little smile. On auto, my hand adjusts my crotch. Shit. Not good.

She's slightly off form. Her ass is up a little too much in the air, but other than that, her legs and back are flat. And I'm not about to tell her to lower that curvy ass.

The woman on the phone dictates instructions for another pose, but Sage pushes up onto all fours and crawls to me. I have to blink a few times to confirm it's not a hallucination.

She palms my thighs, just above my knees, rising from the floor.

Fuck, I want her. But no. She's got to be sore.

"Taking a break?"

She smiles, and I have to say, there's nothing timid about that smile. Her hand cups my shorts, pressing over my erection.

"Do you understand you're playing with fire?"

Her teeth sink into her lip as her lips curve into a flirty smile.

"Babe, it won't feel good today. You're going to be sore." And I'm not that big of an asshole. "We aren't—" Her grip tightens over my crotch, effectively cutting off oxygen to my brain.

"What about oral? Last night, you tasted me. But I didn't get to taste you."

Boom. Explosion. All thought obliterated.

CHAPTER 26

Sage

The expression on Knox's face is one I hope I never forget. He's enthralled. With me.

"I don't have a lot of experience with this," I admit as I unsnap his shorts and tug on the zipper.

"You..." The strained word is garbled. He places his hand over mine. "You don't have to do this."

"But I want to." And I really do. I want to return some of the pleasure he gave me last night. I take him in my hand. He's not wearing briefs or boxers. His silky skin stretches taut. My thumb traces a thick vein running his length. His breathing comes out in sharp, shallow breaths. I push off on my knees, rising closer to him, and he spreads his thighs wider, giving me ample room. His shorts pull tight around his thighs.

I probably should have removed his shorts, but based on the way he's zoned in on my every move, he doesn't seem to mind.

I press my lips to his shaft. His chest trembles. My gaze shoots upward. Is he laughing?

But there's no humor present in his hooded eyes. I lap my

tongue from the base of his shaft to his tip, where I circle the head. Pre-cum forms, and I circle it with my index finger, then place my finger in my mouth and suck.

His eyes are impossibly dark. His chest still. I squeeze his shaft harder and lower my head, taking his tip into my mouth.

"There you go," he gasps. "Just like that."

My mouth stretches around his girth. I grip his base and then, remembering something I read, use my other hand to cup his balls. His hips lift.

"Yes, yes."

It's amazing that I can do something that has him tilting his head back, eyes half-closed, torn between watching and losing himself.

I pull off him and glide my hand up and down, over his now wet shaft. "Tell me what you like."

"Jesus. You're going to be the death of me."

"I hope you mean that in a good way."

"Only the best of ways, trust me." His hand brushes over my hair, then his fingers loop into my ponytail. There's a slight pull on my scalp. "What you're doing is mind-blowing."

"I'm doing it right?"

"Perfect."

He guides my head, softly, up and down. I push myself to take him as deep as I can, over and over. His balls tighten in my hand, and he grows wider in my mouth.

"I'm gonna..." There's a sharp tug on my hair and I'm pulled off him, but not before my mouth fills with a taste of his cum. It's not the best thing I've tasted...but it's him. I brought him to the brink.

I've given two blow jobs in my life. One to a friend with cancer who told me he'd never had one. I clearly did something wrong because he went soft while I was trying. We were in high school. And then the guy freshman year who was into me until my shirt came off. Those experiences sucked.

Long, white spurts stream across Knox's heather gray cotton shirt. Thick, white streams. "Fuck, that felt amazing."

Pride surges. I did that.

He carefully rolls up the hem of his shirt, covering his release, then removes it, setting it down on the floor. He repositions his shorts and grins down at me.

"Now, it's your turn."

My arms clamp down against my sides. But his hands are nowhere near my chest. His fingers slip below the band on my shorts and he lifts my bottom, and it's goodbye shorts and panties. He's really good at removing clothes.

His jaw grazes my calf. There's a slight burn as his rough growth collides with my skin. "Don't look too closely. I haven't shaved today." But thankfully, my hair typically grows in a little soft. Although, that doesn't make the dark hairs attractive.

Based on the way he's nipping and licking his way down my legs, whatever growth is there doesn't seem to bother him. And then he's there, between my legs.

His tongue…it's…*god, that feels good.* My back curls, thighs wide.

Muffled voices from the beach carry through the glass door, a reminder there's no covering on the door. If someone walked up on our deck, they'd see me spread wantonly on a sofa.

Knox thrusts a finger inside me. One finger and a twinge of discomfort has my muscles tightening, but he applies pressure on my mound, and I loosen right back up. He's down there, doing the best things, for the longest time. Rough callouses ride over my belly, below my shirt. He captures a breast and tweaks the nipple. It's like a direct line to my center, where I seize around his fingers as his teeth graze my clit.

The room blackens other than a burst of scattered orange glow.

Wet lips press against my inner thigh. My eyelids flutter open. Blazing eyes peer up at me, his smile wide and carefree.

"God, you're gorgeous when you come."

Inside my head, a girly squeal exalts pure joy.

He crawls up my body, and my legs wrap around him, welcoming him. He drops his head and kisses me. My heart flutters…heck, all of my insides perform a contented, happy dance.

"Getting hungry?" he asks, then rubs the tip of his nose over mine.

My stomach growls loudly in response, and he chuckles.

Breakfast consists of coffee and a cheese omelet for me, but he eats a frozen meal with chicken. He also adds protein powder to his coffee.

And he insists we eat breakfast in bed. "It's the least I can do, you know, since none of this has gone as I would've preferred."

Magical. The morning, last night, it's the only word for it.

"Why are you looking at me like that?"

"It's nothing. You're sweet, that's all." How is Knox not married? With a bushel of kids? The side of my hand rubs my sternum, pressing down on the warmth building. Soon, I'll be across the country, and he'll be taking women on dates. And returning favors and… "What's going on with Sloane? Is there anything I can do?"

"No." He lifts my hand and rubs the pad of this thumb over my nail.

"Is it just me, or does it feel like we're not making any progress?"

"These things take time. A missing person. Last heard from two weeks ago in another country. It's gonna take some time."

"I feel like I should get on a plane and go search for her myself."

"Definitely not," he says, pulling me against him. "There's no way I'm letting you put yourself at risk. The best thing we can do is to stay low." A smirk plays across his face. Yeah, we've been lying low pretty well. "We've got men on the ground. They're doing the real work."

"That's the stuff you usually do, right?"

"Yep."

I remember how hard Sam worked to make special forces. The

elite of the elite. The hell he went through to qualify. All the sacrifices once he made it. A labor of love. "Was it a hard adjustment? Leaving the military?"

He scratches the back of his head and grimaces. "I think I'm still adjusting. It's different. A different way of life. Still trying to figure out where I fit in. What my day-to-day routine is."

"What do you mean?"

"Well, in the military, it's structured. You get used to that. Trevor has most of us on a structured workout regimen, but you know, in between assignments, it can feel a little… Arrow pays us well. The idea is we're on staff as resources when needed. Max will likely transition to specializing in intelligence in a tech capacity. It's kind of his thing. Can't say I share the same love."

"That's where the dogs come in? You're thinking you might train dogs for Arrow to use?"

He lifts his shoulders and stretches the fingers of one hand wide. There's a band of pale skin around his right wrist where he typically wears a watch. "It's a thought. Although it's doubtful Arrow's going to need trained dogs. If they ever need them, we have law enforcement partners who could provide them. Security is a big part of what Arrow does. It's possible I'll get assigned to someone's protective detail and then…you know, my days will be regular."

"I get that." When Sam returns, I bet he'd love to work for a place like Arrow. "So, it's conceivable you'd need to move again?"

"For sure. It's one of the reasons I'm in temporary housing. Owned by Arrow. What about you?"

"Me?"

"What's a day in the life like for one Sage Emory Watson?"

"You remember my middle name?"

"Well…" He looks sheepish as his right shoulder rises. "I looked it up."

"Where?"

"It's on our portal. All the basic background information. It's just...standard."

"They did research on me?"

"Of course. Part of taking the case. Also part of figuring out what's going on."

"They're spending a ton of money on me, aren't they?"

"They are...but that's one of the things I like about these guys. They are much more into doing the right thing than making money."

"That's got to be refreshing."

"It is. When you pick this line of work, it's important to believe you're on the good side."

For someone like Knox, I'd expect basic goodness and integrity to be critical. He links his fingers with mine and tugs me up, holding me against his side.

I look up questioningly, and he brushes his lips against my temple. "Just want you closer."

With those four words, my heart's no longer mine. It becomes his. Although, who am I kidding? I've been serving my heart up to him ever since I arrived.

CHAPTER 27

Knox

"How're things going there?" Max's question in my earbud has me taking stock.

I've got a gorgeous woman snuggled against me. Outside the narrow rectangular window there's only blue sky and stray, puffy, white clouds. And what have I been doing all day on a weekday? Hanging out. Talking. Touching. All things considered, things are pretty fucking fantastic.

She peers up at me, and her gaze lights a wick deep inside me, building on the warmth. It's not just sex. I like talking to her. Lying next to her. Fostering a connection.

Of course, her sister is missing, and we're currently evading what appears to be hired guns. Perspective.

"It's good."

"Nothing suspicious?"

Guilt nudges at the corners of my conscience. "We've mostly stayed inside. This beach is vacation central. No one stands out."

"Well, I've got good news. Time to pack up and go."

His tone is all business. I nudge Sage, and she pushes off my chest. I get off the bed and peer out the window, scanning the crowded shoreline. "What've you got?"

"We've identified a probable location for Sloane Watson. We're putting together a team now."

"Where?"

"Cayman Brac. High-level security detail. Eyebrow raising for an island with a population of two thousand. Ownership traces to a shady shell corporation. We're putting together a team of eight. Plan is to go in at night, undetected, and if she's there, extract. We're tight on resources. We need you."

"When do we head?"

"We'll fly out overnight. Tomorrow review and prep. If we're feeling good, go in tomorrow night. If not, we'll pause, go in the next night."

"Who's gonna stay with Sage?"

"Did you find Sloane?" Sage's eyes widen. "Where is she? I want to come with you."

There's no way in hell. But she doesn't understand. The plan will be to get in and out undetected.

"You talking to me?" Max asks.

"No, man. Sorry. Sage is here. What's the plan?" I shoot Sage a stern look to convey I'll update her after the call.

"Felix is going to cover for you."

"He's not coming with?" Felix is an experienced asset.

"He's got a family obligation. He'll take day shifts with Sage. Still up for discussion, but we're leaning towards relocating her to Stella and Trevor's condo."

"Logic?"

"Well, your dog, for one. Stella's already taking care of it. But the condo is secure. It's also convenient for the team to swap off coverage. And Trevor said he and Stella can stay there overnight, so there won't be a need to put resources against overnight security."

Trevor and Stella are good people.

"Makes sense. Any updates on the perps?"

"No. Current theory is the goal wasn't to kill."

"Wasn't to swap recipes."

"Good one." Max snorts. As if it's funny. "Leading theory is they want her for Sloane's compliance."

The abduction theory. "No one else watching our place?"

"No. But Kairi believes there's got to be a job post on the dark web. Her team hasn't found it. But it fits. Which means others could be out there looking for Sage. To be safe, neither of you will return to your apartment. There's covered parking at the condo. You'll park there, go up in the elevator."

The second I end the call with Max, trusting, hopeful brown eyes await, full of questions.

I'm going to bring her sister home. And that's a good thing. It's fulfilling a promise to Sam. But I'm reluctant to pop our bubble. When this is over, she'll return to Asheville. And then what? Long-distance? It'll be better than the guys had it on the team, but long-distance wears on a relationship. I've seen it time and time again over the years. Long-distance means separate lives. I wanted more time.

"They found her?" Sage prompts. She's touching me, her hand on my forearm, like she knows everything's not one hundred percent fantastic.

"Looks like it."

"Where?"

"Our team on the ground located a facility which could conceivably serve as a place to hold someone against their will." She doesn't need the worry of knowing the location we've identified has military grade armed security.

"So, you think it's her company that has her? Is she being held captive?"

"It fits with her company concocting a story about her resigning. Because you never believed that, right?"

She gives it consideration. Her gaze falters, tongue flits out between her lips. She looks me directly in my eyes. "No. Sloane loves her job too much. Don't get me wrong. I do believe the right guy is going to come along and she'll fall in love. But when it happens, it won't happen quickly. And she'd never prioritize a guy over her work. Aside from that, she'd never quit her job and not call me. She'd never move and not call me." I caress her chin, her cheek. What she's not saying is that Sloane is the last of her living family. She wouldn't turn her back on her. "If she's done anything…if she's involved in something that's illegal, what will happen to her?"

I drop my duffel on the bed and unzip it, considering the question. If she was one hundred percent on board with her employers, she probably wouldn't have gone MIA. "Interpol might want to talk to her, but they've only been monitoring her company. From what I've gathered, this isn't a case where anyone's gearing up to prosecute. We just want to bring your sister, an American, home safe." Her sister might have experienced trauma. Kindness and hostage situations rarely go hand in hand. "You know, your sister might need you when she gets back." And she doesn't have a home to return to. "Maybe while I'm gone, you can spend some time looking at places for you and Sloane to stay when you return. Find yourself a builder."

"So, when you bring her back, you think it'll be safe for us to return home? To Asheville?"

"If Sloane knows something they don't want to get out, the cat will be out of the bag, so to speak, once we rescue her. No need to keep coming after her. I mean, there's a potential witness scenario, but I doubt it. You'd be dealing with international courts. Whatever intel she has would probably be of the variety you can prove with files. If they were simply forcing her to do work she didn't agree with, it's hard to imagine they'd try to recapture her once she's Stateside. But right now, we're dealing with way too many unknowns." She's skeptical. Worried. Possibly fearful. "I promise you, we won't let you go back to Asheville until we know it's safe."

The trust in those eyes hits me square in the chest. She's depending on me. I bend and press my lips over hers, close my eyes and let my fingers sift through her hair, giving us a second before we shift gears. With an exhale that releases all hesitation, I open my eyes and give her a quick reassuring smile. "Let's get packed up."

"Where're we going?"

"I'm going to get you settled in a new place. Millie will be there. Stella, you remember her from the soccer game, right?"

"Yes. Of course."

"Well, you're going to stay with Stella and Trevor. Felix will hang out with you during the day. Won't be as good as yours truly, but..." I shoot her a cocky grin.

"But you're leaving?"

"We're flying out this evening. You'll be in good hands. Don't worry."

"And then when you get back, you'll have Sloane."

"That's the plan."

"And then I return to Asheville?"

"Not until we know it's safe. But yes. Didn't you say you need to go back? School's starting?" Hell, if she wants to stay—

"Yes. I need to be back. Actually, on Monday. A week from today." Six days.

"Well, we should return with Sloane in three to four days, tops. You'll be good to go."

"Do we need to go pack immediately?"

It's a little after noon. My team's prepping for the trip. "We can fix lunch here if you want. I'd rather not walk on the beach. I don't like how exposed we are out there, even if theoretically we're safe."

"I was actually thinking..." Color rises to her cheeks and along her neck, all the way to the rim of her T-shirt collar. "Would you... could we maybe...one more time? It just...it feels like this is over, and I don't have any expectations. I know we live on different sides of the country and..." She's staring down at the comforter, full of uncertainty, and if there's one thing she doesn't need to be unsure of, it's my desire and willingness.

"Hey," I say, stepping close to her, "trust me. I'd love nothing more. But I was worried about you."

"Me?"

"You said you're sore." I touch her shoulder, stepping closer, breathing her in.

"Maybe, but…when you get back, everything will be different."

"No. It won't. We'll work something out."

Her expression has me wondering if she can hear my self-doubt at that statement. I've got a long history of relationships petering out when faced with the prospect of distance.

"But if everything's about to change…" She turns in my arms, her palms flat against my chest. "One more time?"

The duffel bag hits the ground. She and I have more than one more time in our future, but I'll be damned if I'm going to leave her wanting. And as we come together, sweaty and out of breath, I know without a doubt she is someone I will never get enough of.

CHAPTER 28

Sage

Stella and Trevor's apartment boasts a modern, clean design. The sofa and chairs in the living room are leather. Black-and-white-framed mountainscapes decorate white walls. One of the framed portraits is an aerial shot of two men hanging on rope off the side of a mountain, rappelling downward. Stella told me the two men pictured are Trevor and her son Ethan. He's currently serving in the Navy with a goal of becoming a SEAL.

This apartment was Trevor's before they got married, and they keep it because of its proximity to Arrow's offices. They stay here when they're going out at night in the area. And Arrow employees stay here when they're visiting from out-of-town.

She swore up and down staying here with me wasn't an imposition at all. I promised I'd be okay staying here by myself. And she cocked her head and grinned. "Honey, I know that. But your guy wouldn't be okay with that. When he knows you're safe, he can focus."

But he's not my guy. It had been on the tip of my tongue. But there was no point in divulging the truth of our relationship. I mean, he'll always be my guy. I'll always love him. He's my first and will likely be my only. I can't imagine being with anyone else. Not after being with Knox. But still, she's making it sound like we're in a committed relationship and we aren't. We're navigating seeing each other once I return home. But, there's no reason to clarify the state of our relationship to Stella.

With each passing hour, my apprehension intensifies. Sunlight streams in through expansive windows, and the tops of palm trees sway across the street. Knox should've landed by now, but I haven't received a text. Stella warned me this morning that the men don't communicate frequently when they're working.

This morning I woke to the smell of coffee and bacon. Stella greeted me in the kitchen, saying Trevor leaves early in the morning. After breakfast, Stella suggested that the two of us go for a walk outside. She said no one should have to spend the day cooped up inside.

I questioned her, remembering how Knox had changed his mind about a walk on the beach yesterday, but Stella assured me that she works with these men day in and day out and that they can be over-the-top cautious. While on our little walk around the neighborhood, we stopped in Arrow's offices, and I had the opportunity to thank Ryan. Well-funded or not, they were doing more than I could have ever expected.

"It's an honor to help a fellow brother's family. I didn't know Sam personally, but I heard good things." Ryan believes Sam is dead. Everyone believes Sam is dead, except for me. Dead or alive, he's still in Ryan's military brotherhood, so I smiled and thanked him. "You know, my partner, Jack Sullivan, met with Sam. He held him in high regard."

The thank you I uttered felt weak and inadequate. But I've learned over the years that few people know the best thing to say. I appreciated his willingness to talk about my brother. Some people refuse, as if bringing him up in conversation might hurt.

Felix sits at the kitchen table, a laptop open, tapping away.

I circled him about an hour ago, expecting to see a streaming chat or possibly a report document. His screen showed an illustrated man in fatigues with a scary-looking long gun in his hand and blown-out buildings in the background. The gun lifted, and a man went flying backward through the air. I passed quickly so he wouldn't know I caught him playing a video game.

He's been on the phone several times with his wife, Maria. Based on some of the things I've overheard, I suspect she's the reason he stayed back. He asked her if she's doing okay and reminded her he'd be home tonight.

Millie stretches out on the sofa, her nose a hair's breadth from my leg. Of all the occupants in the condo, she's happiest. And the most relaxed. Pinpricks of dark hair cover the shaved area, and the corner of the glue taping her injury flicks up on the end, as if it's ready to peel. The instructions were to let it fall off on its own. The injury is close enough to her head she can't lick it, which is a good thing. Otherwise, she'd need to walk around with a cone.

"They're set to go in after dusk," Felix announces.

"How long do you think it'll take?"

"Unclear. They're reviewing drone footage and building floor plans. They're going in by water. If all goes well, they'll surface, approach, wait until it's lights-out on the island, and go in via the beach where there's no border wall. Retrieve her and head out. I'd say when you wake in the morning, you'll have good news."

As if I'll be sleeping tonight. "That's if things go well. What if things don't go well?" There's always a worst-case scenario. With medical procedures, you have to read the fine print, but that worst case is often death.

Felix twists in his seat. "Our guys are some of the best trained in the world. Yes, there's security they need to get around, but typically, the folks hired for security lack training. We've also got the element of surprise. One that, ideally, we won't need to leverage. But you asked if things don't go well, what does that look like?" I nod, fully aware I'm going to get a softened answer, because Felix is talking to me like he has bad news that he doesn't want to share. The sloping shoulders and the curved spine, an attempt to get down to eye level and reassure, are all familiar postures. "A less than ideal outcome is if we're exposed. If our guys don't get in and out unseen. But we know what we're doing. Our guys will be fine. We're equipped and skilled."

He's talking about gun skills. Hand-to-hand combat skills. *Dammit, Sloane.* If she'd taken any number of the jobs Stateside, none of this would be happening.

I close my eyes and pinch the bridge of my nose while focusing on my breathing. *Please let Knox and Sloane be safe. Please keep the Arrow team safe. Please let Knox come home safe and unharmed with Sloane. Please.*

"You know, I've always thought Maria had the toughest role. Staying back home. It's hard to keep your mind off what may or may not be happening. But like right now, I bet you they're kicked back studying plans. Drone footage. Safe as can be. And here you are stressing yourself out."

If something happens to Knox because I showed up here, I won't be able to live with myself. Knox should have a full life in front of him. Why did Sam have to send me to someone I care about?

"You love him." Felix says it like it's a fact.

"Everybody loves Knox." He's got one of those smiles that warms people. More than that, he's loaded with charisma. When he walks in a room, everyone takes note. When he speaks, they listen. He's trustworthy and kind. And dependable. Just look what he's done for me. The same traits that earned his place as Sam's best friend are the traits that shine through to everyone.

"There's some truth to that." Felix crosses one ankle over a knee, cocks his head, and gives a friendly smile. "I'd take a bullet for the guy. But my guess is you and I love him in different ways."

Why is Felix choosing this topic for discussion? He's observant, meaning he possesses highly refined observational skills. That's how Sam would describe it.

"Hey, I approve. Glad to see it. Knox needs someone in his life, and he says you have a heart of gold. Which is good. He deserves that." The side of my hand digs into my sternum. "You're a good one. That's all I meant. He loves you, too."

I jerk back at that. "No." I smile, but the reaction is wrong. Out of place. "We're close," I tell him, explaining. "He's...we've got history." Given he took my virginity, we've added to our history exponentially in the last two days. "We go way back. But we live on opposite sides of the country, and he's got a job like..." He's got a job like Sam's. The kind of job that can take him away for days, weeks, months at a time. In Sam's case, years.

"Our job used to be pretty intense. I'll give you that. Takes a hit on relationships for sure. But that's...it's a different world now. Look at me. I'm here so I don't miss Rafe's birthday. Four years old." Felix beams. "The guys didn't bat an eye. Arrow's also big into professional development. And your man, he's already got a couple of side gigs going. He's in a better place than ever before to invest in a relationship."

"Invest?"

"Yeah, invest." His brows knit together, and he nods with emphasis. "I've been married going on ten years now. You don't pull that shit off without some investment. Lots of give and take. But it's worth it."

One day, Knox will have that with someone. He'll be the one telling someone that yeah, sacrifices are required, but it's totally worth it. I can see it clear as day. And whoever he's saying that to will be a lucky woman. But it won't be me. Knox deserves a lifetime of love. A healthy love with someone who...I stall, searching for what he deserves that I'm not. The truth is, I've done all right for myself. I'm giving back in my career. But I look at what others have done in my social groups, and I trail them all. Some have run marathons. Some are CEOs. There are some who have raised millions of dollars for research. And then there are people like Sloane, who hasn't even had a transplant, leading the charge on regenerating human heart tissue.

Felix raps the table and lowers the lid on his laptop. "I'm gonna head to the restroom." He rubs his belly. "My stomach. Man." He grimaces as he walks backward to the hallway bathroom. "You wanna watch a movie or something? There's a remote on the table. See if you can't find something for us to watch. Will make the time go faster."

I doubt that. Time slowed to a standstill the moment Knox whisked me upstairs to the rooftop deck and kissed me goodbye. The condo had been full of people, and he'd said he wanted to have a private word. Instead of the remote, my fingers roam my lips, remembering. I'd wanted to beg him to stay, but I couldn't do that.

He and his friends left to rescue my sister from a situation she likely contributed to in some way. Of course, if Sloane crossed any ethical lines, it's because she believed it was for the greater good. Maybe she discovered a way to create a synthetic organ, or she used stem cells in some unethical way that would help people like me live longer. She loves science, but she loves science because she sees it as a way of keeping me alive.

There's a knock at the door, and I catch a reflection of myself in the hallway mirror. The side of my hand presses between my breasts. Felix is right. Sitting around waiting for updates sucks.

Two bikes hang on the wall near the apartment door. There's another bedroom with more bikes and gear in the back. As I approach the door, Millie lets out a series of loud barks, as if she's just realized someone is here. She's barking so loud I don't stand a chance of hearing whoever is on the other side of the door.

I grab Millie's collar in my fist.

"Shh. Stop, Millie."

Ruff. Ruff. Ruff. Ruff.

She's loud. Too loud. I unlock the deadbolt with one hand and crack open the door.

A man in a pale blue uniform and a plastic construction helmet glances between me and Millie.

"Hey. Sorry." Millie's tail wags and her barks slow to a rhythmic bark, pause, bark. I let her collar go. "How can I help you?"

I keep the door partially closed on the off-chance Millie might charge the man.

"Hi, miss. I'm with SoCal Gas. We got a report that there's a gas leak in the building. We're checking each of the units. Would you mind waiting outside while we secure the building?" Gas leaks can be serious. "Are you here by yourself?"

"Oh, no. Ah, let me get…" I look toward the bathroom. The door swings wide and the man steps inside. A man with a small hoop earring in an identical uniform steps into the doorway.

Millie's hackles rise and she growls.

"I'm sorry," I tell the men. "She's a rescue dog. Maybe it's best if you wait outside while I get my friend." Both of the men wear thick leather belts. The worn leather hangs loose on the waist of the man closest to me.

"We've already checked the downstair units. Do you know if anyone is next door?"

"Oh, no. That unit is empty." Ryan owns the unit next door. Trevor and Ryan lived in these two units before they got married, but Stella told me that now they use them mostly for guests of Arrow Tactical.

A toilet flushes, and the sound echoes through the open living area and down the hall.

"Why don't you come with me, ma'am?" The man in the doorway asks. "Johnny will wait for your friend."

They're both wearing sunglasses. The man closest to me has a black beard and a mustache, and short black hair. But the hair protruding below the helmet, on the base of his neck, is a sandy colored brown.

A hand wraps around my wrist and tugs. The visual has a

surreal quality. As if it's not my wrist beneath his hand. Pain sears my lower arm.

"Let go of her." Felix's voice is calm. Eerie.

The black bearded man lifts a gun. Where'd that come from?

"If you want to live to attend your son's birthday party, you're going to put that gun down."

"Right." Amusement drips from the single word.

A gold chain glimmers.

Grrrrr.

"I'll go. Just let—"

"You're not going anywhere, Sage. Back up. Slowly."

A harsh pull on my arm hurts. I stumble forward and smash into the uniform of the man with a hooped earring. Pungent body odor fills my nostrils. I get a good look at his rope chain necklace and a silver cross pendant. Across his waist, in the leather work belt, there's a handle to a gun.

"You need to let her go," Felix says. "We're a block away from headquarters. Within seconds, our team will be here."

"Did you get a response to your text? Didn't check, did you?"

I can reach for the gun. The holster isn't a gun holster. It's too wide. The gun isn't secure.

"We blocked the Wi-Fi signal. No cavalry is coming, my friend. We're not going to hurt her. Put the gun down. Live to see another day."

"You're not taking her." Felix sounds like a movie action hero.

If I go for the gun, these two might shoot each other.

"What do you want with me?"

Keep them talking. It's Sam's voice.

"You've got a sister who wants to see you. We're taking you to her."

"And I'd love to see her. But why do you have guns?" *Take the confrontation down a notch.*

"Can we all put down the guns? Let's talk this out."

"Sage. You're not going anywhere. Back. Up."

In my peripheral vision, Felix comes into view. Gun outstretched. A two-hand hold.

If I back up, I can't get that gun.

Pop.

The charged sound is muted. Yet unmistakable.

Black beard lunges forward.

I reach. Grip the gun. Tug. Lurch backward.

Felix and the man with the earring are on the ground. Rolling. Grunts. Punches.

Crunch.

A shadow crosses the floor.

I flip the gun. Wrap my finger through the hole.

Hold it steady. Squeeze.

Pop.

It's a muted discharge.

Keep shooting until he's down.

Sam's voice. My arms shake. But I keep the gun pointed, my finger tight around the trigger.

Black beard steps back. It's as if I punched him. But I didn't.

I aimed at his chest. Below the cross. But the kickback. It went higher. I didn't have a good grip. I hit him right above the clavicle.

Blood spills. Spreads. Soaking the light blue.

The whites of his eyes flash.

I didn't mean to.

He falls back against the wall. His head misses a bike wheel by inches.

On the floor, the other man lies still near Felix. He's face down. A stream of blood flows from his body. A narrow bloody river over a white pine floor.

"You okay?" Felix pushes back from the man. His legs are sprawled near black beard's body. Felix clutches his side. Blood seeps between his fingers.

"You're hit." My voice isn't my own. But it is. My hand comes into view. Both of them. Clutching a gun.

"See if you can get a signal. Call Arrow."

The man in the corner breathes. His gaze follows me. I feel it on my back.

I set the gun on the table. It's a Glock.

No safety. All you do is point and shoot.

The end of the gun points in Felix's direction. I spin it. To the window.

"Where's your phone?"

Felix gestures to his back pocket.

I find it, careful to avoid his wound. "There's no signal."

"They weren't shitting. You're going to need to go to the offices. Do you know where they are?"

Stella took me to the offices this morning. I nod.

Millie wanders around the room, head down, sniffing.

"Go. Get help." My eyes bulge. Burn. "Hey, Sage, I'm gonna be okay. But maybe don't take your sweet ass time."

What he's saying is...*Move. Those. Legs.*

CHAPTER 29

Knox

"This isn't at all what I was expecting."

Cayman Brac is a typical small Caribbean island. The homes whizzing by late at night are a mix of cinderblock and stucco. Shrubs and low-lying trees dot the sandy landscape.

"You spend much time in the Caribbean?" Mateo is so relaxed, arm halfway hanging over the rolled down window, you'd think we're shooting the shit while zipping around the island on vacay.

"Not a lot." It's been a long time since my folks took me on a family vacation to the Bahamas, and the vacations I've chosen to take as an adult are more of the adventure variety. Rock climbing, camping, whitewater rafting.

"It's glam and glitz if you're resort side. Once you leave the resort, shit gets real."

"I get that," I say, scanning the area as Max slows.

Given our objective is to get in and out undetected, after further analysis, we opted for a four-man team. We also canned the swim-in plan as unnecessary.

Our contact at Interpol sent over blueprints of the building. All they want in exchange is information. Apparently, they like to keep tabs on shell companies and businesses exercising shady accounting practices.

The Caymans are known for harboring all kinds of law-skirting operations, but it's not one run by organized crime with big guns. In this country, accounting crimes are the norm. Violent crime isn't.

"Doesn't feel like we're in the right place," I say. The salt-tinged, humid night air and the swaying palms remind me of a small Florida beach town, the kind where all the doors are unlocked and during the day there are as many cyclists as motorists.

Back in the hotel, when we were reviewing blueprints and aerial shots, I suspected our intel was off. Being out here on location only serves to underscore that suspicion.

"Eh, you're picking up on the friendly vibe. All the locals know each other. Doesn't mean they wouldn't look the other way with the right incentive," Mateo says.

Mateo is an independent contractor Arrow hired. He's got a military background but does mostly surveillance work now.

The stretch of road ahead darkens, lit only by our headlights and a sliver of moon. The faint sound of waves crashing blends into the hum of the combustion engine. Given the widest stretch of island spans one mile, we're surrounded by ocean.

Max veers off the asphalt road onto a stretch of dirt mixed with shell. Winding, curly branches with green foliage provide cover. He cuts the engine and the four of us climb out.

From the rear, we gear up, strapping on Kevlar vests, holsters, guns, knives, and night vision goggles.

Rex, another independent contractor, points past the hood of the Jeep. "We'll take that trailhead. Mateo and I scouted it two days ago. Direct route to the buildings."

Aerial views from a drone counted four men with assault rifles patrolling the perimeter of the grounds.

As we prepare to head off down a narrow path, I'm hit with regret that I didn't find time to call Sage earlier. Which is proof she's different from anyone else I've dated. It's not like me to regret anything, or for that matter, to be thinking of anything other than the mission. Three teammates rely on me to maintain focus.

"You take the heat sensors. Okay?" Rex hands the goggles to Max. "I'll take the lead, as I've taken the path before. We'll go in one by one, as up ahead the trail narrows. Order goes me, Max, Knox, and Mateo takes rear."

Rex extends a tube of camo face paint. "You want?"

There's not a lot of light in the area we're moving into. I squeeze some out on the tip of my fingers. Mateo has dark skin, and he waves it away. Max's nickname was Viking thanks to his height, build, blond hair, and blue eyes. He rubs the paste around, taking care to get the white areas below his eyes where his sunglasses keep him from getting color.

Mateo lives in Puerto Rico, and Rex lives somewhere on the East Coast. He didn't specify the location. We're trained to seamlessly function as a unit, even if we haven't worked together before.

Geared up, we head out.

There's a decommissioned lighthouse nearby. I saw it on the map and the aerial photograph but can't see it through the trees. Fifteen minutes in, we come to a stop at the tree line.

Max lowers the heat sensing goggles. Painted white cinderblocks form the exterior for all three buildings. Two of the buildings are smaller, with one thousand square feet interiors. The largest building is shaped like a traditional schoolhouse from the eighteen hundreds.

All lights are out. The occupants should be sleeping. To the front of the schoolhouse building is a gravel parking lot with a beat-up Land Rover, an open Jeep, top off, and a circa nineteen-eighties Cadillac.

This feels off.

"All the tangos are quiet," Max reports. "No sign of movement."

The property encompasses two acres according to tax documents. Security could be roaming the perimeter.

"I count an estimated twenty in horizontal positions in the big house. Cold in the two small houses," Max says.

"Rex, cover my six," I say, ready to get this done. "I'll clear the two small houses. Max, Mateo, stay back. Let's see if movement stirs anything."

"Copy."

The knob on the door to the first house twists easily. Unlocked.

Inside, there are two tables with charging cables. There's a world map hanging on one wall. Pens. Blank pads of paper. No phones. A small table in the corner holds a dated printer. It's someone's office. The windows are high on the wall, so whoever works in here has no view. A dusty bikini-model calendar hangs on a single nail. I step closer. It's open to May. Lean a little closer. 2022. This office doesn't get a lot of use.

Outside, I point to the next house, and Rex falls in line.

The white paint is peeling, and there's rust forming where the nails are below the paint. The knob twists. Locked. I shake the knob, and the door shifts. Based on the degree of movement, the lock is weak. I scan the perimeter. The tree line. Listen to the hum of crickets and crashing waves. On the count of three, I ram my shoulder against the door. The flimsy lock snaps. Stacked boxes line one wall. I flip open a cardboard lid. Water bottles. The brand logo for Frito-Lay is stamped on the side of another box. Some boxes are plain.

Odd. But the contents aren't important. Sloane's too big to fit in a box. I pull the door closed.

We retrace our steps back to Max and Mateo.

"*Nada*," I say as I approach. "If she's here, she's in the big house."

Rex and Mateo described this place as having military grade security detail. So far, I disagree. Assault rifles don't equal military grade. Max and I exchange glances. My interpretation of his unamused expression is he's coming to the same conclusion.

One more building to go. But my instincts tell me it's highly unlikely she's here. And if she is, they haven't held her here against her will.

Based on the floor plans, the schoolhouse building has one central room, but on the south side of the building is a series of four square rooms without windows.

No security system. Lights hang in the corners below the eaves of the big house. They could be motion-detector lights.

We approach the double door on the side of the building with care. By silent agreement, Rex and Mateo cover, while Max and I breach the thirty-foot perimeter.

A light flicks on. We crouch.

No movement. No sound.

We continue to the double doors. Locked. Max unrolls his lock kit. In thirty-five seconds, we're in. We lower our night vision goggles, raise our guns, and enter.

A television and two sofas are to the left. The cinderblock wall behind the sofa doesn't reach the ceiling. To our right is a kitchen and a long table with around a dozen chairs. The cinderblock wall behind the kitchen reaches the ceiling. The floor is concrete.

Silence. It appears all the occupants are sleeping. Past the half-wall, there's a series of metal bunk beds. Adult men and women, maybe some teenagers, sleep. All have dark hair and olive skin.

I twist the knob on the first door to my right. Peer inside. One narrow bed. A man with a shaved head sleeps. Mouth open. Snoring. There's a rifle propped against the far corner. A table with an AK-47 and ammunition.

Behind door number two, a person with long hair sleeps on the side, face to the wall. Sloane? The door was unlocked. There's a Bible on the bedside table. The person shifts. A dark beard. Not Sloane. I back out.

In the third room, two people sleep in a larger bed. Possibly queen size. I let my eyes focus. One male and one female sleep in the bed, but judging from the blend of white strands and the wrinkled skin, I'd estimate the woman is in her sixties. Not Sloane.

The last room is a bathroom. A line of four open showers, two bathroom stalls, and four sinks. A ring of rust rims the bases of the sinks.

We exit the building. I flick my finger, giving the hand signal to depart.

Floodlights shine on our backs, casting shadows to our fronts. The light clicks off five feet from the edge of the tree line.

"Nothing?" Rex asks. At least, I think it's Rex.

Max answers. "No sign of Sloane. Or anyone being held against their will."

We're in the Jeep, gear stowed, faces wiped clean, before anyone speaks again.

Fuck. Not only did we not find Sloane, we have no leads. No evidence Sloane was ever at this site. It's been over three weeks since Sage has heard from Sloane. She could literally be anywhere in the world.

"She's not in the Caymans," Rex says as we pull away, reading my thoughts.

"What is that place?" Max asks.

"Did you see any of the guns?" Mateo asks.

"Two," I answer.

The people sleeping in the cots might not have been native to the Caymans. Maybe a resort shipped them in for labor.

I'll give Rex and Mateo the AK-47s raise suspicion, but owning a gun isn't a crime. The owners may just want any wayward guest to know they can't fuck around on premise. Or hell, maybe the owner is a gun aficionado.

"Those bedrooms don't have windows," Rex says, sounding defensive of the goose chase.

"It's a shitty building," I answer. "Place doesn't have a lab." Yes, the last part is a pointed dig at our two contractors who fleshed this location.

Max gives Mateo and Rex a rundown on everything we saw inside while I stare out the window.

Sage will be so disappointed. She thought this was over. That we'd found her sister. She's supposed to return to work in less than a week. I can go back with her. But is it safe to do so? What am I going to do? Sit in her classroom?

We don't have a fucking clue who is coming after her or why. Or where her sister is. She could be at the bottom of the ocean feeding the fishes. We have no clues.

"What a fucking waste." My assessment gets Mateo and Rex's attention. It's Rex who takes the bait.

"Look. You all told us she was here. You said, she's somewhere on these islands. We found the one place she might be. The only place." He twists in the seat. Questioning his skills clearly pisses him off, but they should absolutely be questioned. "And it wasn't useless. You know she's not here now. You suspected. We narrowed the scope of your search."

Yeah, we narrowed it to the rest of the fucking globe.

It's almost three a.m. when we return to the Grand Cayman marina. A man dressed in black suit pants and a black button-down Oxford with monogrammed cufflinks awaits on the dock. His pale skin glows in the moonlight. His dark hair looks like it's brushed back and held in place with gel. He's a businessman.

The four of us approach. No one else is out here at this time of the night.

"No luck?" The man's accent is distinctly European.

"Who are you?" I ask.

"Jack Sullivan sent me. Did you learn anything?"

Rex gives a quick shake of his head.

"Mateo. Rex." The man's authoritative tone has us all stopping on the wood plank boardwalk. "You owe me a debrief."

"Now?" Mateo asks.

"You two." The suit points to Max and me, ignoring Mateo's question. "You're going to want to call home." Stone cold tendrils crawl over my skin. "There's a private plane waiting for you. The driver in the black sedan will take you."

CHAPTER 30

Sage

What have I done?

I should've never come here.

I should've stayed in Asheville. Letting them kill me is preferable to this.

No one else should die for me. I've already exceeded my life expectancy.

But no, I had to follow Sam's direction. But Sam couldn't have known what I would bring to his friend's doorstep. He couldn't have known what would happen. The tragedy I would inflict on others.

The cracked bedroom door opens wider.

Ava Sullivan, a dark-haired woman with shoulder length hair and thick bangs that frame enchanting, concerned eyes, enters with a tray.

I wanted to go to the hospital to be with Maria, but they didn't let me. I'd been ready to argue, but Ryan snapped, "It's not safe."

He didn't shout, but I cowered in response to his stern command and glaring ice-blue eyes.

Pandemonium surrounded us. Paramedics. Police. The local news van parked on the street.

One officer asked me questions. Stella wrapped a blanket around my shoulders. The temperature must have dropped fifty degrees. I couldn't stop shivering. Still can't.

They put me in the back of an SUV with tinted windows and delivered me to an awaiting helicopter.

"We don't know how they found you, but they won't be able to follow a helicopter. Is there anything you needed from the condo?"

"No." Ryan had to hate me. His company spent so much on my protection, and then his friend…

"Sage, I know it's hard, but you need to drink something warm, okay? I added honey to the tea. And…" Ava kneels on the plush carpet and adjusts the blankets over my legs, "You're safe here. You don't need to be scared."

Ava has been incredibly sweet to me. Her husband, Jack Sullivan, isn't home. She insisted I stay in their daughter's room. Ryan told her to put me in the guest room, but Ava wouldn't have it. I probably should've spoken up, but when Ryan is around, I lose my ability to speak.

Ava said she wanted me to have a view of the ocean, and she thought I'd feel safest in this room. There's no balcony, and it's not on the ground floor. She admonished Ryan, saying Sophia would want me to stay in her room. I take it Sophia is her daughter.

Given there's nothing in the room to indicate a young girl lives in it, I wonder why Ryan argued against me staying here. Sophia has to be an adult. The room is essentially a guest room, and it's nicer than any bedroom I've ever been in. But I suppose if I were in Ryan's shoes, I probably would've sent me on my way. Told me to get in my car and drive far away. I too wouldn't have wanted me to stay in a close friend's child's bedroom.

But I'm sitting in a stunning mansion overlooking the vast Pacific. I might feel intimidated by the grandeur, except Ava's torn jeans and tattoos remind me of Asheville. Maybe I'm asleep. Trapped in a nightmare.

"Here. Drink this, sweetie." She lifts the saucer to me. "Drink it. Then I'd like to get you under the covers. You're in shock, and sleep will be good for you."

"Have you heard from the hospital?"

"He's still in surgery."

It's a cloudy night with limited visibility, but the distant sound of crashing waves infiltrates the room.

"Come on. You've had a full day. If I can't get you to drink, let me get you beneath the covers."

"Why are you being so nice to me?"

"Why wouldn't I be?" She stands and places pressure on my shoulders, urging me out of the armchair. "Do you think this is your fault? It's not. No one blames you."

Ryan seemed to. And Maria…and her son…*please let Felix pull through.*

My eyes burn, but there are no tears. A shivery apprehension coats my skin.

"Do they have good surgeons?"

"Yes." She sounds confident, but people don't know.

"Have you researched them? If you give me their names…" And what? Mid-surgery you're going to swap surgeons?

"I promise you, we got the best. Ryan and Jack wouldn't have it any other way." She pulls back the blanket.

She guides me like I might fall. Like I'm the one in the hospital.

Knox is safe. For that, I'm grateful. One good thing from today. But they didn't find Sloane. I didn't ask questions, but I overheard snippets of conversations. The facility they suspected held her is shady. Local police are investigating to ensure no one is being held there against their will. But the men they hired to search for Sloane jumped to conclusions without doing proper diligence.

They don't know where to look next. But the fact someone's after me leads them to believe she's out there.

What if it's not Sloane at all? What if it's something Sam is involved in? But that makes little sense. Sloane would never go weeks without calling me. Unless they came for her, like they came for me, and Sloane didn't get away…

The ache in my chest intensifies. I can't…there's no way. I can't think like that. It can't be. If Sloane wasn't alive, I'd feel it. My siblings and I, we have a connection. My fingers tremble and I close my eyes, seeking the intangible bond.

A warm, thick comforter surrounds me. I'm in Ava's silky pajamas and cocooned in plush warmth. She brushes my hair with her fingers. The tenderness stirs a memory…Mom.

Cerulean silk curtains, shades lighter than the deep blue sea beyond the picture window, shimmer in the morning light.

Where am I?

The ceiling height is much taller than in my home, and the elegant crown molding, while painted the same color as the walls, bears a permanence. The luxurious blue-gray velvet chair is oddly familiar.

Is this a dream?

The weight of a gun. The lift of the barrel. A man's eyes, widening. Felix. Holding his side. A bloody river. *Move. Your. Legs.*

It all comes back to me in a rushed blur. I close my eyes, curve my shoulders inward, and press against my sternum, wishing it away.

"Shh. You're okay." A soft touch accompanies the deep voice.

"Knox!" He's lying on the bed, over the comforter. The blanket I'd had wrapped around me now covers his legs. "You're back."

He cups my jaw and caresses my face. I've pushed up off the bed, and he's still lying back on a pillow, looking up at me with tenderness. His facial hair has grown longer, even thickened. The strands on his scalp go every which way. But it's those eyes, nearly ebony in this dim light, that catch me and hold me. There's pure warmth in those eyes.

"Came straight back. The entire flight, all I could think was... what would I have done..."

I slowly lower back down to the pillow, facing him. His fingers twist through my hair.

"Felix? Is he—"

Knox's lips tense, his gaze falters.

Oh, my god.

"They did everything they could. It was close range. Too much damage. It's a miracle he made it to surgery. Got to see Maria before... Hey. Shh."

Tears spill over. My heart hurts. Aches. It's...I did this. I'm as much responsible for his death as if I pulled the trigger myself. If I hadn't come here...

Knox pulls me into his chest. My nose smashes against his neck. Strong arms wrap around me, like he's trying to save me. But he can't.

After a few minutes, he pushes off the bed and returns with a box of tissues in a silver container with an ornate base and offers me one.

Knox's touch roams from my face, along my throat, and over my shoulder. He's concerned. For me. But... "He was your friend."

"Yes. A good man." He nods, and I watch as his Adam's apple shifts with his swallow. "A good family man."

"I'm so sorry." A fresh round of tears spills over. I should've never come here.

"You didn't pull the trigger."

My index finger feels the pressure. The whites of the eyes.

"I killed a man." Two, no three men died because of me yesterday.

"I read the police report."

"Do they have the gun?" I don't remember what I did with it. It wasn't my gun.

"The police? Yes. Standard procedure in a homicide." A sob escapes and he holds me tight against him until I gain control. When I pull away, he places a hand on my thigh. "We were able to learn more about the assailants."

I pull my knees up to my chest and wrap my arms around my legs. The pain. It hurts so much—

"Hey. Look at me. Those men were not good men. Both had records."

"They said they weren't going to hurt me." And then I pulled the trigger. Did I do that before or after they shot Felix? I strain to remember, but my memory, the images, are shrouded in blurry darkness.

"Their goal was to abduct you. They found enough tranquilizer in the back of a van to take down three horses. Rope. Handcuffs."

"For me?"

"That's what it looks like. We're working with the cops and feds to access their phones. They had an iPad in the truck. Our tech team should be able to pull a lot once we get our hands on the devices."

That won't help Felix. Or his son. That cute little boy with a huge smile and bowl-shaped haircut.

"Hey." He manhandles me, situating himself against the headboard and me against his side. The ten-foot wooden door is closed. The crystal doorknob sparkles. "You can't blame yourself."

"How can I not?" I push back so I can see his face. He has to understand how the world would be different if I never drove here. If I didn't heed my brother's instructions. Why did Sam leave me a bag filled with cash and fake passports? Why couldn't he have just told me to go to the police?

"Listen to me. Men like Felix. Me. Max. We chose this. We're—"

"Don't tell me he gladly left his wife and son."

"No. But he'd do it all over again."

A slight dizziness and nausea arise.

"We're going to figure this out. Discover who orchestrated this. We're going to find Sloane."

"What if it's not about Sloane?"

My thumb gently caresses his lower lip because…he's beautiful. I exhale, close my eyes, and blink back emotion. He may think I've lost my marbles, but I've got to tell him about my alternative theory.

"What if it's not about Sloane? What if it's something Sam is doing? What if they sent the same men after her and she didn't get away, which is why she hasn't called me?"

His palm covers my cheek, and his eyes go soft. His lips press together. Pity. He pities me. "Pretty sure Sam's not causing trouble from the other side."

"What if he's alive?" He drops his hand and tilts his head, skepticism clear. "Hear me out. The last time he stayed with me, something was different. He packed that baffling black bag. With fake passports and cash and an alternate license plate. He made me pick clothes to pack. Clothes I would need if I had to leave in a hurry but that I wouldn't be tempted to take out and wear before… I don't know, I guess before I needed the black bag. And you know, I told you…he always mailed me letters. And a lot of times, not through the military. He'd go somewhere else to mail them, because he said the military had people that might read them." He opens his mouth, and I push my hand over it. "Listen. I didn't tell you about the last letter. I mean, I told you he said to go to you if I was ever in danger. But the last letter…it was like he thought someone might read it. He was cryptic. He said remember where I told you to go. Don't hesitate. He'll be there for you. I'd show you the letter, but I bet it burned."

"That definitely sounds like he was involved in something. Maybe he was…there are groups who recruit from within the SEAL ranks. That could be why he met with Jack Sullivan. Jack went from the Navy to the CIA. He's retired now, but…" He reaches for my hand. “Sage. I was there when Sam died. I can promise you, what is happening right now is not due to Sam.”

“If he was dead, I would feel it.” I rub my sternum. “I felt it when my parents left. Each of them. Sam. Sloane. They’re both still here.”

He doesn’t believe me. Jimmy didn’t either. Sloane and I never talked about it. I tried, and she shut me down. I understand why. She was hurting and she’s someone who needs to close the chapter. She’s stronger believing he’s dead, and I’m stronger believing he’s alive. The reality is, neither of us know. No one knows. His body wasn’t found.

“The day of the explosion, we were off duty.” His gaze is on my hand. He’s toying with my fingers, and sorrow is the word that comes to mind when I take in his expression. Deeply sorrowful. “The bar…it was…a dive. Filled with mostly off-duty military. We weren’t supposed to really be drinking but… I had this woman…I didn’t know her name. Don’t know her name. But she made it clear she’d… go out back with me. It was…” He lets my hand go, and his gaze travels to the ceiling. “I’m not proud of it. I’m not a saint. Wasn’t one. A call came in. Sam took it. Said they’d had reports there might be trouble next door. A partially abandoned building. Sam said it was probably nothing. He’d go check it out. I told him not to, we were off duty. Wasn’t something we should do. He said nah, he’d check it out. He told me to have fun. Enjoy my…”

I can read between the lines. There’s no need to add details. “It’s okay.”

“No. It’s not. I downed my beer and told the woman I’d meet her in the back. Went outdoors. Saw Sam. Called out to him. He entered, and seconds later, the building exploded. The force of the blast threw me back ten feet.”

This is what he thinks happened, but it doesn’t mean that’s what happened.

“If I’d gone with him, we would’ve circled the building, checked for trip wires. I was always better at seeing the wires than Sam.” He rubs his face with his hand, over and over. "I'm so sorry, Sage. But that's the truth. That's what happened. There is no way Sam survived."

I don't believe it. He's wrong. But I don't have the strength to argue. I feel dead inside.

CHAPTER 31

Sage

"What are you thinking about?"

Ava's at my side, on her deck. She brought me tea and set it on the small table beside my chair. The space overlooks a manicured back yard with a lap pool and, beyond the hedge, a stretch of white, sandy beach and ocean. Palm trees sway along the sides of the property. I've learned she's a therapist. She's not pushy, but she asks probing questions.

For the last several days, she's been the consummate hostess. Always checking to ensure Knox and I are hydrated and well-fed. Suggesting things we can do, on the Sullivan property, of course. Swim. Work out in the gym. I've had no energy, but she's been gently encouraging activity to stimulate endorphins.

Typically, she's dressed casually. Today, she's dressed in an elegant black dress and thick fuzzy socks. Today is the day of the funeral.

I pull my knees tighter against my chest. There's a surfer far off in the distance. He, or she, is in a wet suit, and they're so far out they're a speck in the water. The distance from the shore can't be safe.

"The information they're getting this time...they have good reason to believe it's accurate. They're going to find your sister and bring her home." *Sloane.* "This is all going to be over before you know it."

Maybe. I contacted the school and spoke to our headmaster. He'd known about my house fire and, without my getting into specifics, he graciously gave me an extra week. I assured him I could get the classroom ready and be prepared for the start of school. I could've been working on name signs for the cubbies and for desks. We received our classroom lists days ago. But I've been in a funk.

And my funk has nothing to do with Sloane. I'm worried for my sister, but concern isn't the only emotion percolating. I keep coming back to questioning how she got herself into this. How she could agree to work for someone who is breaking the law and willing to murder to avoid getting caught. I don't doubt she rationalized her decisions, whatever they were. While we obviously never had the conversation, I can hear her telling me the morality rules limiting her research held back science, and the path they chose would be better for humanity in the long run. She'd tell me, dripping her self-righteous, no-fault attitude. Something along those lines is why she went to work for monsters. Why she left to work in a country with notoriously lax governance. If I know my sister, and I do, that's the only explanation that explains everything that has happened.

When she returns, she'll explain her reasoning. I'll disagree. And we'll move on because she's my sister and I love her. She's all I have. We'll move forward and put this behind us. But that thought alone is where I stumble over guilt. I could drown in the guilt.

"It will never be over for Maria. Or Rafael." My chest aches. An unrelenting pressure emanating from my thoracic cavity. It's one thing when someone dies from an illness. It's horrible, but there's no guilt. This time, guilt gnaws a sensitive place, intensifying the pain.

"True." She sips her tea. Her dark eyes watch me closely. I'm sure there's more she wants to say, but she's hoping I say more.

But what is there to say?

I keep thinking of Maria. At the soccer game. At lunch. And I ask the question that's been weighing on me but that I haven't been brave enough to ask. "Is Maria pregnant?"

"She miscarried. That's one of the reasons Felix stayed behind. I don't think she was very far along, but she'd had trouble in the past. How did you know?"

"She didn't drink alcohol at lunch." Ava listens intently. "And I heard Felix asking if she was okay. I didn't think…he said it was Rafael's birthday."

"Sage. None of this is your fault."

The automatic sliding door emits a low mechanical whir as it opens. Knox steps out onto the deck. His black suit accentuates his broad shoulders and height. He borrowed the graphite tie from Jack Sullivan, our host. I overheard them talking about it. Freshly shaved, he's as handsome as ever. The lines around his eyes and a more muscular build are the differences from his high school days when he'd dress up for game days in a far less tailored suit.

He's been attentive and caring since his return. Doting over me when he's not in Jack's office, on conference calls, or working with the other guys in the security room downstairs. Yes, there's an entire room on the basement level of this house dedicated to the security team. The men Jack hires for security are Arrow Tactical employees, therefore they're all Knox's colleagues.

He's been treating me with kid gloves. I'm quiet. Despondent. Melancholic. But I did this. It's my fault. Felix's life ended because of me. His son will grow up without a father because of me. His wife is now a heartbroken single mother because of me. As if I haven't already done enough during my life just by living. The heart and lungs inside me belong to a twenty-six-year-old woman who died in a car crash. Another match didn't get her organs because I was higher on the list, and that person may have died. I don't know, but it's likely. Approximately six thousand people die each year in the U.S. alone awaiting organs.

I shouldn't be here. If I wasn't here, if I had died waiting for organs, Felix would be alive today. Maria would have her husband, and Rafael his father.

Each night Knox holds me close, and I stay in his arms until his breath evens out, and then I push away, finding reprieve between the crisp, cool sheets close to the edge. Last night, we made love. He was tender, attentive. Quiet. Toward the end, when Knox was close, he saw my tears. I don't know why I teared up. I shouldn't have. I haven't been crying.

He froze. Concerned. Probably the worst sex of his life. Neither of us came. I got up and went to the bathroom, and then he went to the bathroom. It was awkward. Not what a guy like Knox wants. Or is used to.

"I guess I should go change my shoes," Ava says to Knox. They've been talking about today's travel plans. They're flying in a helicopter to the funeral. Knox didn't want me to go. He doesn't trust that it's safe. I'm not about to bring risk to a mourning family, but I imagine they don't want me there, anyway. I expect I'm the last person Maria wants to see.

"We've got a video for you to see. It's one we found on the phone of Omar Cardenas."

Yes, they identified the two assailants. Omar Cardenas and Alexis Flores. I shot and killed Alexis Flores. Both men were American. Records show ties to hate groups and gangs. Omar served time previously for grand theft larceny. Alexis was previously charged on two different occasions with assault and battery, but both times, charges were dropped. Omar Cardenas lived in New Mexico and Alexis Flores lived in Arizona. It's not clear how the two ended up working together.

"Sage? You okay? You don't need to see it. I told the guys—"

"I'm coming." Frustration escapes through my exhale. I've been moving slower. My head isn't right. I shouldn't take it out on Knox. Two steps toward Knox and I realize I left my tea on the side table. A guest shouldn't leave glasses out and about. I return, pick up the lukewarm mug, and follow Knox.

He leads me into Jack Sullivan's ocean-view office. Dark walnut adorns the walls. Leather-bound books fill one bookcase. There's no dust, but the matching gold lettering and smooth bindings give the volumes a decorative feel. There's a flat-screen television mounted on one wall. The screen is black, but there's a click clack of keyboard keys, and the screen comes to life with static.

"We think this is staged," Jack says. He's wearing tortoise-rimmed glasses and a dark suit. The grays soften his wavy brown hair, but I can imagine not too long ago he was a formidable person.

The static clears on the screen. The visual sharpens on a corner of a metal desk. The background is black. The camera view swings.

Sloane.

They have a dirty white rag tied over her mouth. Her dark hair is flat, bound tight around her scalp by the rag. She's not crying.

No, I know my sister. Molten anger blazes in her eyes. Whoever she's looking at, maybe the man holding the camera, she hates.

"What do you want to tell your sister?"

She lets out a loud garbled sound.

A shadow steps out from the darkness. A beige thermal bunched on a forearm comes into view, reaching behind her head. The olive skin is covered by a rather thick coat of black curly arm hair. The rag falls below her chin, and the man backs out of camera view.

Sloane glares at the camera with a lethal expression. My sister isn't one to put up with bullshit. I halfway expect her to leap out of the chair and bite someone. But her arms are behind her. They strapped her to that chair. If her hands weren't strapped down, I don't doubt she would attack.

"Do you want to find out what we do to disobedient women? We don't have all day. "

My insides cringe. Have they been hurting her? I've been telling myself she played a role in this, but that's not what I'm seeing.

"Sage, do whatever they say. Don't fight them." She directs her gaze to the right of the camera. But then, she shifts, and her gaze centers on the camera lens. It feels like she's looking at me, as if she can see me. "It's going to be okay. Just do what they say. They'll bring you here, and we'll be together. Together. We'll get through this together. Do what they say, and they won't hurt you."

The video ends.

"Was there a hidden message?" Jack asks.

"Hidden…what do you mean?"

Jack runs a hand through his hair. He's also in a suit, but his is a three-piece suit. He paces in the space between the back of his desk and the window. "I just thought…sometimes siblings have ways of communicating. My brother and I…we had code words. Maybe it's just something brothers do."

"Play the video again." Sloane and Sam played together. They'd play all kinds of games, running through the house. I was too young. And I wasn't allowed to run. If I tried, Sloane would yell for Mom or Dad. In some ways, she was my third parent.

Together. We'll get through it together.

She'd said it to me at the hospital. Many times, actually. It never made sense to me. I was the one being poked and prodded and stuck in the hospital.

"Nothing?" Knox asks, hovering close. With a deep inhale, I smell the scent of the guest bath soap, a soft floral, wafting off his skin.

"No." There's no point in telling them about the together reference. It's doubtful Sloane remembers. It means nothing.

"Well, the good news is," Jack says, "with this video, and others on their phones, we're getting closer to her location. Omar didn't film this. They sent it via an encrypted text to him. They blacked out the perimeter, but we have experts reviewing the video for things we might not pick up on. Sounds. Details. Interpol is assisting. Did Sloane ever mention Laos? Or Cambodia?"

"No." The Caymans are nowhere near those countries. And to my knowledge, they aren't hotbeds for scientific research.

"Her passport doesn't show that she ever traveled to those countries." It's a statement, but Jack says it like he's asking for confirmation. As if I kept track of her whereabouts.

"She thought about taking a vacation to Thailand one year, but she canceled last minute."

"Why?" Jack asks, coming around the front of his desk.

"Work." I try to remember what she said. "It was years ago. Before the Caymans. She worked for a company based in New Haven, Connecticut. It was typical Sloane. The date got closer, and she got nervous about getting behind. I think. Or maybe something in the data… I don't remember. And it wouldn't help you, anyway. Sloane never gets too detailed with me. Her work is complex." And I am a kindergarten teacher.

Knox's phone vibrates. He pulls it out of a pocket and checks it. I see Max's name on the screen. He taps back.

The click-clack of heels over marble sounds and Ava appears. Gone are her comfortable plush socks, and in their place elegant black high heels and sheer black hose.

"Are you sure you don't want to come?" Ava asks, her question directed at me. "I can find you something—"

"It's not a good idea," Jack interrupts.

"I'm good hanging out here," I tell her.

"It's going to be a lovely day. Why don't you walk around the grounds? Get some fresh air. The chef is going to be working from here today. You can ask him for anything you want. Anything at all."

"Thank you."

I walk them to the door to the garage. Jack and Ava climb into the back seat of a sleek black Range Rover. Another Arrow man, a man who works security here at the house, gets behind the wheel. Knox lingers behind, lightly touching my elbow.

"You going to be okay?"

"Yes. I'll be fine. Go. Don't keep them waiting."

He brushes his lips over mine. "I love you."

I think he said it last night too, maybe. Last night was…but this I can't mistake. I love him too. Too much to bring him into this mess. To kill his friends.

I want to reach for him. To touch his smooth, clean-shaven skin. To breathe him in. Not the floral guest soap, but his scent. My hands remain by my side.

I look him directly in his eyes, hoping he senses that I love him, too. That I'll always love him. And a part of that love is looking out for him. I won't drag him down or lock him to me. He can do so much better.

After the garage door closes, I turn and head down the hall to Ava's daughter's room. The room we've been staying in even though one of the guest rooms would've been sufficient. My plan crystallizes as I change into a pair of jeans, a sleeveless top with a high neckline, and a pair of sneakers that are more for fashion than exercise.

Ava brought me a ton of clothes to choose from. They suspect that there may be a hidden tracking device somewhere in my bag or in my clothes. I doubt that. I packed my bag two years ago, except for a handful of things I threw in when running out of my house.

I'll mail these clothes back to Ava when I can. If something happens and I can't, she'll be okay. I've gathered the Sullivans don't want for anything.

I could leave a note, but that would not be wise. When they go looking for me, it will confirm I'm gone. With no note, it will take them longer to confirm I'm not on the property. I do not want to endanger anyone else.

On the laptop, I search for cab companies. I don't have a credit card, but I have cash. Max sent my cash to Knox, who gave it to me. Along with my identification. The valid identification and the false passports.

There are no phones in the kitchen, but I remember seeing a desktop phone on Jack's desk. His office doors are open. Presumably, all the security men are downstairs.

I dial the number and request a cab.

"Yes. There's a gate out front. Can you please ask the driver to wait in the street? I'll be right out. There's no need to ring at the gate."

"You got it. It'll be there in about fifteen minutes. Thanks for calling California Cab."

The line disconnects, and I breathe out. My skin tingles with the sensation of reawakening. This is the right thing to do. Whoever is doing this has been adept at finding me. They'll find me again. This time, I'll make it easy for them. And Sloane is right. She and I can get through this together without bringing anyone else into it.

Whatever this is, Sloane and I will get through it. If anyone else needs to die, it'll be me. It's my turn.

CHAPTER 32

Knox

"Dear friends and family, we are gathered here today to honor the life and memory of a hero. Felix Serrano dedicated his life not only to the service of his country but also to the pursuit of justice, security, and peace. While his uniform changed over the years, his commitment never wavered."

Ryan Wolfgang, the leader of Arrow, the man who recruited so many of us, stands before the small crowd gathered for the graveside funeral. Maria requested that she have one private service with family in her church, and another service graveside with her Arrow family, friends, and neighbors. Towering palm trees fill in the corners of the cemetery, the fronds swaying softly in the breeze.

"In the Navy, he was the embodiment of honor, courage, and commitment. The waves and vast expanse of the sea were not just a workplace, but a testament to his resilience and dedication. He transitioned to the world of the private sector, where he served with equal valor and distinction.

"His path was not one chosen lightly. It was a path of sacrifice. A path that demanded everything, and Felix gave it willingly. He believed in a world where justice could be upheld and where innocent lives could be protected."

Ava dabs at her eyes, and Jack holds her to his side. A steady stream of tears runs down Stella's face. Trevor stands close, on guard, his front melded to her back. Max and I stand side by side, heads bowed.

"Serving in the Navy taught him more than just the art of warfare or the nuances of strategy. It taught him about brotherhood, about selflessness, and about the immeasurable value of human life. It's no surprise, then, that he continued this service, venturing into roles that few dare to take, but which he took on with honor and determination."

After reading the police reports and seeing the scene photographs, I can envision how it went down. Hand-to-hand combat, Felix struggling with a gun. He may have been restrained in combat, aware a stray bullet might hit Sage. The protector instinct comes naturally to a guy like Felix.

"Yet amidst the stories of bravery and daring, let us not forget the man behind them. A loving husband and father, a trustworthy friend, and a mentor to many. In his career, where actions often remain unseen and unsung, his impact was profound and will resonate for years to come."

I wish Sage were here with me. I wish she wasn't shouldering the blame for Felix's death. It's not her fault. The person who hired Omar and Alexis is to blame. I'll find whoever did this, whoever has Sloane, and the people hunting Sage.

"In our memories, he will always be more than his accomplishments. He will be the laughter shared at soccer matches and barbecues, the wise counsel offered during challenging times, and the unwavering support given to so many of us.

"As we say our goodbyes, let us remember him not for how he left this world, but for how he lived."

Maria's son buries his face in his mother's dress. Stella sobs. Or maybe it's another woman. A void fills my chest. A deadness tinged with fury.

The phone in my jacket pocket vibrates. I ignore it as the crowd stands. Maria chose to wait until after the crowd disperses to lower the coffin in the ground.

If Felix had died while serving the Navy, this would have been a different ceremony. Far more pomp and circumstance. More like what I assume they did for Sam. I wasn't Stateside when they held his memorial.

Maybe this is better. Maria spelled out exactly what she wanted, and at the end of the day, funerals are for the living.

Clusters form along the sidewalk that runs parallel to the cemetery road. Hands shake and people hug as they say goodbyes. The phone vibrates. Glancing around the cemetery, I realize almost everyone I know who would call me is present. Everyone except Sage and my parents.

I step off to the side, away from the others. I check the phone. Five missed calls from an unknown number. *Sage.*

She could be calling from a line within the house. I'll be the only person on a phone, but the service is over. Something could be wrong. I press to return the call.

"Knox." The male voice throws me.

"Who is this?"

"This is Miles. I'm working security today at Jack Sullivan's home." My skin grows cold. From across the way, Max tilts his head inquisitively. "Sage Watson left."

"What do you mean, she left?" Heads turn my way, so I step down the sidewalk, toward the car and driver who drove us here from the helipad. "When?"

"About two hours ago."

"*Two hours ago?*" My pulse skyrockets. "Where did she go?"

"We're not sure. She walked out the front gate. We thought maybe she was just exploring the neighborhood. Ava said she had suggested she walk for exercise and for us to give her some privacy. After she didn't come back, I sent Reno out looking for her. When he didn't find anything, I checked the footage out front. She got in a cab. I called the cab company, but they won't share where they dropped her off."

Max claps me on the shoulder. I spin, ready to throw him a right hook, but he crouches. "What?" he mouths. He's asking what's wrong.

"Why the fuck did you let her leave?"

"Our instructions weren't to keep her on lockdown. They were to keep her safe while she was here."

Holy fuck, I might strangle this Miles guy the next time I see him. "Did you get the license number for the cab she got in?"

"Yes. California Cab."

"Text it to me," I demand then end the call.

Fuck!

"Why would she leave?" Max asks, clearly having pieced together this fucking shit show.

"I have no fucking clue." Jack and Ava approach, and based on their speed, they've picked up something is wrong. "The only thing I can figure is..." That damn video. Jack may've been right. There might've been a fucking hidden message in that video.

"Sage left your house. She got in a cab and left." I throw the update out there before anyone can ask questions.

Jack pulls a phone out and steps to the side to make a call. Ava's fingers cover her lips. Does she know something?

One of the other Arrow partners approaches. He's an Asian guy, medium height, with an athletic build. I remember his name's Erik, and even though I've exchanged texts and had meetings with him regularly, I don't recall his last name. He's based in Napa along with Kairi. She couldn't make it to the funeral. Something about her husband having a virus that's going around the summer camps.

"When did she leave?" Erik's question is directed solely at me.

"He said two hours ago." My phone vibrates with an incoming text. "After she left, he checked the video feed and got the license plate, but the cab company won't say where she was dropped off."

"Put the license on the team Slack. We'll find her."

CHAPTER 33

Knox

Facial recognition locates her in the gaslight district. In multiple screen shots, she's looking up at the corners of intersections, as if searching for traffic cameras.

Max drives while I scan the sidewalks with Erik's update playing on repeat in my head. There are two Glocks in the glove compartment. A pair of binoculars lie on the back seat, alongside a long-range rifle, scope, and ammo.

We're using the grid search strategy. Methodical. Starting on Fifteenth Street, moving west. The plan is to stay on this side of Harbor Drive because it's unlikely she'd cross the busy roadway by foot. But if we can't find her, we'll cross over. Continue the methodical search to the coastline.

My skin crawls. On edge doesn't adequately describe the physical reactions. My molars grind and my jaw muscles ache.

What the hell is she doing?

Her sister said they'd get through it together. Jack thinks she's hoping to get picked up. He asked if I had a tracking device on her. I don't, but once I find her, she'll be wearing one.

Jack said it was a shame I didn't have a device on her, because then we could follow her and find her sister that way. As if I'd ever risk Sage's life.

On the sidewalk, a tall man jerks and waves his arms. His face contorts, and I'd guess whatever came out of his mouth wasn't nice. He steps past a petite woman in jeans. Brown hair. Sneakers.

"There! There!" I jump out of the moving car. "Corner of J Street and Third," I shout, in case Max doesn't see her, and take off at a run.

She's staring up at the sky. Or more accurately, at the street signs. Searching for a god damn traffic cam.

"Sage!"

She turns, brown eyes wide, pupils enormous. I'm still in my suit. Didn't spare the time to change. By the time we landed, we had the general proximity narrowed, and Max and I took off in one of Jack's spare cars at the helipad.

"Knox?"

"What the hell?" The words are out of my mouth, and my fingers itch to throttle her. The light glimmers over her eyes. A tear falls down one cheek. The effect is one of a wildfire being doused with a helicopter load of water.

"What're you doing?" My voice is softer, but my skin still itches.

She can't answer me because I've looped an arm around her and pulled her into my chest. With my nose in her hair, I inhale jasmine. It's the guest room shampoo, and I don't think I've ever been so relieved to breathe in a floral scent. My hands rub all over her, searching for injury, but there wouldn't be injury because she left of her own fucking volition.

I push back, hands on her shoulders. We're in the middle of the sidewalk in a relatively busy downtown area, and people are dividing around us like we're a boulder in the middle of the rapids.

There's no parking, and Max drives by, shouting out the window, "I'll circle."

"I can't go back with you." Tears dampen both her cheeks. My heart cracks. It's a visceral sensation, one I've never felt before. At least, not for a woman.

"Explain." My thumb wipes her cheek. I fumble in my suit pocket for a handkerchief. Normally, I'd never have one, but I came from a funeral.

"I can't risk anyone else dying. Not for me."

I press her into my chest, arms around her, and scan the street, searching for anyone out of place. Anyone with a bulge below a suit coat. Watching the hands of every passerby. We're sitting ducks.

I maneuver her to the side, next to a building, and scan the street, searching for the black Range Rover.

"I'm sorry I worried you. I thought about leaving a note—"

"And why didn't you?" She opens her mouth to answer. "Not that it would've mattered. Do you have any idea how scared I was? All the shit going through my head. Visions of what they might do to you. You realize I'm trained to know the absolute worst interrogation and torture techniques, right?" Her bottom lip quivers and tears flow heavily. I've unleashed a geyser. "Sage, these aren't good people. They killed Felix."

"I know! That's why—"

"You were going to hand yourself over to them." It's a statement. Not a question. And I grit my teeth, hating that Jack was fucking right. She doesn't value herself.

"No one else is going to die for me. No one." Her palm flattens against my chest.

"Baby, let me explain something to you. Felix didn't die *for you*. He died on the job. A job he loved. You should've heard the sermon today. Ryan explained it better than I could've. He died upholding justice and protecting the innocent. That's you, babe. The innocent. You didn't ask for any of this."

"No, but...didn't you hear Sloane? They won't hurt me. I just need to go to them, and then she and I will get out of whatever she's involved in."

I tilt her chin up to me. Red splotches cover her tear-streaked face. Those brown eyes are glassy. She's sad. Determined. Completely misguided. And I'm completely and totally in love with her. There's no way in hell I'll let those bastards come near her.

"Sage. Babe, I need you to listen to me. Are you listening?" She blinks, and more tears fall. "You can't trust those men. Sloane was under duress. You can't trust what she says. People will say anything in those situations. They have to, to stay alive. You can't trust anything she said in that video."

"But—"

"No." I put my finger over her pale pink lips. "You're not going to them. They aren't getting their hands on you. Not while I'm alive." She looks up at me, and damn if more tears don't fall. "I love you, Sage. Do you hear me? I love you so goddamn much. I don't think I fully realized how much until I thought I'd lost you."

"Don't say that." She can't mean it. "You can do so much better than me. And…and…you don't understand."

A black Range Rover approaches. I give a hand signal for Max to loop around again as I try to process what she's saying to me. "Sage, what are you getting at? Are you not healthy? Do you need another transplant?"

"I mean, no, but it's—"

"Sage. What're you saying?"

"I just…"

"Are you going to need another transplant?"

"It doesn't work like that. You don't just get a new heart." She swipes her nose and sniffles.

"Tell it to me like I'm a kindergartener. Are you sick? Right now. Are you sick?"

"No."

"Well, then—"

"I'm good. Now, I'm good. But my longevity is…it's not promising. And, you know how bad it can get. You were there, before the…" She rubs the side of her hand above her breasts. A familiar movement, one I suspect she does without thinking. "You deserve the best—"

I stop her by pressing my lips flat against hers.

"Do you love me?" She nods. More tears fall. "If you love me, then I have all I want. The best for me." The truth is dizzying. And I hold tighter to her arms for balance. But I've never been more positive about something. Never more sure.

"I debated buying a plane ticket home. Back to Asheville. Figured they'd definitely find me there, but I thought I might put Jimmy in danger."

"Going back to Asheville to draw them out isn't the worst idea. But it's not the best."

"What's the best?"

You and me. Forever. "Interpol sent over another location to check out. Outside Laos. We've confirmed the two assailants have done work for a particular affluent Cambodian. He's got his hands in a lot of things. We're still researching that lead, but it's promising."

"No. No one else gets hurt. That's what you don't understand. Too many people have died for me and–"

"If your other plan is to hand yourself over and to trust these bastards to let you and Sloane go free, then maybe I wasn't clear. Absolutely not. No way in hell."

CHAPTER 34

Sage

"There's the little runaway," Max says cheerfully as I slide into the back seat after Knox cleared it. "Gave us all a scare. What were ya' thinking?"

The door slams, and the car pulls forward. Knox is beside me with a clenched jaw and his dark eyes radiate fury. He's not happy with me. My eyes tear up as if his anger turned the knob on a faucet.

Max's question rattles around. I thought if I walked around long enough, someone would see me and come pick me up. That's what it feels like happened in Santa Barbara.

"Pretty sure my buddy Knox here is going to sprout a few more grays from today alone."

Knox fixes his gaze out the car window. "At least I've still got my hair."

It's a dig at Max, who has cropped blond hair. From here, it looks thick to me, but his hairline might be receding.

"I'm sorry. I should've left a note."

"Not sure a note would've helped, sweetheart," Max says, blinker on.

Knox has one arm around my shoulders, securely locking me against him. It's as if he's worried I'll jump from a moving vehicle, from the middle seat, no less.

"Our Interpol source came through with some valuable intel," Max says, looking back at us through the rearview. "Just got alerted. There's a confirmed sighting of your sister."

A mixture of hope and fear swirls. Sloane was bound and gagged. Her brown hair washed and brushed. She appeared clean, as were her clothes. But they tied her arms behind her. There was no blood. But they confirmed my worst fears in that video. She's gotten herself into something very bad. She needs rescuing. But that means men—Knox—will put their lives in danger to extract her.

I should be the one risking my life. But there's a limit to what Sam taught me. At close range, I still didn't control the kickback on that gun. If I'd been standing farther away, I probably would've missed.

"Sage. You look frightened. Don't be. You're safe now." I meet Max's bright blue gaze in the rearview mirror.

"It's not me I'm worried about. It's everyone else I pulled into this."

"Every single one of us chose this life. Right, Knox?"

"That's what I told her."

It might be my imagination, but it feels like his squeeze tightens around my shoulders.

It doesn't take long for us to return to the Sullivans'. Cars fill the circular drive in front of the house. Max pulls off to the side of the drive, a garage door rolls open, and we pull into the waiting spot. The door rolls down behind us, closing out the California summer sky.

The men gathered in Jack Sullivan's office are no longer wearing suits. As we approach the open doorway, they all look our way. Jack's in a golf shirt. Several of the men are on the security team that I've seen wandering the grounds since I've been here. Men who haven't introduced themselves but have remained on the perimeter.

"I see you found her," Jack says.

Knox answers Jack, his annoyance with me clear in his curt tone and narrowed eyes. "She doesn't want anyone else to get hurt. Thought she'd try to rescue her sister on her own." It sounds ridiculous the way he says it. "She said they wouldn't hurt her."

There's a clear pecking order among the men reminiscent of a classroom. All eyes fall to Jack as if he's the only one in the room with permission to speak.

"Anything we need to know?" He directs the question to Knox.

"Her plan was to be seen and hope they found her."

My gaze falls to the rug. It's a muted oriental rug that I'd normally never notice except the men's weighted gaze has me looking anywhere but at them. Meanwhile, these are the men I was attempting to protect.

A feminine voice breaks the heavy silence. "Oh, thank god, you're okay." Ava places her hand on my shoulder. She's changed from her funeral outfit into shorts, a tank top, and thick socks that reach halfway up to her calves. "I was about to go outside and cheer on my son while he swims laps. He pushes himself harder when someone's keeping time. Want some fresh air?"

"She may join you in a little while," Jack says. "We're in the middle of a meeting."

Ava squeezes my shoulder and steps out of the room.

Ryan Wolfgang speaks, and his square on the screen enlarges. "Nomad, are you still on the line?"

"Yes."

"I know you can only stay with us for a few more minutes. Can you finish taking us through?"

"With pleasure. The LYP Group has questionable work arrangements with migrants. A man recently escaped from one compound, and he's been a valuable source of intel. The international community has been aware of the potentially illegal arrangements for some time, but they remain in operation."

"How many of these compounds are there?"

"Dozens," the voice answers. "But a reliable source claims they saw Sloane Watson enter the compound located near the northwestern town of O'Smach."

"If he saw her, why wouldn't they—" I don't understand. Why watch and do nothing? Did she appear to be there of her own accord?

"Doing anything risks inciting an international incident. I trust this source. Where she's being held is mostly used for cyber scams. Cheap forced labor. But he says there's a small medical clinic onsite. It's my guess they transferred her to that location for something associated with the clinic."

"What do they do in the clinic?" Jack asks.

"Our source hasn't been inside. We've long suspected that when workers are no longer useful, they're resold on the organ black market. But there's nothing to indicate that's what's going on in this compound. We don't suspect drugs. That requires a different setup, and they use different locations for drug production. This compound is one of the larger locations, so if she needed blood or tissue samples, she'd have a good sample size. Another possibility is they're using the workers for medical trials."

"All Cambodians?" A female online asks the question.

"No. Foreign nationals from India, China, Singapore, Malaysia, Indonesia, and Thailand. It's a scam that's grown exponentially over the last ten years. They lure the poor to come work for them, and the migrants find themselves trapped in these compounds by the financial arrangement, threats of danger to those back home, or sheer force. The good news about this specific location is that most of the people on the inside are held by financial obligation. Little force is needed to keep them working. There's security. A gated entrance. But it shouldn't be too difficult to extract her. If she was in one of the drug manufacturing compounds, it could be much more challenging."

"That's the good news," Ryan says. "What's the bad?"

"If we're right on the location, it makes you wonder why she hasn't left."

"Sloane wouldn't willingly do anything illegal." The interjection is automatic. Jack's glare cuts straight to me in a way that says he places no weight on anything I say.

"Unless maybe they've convinced her they'll harm you," Knox cuts in. "Maybe that's what they wanted with you. They promised they wouldn't harm you if she keeps doing whatever it is they have her doing. Does she have surgical training?"

"No. She's a scientist. A cellular biologist. She wouldn't… She couldn't do organ transplants. That requires specific training she doesn't have. It also, by the way, requires specific facilities."

"Well, they want her for something. Do you have any questions?" Jack directs the question at me, and the question feels both dismissive and harsh.

"Me?"

"It's your sister. We're planning an operation to extract her. Do you have questions?"

"I want to help."

"You'll stay here." Jack dismisses me with a commanding frown.

Knox rubs my shoulder and gestures to the door. I'm effectively dismissed.

The men direct their attention to a monitor hanging on the wall. I must have interrupted a conference call. A blueprint of a building flashes on the screen. Someone asks how current the documents are. The door closes behind me, but I'm not alone. A man with a military buzz cut wearing cargo shorts and a black button-down with the sleeves rolled midway up his forearms steps out with me.

"Hi. I'm Milo." He holds out his hand, and I take it. His hand is dry, his grip loose. "I'll take you down to the pool."

"There's no need," I say.

"Everyone can focus on the task at hand if I accompany you." He offers a congenial smile and gestures for me to proceed.

Outside, Ava waves from her lounge chair. A young teen in a swim cap reaches the end of the pool, dives, and comes up a good distance from the wall and resumes his strokes.

"Are you good here?" Milo asks from the lawn. Ava meets Milo's gaze, and I can't help but feel like this is a hand-off.

"Yes, thank you," I answer as the unsettled reality hits. Sloane isn't the only Watson sister being detained in a compound. But leaving again won't do any good. I tried. Sloane's best hope is that in the meeting going on up at the house, they come up with a solid extraction plan.

CHAPTER 35

Sage

"A group of us are going to go see the Barbie movie later. It's a private screening. Want to join us?" Ava's cheerful veneer twists my insides while the surreal surroundings gnaw at me. The blue sky, the luxurious pool overlooking an ocean, laughter floating over the breeze from the nearby public beach. It's all too much. There was a funeral held earlier today. My sister is being held against her will. Men are upstairs in the house making a plan to extract her. And they want me to sit through a Barbie movie?

"I'll take a rain check." I force a cordial smile because none of this is Ava's fault. She's been nothing but nice, and she and her husband have been wildly generous. It's no secret the Sullivans are the funding source behind Arrow Tactical, making nonprofit operations like saving my sister possible.

Her son reaches the end of the pool. Water drips over his swim cap and down his face, around the tight goggles. "Mom? Are you timing me?"

"Tell me when to start," Ava says.

"Mom! Now."

"What is that attitude?" She's smiling as she asks, but there's an underlying warning to her tone. She holds up the stopwatch. "You have to tell me when."

"Okay. Now. Four laps."

"Got it."

He stares at her.

"Are you going to go?"

"Catching my breath," he tells her.

She presses the stopwatch when he dives.

"Do you think there's any chance I can convince them to let me go with them?"

Ava's attention remains on the pool, but she asks, "What would you do? I don't know your background. Do you have any training?"

"No," I admit.

"Without adequate training, you wouldn't be an asset. My step-daughter was in the FBI, and she worked hard. These men, they train daily. There's a lot that goes into what they do."

"I'm sure." My fingers wiggle as a memory of the weight of the gun and the acrid air after I pulled the trigger lingers. "But once they get her, she's…my sister will need someone."

Her son surfaces and twists his head. Ava snaps the stopwatch and yells, "Eighty-two seconds. Good job."

He slaps the water and looks to the sky, mouth open to suck in air.

"One more time. Then I'll do breaststroke."

He pushes off the wall, becoming one with the water. Ava snaps the stopwatch. I can't see her eyes behind the oversized sunglasses she's wearing, but I feel her studying me.

"I can understand wanting to be there for your sister. We can figure something out. Be sure you're with her as soon as possible." Her attention returns to the pool, but she asks, "Is that what's worrying you? Not being there for her when they find her?"

That, and so many other things. Felix's death. I should've never come here, never brought my sister's mess to their doorstep. And soon I'll be saying goodbye to Knox. For good, because it's the best thing for him. I brought my sister's mess to him and his friends. There's no way I'll let him take on mine.

"You know, talking about your concerns helps. It might not seem possible, but it does."

The hospital priest comes to mind. He always encouraged us to talk about our feelings. One of my friends, Jonas, called him the therapriest.

Her son spins through the water, fast approaching the wall.

"I don't want anyone else to get hurt." This is all on me. Felix's death. Maria and her son losing the most important person in their lives.

"Those men have some of the best training in the world."

"It doesn't make them infallible." Heck, Felix had been plagued by an upset stomach. There are so many things that can go wrong. "I just wish I could help. Do something." At times it feels like my whole life has been spent depending on others.

Ava announces her son's time to him, and he tells her he's going to take some easy laps before racing again. I stand and stretch.

"You know, we all have our strengths. The guys," she angles her head toward the house, making it clear who she means, "from a young age, they excelled in athletics, all things outdoors. They're addicted to an adrenaline rush. They work hard for it. Don't get me wrong, but there's natural ability there. They chose careers that leverage their strengths. I couldn't do what they do. Wouldn't want to do what they do. And look at you." There's no way she's about to compare me to them. "I couldn't do what you do either."

"What do you mean?" I'm a teacher. That's easy.

"Put me in a room with half a dozen five-year-olds, and I wouldn't last a day." I look away to hide my grin. It's funny but smiling feels wrong.

"Seriously!" She lifts her sunglasses to emphasize her sincerity.

"When Justin was younger and he'd have one friend over, I'd need to rest after a few hours with them. Sleepovers? Forget about it. No way would I do that unless Jack was home to help. And you deal with those wild things all day, five days a week."

She's right. It does require patience and the ability to treat them with respect and understanding.

"Look. You're not the best pick to extract a hostage. But that doesn't mean you don't do incredibly important work. Maybe the most important work. You know, you're teaching kids to read. Giving them confidence and setting up their academic foundations."

My eyes burn and I rub them, letting her words sink in. Maybe that's what I needed to hear right now.

"I still wish I could do something for Maria and her son. Maybe a Kickstarter campaign or something?"

"Arrow set up a trust for them. They won't want for anything financially. We'll look out for them. Being strong for Knox. That's what you can do. It's not easy, but I believe it helps. Knowing he doesn't need to worry about you will help him and the team."

She's right, of course. That's what I can do. Be there for Knox.

"And we'll be sure to have you in place so you can see your sister as soon as possible."

"I'm not sure I'll ever be able to repay you for all you've done."

"No need. We're family."

She wraps her arms around me in a compassionate hug I didn't expect, but her warmth soothes the twisted frayed emotions I've been carrying around.

"Mom?"

We break apart, and I give her shoulder one heartfelt squeeze, then head to the house.

My feet sink into the luscious lawn as she yells for her son to go. Knox greets me outside the basement doors.

"We've got a plan."

I don't push to go. Ava's right. I don't have any skills that will assist in this particular mission. If I'm not an asset, I'm a loss. An impediment.

"Hey." He steps closer to me. Through the glass, I watch as a couple of the security guys pass through the main room, headed down the hall to the control room. Knox lifts my chin, directing my attention away from the activity inside the house. "Are you okay? I know today's been tough."

Tough for me? What about Maria?

"We're going to find her." He links his fingers through mine.

"Promise me you'll be careful."

Whoosh. We both turn toward the sound of the automatic opening glass doors. Jack looks at Knox. "Ready?"

He squeezes my hand and falls in line behind Jack. I keep a brave face. Being strong is the one thing I can do for him and these men who are doing so much for me and my sister.

In the past, I watched Sam clean his guns and knives. *If you take care of your weapons, they'll take care of you.* I can almost hear Sam's intonations. I close my eyelids, willing the sensation to bring me closer to him.

I imagine Knox and the others are preparing at this very moment, just like Sam would do. *May they not need to use those weapons. May Knox stay safe. May all the men leaving for the Laos compound stay safe.*

I turn off the water and dry my hands, twisting the gold cross-shaped knob. The luxurious bathroom is larger than my bedroom at home. There's a hallway with a desk between the bathroom and the bedroom, and to the side of the hallway is a walk-in closet with a sparkling chandelier centered above a marble island. Ava told me I'm welcome to any of the clothes.

The clothes in here include sequin and silk gowns. Suits. Leather and suede coats. Shelves of handbags and floor to ceiling shelves of shoes protected by glass doors. Behind a solid wood door with a crystal knob are neatly stacked T-shirts. I snag one that falls mid-thigh.

In the bedroom, I leave the drapes open so I can see the moon. The same moon Knox will look upon tonight from Santa Barbara. I wish we'd had a chance to say goodbye. Not the quick one we had, but a chance to smooth things over. He'd been so angry, and then we were never alone.

If this mission, as they call it, is successful, they'll return with Sloane in three to four days. She'll explain what's going on. It will be safe for me to return home, and I'll fly to Asheville. I'll stay in Jimmy's guest room while we work on rebuilding my home, and school will begin. Sloane will join me, but knowing her, it won't be for long. She'll want to work, and she'll move to wherever her new job is. The leaves will turn, ushering in the change of seasons, and everything that's happened will feel like a fever dream.

Stars glitter in the night sky over the ocean. There's a crescent moon, partially obstructed by faint clouds. A system is moving in, and there's a chance of rain tomorrow.

Click.

The odd sound has me rolling in the bed, peering over the stacked pillows on the side of the bed closest to the door. Knox steps inside the room, sending my heartbeat into a frenetic pitter-patter.

He's here. Still in his suit from earlier, or at least, the dress pants and white button-down. The suit jacket and tie are missing.

"You came back."

He scratches the back of his neck. "You're here."

He toes off his dress shoes. His tousled strands point in every direction, as if he's been scratching his scalp or been near a helicopter.

"I thought you were leaving from Santa Barbara."

"We're flying out of LAX. Jack's flying me up. Ryan's flying the other guys down."

"Meeting in the middle."

"Yep." His fingers work the buttons on his shirt. "You tired?"

"I was looking at the moon. Wondering if you were looking at the moon at the same time."

The dim moonlight shadows his firm chest and scattering of dark hair. He undoes his belt and steps out of his trousers, leaving black briefs and dress socks.

"Silly, right?"

He hangs his slacks on the back of one of the wing-backed chairs. His thigh muscles flex as he lifts one leg to remove the sock, then the other. He's truly beautiful. A physical work of art.

"My mom used to say things like that when I was deployed." He piles pillows beside the nightstand and lifts the comforter, sliding in beside me. "This will be over soon. You'll see Sloane soon. Jack said once our plan is finalized, and we know where our return flights will connect, he'll get you there."

"Cambodia?"

He frowns. "Maybe. A Cambodian senator has an ownership stake in the company that owns the compound. He might not take kindly to the off-the-record extraction. I'd feel better if we got her out of the country and then you reunite with her. When there's corruption in government, it becomes less clear who you can trust."

"And you're still finalizing plans?"

He caresses my cheek softly, thoughtfully. "We're still assimilating intel. Travel time is thirty hours. By the time we land, we'll be good to go."

I press my lips into his palm. "Promise me you'll be careful."

"Always." We're lying on two different pillows, facing each other. "When this is over, you'll return home, right?"

"I'll need to." I think about the work awaiting me. Decorating my classroom so a class full of eager kindergarteners has the best first day of their academic careers possible. "There's a lot to do. Really, I should head back now."

"No," he says with the same demanding tone he pulled earlier, but just as quickly as the alpha commander surfaces, he softens, morphing back into my Knox. "Not until it's safe. When it's safe, I'll go back with you. You can put me to work."

"That's sweet." The vision of Knox taping posters on my classroom wall has me smiling. "But it's not necessary. Jimmy will help."

"Well, I've been considering a move to Asheville. Heading out there with you will give me a chance to check out the town."

"You love California. Sam told me you love it here."

"Might love it somewhere else, too. I floated the idea by Jack today. I also have my side business. There's a chance I can work on a project basis for Arrow."

"You're talking about moving. For me?" This man. He's astounding. Risking his life for me, for my sister, and he's saying he'll uproot for me. It's too much.

"I don't like the idea of being across the country from you." His index finger curves beneath my chin, and he gently lifts until my eyes meet his. "Would you be willing to see where this goes between us?"

The ache in my chest, the one that has been ever present since the attack, eases. Warmth soothes those frayed, painful edges.

"You're asking…not out of obligation, but because you want…" I can't finish the sentence because it seems impossible. "This isn't because you were my first, is it? Because that's not something that ties you to me."

"Sage, what I'm feeling isn't because I was your first. I love you. Your heart. Not the organ, your soul. Your strength. Your compassion. I trust you in a way I've never trusted anyone else. I want you in my life. I want to be with you." His lips brush lightly over mine. "You're my first too."

What he's saying doesn't make any sense, and that's not a funny line.

"You're my first that I want to be my last. The first I want to try for. The first I'm willing to do anything for. What am I going to have to do for you to believe it?"

His nose brushes mine as his warm fingers caress my side, sliding higher, to the tender skin below my breasts.

"What can I do to convince you?"

I roll into his warmth. Our tongues tease. Thoughts flee. My body becomes a whirlwind of sensations. Need.

Hot tingles zap through me. He tugs on the T-shirt, lifting it higher, over my head. My breasts are heavy, aching.

He reaches between my legs as his hot mouth sucks on a nipple. My back curls, and I mewl in pleasure. God, the way he makes me feel. My clit swells with need, and he presses the bundle of nerves with his thumb as his fingers find my entrance. As he works magic on my body, my fingers explore the planes of his back, his tousled hair, the coarse growth along his jaw.

He trails wet kisses down my body, to my apex. It takes one, no two slow licks with his tongue and I curl forward quivering. It's mind-blowing, really, what he can do to my body. What my body can do in response to his.

I reach between us, shoving his briefs down to find his erection. I grip him, rubbing my thumb over his smooth tip.

"Je-sus," Knox grits.

He lies flat on his back, fingers in my hair.

"Do you like this?" I lick up his shaft, and he groans. His eyelids flutter closed. I'll take that as a yes.

My fingers fondle his testicles as I lick his tip.

"And that?"

"I'm gonna like anything you do."

I take him in my mouth, deep, as far back as I can go, sucking, moving my head up and down as my hand wraps around his base. He expands in my mouth and mumbled expletives spill from his.

With one quick movement, he pulls me off him and positions me on my back.

There's a rip. His hand rolls over his shaft, and then he's between my legs.

"I want to come inside you. I want to feel you."

I nod and spread my thighs wider. He pushes his tip into my slickness. My clit pulses with need, so much like my rapid heartbeat. He stretches me slowly, carefully, and we both let out a low, satisfied groan.

"God, I love the way you feel. So warm."

Thrust.

"So tight."

Thrust.

"Perfect."

Thrust.

"Don't ever doubt how much I want you." He freezes, poised over me, balls deep within me, his dark eyes locked on mine.

"Same." It's all I can get out. I'm so full. Of him. Of us. Of disbelief, yes, but this is what I want.

We move together. Sloppy, passionate kisses. With each thrust of his hips, he rolls over my clit, delivering pressure where I need it most. We find a pace that feels like a dance, a rhythm that's so natural, I marvel at how something so new can feel so completely perfect.

"Are you close?" He hovers over me, brow next to mine, neck straining.

His hips slow and his thumb massages my clit. The pressure, combined with him, with all of him, with us, and those watchful eyes, the care, the love, it's all so much, and I detonate. My body loses all control.

I cling to him, holding on as tightly as I possibly can, closing my eyes to ride through the blinding release as he pulses deep within me, the side of his face next to mine, his muscles flexed, his hips jerking in uneven movements, all rhythm lost.

He collapses over me, damp skin, chest heaving.

We lie there like that, and all I can think is that I don't want us to move. I don't want time to move forward. I want to stay like this forever.

But that's an unrealistic dream. Time always marches forward.

He pushes up on an elbow and kisses me. Deeply. Slowly.

"I love you." I hold his face, forcing him to look directly at me, so he sees it as well as hears it. "I'll do anything for you."

His eyes brighten and his lips spread into a smile. "I love you, too. So much. Don't ever doubt it."

If I were a sorceress, we would stay like this forever, gazing into each other's eyes, our naked bodies aligned. But I have no such power over time. No spell to hold us here. I can however hold the memory in my heart for the rest of my life.

Almost apologetically, he pushes up and says, "Gotta take care of the condom."

After we each take our turns in the bathroom, he pulls me up against his side, then tucks the comforter around us. "Are you on birth control?"

We've been using condoms, but the truth is, given my medical history, I should use more than just condoms.

"No."

"When we get back to Asheville, do you think maybe you should see a doctor, talk to them about birth control?"

"Do you not trust condoms?" I've read statistics. But it's been years. When you don't have sex regularly, or, ever, it's not something you think about often.

"It's not that. But I want to do a lot more of that with you. And I want to be safe with you."

Is this a conversation he'd have with any woman, or is he bringing it up because of my medical history? "What did Sam tell you?"

"He mentioned it wouldn't be safe for you to have children. I just want to be as careful as we can be. If I should get snipped… that's an option too."

"You'd have surgery? For me?"

He nips at my lower lip. "Absolutely. I know a couple of guys who have done it. Your safety is the priority."

And then my heart overflows. With warmth. Incinerating heat. Hope. Desire. And we make love all over again.

CHAPTER 36

Knox

A short, thin man with thick, black hair in a loose-fitting slate gray suit and white button-down Oxford shirt holds a sign that reads Masterson Party. Together, Max and I approach him.

We're fresh off a thirty-hour flight from Los Angeles to Cambodia. The business class flight highlighted the differences between working for a private security firm and the US government. Business class on Singapore Airlines blew away any government transport. And now a driver will take us to our hotel.

Jack pulled in favors for expedited visas, claiming we have business in Phnom Penh for Sullivan Arms. It was a risky ploy in that he'd prefer to minimize connections between us and Arrow Tactical. But he's invested in a multitude of organizations and claims even if things go FUBAR, he won't take any heat. But he added that he'd appreciate it if we remained below radar, as would the US government.

We have a seven-hour drive in front of us where we'll check in near O'Smach, a town close to the Thailand border.

"Good flight?" The driver asks as he folds his greeting sign. His accent is similar to a Singaporean man I once met.

"No problems," I answer as Max says, "The best of my life."

"Singapore Airlines," the man says appreciatively, as if that's all that needs to be said.

Outside the airport, cabs, buses, motorcycles, and automobiles crowd the street. A white Mercedes van without windows along the sides pulls up to the curb. The driver wears a baseball cap and sports a full beard.

A young woman leans to the side of the black leather passenger seat. "Plans have changed. We're taking you."

She's American. She's also familiar. Her hair is black, and she has trimmed bangs over her eyebrows. She's wearing darkened sunglasses that block any view of her eyes. Where do I know her from?

Max steps forward, scans the interior of the vehicle, and crosses to the captain's chair in the middle row. He speaks to the driver of the van, then says, "It's good. We'll go with the guys."

The Cambodian man who greeted us gives a nod and traverses the sidewalk. He dumps the sign card into a nearby bin.

Max tosses our bags into the van, and we climb into the back. The side door rolls to an automatic close.

The driver scans his side and rear views and pulls out into traffic. The woman climbs back, moving between the two middle row captain's chairs to the bench seat in the back. She removes her sunglasses, and I'm surprised by her vivid blue eyes. She's tan, her skin dark enough I didn't immediately pick up on who she is.

"Sophia?" I glance up at the driver. "Fisher? Are you our support team?"

"Not exactly," Sophia answers. She's Jack Sullivan's daughter. "We're here to update you on the revised plan. They wanted someone you would trust."

"Are you working with Arrow now?" The last time I'd seen

these two, they worked for the CIA, and Felix and I served as an extra layer of oversight. It was a nothing job, one of our firsts after joining Arrow. We stayed off in the distance and conducted surveillance, ready at the waiting should anything go south. The biggest issue we encountered was with some fire ants.

"No," she answers. "And if ever asked, you didn't see us. But the powers that be reviewed your plan and made some changes. They sent us for two reasons. One, you both know us. Two, the CIA has a vested interest in seeing you pull this off. If you need assistance, we're part of the back-up team."

"Why is the CIA involved?"

"We'd like to avoid an international incident. Ready to review the new plan?"

"Ready as ever." Max and I exchange a quick glance before he resumes scanning the street through the front windshield. I focus on Sophia.

"Security outside the Pho Pang compound is hired. A division of the Wagner Group holds the contract. Given who we're dealing with, the powers that be determined your plan to go at night is too risky. You'll be going in as a recently hired guard working for the Wagner Group. When you arrive at your hotel room, a man will meet you and take you through the security protocol. He used to work for them, and he knows the personalities."

"He's on the support team?"

"Why do you keep asking about a support team?"

"Because that was the plan. We're supposed to meet up with an Arrow support team. This is not a two-man op."

"Did you not listen? The plan has changed. If you guys go in there and all hell breaks loose, it could create an international firestorm with China backing Cambodia."

"Arrow runs private plans by the CIA?" I'm not asking to be an ass. I'm simply curious how the CIA became involved. If they hire us for a mission, I get their involvement. This is a one-off.

"Interpol shared plans with us. They, too, are concerned. The revised plan is lower risk. If you'd let me finish."

"We have a seven-hour drive, don't we?"

"Not together, we don't. We bought you a car that fits with your profile. One a person relocating to Cambodia as a mercenary would purchase for personal use. Staying at the hotel fits because you'll be searching for a place to live."

"How long is this revised mission?" She scowls and I hold up a defensive hand. "Go on."

But I also breathe deeply and stretch my fingers because there's nothing more annoying than taking off with one plan and landing with another.

"As a new employee, on your first day, you'll be given a tour. With any luck, you'll gain confirmation she's there. In your role, according to our contact, they should assign you an interior post. The goal is for you to speak with Sloane Watson. Gain her trust. Give her a pill to take. It will induce seizures. You'll call for a medic. We'll intercept the call to the local hospital, and Max will arrive in the ambulance. The two of you will drive away with her. Or, if you can't finagle getting in the ambulance with her, you'll leave on your shift as scheduled and return to our hotel. You simply won't return to work the next day."

"You know, I don't speak Khmer, and my grip on Vietnamese is…" My facial expression relays severely limited.

"We're hoping it works to your advantage. A lot of the Wagner group don't speak it either. Your file says you speak Spanish, French, and Russian."

"French is rusty." I haven't looked at it since training years ago.

"The profile you're slipping into knows Russian and English. Between those two, you should find a common ground. That's the way most of the guards communicate with each other."

"So, let me get this straight. I play the role of a newly hired mercenary. Find a way to speak to her. And convince her to take a pill that's going to give the illusion she needs emergency medical care."

"That's the plan."

"And someone thought this is a better plan than us moving in at three a.m. and simply extracting her?"

"We don't have enough intel on what's going on behind the compound walls."

"Which is why Interpol wants us to share what we find?"

"Interpol and several other organizations. When you disappear with the ambulance, they're going to know the Wagner Group was infiltrated. We won't get back in the same way. So, you asked how long? We're hoping you'll spend a couple of days getting as much information as you can. But not too long. The deadline is five days."

"What happens in five days?"

"We've got a VIP watching this, and his patience is wearing thin. The sooner you can get her out, the better."

"VIP?"

"Above your clearance. But trust me when I say there's more riding on this than just getting an American out of a forced work arrangement. We have a deadline. If she's not freed within five days, a tangential operation that we're invested in blows. You asked why I'm down here? Our boss," she gestures to Fisher, "wanted to send someone you would trust. Plus, apparently, as a rookie, I'm given all the easy ops." Fisher keeps his eye on the road but holds up an index finger and shakes it in her direction. She smiles. I let their little joke go because I'm not loving this plan and need to focus.

"And there's no backup?"

Max's studious expression tells me he's listening, and he's as uncertain as I am.

"We've got three teams on standby on the Thailand side of the border. But no one, and I mean no one, wants us using them."

"SEALs? Delta?"

"Does it matter?"

I take her question to mean when briefed she didn't ask.

"No." But I would like to know.

"The point is, if this goes south, no one's going to let you waste away in a Cambodian prison."

"Good to know," Max says.

The worst-case scenarios I'd imagined involved being discovered and shooting our way out. The plan changing drastically while in transit hadn't been one of my fears.

"There's one more thing," Sophia says. Max and I exchange a glance. As SEALs, we've been through enough briefings with the CIA to be wary when they have one more thing to add. "Our sources are divided on whether or not Sloane Watson is being held against her will."

Shit. "Anything to back that up?"

"She was willingly conducting research that violates international law."

Sage had been suspicious she'd grown organs using stem cells or something like that. Doesn't matter to me what Sloane was doing. I want this resolved, so no one else comes after Sage.

"Our running theory had been that they wanted her sister to hold over her head. If she's doing this willingly, there's no reason for them to come after Sage." I'm right on this. Sloane can't be doing this willingly. It's a pointless argument. We're working under assumptions, but Sophia's logic is faulty.

Sophia's hesitation tells me she's debating what she can share. With a sigh, she admits, "It's our leading theory, too. But it's not our only theory. When you approach her, you'll need to be alert."

Fisher speaks up from the front seat. "What she's saying is, if she doesn't take that pill, you need to get out because there's a good chance she'll turn your ass in. This organization has multiple compounds, and the one they have her in is, of all of them, by all informed accounts the lowest security."

"And if that happens, do we leave her?"

"No. If that happens, you get out, we regroup with a forced extraction plan. She's leaving that compound whether she wants to or not."

"Because of the VIP?"

"Exactly."

CHAPTER 37

Knox

"You ready?"

"Ready as I'll ever be. You?"

"Let's do it."

I straighten my shoulders, relaxed in my outfit of old camo fatigues, black leather boots, holster with sidearms, Taser, handcuffs, and zip ties. The outfit has been carefully selected to blend in with the Wagner men per the CIA informant.

I shaved. Not my beard, but my head, and used a touch of Sophia's tinted self-tanner on my scalp so it doesn't appear freshly shaven. In the mirror, a second of shock hits first before recognition filters through. It's still me, just no hair. In a front pocket, I have one photo of Sloane and Sage as kids. The photograph is a safety precaution in case Sloane doesn't recognize me in my current state.

It's been a dozen years since I've seen her, so combined with the gleaming scalp and my presence in Cambodia, I don't expect her to recognize me. If I try to get her alone, she might even think I'm aiming to rape her. Unfortunately, it's a highly conceivable scenario in places like this. It's something that might have already happened. She might've been abused and harbor a deep fear of the guards. I need to be prepared for all possibilities.

Once she recognizes me, I trust she won't turn me in. Even if she has chosen to participate in the name of science, which is Sage's fear, she won't give a family friend a death sentence. In the most realistic worst-case scenario, she'll tell me she wants to stay, but she'll also tell me to be safe and get out of there. Sloane wasn't a close friend way back when, but she's still a Watson, and I trust her.

Max remains dressed in casual clothes. Cargo shorts, a loose button-down Colombia shirt, and sandals. His sunglasses sit atop his head, and he chomps on a stick of gum, the poster child for a relaxed expat.

The CIA acquired an ambulance and outfitted it for our purposes. Shortly after I leave, Max will change into the uniform for the local hospital's ambulance driver. He'll wait for me in the house with the covered parking spot that conceals the ambulance. The off-site team is monitoring calls to and from the compound. Max will have his phone with him. When I call emergency services, I'll be calling Max. For this operation, auxiliary support is remote.

The compound is located outside of O'Smach, within the Cambodian border. The walls of the compound are eight-feet tall, and razor-sharp wire and broken glass bottles line the six-inch-wide flat top.

Two red and gold painted wooden doors block the entrance that's wide enough to let a single car or truck pass through. Aerial views show there are two exits in the south and west corners close to a nearby stream.

At 7:15 in the morning, the sun filters through the treetops. The packed dirt road is muddy. The sky is cloudy, and afternoon rainstorms are expected.

A uniformed guard, about five foot eight, with brown eyes and skin, inspects my passport. He lifts the handset of an old landline telephone. He says something to me in a language I identify as Khmer. Based on his stance and body language, he wants me to stand exactly where I am and wait.

While I wait, another uniformed guard closes the double doors and secures a latch, locking me inside the compound.

A tall man with light skin and sunglasses, wearing mismatched camo and dusty black boots, comes closer. His hands are at his side, loose and relaxed. There's a gun in his right holster and a Taser in the left.

The man who checked my passport converses with him in Khmer. The tones are even. Conversational.

The light-skinned man with short, cropped hair scans me up and down. "English?"

"Yes."

"Why you here? Not back home?"

"Not Russian. Not my battle."

He seems to like that answer. After all, he's not off fighting the war either. Obviously, as paid mercenaries, we'd fight in any war for money, but if there's an easier job, it's going to be preferable to fighting another man's war. "I'll give you tour."

He takes my dark blue passport, one that identifies me as Mattvey Andrei Kuznetsov, and hands it over to the guard at the gate. If that passport was a real passport, I'd be concerned. Confiscating passports is a clever technique to solve employee attrition issues.

"I'm Vlad."

"Mattvey," I say, although he just read my credentials. He didn't hire me. Someone higher up did. The real Mattvey, hired by a recruiter based in Singapore, is en route to an undisclosed location with the possibility of being granted EU citizenship.

"You'll be at the gate at seven each morning. You'll come in, night crew leaves. Small number live on grounds. I live on grounds. Where you live?"

"Not too far from the casino."

Vlad narrows his eyes. "Gamble you?"

"Nyet."

He nods and proceeds inside.

According to my debriefing, Vlad Reinert is a Grade-A asshole. He remained close-lipped around our source, Ninh, a Vietnamese man tempted by the higher pay. He quit after one too many disagreements with Vlad.

Ninh said the men and women held here arrive with the promise of high pay and easy work. Only most are trapped here paying off outstanding loans. Many had to borrow to cover travel expenses, and the company charges exorbitant fees for training. Ninh claims they work fifteen-hour days, seven days a week and have no hope of ever repaying the debt owed. As a trained Vietnamese soldier working for the Wagner Group, Ninh didn't face the same outcome, but he saw one too many fellow Vietnamese trapped by these people. If caught attempting escape, physical punishment is swift and severe.

Ninh landed on the CIA's payroll as an informant, trading intel on both the Wagner group and the Cambodian compound, but when Vlad tasked him with caning a man, he quit. His contacts are currently helping him find new employment.

He's still on the CIA's payroll. I got the sense he might be on a few other countries' payrolls, too. On paper, these compounds are owned by a legitimate Cambodian company, but the people consider one senator to be the owner. Locals refer to him as King, thanks to the number of businesses he owns. Multiple governments have pointed out the Cambodian police never investigate claims of abuse when the rare escapee reaches the media. It's unknown how many escape and never find a media contact.

We walk through the compound together. According to public records, the firm owns over twenty acres of land. The compound is near the center of the land and encompasses approximately four acres. The only road leading up to the compound, like so many Cambodian roads, is packed dirt.

Of the compounds the firm owns, this one is located the closest to a city. Given this compound specializes in cyber scam work, computers and Internet access are required. Reliable access to electricity is a requirement to pull off an operation of this size.

Inside the walls, the ground is tamped dirt. There's no vegetation. All the buildings have concrete walls. The smaller buildings have thatched roofs. Vlad points out the smaller buildings, saying they are staff living quarters.

In the center, there are two taller gymnasium size buildings. The two larger buildings have ceramic tile roofs and are approximately two stories tall.

We enter the first of these buildings and step into an open room filled with rows of tables with monitors and keyboards. Wires spill out behind the monitors and keyboards into rows of extension cords below the tables.

One young man glances our way, and Vlad snaps his fingers and points. He quickly returns his attention to his monitor. There's a song playing from a small black radio with a silver antenna. I don't recognize the song, but it's playing at a low level and serves as background noise. There are no windows in the building. Fans on the ceiling spin, circulating the humid air.

Metal stairs bolted to the far wall provide the only access to the second floor.

"What's upstairs?" I ask Vlad.

"Same. We don't manage the work. Wagner handles security."

I follow Vlad through the building to the door at the end.

Mostly men sit at the computers. At least, based on the hair length, I assume they're men. They all wear loose, tattered short sleeve shirts. Brown leather or cloth sandals. There's a deadness to their eyes. An acceptance of the situation. I search for signs of abuse, but there are no black eyes or busted lips. No scarring on wrists.

Vlad opens the door at the end of the hall and bright sunlight streams in. The man closest to the door lowers his head, wincing from the bright rays. His shirt shifts, and near his collar I glimpse red, swollen skin. The telltale sign of back lashings matches with Ninh's account.

I've expended less than thirty minutes inside the compound, but my gut gnaws at me, telling me we're following another wrong lead. Sloane couldn't conduct any kind of research in this place. The floor is dirt. Packed dirt, but dirt. Something's off. Our intel is off. Once again.

Vlad opens the doors to the next gymnasium-sized building. The stench of urine wafts into the courtyard. "You be here. Most come and go freely. Some…they no earn that right."

Cell blocks line the walls. The iron bar doors are slid open, and the rooms are empty. Like the other building, against the back wall on both sides, there's a metal staircase bolted to the concrete wall.

"More rooms upstairs?" I ask.

"Yes."

"Where are the bathrooms? Showers?"

"Another building." That could explain the stench. Not everyone can hold it until they're released to go to the restroom.

"They plan build more buildings."

I scan the row of cells. At the end of the row, there are four locked doors. As we approach, I see men sleeping on cots. The phrase "skin and bones" comes to mind. At a glance, these men don't appear to be much of a risk, although with the right training, which is often taught in Asia, any one of these individuals could be a competent opponent.

"So, this is it? Two buildings?"

"Easy job, yes?"

Mind-numbingly boring. And no sign of Sloane.

Vlad leaves without an explanation. Tells me to sit and watch. There's not much to watch. The few men locked inside are sleeping. So I wander up the stairs. All the rooms are empty. The barred doors are closed but unlocked. At the end of the hall, on the back side without the stairs, there's a room with a window. The glass is smudged. A linen satchel rests on the end of the bed. A plain cotton dress hangs on a nail. A stack of dusty books rests on a small wooden table.

Vlad said he lives on the grounds. I doubt he lives in this room, but maybe another Wagner hire does?

I step closer. The books are faded, the binding cracked, but the titles are in English. *The Art of War. Pride and Prejudice. The Blind Watchmaker.*

Could this be where they're keeping Sloane? I lift the satchel and tug on the opening.

Creak. Creak.

Footfalls.

Someone's coming up the stairs.

I drop the satchel to the bed and step into the hallway. Out of the smudged glass I see a white woman with long, dark hair pulled back, stepping into one of the smaller concrete buildings with a thatched roof.

Vlad's head appears in the stairwell. He pauses mid-step, gaze on me. "What you do?"

"Just checking things out up here."

"No one's up during day. Too hot."

I can't imagine the people who own this place care about the heat, except for the computers, and even those are in a building with ceiling fans, not air conditioning.

"You hungry? Lunch outside."

We leave the four locked cells and the twelve sleeping people. Outside, I scan the courtyard searching for the woman I saw. The sun is high and the humidity oppressive. I slap at an insect on my neck. Wooden poles holding tarps create shaded areas, and there are tables set up beneath them. Beyond the wall are trees. While the trees aren't as tall as what you'd find in the northwest, a forest grows outside these walls. Why did they cut everything down in here? Trees would provide natural shade and would do wonders for making this place more hospitable.

I follow Vlad past more buildings, toward the end of the compound he didn't show me earlier in the day. We pass one concrete building without a roof. He points at it and says "Showers." Open air showers apparently. The next building has a roof. I see a long metal tray that I recognize as an extended urinal.

Up ahead, beneath one of the shaded areas, are tables, and many of the uniformed Wagner men are eating. Fish sizzles on a metal grate that rests above an open-air fire. A woman smiles a toothless grin and holds out a bowl. She says something in Khmer, but I understand her gesture and take the bowl of rice from her. A man lays a piece of grilled whitefish over my rice. He lifts a ladle from a metal bowl resting on the grill. The sauce is orange red, and my guess is it's curry. But to avoid suffering from an upset stomach, I decline the ladled sauce.

They drench Vlad's rice and fish in red sauce, then add a generous helping of creamy white sauce. If the white sauce is dairy, then Vlad has the constitution of an ox.

Conversation goes on around us. I pick up bits of languages. Russian. French. Khmer. Bits of Mandarin. There's no sign of the white woman I saw through the window.

When I finish, Vlad's still eating.

"I'm going to go check things out. Okay?"

He picks up a chunk of meat with his fingers and shoves it in his mouth and gives a nod in acknowledgement. I'm not a prisoner, after all.

There's a guard in a small, raised platform on the corner of the wall. Binoculars hang from his neck. A cigarette dangles from his lips. There's a long gun leaning against the wall near his leg. The distance is too great for me to identify make and model. He jerks his head in acknowledgement, and I wave.

One uniformed armed guard patrols the perimeter of one of the small concrete buildings. Sweat rings his light brown camo shirt, and he wipes his forehead. A gun is holstered on his waist. He places a sweat-stained hat with a brim down on his head, leans his back against the concrete wall, and pulls out a cigarette pack from his pants.

And then I see her. She steps out of the doorway, wiping her hands down the front of her dress. She shades her eyes, looking across the compound. My gaze catches on her bony wrist and sallow cheeks. The handstitched dress hangs off her shoulders like a curtain, loose all the way to her calves.

In my Wagner uniform with a shaved head, I must look like any other uniformed guard. I step past her to look inside the building she came from. My hope is I'll look like I'm curious and simply checking things out. Inside the room there are two grimy refrigerators and a couple of coolers on the ground. Cabinets line two walls. The counter below the cabinets holds needles, clear tubes, and glass vials. Several hard plastic chairs with rusted metal legs are grouped around a table.

The guard inhales deeply on his cigarette. I step farther inside to inspect the counter. *Follow me, Sloane.*

A shadow darkens the doorway. "How can I help you? Are you here to donate blood?"

"Is that what you're doing? Collecting blood donations?" Perhaps it's my American accent, but her mouth opens slightly, and she steps farther inside.

"Are you…" She steps closer and her voice drops to a whisper. "Who are you?"

"Sam's best friend." I look into her eyes, searching for recognition, while my peripheral vision remains trained on the doorway.

She swallows. "I can't go with you."

"Why?"

"My sister. They have her."

"No. They don't. She's safe."

Her skeptical expression and narrowed eyes match the negative shake of her head. "They showed me—"

"Whatever they showed you wasn't real. She's in California. Safe."

Her hand clenches into a fist and her lips scrunch together. "I knew it!" Then she looks to the ground and shoots a furtive glance to the doorway. "Suspected it. Couldn't be certain."

"What do they have you doing?"

"Taking blood samples. They said they'd kill Sage." She stares out the doorway, voice hushed and calm. "You're here for me?"

"Yes."

"What's your plan? We can't just walk out."

"You take a pill. When it knocks you out, we call for an ambulance."

"Where's the pill?"

I reach into my pocket and pull out the plastic wrapped white pill.

"What is it?"

A shadow darkens the doorway, and I thrust her up against the concrete wall, leg between her thighs, hands around her wrists. She pushes back against me, teeth bared like she's going to bite me, but her gaze catches on the guard and she freezes.

The guard puffs on his cigarette, staring at us. He steps back, and her wrists relax.

Vlad pushes past the guard, cigarette dangling from his lips. "You want sex, are others. Not that one. Time go work."

I back away with an expression I hope she interprets as a promise to return. Tomorrow we will talk further.

Her fingers curve around the pill. She's careful to use her body to shield her hand from Vlad.

"Move," Vlad commands.

I comply. Both Vlad's and the guard's hands are relaxed.

At least Sloane isn't here of her own volition. But what the hell do they have her doing? Phlebotomists aren't so rare that they'd need to hire an American scientist. What is she testing for?

From the courtyard, I give her a discreet salute. A casual nonverbal goodbye.

She remains in the doorway, watching me. Her fingers go to her lips. My breath catches. *No. Not now.*

Time slows. She swallows. Leans against the wall, much like the cigarette smoker.

It's oppressively hot. A sheen covers all exposed skin. I'm two feet behind Vlad. I bend to tie the laces on my boot to buy time.

The pills act quickly, but how quickly? What did they say? Three to five minutes?

I'm a five-minute walk from a building without windows. Once I'm inside, all hell could break loose, and the only way I'd know is if I went upstairs to the one room with a window.

If she passes out moments after I touched her, will they suspect me? Will they let me jump in an ambulance with her on my first day here?

My fingers graze the firearm on my side. It's loaded. No safety. One armed man to the front, one to the back. There's a sniper on the elevated platform.

Sloane wobbles. Crashes to the ground. The guard shouts. I run. Find my phone.

I press Max's pre-entered number.

White foam oozes from between Sloane's lips. I place two fingers on her neck. Make a show of holding out my phone and calling.

Her pulse is strong.

"We need an ambulance," I say in English. Then repeat it in Russian. Then repeat it in English.

I lift her in my arms. She's dead weight. Unconscious.

Fuck. It's not real. It's not real. It's for show.

I take off at a steady jog for the gate at the front of the compound. Today was not the plan. Yes, Max should be close by, but this was not the plan.

"Wait," Vlad barks.

I've reached the second large two-story building when a siren sounds in the distance. *Max*.

Vlad's hand falls to his waist. His gun.

"She's having a seizure," I yell.

A lock dangles over the metal bar locking the entrance doors.

The siren draws closer. Louder.

I could shoot the lock, shoot Vlad. But then we would have the international incident they instructed me to avoid.

Think, Knox.

"Open the gate!" I shout in English.

The guard from this morning steps out of a small building.

One in the corner reaches for his rifle.

"Open the gate!" I shout again.

The guard by the gate understands English. He met me this morning.

Sloane's head lolls against my arm.

The siren grows louder.

Vlad is behind me. His strides are long. Walking. Not running. Hand on his gun.

The guard pulls on the large door, sliding it backward on the metal track. The dirt area outside the compound comes into view. Sirens blare. A white van with the word "Emergency" in English along the side pulls up. One row of red lights sits atop.

The driver is a dark-skinned man with black hair.

Fuck!

The ambulance's back door swings open. Max wears a blue short-sleeved shirt with navy slacks and black shoes. His shirt has the local area hospital logo. He glances behind me, hands on a stretcher.

I don't give him a chance to pull the stretcher out. I jump into the van and lay Sloane down across the stretcher.

Max pushes me out of the way, checking her pulse and doing whatever else medics would do. For our team, Max was the medic. I leave him to it, closing the back van doors.

"Wait!" Vlad shouts.

"Go, go!" I shout loud enough for the driver to hear me.

The last thing I see as the door closes is Vlad aiming his gun. At us.

But his expression is one of indecision. Lost seconds. His loss.

If he shoots, I don't hear it.

The siren wails.

The employee parking lot is a good five-minute walk from the entrance. We'll have a decent lead time, should Vlad pursue us.

By the time he realizes we aren't headed to the hospital, we'll be long gone. Once this vehicle is closed in the garage, we'll change cars. Cross the nearby border. And head home.

No kill shots. No international crisis.

Max opens Sloane's mouth, breathing in while pinching her nose.

"I'm losing her. Charge the paddles."

CHAPTER 38

Sage

"Hey. Sage." Knox's voice bears a raspy quality.

He's alive. "Are you okay?"

"Yeah. I'm fine. We're all fine."

"Oh, thank god." My palm flattens over my chest. My lungs expand, breathing freely for the first time since they left.

"We, um...we, ah, encountered an issue."

"Sloane wanted to stay?" *Please, no. Say she didn't. Say she left willingly.*

"No, no. She wanted to leave. She was definitely being held against her will. But, ah, the plan we hatched. We had her take a pill, so she'd need a medic." The raspy voice means bad news. The side of my hand presses hard against my sternum. "She had an adverse reaction to it."

Oh, god.

"She's in a medically induced coma."

"Where are you?"

"In Kuala Lumpur. They're doing everything they can."

"What do you mean?" I hate that phrase. "Is she—"

"They fully expect her to wake."

"She's in a coma?"

"Until they stabilize her. When we found her, apparently, she was severely dehydrated and hadn't been eating. We didn't factor that possibility in, and…I don't know. It's…but she's going to be okay."

"Where is she? I need to get there." Ava stands behind me, arms crossed, listening intently. "Kuala Lumpur? Where is that? How can I get there?"

"We might move her back to the States. We're still figuring it out. They'd like for her to wake up before they move her."

"I need to be there. She'll know I'm there."

Ava taps me on the shoulder. "We'll go," she mouths.

When I deboard the plane, the first person I see is Knox. He's got the shortest buzz cut I've ever seen, and his overgrown beard is unkempt. Shadows lurk beneath his gold-tinged brown eyes, but he's safe. And he's the most beautiful person I've ever seen. I blink away tears as I throw myself into his arms.

He engulfs me and I breathe him in. He's okay. He survived. No one got hurt. Sloane's okay. She's in the hospital, but she's okay. She will be okay. They've been sending me updates while I was in transit. And I owe it all to this man.

My feet are off the ground as I'm crushed to his chest. And then he's kissing me like I am his oxygen. As if he missed me as much as I missed him. All that worry I've been holding onto evaporates. There's no worry to weigh us down. Not anymore.

We're on a tarmac for private planes. The Sullivans pulled out all the stops to get me here as quickly as possible, calling in favors from what I can only imagine are very important people.

A black Mercedes limousine awaits us. The driver wears a suit and tie and a subdued smile that says he shares our joy.

He helps us in the car, and when he's in the driver's seat, he tells us, "There's chilled water for you in the cooler in the cabinet. Based on current traffic conditions, we're about thirty-five minutes from your destination."

Knox holds both my hands, and we sit as close as possible on one corner of the spacious back bench seat. Another black leather bench seat faces us and a lacquered wooden cabinet with doors extends like a small table, nested beneath the extended tinted window.

"Thank you," Knox says.

"Would you like for me to raise the privacy screen?"

"Yes. Thank you."

I watch in awe as the screen rises between us and the driver.

Knox pulls me onto his lap so I straddle him. He fingers my hair, finds the ponytail holder, and my hair tumbles around my shoulders. In turn, I explore his new look. The fine hairs are soft to the touch, and he closes his eyes as if what I'm doing feels good.

"I figured you'd want to go straight to the hospital."

He's right. I do. I need to see Sloane. But time is on our side.

"I guess we need to make the best use of these thirty-five minutes, huh?"

His eyes blink open, my words perhaps taking him by surprise, and his smile blinds me.

"Have you got some ideas?"

"I do."

Outside the window, we're passing tree-lined streets, and it appears we're near an office park or parts of the airport.

"These tinted windows. People can't see in, right?"

"No. They can't." He takes my hand, lifts it to his mouth, and kisses my palm. The prickling of his beard gives me goosebumps and the tenderness in his eyes sets my heart fluttering. It's a good thing I'm sitting because I'm not sure I could stand.

I wore loose, soft clothes for the flight. His touch beneath the light sweater, directly on my skin, sets off a flurry of sensations.

Slowly we kiss. Our breaths quicken. A mix of hard and soft kisses rain down over my neck to my chest. He tugs on the sweater, and I lean back and pull it over my head, letting it fall. I reach behind me and unclasp my bra.

Love. That's what I see in his eyes. And that's what I feel as his lips press against my scar. He cups my breasts and sucks on an exposed nipple and my entire body twitches.

I tug at his shirt. It's a three-button short sleeve henley, and it's in the way.

"Fuck, baby, I need you."

My clit pulses in time with my heartbeat. Yes, that's my body, answering him. I need him too.

He maneuvers me onto the seat, legs together, in the air, and with one swift tug my loose pants and underwear are gone. God, the way he looks at me. I can only imagine it's how I look at him. The rough pads of his fingers trail along my thigh, and my hip, over my curls.

I push up and struggle with his cargo pants. He toes off his shoes and then he's up, helping me to remove everything and then I'm back in his lap, his erection standing tall, nestled between us. I wrap my hand around his length, and he groans. He fists my hair and forces my mouth back to his. I rise up and my knees press into the leather seat. I drag him along my seam and his hands clutch my ass and then I sink down onto him.

Oh, fuck, he feels so good.

"Holy shit," he breathes against my neck, giving me a second to adjust, for my body to accommodate him. "You feel so fucking good, baby. But hold on. Stay right there."

He reaches around me, grabs his pants, a wallet, there's a glimmer of foil, and he rips it with his teeth.

"Raise up."

I don't want to. No part of me wants to, but I have to meet with my doctor. And I love him for thinking about that when I completely forgot. I lift back up onto my knees, pressing my hands on his shoulders. I'm not embarrassed. I just want him. Now.

In a flash, he's covered, and I sink back down, stretching around him.

The world outside blurs as we find our rhythm. His fingers work in tandem with our hips and his mouth covers mine to squelch the sounds of pleasure I can't control. Blood rushes hot and thick through my veins. Perspiration coats my skin and sticks to the leather. My legs wrap around him. I'm somehow on my back and our kiss is sloppy and sweet, and I don't think I could ever be closer to anyone than I am to him right now. In this moment.

Tremors spread slowly, from my core, through my muscles forcing my toes to curl until my breath comes in choppy pants that I fight to control.

"It's okay, baby. Let it go."

Bright lights flash behind my eyelids, and deep within me he throbs and my muscles convulse.

He brushes my hair away from my brow and presses kisses along my nose and cheeks as our breaths even out.

"Wow. I can't believe what we just did." I look to the front of the limousine. "You don't think he could hear us do you?"

He grins. "No."

My fingers scrape through his beard and he captures them and presses the tips to his lips.

"That was…just…wow." I can't believe what came over me…us. Being with Knox…he's incredible.

"Baby, with us, it just keeps getting better. Trust me, what we have, it's special."

"I don't want to know what it's like with anyone else."

He stills and those earnest eyes burn into me. "You're mine, Sage. Only mine. No one else gets to have you."

"Yours," I confirm. "And you're mine."

Seven hundred and twenty-six days. That's the number of days I've spent in a hospital bed, attached to monitors with an IV-line protruding from either my arm or the back of my hand. In all of that time, I never imagined what it would be like to be sitting in a chair watching Sloane.

I'd much rather be the one in the bed. The doctors say she's going to be all right. That she's going to wake up. But what if they're wrong?

Knox and Max are in the adjoining den. Knox sits in a chair that allows him to see both the television set and me. His concern for me is evident, and it's touching, but I'm not the one who is in a coma.

Once again, I'm blown away by Jack Sullivan's generosity. We're in a VIP Suite at a hospital in Kuala Lumpur, and while I've spent far too much of my life in hospitals, I didn't know suites like this existed. It would've been so much better for my family if they'd had this kind of space when I'd been living in a hospital.

The suite boasts two full private bathrooms. Back home, the bathrooms were large enough to accommodate wheelchairs, but not much larger, with toilets and showers equipped for frail people. And there was no real thought or accommodation given to space for visitors.

This suite is nicer than many resorts I've stayed in. The view is of a golf course. *A golf course!*

If Sloane would wake up, she'd appreciate it. Or maybe not. But I imagine she'd see the stark difference between this palace and Duke. We might laugh about it. If she'd wake up.

My phone rings. My phone is once again on. I've been told that no one should be able to trace it. They don't believe Sloane and I are still in danger, but there are a lot of open questions. I want Sloane to wake up because she's my sister and I love her. But there are many people waiting for her to wake up to get questions answered.

"Jimmy? How was school?"

Jimmy far prefers text over speaking on a phone. But, for the time being, we're limiting our communications to verbal ones.

"No complaints so far. Everyone's asking about you." Jimmy teaches high school English, and those kids don't know who I am, so I know he's talking about the faculty. We teach at a private school that's kindergarten through twelfth grade. The pay is better than public school, so when we both landed jobs there, it felt like we'd won the lottery.

"Did you stop by my classroom?"

"It looks great. I took pics. Is it okay for me to text them to you?"

"Supposedly." My gaze meets Knox's. His brow furrows. I doubt he can hear me from the armchair. He's technically sitting in another room, although the space between the bedroom area and the sitting area is wide open. "I'll wait. Better to be safe," Jimmy says. "Just trust me. We did a good job. You're gonna be happy." When Jimmy told the other teachers about my sister, the lower school teachers pulled together and decorated my classroom. A retired teacher returned as a substitute teacher until I can make it back home. "How's Sloane?"

"The doctors expect she'll wake up soon. We still don't know why she had such a horrible reaction. If they were drugging her, it could be a drug interaction." My fingers trace the outline of Sloane's knuckles. "We're waiting on the toxicology results."

Beneath my fingers, Sloane's hand twitches. My breath catches.

"Jimmy, I think she's waking up."

CHAPTER 39

Knox

"I heard she's awake."

Various doctors have been in and out of the suite. I've been relaying updates to the team as I get them, stepping out of the room as needed for quiet.

The tall lean man in the corridor outside the suite is not a medical professional. He's in dark jeans, black leather loafers, and a navy and black plaid sports coat. His hands are relaxed at his side.

"I'm not sure we've met," I say, tilting my head, openly studying the stranger.

"We haven't, officially." He scans the hallway, dismissive of me. "Is the doctor with her?" he asks, gesturing to Sloane's hospital suite.

"There's a nurse. And my girlfriend." It's the first time I've applied that word to Sage, but I'm not about to give this stranger her name. Hearing the word, though…I like saying it.

"Can we go outside?" he asks.

"Why?"

His hands remain relaxed in a non-threatening position. "So we can speak. Without being overheard."

"Who are you?"

"Forgive me. Tristan Viognier." The name triggers nothing. "When we met on a call, I went by Nomad."

Ah. Interpol. He's a part of an elite group within Interpol. Chances are Tristan Viognier is an alias.

"She's groggy. She's been in and out of sleep all day. We don't know anything yet."

"May I speak with her privately?"

"No."

"In your presence?"

"You flew to Kuala Lumpur for an update?" Given he hasn't shown any identification, my skepticism is warranted.

"I was in the area. Jack Sullivan has kept us updated." He steps closer and offers a card identifying himself as an Interpol officer. "I'd like to hear her story."

The nurse exits the room. Recognizing me, she smiles and says, "Everything's looking good."

"Do you think she's up for a guest?" Is she up for an interrogation? That's what I'm actually asking the nurse.

With a pleasant smile, she says, "Yes, sir. She'll tire easily, but loved ones will do her soul good."

With her blessing, I lead Nomad into the suite.

Sage has fallen asleep in the armchair.

Sloane rests against pillows, propped up by the hospital bed.

"Sloane, this is Tristan Viognier. He's part of the team that helped us find you. If you feel up for it, he'd like to ask you some questions."

"The nurse said they may discharge me in the morning." Sloane's attention is on me, but her gaze centers on something behind me. I follow her gaze to Max standing guard in the doorway.

"That's good news." Sage needs to get back to Asheville, and we need to put this behind us. "Do you feel up to answering some questions?"

Sloane stares out the window. She's Sage's sister, and there are similarities if you look closely. The shape of the eyes and nose bear a resemblance. Sage's hair is a lighter brunette shade, and her eyes are a warmer brown. When Sage smiles, her face lights up and inner warmth glows. There's an absence of warmth from Sloane.

"Do I have a choice?"

She does have a choice, but we all have questions, so I yield the floor to Tristan.

From Arrow's perspective, we weren't hired by a US agency to find Sloane. We aren't law enforcers. If she broke any laws, she did so outside US territory. If anyone is going to investigate the matter, it would be Interpol or the Cayman Islands police. And the Cayman Islands will not send investigators to Kuala Lumpur.

Tristan drags a chair beside her bed. He removes his sports coat, leaving a close-fitting black dress shirt with gold cufflinks engraved with what looks to be a family crest. He positions himself lower than Sloane, presumably to set her at ease. The effort seems lost on Sloane, who continues to stare out the window.

"How are you feeling?" Tristan asks. I back up to the wall and lean against it. This is his game, but I slide out my phone and hit record. Our team will want to hear these answers.

"What do you want to know?" She jabs her temple with her index and middle fingers. "My head hurts."

"I'll strive for expediency." Tristan leans back in the seat and crosses an ankle over his knee, exposing purple paisley dress socks. "What led to your abduction?"

Sage shifts in the chair, blinking herself awake. Sloane remains transfixed with the window.

"Do you know why you were abducted?" Tristan asks again.

"He took me on a boat. I told him I get seasick."

"Does this man have a name?"

"Anton. That's what he introduced himself as. I overheard others address him as Solonov. I assume his name was Anton Solonov."

Tristan turns slightly in the chair, meeting my gaze. I don't recognize the name. But maybe I should. "How did you know Mr. Solonov?"

"I didn't know him." Tristan appears unfazed by her attitude. Sage comes to stand beside her sister, physically blocking her view of the window. She brushes her sister's hair behind one ear and leans closer, setting her face near Sloane's.

"Sloane. Do you think you could tell us what happened? Just start from the beginning." From this angle, it's difficult to read the exchange between the sisters. "Where did you meet this…Anton?"

"The man is a psychopath. Possibly a sociopath."

Sage picks up her sister's hand and rubs her thumb back and forth over the back of it. "Let's start from the beginning. Where did you meet him?"

"The lab. It was a Sunday. An hour and thirty-three minutes before our Sunday video chat. He asked me to go for a ride."

"Had you seen him before?" Sage asks.

"No."

Sage looks distraught. "You got in a car with a man you don't know?"

"He looked like a cover model for one of your romance books. You would've gone, too." Sage's eyes cut to me, and I tap down my smirk. I'll need to ask about this later. "And no, I didn't get in the car. I'm not stupid. I agreed to meet him. I had my bike. He showed up after I finished a report. I'd been working on it nonstop. I needed a break before I double-checked the numbers in my analysis."

"You met him in your lab?" Tristan asks.

"I thought he was an investor. I overheard them in the lobby. They were referencing incorrect financial projections. I didn't want them to cut funding, so I dug deeper into the data."

"What data?" Tristan asks.

Sloane's lips purse as she presses her temple.

Sage leans closer. "Sloane?"

"Transplant survival rates. I overheard people talking in the Bodden building. And the numbers cited were significantly off. Yet familiar. It bothered me. I went back and checked peer reviewed research. I was right."

"About what?" Sage combs her fingers through Sloane's hair, the movement as soft and comforting as the tone she takes with her sister.

"It doesn't matter." Sloane's gaze settles on the top right corner of the room. "You won't understand."

Sage smiles. It's a smile reminiscent of a kindergarten teacher helping a frustrated child learn to read. "You're right. I probably won't. Can you still tell me? Simplify it. Tell me like I'm a third grader."

Sloane's shoulders rise and fall.

Tristan leans forward. "Sloane, the Bodden building. Is that part of Origins Laboratories?"

"Yes. We don't do research in that building, but they hold meetings there. Investor meetings."

Sage touches her sister's arm, as if bringing her back to the topic. "So, I'm a third grader. What were they wrong about?"

"The survival rates they were referencing were wrong. Five to ten percent off. More. The complications. Hepatitis C. Cancer. And they weren't comparing live versus dead donors. They were just. Wrong. I went to the server room in the Bodden building to pull a report. I needed to show them they were wrong, because if they believed those numbers were right, they might not continue funding my research."

"And exactly what research do you do?" Tristan interrupts.

"Organoid research. I'm working on growing organs from stem cells."

"Past fourteen days?" Tristan asks.

"Yes, past fourteen days. We're making progress, too. Growing organs in a lab is an ethical solution to the world organ shortage. But the survival rates the investors touted were off. And I went to find out why. I figured it out."

"What was wrong with their numbers?" Tristan prompts.

"They were touting numbers from studies coming out of both India and Taiwan. Both studies attempted to discern variations in results on black-market organs. Gathering black-market data is quite difficult. For obvious reasons. Anyway, I compiled a report on all black-market transplant surgeries versus both live and dead organ transplant surgeries in the United States and the United Kingdom and prepared a discourse on the variations and how lab grown organs would not suffer the same results as those in alternative countries. I also located more recent data on our server from non-specified locations. The location field had been deleted, but I located the source file. The results were noteworthy and worth peer review. It appears survival rates on black-market organs are trending downward in specific source regions. The cancer rates for three years post-surgery for recipients with organs sourced from specific regions in Asia were extraordinarily high. Twenty to thirty percent higher than standard norms. Obviously, it needs to be shared broadly. Peer review. I might have missed something. Tabulated something incorrectly."

"Did you share this report with anyone?" Tristan asks.

"No. The psychopath arrived before I double-checked my analysis. I'd been working on it for days. I saved it to the server, but I wanted to review it again before sharing it with my boss."

"Did you talk to Anton Solonov about your work?"

"No."

"Did he inquire about your research?"

"No."

"So, what happened? After you left the lab?" Sage prods.

"I woke up vomiting in the bottom of a boat. I thought I would die. When we made it to land, I told him I would do anything as long as he didn't make me ride in a boat again."

"I thought you said you didn't get in the car–"

"I didn't. He gave me a water bottle. The last thing I remember is him driving alongside me while I walked my bike on the sidewalk. I could see the marina, but I was so tired. He must have drugged the water."

"How did you end up in Cambodia?"

"We docked somewhere and boarded a small plane."

"Did you…did he touch you? Hurt you?"

Sloane shakes her head slightly. "I couldn't stop vomiting. Dry heaving."

"What about the people in Cambodia?"

"Anton told them he'd be back to get me. He told a guard no one was to hurt me. Before you ask, I don't know why. Whoever his boss is gave specific instructions I wasn't to be hurt. I heard him instruct more than one person."

"Were you ever held against your will in the Caymans?"

It's a point I've been curious about, so I'm glad the Interpol officer asks.

"No. How quickly can we get flights home? I need to get back to the lab."

Sage places her sister's hand, the one without an IV, on her thigh. She's leaning on the bed, and she seems to be working to get her sister's attention. "They believe you resigned."

"I didn't resign. I need to get back."

"Not so fast, love," Tristan says with quiet calm. "Anton Solonov is a known assassin. There's what's called a Red Notice placed on him. Which means he's considered to be highly dangerous. We've been quite aware of him for years. Someone hired him. Someone with extensive means because he doesn't work for just anyone. Can you think of any reason someone would hire him to abduct you?"

"No. I mean, I figured out why they had me doing blood tests."

"Why?"

"Organ matches." She licks her lips, and Sage gets up to get her water. "The people in the compound will be harvested for organs. Or at least, that's my assumption based on the records they were keeping on them. But anyone could do those tests. Once I figured out what they were doing, which was like on the first day when I saw the data they were collecting, I refused to be a part of it. But then they told me they'd hurt Sage."

"And you don't have any idea why they picked you?"

Sloane shakes her head, lips firm and tight, gaze downward.

"Could it be this report you created? Is there someone who wouldn't want it shared? Data, perhaps, that someone might not want uncovered…"

Sloane takes the glass of water from Sage and sips. She closes her eyes and rests her head against the pillow. "It wasn't our research. I accessed a database we pay to access. Multiple parties contribute data. I was making the case to the investors that organ development will be profitable because I overheard one of them questioning the financial return. If anything, the risks inherent in trafficked organs will be absent from lab grown organs. And based on the data I was putting together, the risks of black-market organs are increasing. Significantly high cancer rates. Like I said."

"How closely does Origins Laboratories work with Lumina International?"

"They're an investor."

"So you don't work closely with them?"

"I never work with them. My old supervisor took a job with them in Geneva. The headquarters." Her gaze drops to Sage's hand over hers. "I was close to him."

"Has he remained in contact with your project?"

"No."

It could be my imagination, but Tristan appears relieved.

"And your supervisor's name?" He reaches in his coat pocket for his phone.

"William Salo."

He taps the name into his phone.

Knock. Knock.

Max raps his fist against the doorframe to get my attention. I wave him inside. "Tristan, this is Max Hawkins. He's a colleague of mine."

Max peers in Sloane's direction. "How's the sleeping beauty?"

"Grumpy," I mumble low enough the women can't hear.

"Well, I think I've had the most pressing questions answered," Tristan says. "Nice to meet all of you. My department would appreciate inclusion on any reports or summaries."

"Absolutely. We appreciate your help," I tell him. "I'll walk you out."

At the elevator, I ask Tristan, "Based on what she said, what do you think?"

He shrugs into his sports jacket as we wait for the elevator. "I think our suspicions were correct. Someone believed Sloane Watson was compiling a whistleblowing report. If your write-up clarifies that wasn't her intention, and you share it widely, or post it in a hackable location, whoever hired Solonov should call off the hounds."

"Are you going to research further?" He raises a questioning eyebrow. "Isn't the black-market organ trade of specific interest to Interpol?"

"It's a prevalent societal problem, but not one with simple solutions. If you get your hands on the report she compiled, send it to me. The databases she accessed to pull the data might lead us somewhere. But, if I were you, I'd focus on ensuring interested parties don't believe she possesses any damning material. It's a billion-dollar trade." His brow creases. "Her presence in Cambodia is an odd turn of events. The order to keep her alive is intriguing. If you gain more information, please do share. But if you're asking about Interpol's next steps?"

I stare him head on for an answer.

"She's most likely correct about the compound. Intel has indicated migrant captives are sourced for organs. Interpol won't engage without evidence of a crime crossing borders, and right now we have none. My best guess is if they are using those people for organs, they'll use them for medical trials too. The cancer component." He raises one eyebrow. "That's what caught my attention. It would have to be preliminary testing, of course. Something off the record. Only useful if it paves a smooth path through for on-the-record clinical trials." He scratches his nose. "I'll continue looking into that angle. A scandal of that nature could bring down a pharmaceutical giant. Do you know much about pharmaceutical companies, Mr. Williams?"

"No."

"Think money. Loads of it. Of course, this is supposition."

"But why target Sage?"

"From what I've read of the case, the men who came after Sage wanted her alive, right?"

"Yes."

"And those men were not Anton Solonov. But they were the kind of men Solonov would hire if he chose to outsource a project. My guess is someone, either Solonov or the party who hired Solonov, put out a hit with a higher reward if Sage was brought in alive. She's a more useful tool for coercion if she's alive. Yes? The thing about these contractors is that they don't always do reliable work. They often get caught. Or killed. As was the case here."

"If someone wanted Sloane unharmed, does that say to you that whoever is behind this knows her?" Why else insist she be unharmed?

"It's conceivable someone cared for Sloane. Didn't want her murdered." He crosses his arms over his chest and his lips purse. "On the outset, this doesn't appear to have been well planned. Reactive to a situation. I'll investigate this William Salo fellow. Look for connections. Lumina is a sizeable multi-national conglomerate, but their main skillset is helping pharmaceutical companies bring products to market. They act as a third party guiding the clinical research. The coincidences make for an intriguing case. But, I'll be honest with you, I'm not optimistic I'll uncover anything. If my theory is correct, and this was all about preventing external scrutiny, possibly blocking that peer review she was gunning for, then they've had plenty of time to destroy evidence."

"And without evidence of a crime crossing borders, Interpol won't get involved?"

"Even with evidence the organization doesn't always get involved." He presses the elevator button. "It's the way of the world. Politics are always at play."

When I return to the room, Max has claimed the chair beside Sloane, and Sage stands at the end of the bed with a look of confusion. Dark circles below her eyes highlight her exhaustion, as I'm sure the extended travel is catching up to her. Her fingers are freezing, something she assures me always happens in hospitals.

"What's going on?" I ask as I reach for those iceberg hands to warm them.

"Max is insisting I leave."

Sloane's eyelids are closed, and resting against the pillow, she gives off the appearance of sleep, but she says, "Max says she hasn't left the hospital room since arriving. Take her back to the hotel. Make her rest, shower, and eat."

"You don't get to tell me—" Sage interrupts.

"Have you been taking your medication?" Sloane asks, eyes still closed.

"Yes," Sage bites out. "You can't kick me—"

"Talk to the hand," Sloane says, palm up, eyelids closed. "You're not getting sick or worn down on my watch. With luck, we'll fly home soon. You need to be rested before we board a long flight. It's important for your immune system."

Up until this moment, my feelings toward Sloane had been lukewarm at best. But her insistence that Sage leave and rest, well, it alters my opinion of her. Warmth may flow beneath that dark-haired, brash exterior after all.

Taking Sage back to the hotel to take care of her is exactly what I want to do. There will be time to review the case information and explore next steps. At this point, my priorities align with Sloane's. Caring for Sage is my highest priority.

CHAPTER 40

Knox

Six days later

The broadleaf maples lining the street are haphazardly dipped in bright red and yellow, but green prevails as the dominant color. There's a chill in the air in the morning, and in the evenings, the distinct scent of wood-burning fireplaces permeates the air. Fall is coming to the mountains.

Sage and I arrived in Asheville four days ago. We've been staying in her friend Jimmy's guest room. The fire department salvaged the walk-out basement and much of her home, but the extensive damage requires that her house be demolished and rebuilt. Insurance will cover the expense, but it will take at least a year, if not a year and a half to rebuild.

It wasn't easy for her to tour the charred remains of her home, but Jinx, her cat, returned within minutes of her arrival, as if he'd been in the woods on lookout. Her neighbors kept him fed by putting food out in bowls, and now that she's returned, she's taken over the duties. She considered taking him back to Jimmy's, but decided he wouldn't be happy with the arrangement, so he wanders his territory and shows up each day Sage returns with food.

Sage has worked the last two days, and I've patrolled the parking lot and surrounding area, but I've done so without her being aware. There's still a chance this isn't over.

I'd like to believe she feels safe, but she repacked her black duffel bag and replenished the cash in the side pocket. When I asked her if she was scared, with a timid smile, she answered, "No. But when Sam comes home, he'll be happy I listened to him and kept it on the ready."

I didn't argue. But Jimmy and I locked eyes over her head. One day, she'll accept the truth, and Jimmy and I will both be there for her. I've decided Jimmy is an all-right guy.

He hooked me up with a guy who owns a property on Sage's street. The man has been using the home for rental income, mostly on Airbnb. A former vet, he was stationed at Fort Bragg for almost fifteen years. Proof it's a small world, he knows my dad. And he offered to rent the house to me and Sage. It's a cute two-bedroom craftsman, but most importantly, the proximity to Sage's house will make for easy monitoring during the rebuild. It's possible Jinx will make the move too.

At least, I believe this option is ideal. After work today, Jimmy is going to drop her off. We shipped her car back, but it won't arrive until next week, so she's been hitching rides to work with Jimmy, and I've been using a rental. My car remains back in Santa Barbara, but if she agrees to moving in together, I'll ship my stuff out East.

I've thought about all the reasons she might say no. She'll say it's fast. It is. She'll question if I'm suggesting this out of fear someone might come after her. I'm not. Knowing Sage, she'll try to tell me I can do better with a—to use her words—healthier person. I can't, and I don't want to.

Being with her is where I am meant to be at this point in my life. The years climbing the ranks, deployments, and operations were all bound to end. Those years ended, I've transitioned, and now this is where I belong. Now that I've found her, I have no intention of ever letting her go.

My phone vibrates in my pocket. Seeing it's Max, I sit down on the front porch of the rental to keep an eye out for Jimmy driving up with Sage.

"Mad Max," I say in greeting. "How's it going?"

"I might kill her." I snort. "I'm serious. She makes me want to strangle her."

"What's she doing now?"

Max and Sloane didn't return to Asheville with us. Sloane got it in her head that she needs to find her boss. That her boss might be in danger. That if her report caused all of this, then her boss had access to it. Max argued that her boss is probably the one who hired Anton Solonov. They agreed to disagree. But when she made it clear that she and Sage would get to the bottom of it, he balked. Like the good friend he is, he volunteered to join her on her fact-finding mission, insisting that Sage needed to get home.

Sage thinks Sloane has resumed work on her precious research. She believes Max accompanied her as a safety precaution. That's mostly true. Except Sloane isn't working. Sloane is determined to figure out who hired Solonov and why. None of us want to worry Sage, but we would all like to find those ultimately responsible for Felix's death.

"She's concocted a plan to break into the lab."

"Why?"

"We haven't been able to hack through the server wall."

"Erik hasn't been able to?" Our guys are the best.

"No. And they're employing some serious firepower. But she claims if she can get onto the network from inside the building, she can get everything she needs. She's like a dog with a bone."

His reference to a dog has me thinking of Millie. She's been with Trevor and Stella, but if Sage agrees, I'll bring her out here. She'd like the mountains.

"So, you gonna do it?"

"We are. I told her I'd do it. But she insists she has to be there. Like computers are some foreign object to me. Pisses me off. I've been trained."

"But she'll know what she's looking for." I get his frustration, but she's probably not wrong that she'd be able to get what they need a lot faster than Max, who's a stranger to their databases. "You know, if Tristan is correct, whatever she's looking for is long gone."

"Oh. Trust me. I know. It'd be so much easier to deal with her if she weren't so stubborn." A loud, frustration-filled huff crosses the line. It sounds like he's walking on a beach. "The one reason I'm willing to play along is there's no sign of her boss. We've been searching. Intriguing, right?"

"You need me to come there?"

"What, you think she'd listen to you?" Another huff. "Not a chance. Nothing gets through that thick skull. She never listens. But enough of that. We'll either unearth something useful or we won't. How're things going there?"

"Good. Nothing suspicious on this end." I wave at a cyclist coming home from work. He's wearing a helmet and a messenger bag and nods as he passes.

"You heading back to Santa Barbara soon?"

"Depends on Sage's answer to a question I'm planning on asking."

"Get the fuck out of here."

I grin, knowing exactly what he's thinking. And he's right. Sort of. I bought a ring that caught my eye in a store window yesterday and have it in my pocket. I want forever with Sage. But I get this is fast. We've been together for less than a month. Moving in together is a big step, but if things go south, we can more easily adjust than if we tie the knot. Marriage is permanent.

But things won't go south.

It's an internal dialogue I've had going on in my head nonstop since we booked a flight to Asheville. What's more romantic? To make the sweeping proposal, offering everything, or to understand she's still gaining her confidence in us, and to give her time and take things step by step?

I believe we could make long distance work if needed. But that's not the case here. We have options.

"You really going to do this?" Max sounds incredulous. I get it.

"She's the one."

"Well, her sister is a menace, so I'm telling you straight up, you're taking on one pain in the ass sister-in-law."

"You know, you don't need to stay out there. She's a grown woman. If she digs herself into another hole..." Wait. If she digs herself into another hole, Sage might get pulled in.

"That's right. Connect those dots. I wouldn't do that to you, man. Besides, you know me. I don't half-ass anything. And she may be a PITA, but she's right. If her data can help us bust an illegal organ trafficking ring, or save those people back in Cambodia, it's a worthwhile thing to do. Arrow is backing us. Jack and Ryan want me here. Interpol's on standby if we obtain evidence. Or something more than conjecture. It's just this whole op would be a lot easier if she would fucking listen."

A bright red vehicle turns onto the street. My pulse picks up. *It's go time.*

"Keep me updated and be careful. If you need me, I'm there."

"Nah, the work here is mostly surveillance. Looking to see who comes and goes. She's agreed to not let anyone from the office know she's back until we at least locate her boss. You'd be bored out of your mind if you were here."

"Yeah, I'm sure hanging out on a Caribbean island is torturous."

It's his turn to snort. "I've definitely had worse assignments."

The fire engine red Jeep turns onto the paved driveway. "Sage is here. I gotta run."

"Is today the day?"

Jimmy gives me a two-finger salute from behind the wheel, a smile plastered on his face. He's all in on this. I hope he hasn't given anything away, but judging from the confusion playing across Sage's face, I'm guessing he's pulled off the surprise.

"We'll see," I say to Max and slip the phone into my back pocket as the passenger door opens.

I catch the handle and pull it wide. "How was school?"

"This place is a rental," Sage says, peering around me. Jimmy grins and gives me a thumbs-up signal. Sage looks from the Craftsman style house to me and then to Jimmy. "Why are we here?"

"I'm outta here," Jimmy announces. "I'm meeting Alex for beers. You two are on your own."

He grins, and I shake my head. *Subtle, man. Subtle.*

"Thanks, Jimmy," I say as I lift Sage's leather satchel and close the door.

This house is four houses down from Sage's property, but on the opposite side of the street. Tarps hang over holes in the roof where the fire burned through and from here, her place is an eyesore.

"Why're we here?" she asks as the door opens on a house two doors down and a scrawny kid runs outside, lifts his bike, and jumps on it, pedaling away, barely sparing us a glance.

Here goes.

"If you like this place, we can rent it until your house is rebuilt. The owner will rent it to me for as long as we need. Open-ended rental agreement." Of course, those specifics aren't the important ones. "Want to come inside? Check it out? See if it works for you?" *For us?*

The glints of gold in her brown eyes shimmer in the waning sun. She's taking in the house's front. The eight-foot-deep wooden porch is painted a rich, deep navy. The roofline extends over the porch, supported by thick, square white columns.

"Do you want to look inside? It's furnished. The front porch isn't, but inside is, and he said we can keep any of it we want to use. He has a farm not too far away and said we can store any furniture we don't want in a shed he has—"

"You keep saying we?"

"Well, I'm hoping for we."

"You want to live here with me?" She's back to taking in the house. I wonder what she sees, what it looks like in her eyes. I can paint it if she doesn't like the colors. The bright white trim could stand to be toned down, but what do I know about color? "What about your job?"

"I told you. I have my own company. I can run that from anywhere. Arrow will work with me. I can take on contract work with them."

"For how long?"

"What do you mean?"

"Knox." She's flustered. Her answer may be no. "Sam didn't expect you to give up everything for me. I'm safe now. I mean, don't get me wrong…I love having you here. Every night I go to bed hoping I get one more day with you, but you can't…this isn't… you don't have to move here to keep me safe. After this school year, I can move for you. If you want."

She links her fingers with mine and tugs me to the steps on the front porch. She pats the painted wood, and I take my place beside her. The box in my pocket digs into the side of my thigh. There's a look of steely determination on her face, and I brace myself.

"There's something we haven't talked about. I didn't want to bring it up because I didn't know if we were there yet. But if you're considering moving here…and I guess that would be for me—"

"You'd be guessing correctly." I can't stop the grin that breaks out. My heart pounds in my chest from a mix of nerves, excitement, and anticipation.

Her cheeks flush, and I take her hands. "Go on."

"Well, I want children. Or, at least, a child. And we haven't talked about it, but—"

I squeeze her chilled hands to halt her uneasy words. "You think I don't want kids one day?"

"Well, no, I imagine you do. But, well, I might not be able to give them to you. I mean, I need to see a doctor, and obviously we'd want to avoid having a child with the same issue I had, but they can test for certain issues now, and there are options with invitro fertilization that didn't exist before, but it's a lot. I hadn't said anything yet because that's a big talk, and it's very presumptuous, and we're in the early stages, but if you're serious about moving here, then it probably needs to be said, right?" Her nose crinkles and her eyes squint in uncertain question.

"Are you done?" She blinks and gives a shaky nod. "None of that scares me. I'd expected pregnancy would be an issue, and it doesn't bother me. We can adopt or look into foster kids. It really…my thoughts, my focus, have been on us. On finding a way to be together. I wasn't…my thoughts didn't jump there, but if a child is something you want, I'm all in."

"Really?"

"Yeah, I mean, I was an only child, and until I met your family, I thought that was the absolute best. But I also guess growing up I sort of assumed one day I'd have kids. Finding the person I wanted to spend the rest of my life with seemed like the bigger challenge, one I wasn't in a rush to conquer." She sinks her front teeth into her lower lip, smiling like she's holding back a laugh. "But maybe I was just waiting for the right woman to come along and for it to not feel like such a challenge. And with you, Sage, it doesn't feel like a challenge at all. It feels like maybe some part of me has known all along that one day our paths would cross again. That it was just a matter of time."

She narrows her eyes in teasing disbelief. And yeah, I get the disbelief. There's a part of me that wonders if maybe I'm now one of those guys who has lost all common sense for a woman. And maybe I am.

My lips brush against hers, and my thumb caresses her cheek. The wind rustles the leaves as dusk falls, and a vision of us sitting like this years from now, looking down the street, waiting for our kid to return on his bike hits. I remember my dad checking his watch, frowning at how close I cut it, pushing it right to the limit on making it home for dinner. And yeah, I can do that. Put on the scowl. Be the disciplinarian, because yeah, Sage will be the one who makes the cookies and tells him it's okay to cry.

"I need to go to see the doctor. There are plenty of people in my Facebook groups that have successfully carried children to term. There's no reason to believe I can't, but before you agree to move out here, I should probably check and—"

"Hey." I tilt her head up so she's forced to look in my eyes. "Do you really think I'd change my mind based on whether or not you can have kids?" She's unbelievable. "What if it turns out that I'm infertile? Have you ever thought of that?" I mean, I assume I'm not, but I've had a lot of sex and no accidents. It's in her nature to put it all on her shoulders. My fingers tangle in her hair at the base of her neck. "But, if the doctors say no, or even question it, my priority is and will always be you. Are we in agreement on that?"

Her lips press together, pensive. But they soften as she looks down at her leg.

An enormous gray cat with wispy white hairs around perky ears curls around her calf. In truth, he looks more like a wild mountain cat than a domestic one.

"Jinx."

"Think he'll like this house?" I ask with a glance back at the front door we have yet to cross. I'd like to get her inside, to let her see the place and decide if this can work for a temporary home.

"No," she answers as his head tucks up under her palm. He stares at me with vibrant green eyes that say she can pet him, but I'd better keep my hands to myself. "This guy thrives on being outdoors. If the weather turns super cold or snowy, he'll come indoors. Or, you know, heavy rains. But he'd be miserable if we locked him indoors."

A Subaru appears down the street and turns before reaching us.

"You don't worry about him with cars?"

"I do, but for Jinx, it's a quality-of-life thing." She rubs her finger over his furry nose. "And he'd destroy my furniture if I forced him to remain inside. Not that I have any now, but..."

"Well, we can go inside and check out what's in this house," I say, once again prompting her.

"We can," she says and looks up at me, but this time, she's the one who angles my face with a gentle touch. "I'm not trying to rush you with the kid talk. But if we're going to move forward, and, well, take big steps like this so quickly, I think it's important we do so with total honesty, you know?"

"For someone who hasn't been in a relationship before, I'd say you're a natural." She smiles and my conscience kicks in. She wants total honesty, and she's right to ask for it. But I haven't been honest with her.

"What's wrong?" Her nails scratch into my rough beard, and I flatten her fingers against my cheek and close my eyes to take stock.

I've got to come clean or one day she'll have the right to be very angry with me. I let out a determined sigh and shift on the step, rest my elbow on one bent leg, and shoot off a quick prayer to the universe this goes well.

"In the spirit of total honesty, Sloane isn't back at work this week." Those trusting eyes narrow, but she's silent, waiting for the explanation. "We decided not to tell you, as we all knew you needed to get back for the start of school."

"And you wanted to protect me." She pulls her hands out from mine and places them on her lap.

"Yes. I'll always want to protect you, and I'm not going to apologize for that."

"What is she doing?"

"She's trying to get to the bottom of who hired those men to come after you."

"And her."

"Yes." I nod and reach for her hands. She doesn't pull them away, thank god. "She believes she can figure it out. She has the full resources of Arrow at her disposal."

"That's why Max is there." She says it more to herself than to me, like she's putting it together.

"Yes. We all want to find who did this."

"To avenge Felix."

"Yes, for one. Absolutely. But also because right now it's an open case."

"Should I be with Sloane? Helping her?"

"No." I don't want her anywhere near Sloane's mess.

"Don't look at me like that."

"Like what?"

"Your jaw muscles are flexing. The blood vessels in your forehead and your neck are bulging. You don't have a poker face."

She's right. I don't. Never have. "Sage, what exactly could you do? She's the one who knows what to look for. Max has been trained by one of the most elite militaries in the world, and if he needs backup, he'll get it. But right now, all they are doing is surveillance. Basic investigation."

"That's it?" She gives me a firm expression. One with strength and determination. I stretch my fingers and ball them up and stretch them again.

"Knox."

Fuck me and my honesty. "She's hoping to gain access to her company's computer network. See if she can figure out who accessed that report of hers. But you can't help with that either."

"And that's all she's doing?"

"Yes. They're conducting an investigation. That's it."

"And that's why you've been circling the school grounds and parking near the street? You're worried?"

"You noticed that?"

"You kind of stand out to me." She's teasing, but the love in her eyes soothes me. We're going to be just fine.

"When we first got here, I was concerned. As each day passes, I'm less so." She glances over her shoulder at the front door. "To be clear, that has nothing to do with why I'm proposing that we move in together. Or that I move out here. I want to be with you." She doesn't get it. I'm not great with words, but there's a box in my pocket that might say it better. I pull it out, push off the step and bend my knee, kneeling before her.

"Sage, this has nothing to do with keeping you safe." My fingers tremble. Hers cover her mouth. I haven't opened the box, and suddenly the box doesn't feel so important. It's not important to someone like Sage. I peer up into her sweet brown eyes, hoping she can grasp what I'm struggling to say. "I mean, I'm going to keep you safe. Absolutely. I'll kill anyone who–" Her head tilts, and I'm fucking this up. "Sage, I love you. And I know we haven't been together long. But I want to be with you. Forever. If you'll have me, I want you. You are the future I want. Everything else...it's immaterial. This ring, if you don't like it, we'll pick out something else. If you don't like this house, we'll find another one."

She wipes tears and sniffles. That's gotta be a good sign.

"Sage, will you marry me? And you don't have to answer right now. I wasn't going to ask today. I know you might need more time. But I don't. I'll wait. I'll prove myself. But I need you to see that for me, you're everything."

Her bottom lip trembles.

I push up off the ground and tug her into my arms. "Don't cry."

"But you deserve..." She buries her face into my chest, sniffling.

"I deserve what, Sage? The love of a lifetime?" I nudge her chin up so I can peer into those warm, brown, love-filled eyes. "I believe that's what I've found in you. I want my tomorrows to be with you.

For however long we have, I want to be with you. What do you say?"

"I want the same. However many more days I have, I want them all to be with you." Her eyes glisten, full of emotion. My heart aches. But it's a good ache, a solid ache, one that says I've put my heart out there on the line and won.

In all the things that matter, I've won.

EPILOGUE

Sage

Two Years Later

Golden yellow leaves scatter across the painted wooden porch. Rain is in the forecast, and I clutch the cardigan around my shoulders, scanning the yard. Jinx jumps up on the porch from wherever he has been. He circles my leg, letting his tail drag around my calf, then heads to the door.

"That's right, buddy. You know the storm is coming in."

He still prefers spending his time outdoors, but with each passing year, I've noticed he spends more time indoors, especially when the weather turns sour. I open the front door, and Millie sits back on her haunches, tail wagging as she thinks I've changed my mind and am staying home.

With careful steps and a commanding eye, Jinx strides past Millie. Our family dog glances from him to me, tail wagging. She won't do more than watch him. She learned he's the boss after one encounter with his claws.

Jinx disappears up the stairs. "I'll be home soon, girl. Gotta go get Daddy."

Millie's tail slows as I close the door. When I descend the steps to the car parked in the driveway, I glance back at the house and see her face in the window, paws on the back of the couch like she's not supposed to do.

The golden hues of the leaves reflect off the picture window, contrasting beautifully with the Hale Navy exterior. We chose to paint our home in the deep blue color, a similar hue to that of the rental we first moved in together, and I love how the color transforms throughout the day depending on the location of the sun.

I adjust the seat once again and rub my growing belly. At almost six months pregnant, my belly protrudes like I'm carrying basketballs below my dress. I haven't gained as much weight as the doctor would like, but I've also struggled with nausea.

Knox's parents are over the moon. As is Knox, but he's in worry overdrive mode which shows in his overly attentive behavior. My doctor doesn't consider this a high-risk pregnancy as I'm under thirty-five and am doing remarkably well. But you can't convince him of that, probably because of Sloane's frequent intrusions.

As a sickly child, I didn't dare to dream of pregnancy—or marriage, for that matter. Back then, no one mentioned it as a possibility. Quite the opposite, actually, as the going the lingo discussed how many years the surgery would provide. But medicine is a marvel, and my doctors assured us my heart is healthy and I can do this. It all feels like a miracle. So much of my life feels like a miracle. I didn't expect to be alive in my thirties. I especially didn't expect I would be married to my older brother's best friend, a guy I crushed on for as long as I can remember. The man who is my first and only love.

Traffic is light, and I reach the airport about fifteen minutes early. Knox told me he'd grab a cab, but there's no way I'd let him do that. Not when it's a Saturday and I'm not working. My plan is to work through the end of this semester, and then take maternity leave for the rest of the school year. It's hard to believe that next year our baby will arrive. Next Christmas will be our baby's first Christmas.

Do all women think like this? Jumping ahead. I shouldn't jump. If I've learned anything in my life of unexpected events, I should enjoy every moment.

Knox works for Arrow Tactical on a contract basis now, meaning he's someone they have listed to call if something comes up in our geographical area. He took a job with Sullivan Arms, working for Jack Sullivan's brother, Liam. He's in heaven. He's always loved developing weapons, not only the knife blades and handles that he still sells from his privately owned company, but in more advanced weapons that I don't want to think about.

The great news for me is he works remotely from the office we built over the garage at the end of our driveway. About every other month, he flies to the Sullivan Arms headquarters, based in Texas. The rest of the time, he's here. And when he's there, he's safely working in an office building or testing products somewhere in no man's land. Wherever he is, he's safe.

My phone vibrates as I approach the stacked stone columns in front of the Asheville Regional Airport entrance.

KNOX

Landed. Cannot wait to see you.

An uncontrollable smile blooms. God, I love my husband. The regional airport is small, and it won't take him long to deboard and make his way through the hallways behind security.

ME

I'm here. Eagerly waiting.

KNOX

Do we have plans for tonight?

ME

No

I grin. That answer will make him happy. I've noticed that of the two of us, he's more introverted. I'll make plans with neighbors or Jimmy or other teachers, and Knox will be a good sport. He's happy when we have people over. But he's happiest when it's just the two of us.

KNOX

Excellent.

KNOX

I've got plenty planned for both of us. And the plans do not involve leaving the house.

ME

Now you're getting me excited.

KNOX

I'm not sure we'll make it home.

I glance up from the phone and see a stranger by the luggage track watching me. Can he tell I'm blushing? Does he know what I'm thinking about? *It's my husband,* I feel like telling him. But the luggage track moves and the man's attention shifts. I move closer to the doors, searching. My heart beats a little faster, like it knows he's going to be here any minute.

It's silly. He's only been away since Monday, but it feels like forever. More than once I've wondered if we had connected earlier, when I was younger and he was still serving, subject to leave at a moment's notice and gone for months at a time sometimes, what that would've been like. Would I have grown accustomed to the ache and the worry? With my brother, I always worried, but I knew he was doing what he loved. What he excelled at. He lived his life doing exactly what he wanted. And while I love my brother deeply, there's a difference with Knox, with my husband. I miss him when he's not with me. Heck, even during the school day we text each other, in constant contact.

Lately, I've been texting Knox photos of the kids at school touching my belly with big eyes, blown away that a baby is inside. My palm absentmindedly rubs over my taut, round belly as I scan the exit doors, waiting for Knox.

And there he is. Bursting through, his smile wide, and like a sun's ray, the warmth from his gaze heats my skin.

He gathers me in his arms, careful of the belly, and holds me close. I breathe in his evergreen scent and run my fingers through his hair as my feet leave the ground.

"God, I missed you," he groans. His rough beard scratches the side of my face, and then as my feet meet the floor, he's kissing me.

It's a slow kiss meant for public places, but it's a kiss that tells me he's speaking the truth, and he's missed me in an aching way, just as I missed him.

He pulls back, and his fingers spread over my firm belly, hands planted on each side.

"How are you feeling?"

He glances between me and my belly with tender concern.

"Good. Now that you're back."

"And I'm not going again for a long while. Liam told me to stay until after my paternity leave is done."

"That's great news."

"Eh. It's not like I can't get shit done working remotely." His mouth opens. "Whoa. Did you feel that?"

The thing is, I did. Movement. In my belly.

"I think she moved." I can't believe it. My hands spread across my belly beside Knox's.

An announcer chatters on the overhead speaker, but we're in our own world, mesmerized.

And there it is. Another kick. But this one stretches my gray cotton flannel dress.

"She's lively," Knox says. "Feisty."

This will most likely be our only child, and we've decided to wait to learn the gender, but I've noticed Knox almost always refers to our baby with feminine pronouns. Sloane strongly disagrees with waiting to learn the gender, but this is my experience, and this is how I'm choosing to live it. When she has her child, she can choose a different path.

I refer to our baby with masculine pronouns, I suppose mostly to balance Knox calling her a girl. Do I want a son? There are days when I fantasize about Knox throwing a ball in the front yard with our little boy. But then an hour later I'll imagine Knox running alongside our daughter as she learns to ride a bike. Really? I just want healthy. Boy or girl, I'll be thrilled.

So far, all signs point to healthy. But my parents didn't know I was sick at first. It's a scary thought, but my doctor assures me they know more than they did back then, and her heart is perfect.

My classroom kids couldn't be more supportive. Crayon colored cards line our refrigerator. One shows me in stick figure form with my baby. Another shows a baby head and blue blanket. And many are squiggly lines or the sun and brown trunks with green circles. All are given to me with an endearment along the lines of "I'm gonna miss you, Mrs. Williams."

Yes, I took Knox's last name. It's yet another thing Sloane disagrees with. She said he should take my last name, or I should hyphenate. Knox would've gone along with either option, so long as I wore his ring. But before we even discussed it and before Sloane got her two cents in, I was scrawling out Sage Williams in my down time at school. When I told Sloane my final decision, she grumbled something about that on the bright side, my monogram won't change.

I believe Knox is my destiny. Sloane says there's no such thing. But I point out that if our last name, Watson, wasn't close to Williams, then Sam and Knox wouldn't have ended up in the same home room all those years ago. For that matter, if Knox's dad hadn't taken a job in Rocky Mount after retiring from the military, our paths would've never crossed. To me, that's destiny. To Sloane, it's chance.

I believe one day Sam will come home. Sloane—and everyone else, for that matter—disagrees.

What do Sloane and I agree on? That Knox and I are good for each other. That I'm happier than she's ever seen me. That finally, I'm more confident than I've ever been. Love will do that. I no longer hide my scar. I've even been known to wear tops that reveal the raised scar tissue along with dangly necklaces that draw the eye to the raised skin. What I once thought of as ugly, I now don't mind. If anything, I'm proud. As Knox says, it's a symbol of my strength and perseverance.

I informed Knox the other day that I'm getting stretch marks. They're faint, and I swear I'm using the creams, but I worry they won't go away. And he said if they don't go away, they'll be additional battle scars and will only make me more beautiful to him.

"Has she calmed down?" Knox asks.

"I think so?" Our hands link over my belly. "She's my first. That's the first time I've felt her kick. I don't know what's normal or what to expect." I beam up at him. "She must've been as happy as me that you're home."

"God, you are so beautiful." The comment takes me off guard. Knox is sweet and kind, but he's not one to throw out daily complements.

"Knox, I'm approaching beached-whale status, and I'm wearing one long sheath of cotton."

"Yes, you are. And you want to know something?" I raise an eyebrow. "I can't wait to get you home and take it off."

And then he gives me a kiss that's meant for private places, and the kiss goes on until my knees grow weak and we're both breathing heavily.

The tip of his nose brushes over mine, and his fingers caress my cheek. "Baby, don't ever doubt that, to me, you'll always be beautiful."

The End

Up next is Sloane's story in *Savage Beauty*.

She lives by the rules of science. He operates by a code of duty and honor. But when their worlds collide, the heat between them will melt every rule in the book.

NOTES

What's real? What's not?

The Cambodian compound is real. You can read about it more in the *New York Times* article "The Online Scam Industry Is Thriving. Cambodia Plays a Key Role."

https://nyti.ms/3I1B3j9

Obviously, I don't know what goes on inside those compounds. This is a work of fiction.

My father was denied twice for a heart transplant, once in Florida and once in North Carolina. The numbers on the wait lists for organs don't include those who don't qualify for the list. I suppose my experience watching my father go through the extensive testing required to see if he could qualify for a transplant has stayed with me. I've thought a lot about the people who need organs over the years. There's no easy solution, but I do hope that one day we have more options. And science is making headway. It's not unrealistic to believe that one day we will grow functioning organs in a lab, and indeed we are moving down that path.

New Guidelines Suggest Lifting 14 Day Rule — https://nbcnews.to/49wgasJ

New tissue engineering process brings lab-grown organs one step closer — https://bit.ly/3SXWrw4

Lab Grown Mini Organs Help Model Disease and Test New Drugs — https://bit.ly/42O8S0H

In later books, it will become clear that Sloane's research had nothing to do with her abduction. She became a target based on what she unwittingly unearthed when diving deeper into the data, and what others would question if she shared her findings for peer review. But more on that in Sloane's story, *Savage Beauty*.

FROM THE AUTHOR... AKA IZZY

If you enjoyed the story, I hope you'll take a moment to leave a review. Five-star reviews truly do sell books, bringing me closer to the day when I might be able to do this full time. So I'm deeply grateful for them.

In case you are curious...

Stolen Beauty is technically the fourth in the Arrow Series, but it's the first in what I'm calling the Beauty trilogy. Savage Beauty is up next, and it's Sloane's story.

The first three books in the Arrow Series are what I'm calling the Wolf trilogy, and these books are, in order, *Better to See You*, *Sure of One*, and *Cloak of Red*.

The Arrow Tactical series is a spin-off from the Twisted Vines series. And the Twisted Vines series is a spin-off from the Haven Island series.

GRATITUDE

With every book I write, my process evolves. The circle of those who help me create the best story expands. And the more I realize I can't do this in a vacuum.

This one evolved slightly differently than others. Jessica Snyder read it first and provided great insight and direction. After massive revisions, my beta readers from Hidden Gems weighed in. Big thanks go to Lori Whitwam, my editor, and to Karen Cimms, a proofreader. Although Karen's official title on this is proofreader, she really did so much more and I send her so much heartfelt thanks.

Mr. Jolie also weighed in. The scenes with Millie are now shorter and some are cut…as a matter of fact, he pruned this one. At over 90,000 words, it needed pruning!

Last, but most definitely not least, I am so grateful to my ARC readers. There are so many books out there, and when a book first releases, those reviews can make all the difference. I'm so grateful that I have ARC readers who want to read my books and sign up to get them with each release.

And of course, to my readers: Thank you for reading!

ALSO BY ISABEL JOLIE

Arrow Tactical Security Series

Better to See You (Wolf and Alexandria)

Sure of One (Jack and Ava)

Cloak of Red (Sophia and Fisher)

Stolen Beauty (Knox and Sage)

Savage Beauty (Max and Sloane) - Releasing June 6th

Sinful Beauty (Tristan and Lucia) - Releasing September 12th

The Twisted Vines Series

Crushed (Erik and Vivi)

Breathe (Kairi and David)

Savor (Trevor and Stella)

Haven Island Series

Rogue Wave (Tate and Luna)

Adrift (Gabe and Poppy)

First Light (Logan and Cali)

The West Side Series

When the Stars Align (Jackson and Anna)

Trust Me (Sam Duke and Olivia)

Walk the Dog (Delilah and Mason)

Lost on the Way (Jason and Maggie)

Chasing Frost (Chase and Sadie)

Misplaced Mistletoe (Ashton aka Dr. Bobby and Nora)

Standalone Romances

How to Survive a Holiday Fling (Oliver Duke and Kate)

Always Sunny (Ian Duke and Sandra)

The Romantics (Harrison and Zuri)

ABOUT THE AUTHOR

Isabel Jolie, aka Izzy, lives on a lake, loves dogs of all stripes, and if she's not working, she can be found reading, often with a glass of wine. In prior lives, Izzy worked in marketing and advertising, in a variety of industries, such as financial services, entertainment, and technology. In this life, she loves daydreaming and writing contemporary romances with real, flawed characters with inner strength.

Sign-up for Izzy's newsletter to keep up-to-date on new releases, promotions and giveaways. (**Pro-tip** - She offers a free book on her home page...just scroll down after arriving at her site.)

Want to say hi? Email her through her website or reply to her newsletter...she loves to hear from readers.

Made in the USA
Monee, IL
20 July 2025

21487437R00215